Dark Mountain

Perilous Friends

Perilous Friends

A Barbara Simons Mystery

Carole Epstein

WALKER AND COMPANY
NEW YORK

All the characters and events portrayed in this work are fictitious.

First published in the United States of America in 1996 by
Walker Publishing Company, Inc.

Published simultaneously in Canada by Thomas Allen & Son Canada,
Limited, Markham, Ontario

Library of Congress Cataloging-in-Publication Data
Epstein, Carole
Perilous friends / Carole Epstein.
p.   cm.
ISBN 0-8027-3287-9 (hardcover)
I. Title.
PR9199.3.E65P47   1996
813′ .54—dc20   96-23322
CIP

Printed in the United States of America
2 4 6 8 10 9 7 5 3 1

For my father

For wisdom will enter your mind
and knowledge will delight you
Foresight will protect you
and discernment will guard you

2 Proverbs 10:11

Acknowledgments

Barbara Kain listened to my ramblings and Barbara Freiheit read and reported. But they were not the only ones. All my friends were unflaggingly supportive, urging me on when this tale was only a fantasy. To all of them who believed in me when I didn't, I give my eternal thanks. Without their support it would not have been possible.

Perilous Friends

1

BEING UNEMPLOYED WAS alarming at first. It progressed slowly through depressing to downright tedious. I had always dreamed of the day when I could do all the things that I never seemed to find the time for, but now that the occasion presented itself, I couldn't for the life of me remember what all those important things were. More to the point, there was the question of how to finance whatever it was whenever it was that I finally figured it out.

So I took the coward's way out. For the first week I rarely got out of bed. Then I took to wandering slowly around my apartment, looking at things I had seen a million times and alternately trying to remember where I had got them and trying to figure out exactly how much they would fetch on the open market. Sentimentality never entered the picture, and no memento was spared my financially critical eye. But the arithmetic was too much for me, so mostly I watched daytime TV, which depressed me even more since those people were getting paid to talk about their problems and here I had all this spare misery that no one would give me a cent for. It was all just too unfair.

Having always been an optimistic, upbeat sort of person, I was totally unprepared for the lethargy that gripped me like a vise and squeezed out all my energy. I really believed that if I stayed home and hid from the world the evil demons of bad luck and misfortune would no longer be able to find me. And I was sure they were looking hard. The only excursions I made outside in that three-and-a-half-week period were quick, furtive trips to the convenience store next door to stock up on Diet Coke and cigarettes, my two new best friends. I ate little, subsisting on foodstuffs found in the pantry on the few occasions that I found myself hungry. As the food supply dwindled I invented strange combinations, or rather concoctions, but it made little difference; I hardly noticed the taste. All I was doing was stoking the furnace to fuel the cloud of doom that hung over me, threatening to burst at any second.

Finally I decided that I was boring even myself. It was no longer fun to wallow. My taste buds, now inured to the shock of caffeine and nicotine, were reactivating, while my culinary creations were becoming progressively more revolting. It was finally time to gird my loins and make a foray out into the real world.

But first my loins badly needed cleaning. Wallowing in self-pity is a dirty, smelly, pastime, and I was stunned when I finally looked in the mirror and saw the old person who stared back. Depression I could abide, but premature aging was definitely out of the question. Here was a situation that I could actually do something about, and it was even easy. All I had to do was clean up, and I could lose at least ten years. Well, maybe five if I squinted.

As I stood in the shower and let the fragrance of shampoo fill my nostrils, I decided that taking stock of my life was futile. I'd been doing it for what seemed like ages and got nothing but depressed and dirty for the effort. I dried my hair, put on a little makeup, slipped into gray flannel pants and a soft pink cashmere sweater that had faint delicious traces of perfume lingering. The outfit almost tricked me into feeling successful again. I looked in the mirror and was no longer frightened. I wasn't exactly beautiful, but I had turned a few heads in my time and today I actually felt that given the opportunity, I might still be able to swing it.

Recognizing myself for the first time in weeks, I came to the conclusion that I hadn't fared badly through the siege. If anything, I had lost some weight, which any woman knows is never a bad thing, especially if it can be accomplished without the trials of dieting. I was about to consider what the next step would be in my resurfacing expedition when I heard a definite banging at my door. This presented me with my first decision in weeks: Should I or should I not answer the door? In my frame of mind this was a ponderous proposition; somehow I knew it couldn't be good news. Nothing that insistent and persistent could bode well.

"Barbara, open the damned door. I know you're in there and I'm not going away!"

I stood there agonizing at my next move, thankful that most of my neighbors were at work getting on with their lives, and not home to hear the clamorous pounding that resounded through the halls. Next condo association meeting I was going to suggest thicker carpeting and perhaps some kind of fabric on the walls. Then people could pound like hell and not disturb the rest of the building. This seemed much more engrossing a topic than addressing the caller. The nosy biddy who lived across the hall would definitely be home and alert to any activity from my side of the corridor, but she'd likely be thankful for the diversion. Spying on me must have been deadly dull of late.

I refocused, puzzled. In my recent incarnation as an affluent employed person I had taken up residence in a classy building, fully loaded with all the amenities—an upscale dream dwelling with pool, sauna, whirlpool, exercise room loaded with useless but impressive-looking machines, sundeck for those few months of summer and those too dumb to fear skin cancer, and twenty-four-hour doormen and security. How had Susan ventured this far without my being alerted? Anger at services I could no longer afford but was still paying for and definitely not getting propelled me to open the door.

"How did you get in?"

"Nice to see you too. Easy. Just hung around the garage door until someone drove out, and I snuck in." The shit-eating grin on her face did nothing to alleviate my already nasty disposition.

"But the door from the garage to the building is locked," I persisted. "You need a key."

I wouldn't let go. I needed to know just how badly the service in the building had let me down, just like everyone and everything else I knew had. Hey, I had been practicing this wallow for three weeks, and just because I was clean and presentable I wasn't giving up the mood that easily.

"They're taking out the garbage. The door was open."

I countered truculently. "Why didn't you just ring the door-bell like a normal person?" I didn't move. I figured the doorway was blocked, and if I was obnoxious enough maybe she would just leave.

"Well, you won't answer your phone. I've left tons of messages, and I finally decided to come see for myself."

True enough. Aside from soap operas and talk shows, my other diversion and entertainment during my self-imposed incarceration was listening to my machine take messages. First came the sympathetic calls as word got round, then concerned calls, then insistent, worried calls, and then finally, practically no calls at all. Which only fueled my lethargy. Even my friends gave up on me easily. Which absolutely proved no one cared about me. I'd teach them. What it was that I was going to instruct I didn't even try to figure out, but nonetheless, they would learn. My reasoning powers seem to have been in as great a disarray as my surroundings.

However, in cleaning myself up I had managed to sweep some of the cobwebs from my head, and I could now think almost rationally, albeit not graciously.

"I didn't feel like talking to anyone. Go away."

"Hey, are you hiding someone delicious in there?" she asked, trying to peer around me.

"Yeah, he's about twenty-five, gorgeous, hung like a horse, and doesn't say much. You may as well come in," I said almost civilly as I backed away and opened the door only a notch wider to let her in.

She looked around, her eyes wide.

"Two choices. You've been robbed or you really are the world's all-time greatest living slob. This is amazing. How can you find anything? Where should I sit—or should I correct that to stand, as every chair seems to have something suspicious on it?"

For the first time in weeks I looked around the room with objective eyes.

"At least you have the decency to blush," she said with a malicious grin.

It truly was a disaster area. I hadn't put anything away for three weeks of constant habitation, and scattered everywhere were dirty dishes, soiled clothes, overflowing ashtrays, and weeks' worth of unread newspapers. The pièce de résistance was, by quick calculation of average consumption, the approximately 200 empty cans of Diet Coke that littered the entire apartment.

"At least it doesn't smell," I said defensively. I didn't quite believe it myself, but my stare dared her to argue with me. Although I had recently resurfaced, I wasn't yet ready to be confronted with the worst of my bad habits. My slothfulness always simmers just below the surface, threatening at all times to bubble over.

"What happened to Mme Jacqueline? Did she finally give up on you?"

Mme Jacqueline was, is, and, I fervently pray, always will be my cleaning lady. My pathological inability to return things to their proper places, countered by my desire to have things at all times orderly, led me on a long search that culminated with Mme Jacqueline coming on Mondays and Thursdays to repair the damage created between.

A sturdy French-Canadian woman of uncertain age, Mme Jacqueline speaks English poorly and writes French atrociously. With her brood of grown-up children gone, she looks on me as all of them rolled into one, and once again she knows she's needed. She's not mistaken. She picks up my clothes, washes, irons, vacuums, and scrubs floors and toilets cheerfully, all the while muttering to herself how incorrigible I am. But she mutters affectionately. At least I hope she does. The present condition of my apartment was enough to attest to how quickly and badly things around me degenerate without her.

Her main drawback is that she loves to talk. A calamity is always brewing somewhere in her seven children's extended families. Having thrown her husband out of the house the day after her youngest daughter got married, she fills the time she no longer spends in argument with self-help groups, volunteer work, and martial arts courses.

While I was still working I didn't see her often, making sure to leave before she arrived. Every now and then she purposely comes early, and I have to spend an hour catching up on everything. Generally, we communicate with notes she sticks to the refrigerator door informing me of the cleaning products I need to buy and passing editorial comment on any acquisition made since her last visit. Mostly, I need Windex. I could swear she drinks the stuff

When I went into hibernation I couldn't face the prospect of her incessant chatter and I no longer had anywhere to go to escape. So I told her not to come and the systematic destruction of my apartment went unnoticed by anyone, particularly me.

"I told her I was going away," I mumbled.

"Yeah, like she'll really believe you when she comes back and sees this." Susan swept her arms around the room unsympathetically. "Look, either you clean this mess yourself, which you know is impossible, or you tell her to get herself over here immediately. I'll pay for it if I have to, although you can't convince me that you're that broke. Jeez, this is unbelievable." Her head shook from side to side slowly, overwhelmed by the sight before her.

"Sure you'll pay. You're just rolling in it." I wasn't relinquishing my long mope just yet. Although I knew she was trying to help, she made me feel like a charity case.

It was as if she read my mind. "It isn't charity, if that's what you're thinking. I need you, and I need you fully operative. No one, not even you, can function in this mess." She rooted around and found the buried phone. "Here," she said, handing it to me. "Call her now. It's still early, and she can probably come in today. There's at least a month's work for a normal person, but knowing her, she can make a serious dent. How do you find anything?"

"I know where everything is," I muttered untruthfully, slightly abashed.

I don't like anyone confronting me with my slovenliness at the best of times. It's a bad trait that I usually suppress, and few people know what a slob I really am. This isn't a case of feeling sorry for myself. It's a truth I have learned to accept and have invented ways of concealing from almost everybody. I'm the fat person who never eats in public or the closet alcoholic who only drinks alone. But with the irrefutable evidence surrounding me, I was embarrassed at being caught with my pants all over the place.

"Call her now," she commanded, "and then I'll tell you why I came over. We can be out of here before she arrives. I imagine even you are too embarrassed to face her. Think of it"—she let her eyes go dreamy—"when you come back you'll actually be able to see the floor."

I should have been alerted then and there. "Come back" implied that I would be going somewhere, something I was not at all prepared for. But the concept of having order restored with no significant effort on my part was indeed seductive, far outweighing the realization that the return of Mme Jacqueline would signal the official end of my self-imposed mourning. I dialed.

"She'll be here in an hour," I said, almost smiling as I hung up.

I felt curiously cheered. I had made a decision, albeit a forced decision but a decision nonetheless. I was definitely moving forward and it hadn't even been that difficult. I would see where this would lead. I felt so confident about my ability to cope that I looked on Susan pleasantly and no longer resented her intrusion. Much.

Cleaning ladies are the true saviors.

I noticed that Susan had swept away a pile of newspapers and aged, empty pizza boxes, unearthing a chair. She was trying to arrange herself neatly in this newfound place, creating a semblance of order in the sea of sloth. Clutching her handbag closely to her chest as if afraid of contamination, she looked uncomfortable and foreign. In a childish, vindictive fashion I was pleased to note her discomfiture. She's always so self-possessed.

"What can I do for you?" I said with the hint of a smile.

"It's Frank."

"It's always Frank."

Frank is her ex-husband. Technically, he is still her husband. They have been separated for six years now, but never actually divorced.

"What new technique has he come up with to annoy you?"

"Nothing new. Same thing as always. Money. I know the bastard is socking it away somewhere, and I can't find it. He keeps whining about how poor he is, but Bimbo is living way beyond her possible income, with no visible means of support besides him. It bugs the hell out of me that she's living better than I am. Do you know Robert's school called and informed me with glacial certainty that if Mr. Porter didn't come up with the money for last semester within a week they would kick Robert out? Notice I said last semester. She knows better than to ask for this semester's money up front. I'm too embarrassed to go to parent-teacher night. I think they all know about me."

Her discomfort bested her intentions, and she immediately stood up and began to pace, crunching hidden mysteries as she walked.

"I don't care if he stiffs me. Not true, I care a lot. But doing this to Robert is unthinkable. Frank always pretends to dote on him and tells everyone what a great father he is. I have a piddly job that barely covers the cost of the housekeeper, who needs to be there when Robert gets home from school. I can't take it anymore. He's hiding something, and this time I mean to find out."

Susan has never divorced Frank because of those alleged hidden assets. He is the master of bankruptcy, having honed the technique to a fine art. He goes into business and within three years is gone. It is such a constant pattern that it surprises me that he isn't in jail. Susan knows that if she files for divorce she'll get nothing except lawyer's bills. This way, he at least pays her basic expenses, although he is generally in arrears. Bailiffs at the door are no strangers to her.

She appears wealthy enough. Shopping on Frank's credit cards is her revenge. When the cards are seized, which has happened often enough for her to have gotten over the humiliation a long time ago, she just badgers him until they are reinstated and the pattern begins all over again. It's a convoluted arrangement, but it seems to satisfy them both.

Frank, for his part, actually prefers to stay married. It prevents women from pressing him too hard for wedded bliss. He can claim a neurotic, suicidal wife and a child who won't survive further damage, and that usually keeps them off his case for a while. He maintains a good front, always blaming his failures on others. The testament to his excellent salesmanship is that most people believe him. The consummate promoter, he stages fashion extravaganzas on a scale rarely seen outside New York, Paris, or Milan, certainly not in Montreal. You *have* to believe he is successful. Normal businessmen don't mount such hooplas in the hope of getting an order; it's simply too expensive for no guarantee of return. But Frank doesn't hope for the orders, he *knows* they'll come pouring in. Only they never do since the product is shoddy, and so periodically he quietly folds his tents, finds a new sucker to back him, and begins the charade anew.

Susan certainly would never be caught dead wearing any of his creations. They are inevitably ugly and cheap, though with dramatic lighting and flashy staging he always manages to pass off his monstrosities as the latest thing in Paris. Vladivostok more likely. He produces an excellent rendering of K-Mart styling at Neiman Marcus prices. P. T. Barnum would have been proud.

Pretty despicable way of conducting business, in my corporately trained eyes.

I have never liked him, and can't hide the fact from Susan, though I try. He is her problem, not mine, and my opinion doesn't matter at this stage of the relationship. Physically I find him revolting. He has too much red hair, thick Mick Jagger lips, and eyes that never settle on anything. They dart around like a Secret Service man's, always eyeing the exits, never looking directly at you. It is disconcerting to try to engage in a conversation with him, since he always makes you feel that something much more interesting is happening across the room. Baggy pants with tapered cuffs, shirts buttoned to the collar, state-of-the-art sneakers. Mostly black or charcoal gray. Sometimes shiny.

But it's that hair. Teased, carefully arranged, and sprayed

into an immovable cap, it is a testament to the seventies and gives him a painfully large head on a small neck.

I've never been very generous when it comes to Frank.

"He's been hiding something his whole life. When he was a kid he probably lied about what he got for Christmas so he could use the other kids' toys rather than share his own," I said.

"No. This isn't the usual. This is something bigger," she said, her voice taking on an unaccustomed grave tone.

That caught my attention. Susan is rarely grave. She has a natural gregariousness and infectious enthusiasm, coupled with a wry sense of humor. She makes light of almost everything, which for her is an effective coping mechanism. That is, everything except her son. Robert is the light of her life, and she loves and protects him fiercely. She's even forgiving toward Frank because without him she wouldn't have Robert, and she couldn't imagine life without him.

I'm childless myself, never having taken the time from the fast track to get married, but I admire her devotion.

We were still standing, since there truly was no fit place to sit. Susan continued pacing, stepping on things without feeling them, looking everywhere and not seeing anything, picking up objects and discarding them.

"What is it? What's wrong?" I was impatient with the buildup.

"I'll give you the short version."

For this I was indeed thankful. Susan can spin a yarn to astonishing lengths with hilarious results, but I was in no mood for an extended tour. Anyway, it didn't sound like a funny story.

"As I said, he's been spending a fortune on Bimbo."

Susan calls all Frank's girlfriends Bimbo and Bimbette, by turns. This way she can distinguish the current from the past and anticipate the future. She pretends not to know their real names, although being Susan, I'm sure she has more information about them than their own mothers.

"And I do mean a fortune. Furs, trips, jewelry, the whole kit and caboodle. Meanwhile I'm getting nothing. The rent check bounced again."

"Have you discussed this with him?" I asked stupidly.

She looked at me like I was seriously mentally deficient.

"You know him. It's an accounting mistake. Shit. I called his accountant and he says Frank is going bankrupt again. He also says he's been trying to reach Frank, but Frank never calls back." She looked directly at me through narrowed eyes, implying that I wasn't much better. I was so intrigued with the story that I didn't take umbrage. "The accountant says there's no money. But there is. I know there is. He just spent twenty-two thousand dollars on a new Rolex watch for himself."

"How do you know it isn't a fake? And he's not just bull-shitting you as usual?" Frank has been known to flaunt his self-proclaimed affluence with Taiwan copies of designer anything, which stand only cursory inspection. A gift from Frank generally has a shelf life of two months.

"It's real enough. Last week I brought my pearls in to be restrung, and the jeweler asked me if I was pleased with Mr. Porter's new watch."

"What did you say?" I felt a smirk rising but suppressed it. At last, a television situation come to life.

"I said it was gorgeous and I was thinking of buying one for my father, and how much was it."

"Your father's dead."

"He doesn't know that, dummy."

"And he told you?" I couldn't believe it. Somebody should buy this man a *TV Guide* and let him read plot summaries. He has a lot to learn.

"Okay, the guy's not brilliant. All he saw was more dollars and I guess he thought if Frank could pay cash for one watch he could pay cash for two."

"Cash!"

"Yeah, cash. Close your mouth and tell me where he's getting all that money all of a sudden. His accountant sure as shit doesn't know anything about it."

I thought about it but could come up with no decent answer. Admittedly, all kinds of indecent ideas flashed through my head. Frank was sleazy, okay, maybe a little larcenous, but surely not criminal. Yet only some sort of illegal activity could account for all that cash. He had to be an idiot to flash that kind of money around so publicly. Actually, the only smart thing he had ever done was marry Susan, and even that he couldn't manage to sustain for long.

She kept pacing, having by now worn a path through the debris. This was really bothering her. I knew she was always after him for money and resented the bind he had her in, but this was beyond normal resentment.

"Give me a cigarette," she demanded.

"I thought you quit."

With a sweeping gesture around the disaster scene that surrounded her, she proclaimed malevolently, "There's so much smoke hanging in the air in this pigsty. What's the difference?"

She was immediately contrite.

"Sorry. You don't deserve that. I know you've been going through a hard time, but I need your help. I'm obsessed with this cash influx."

I gave her a cigarette. Her hand trembled as she lit it and inhaled deeply; she seemed calmer when she finally exhaled softly.

"God, I miss these. My kid would kill me if he found out I was smoking. What kind of shit are they teaching in schools these days? I'm sure there's a concerted effort to make parents' lives miserable. A grand scheme thought up by teachers as the ultimate revenge for being treated like baby-sitters by the board. Robert thinks smoking is as dangerous as stepping in front of a speeding train and only one very small step up from driving without a seat belt. God, next year, when he's nine, they'll teach him about AIDS and he'll start checking my purse for condoms every time I leave the house. I think he's terrified that I'll die and leave him. I don't think the idea of living with Frank full time appeals to him very much."

She shook herself, realizing she had digressed.

"You remember how we used to play 'What Should We Be When We Grow Up?'" she asked, changing gears.

"Susan, what's this 'used to' stuff? We played that two months ago."

"Whatever . . ." she said, flapping the air.

She wouldn't be diverted and I had given it my best shot. Any talk of age usually snaps her to attention, since Susan has perfected the art of lying about her age. I'm not sure she even knows how old she really is. But I do, I thought smugly.

She continued on track. "We both wanted to be detectives à la *Charlie's Angels,* which dates us badly. We should change that to another program." She thought for a bit. "Shit, there aren't even any decent role models in the crime field anymore. Jessica Fletcher is too old to even consider. What's happened to television anyway?

"Look, stop distracting me," she continued, to my amazement; I hadn't said anything. I remained silent, curious to see where this would lead.

"You're the perfect accomplice."

I didn't like the phraseology but still held my tongue. This was definitely intriguing.

"We're both nosy."

Now this was going too far. "I prefer to think of myself as inquisitive," I said haughtily.

She didn't miss a beat. Turning to face me directly, she said, "You taught me to steam open envelopes."

I couldn't tell if it was an accusation or a compliment. But it was true.

What had finally convinced Susan to marry Frank was reading letters I steamed open for her. They were from some girl who I decided had to be a half-wit, since she was obviously crazy about him and practically volunteered to lay down her life for him. She'd even written nice things about his hair. Susan misguidedly figured that if someone else wanted him that badly, he must have some intrinsic value. So she said yes the next time he asked, which didn't take very long, since he had been asking daily for the past month. She never did think it through. Like when had he met this girl who professed undying love? Susan and Frank had been seeing each other supposedly exclusively for the last nine months. Since we were now here spying, steaming open all his suspicious mail, she should have had some doubts.

Not exactly the world's greatest love match. They had a quick, small wedding—a lot like ripping a Band-Aid off in the hope that it will be painless.

I wasn't invited to the event, and twelve years later I was still secretly insulted.

2

I INSISTED WE take my car. Susan is an erratic driver at the best of times, her attention split between adjusting her makeup in the rearview mirror, looking directly into the eyes of her hapless passenger as she speaks, and lastly, watching where she is going. With her attention on the road for only 30 percent of the time on good days, I couldn't face the tension of the death seat with her this upset. I was too newly hatched from my chrysalis to contemplate almost certain extinction.

As we waited for the elevator to take us down to the garage, she repeatedly jabbed the call button, willing it to come immediately. Her agitation was contagious, and I rooted nervously through my purse for my car keys, spilling and retrieving lipstick, pens, and my wallet simultaneously. We were now both a bundle of nerves.

I calmed down immediately as soon as I got behind the wheel and felt the engine spark to life. Three and a half weeks, and she purred on ignition. Clicking open the garage, I headed out for the first time in almost a month. So far this seemed pretty easy.

Snow had fallen overnight, and my tires crunched satisfactorily on the packed roads. I love my car. It's a 560 SL Mercedes that I bought on a milestone birthday to reward myself for I don't know what. And I don't care what either. It has always had the ability to make me feel special; I feel invincible and beautiful at the same time in that car. Neither its aging nor mine has diminished that power. Previously, I had never had much interest in cars, considering them solely as means of transportation. But with the advent of the SL, driving took on new meaning. I now understand that ridiculous geriatric word "motoring." Whenever I feel the least bit down, I get in the car and cruise around aimlessly. Usually it takes no more than fifteen minutes for the world to be right again. I don't know if all Mercedeses are like this, but I do know that mine is magical.

Comfortably at the helm, I headed down the hill toward Frank's house. I was almost successful in blocking out Susan's anxious presence as she busied herself with the inevitable lip liner. I firmly believe lip liner to be one of mankind's more hideous inventions. I cannot fathom why any woman would perform such an inherently private and unattractive act so publicly. Especially in restaurants. Usually, just as I am about to bite into my sandwich with gusto, I catch sight of a woman who's already wearing too much makeup making an obscene moue and lining her lips in some disgusting shade of purple. Why is lip liner always purple or brown?

At the instant the light changed, the car behind me honked impatiently, interrupting my toilette reverie. I found I was having trouble concentrating on the road, everything around seeming at once foreign and interesting. It felt like I had been away for aeons and was just now rediscovering the city of my past. Flakes swirled gently, making the world look like one of those souvenir-store snow shakers. It really was pretty out here, and I realized I'd missed it.

Turning right, we headed west along Sherbrooke Street,

passing the Museum of Fine Arts on the right. I've always liked that building, with its sturdy pillars and expansive staircase. Today it was crowned with white, which added to its stately elegance. The classical structure commands attention and respect, proudly pronouncing that therein one may find culture and beauty. Directly across the street sits the new addition to the museum. As an offspring it's the prodigal son, clumsy and graceless, a hodgepodge of styles in an ungainly box. It screams "Aren't I clever?" It isn't. It's just plain ugly. I'll never understand why the powers that be have allowed such a travesty to desecrate the centuries-old charm of the street.

Tree-lined Sherbrooke Street between University and Guy is the grand dame of avenues. Its architecture is a tribute to the industrial founding fathers of the city, who considered it the correct place to live and built homes to match their incomes and stature. Most of these mansions have been reclaimed as private clubs and corporate headquarters, but the integrity of the street has been pretty much maintained. There was a flurry of demolition and ugly reconstruction in the early seventies, halted before too much damage could be done, and the Save Montreal committee has done a good job preventing further desecration. Except for the new museum. I'm personally convinced money changed hands somewhere to permit such a conglomeration of facades. I solve the problem of visual pollution by always looking at the other side of the street whenever I pass, pretending the blot doesn't exist.

We arrived at Frank's building in lower Westmount within ten minutes. I hadn't known where he lived, but Susan directed me with that imperious tone usually reserved for newly arrived immigrant taxi drivers. It didn't bother me today; being outside was too exhilarating. I was almost enjoying myself.

There was no doorman posted at Frank's building, one of those blocks slapped up by a developer who understands that the building itself isn't of prime importance, the address is. We let ourselves into the empty lobby, the standard beige marble with the standard stupid fountain tinkling away in the corner. It made me want to go to the bathroom.

The elevator ride to the twelfth floor passed too quickly. Now that my instincts were returning, I began to comprehend just what I was letting myself in for. I wasn't exactly thrilled by the prospect. Although Susan had a key, so it was technically only unlawful entry, I saw the specters of Breaking and Entering loom over my shoulders like little devils in kids' comic books. They were menacing. Years ago, when I last broke into Frank's apartment with Susan, I was younger and braver. And stupider. With the advancing years I've become a more upstanding citizen, with a greater understanding of the consequences of my actions. Sometimes I think that makes me boring, but it's a lot safer than risking real incarceration.

The corridors were thinly carpeted in brown; the wallpaper was a beige-and-brown plaid. A wall sconce announcing each doorway served as the only illumination. The desired effect may have been subdued understatement, but at the moment it felt foreboding.

I was certainly surprised at Frank's apartment itself. I had been kind of expecting a swinger's pad, loaded with chrome and brass, deep gold shag carpeting, stereo speakers the size of Stonehenge, and a conspicuous bar with pinto-covered stools. My prejudices about Frank extend to all facets of his life.

Instead, I was presented with a spacious three-bedroom unit with one of the bedrooms converted into a den/office.

The living room had two deep couches that faced each other on either side of a beautiful burled wood coffee table. The space had a southwestern feeling, warm and not at all overdecorated. *Architectural Digest* would never come calling, but some of the lesser magazines might. Soft peach, turquoise, and creamy beige were reflected in all the accent pieces, with a patterned wing chair tying the whole thing together. The floor was covered with rust-colored Mexican paving stones, and dhurrie rugs were gracefully scattered about. On the walls were tasteful lithos, all of them signed. It was comfortable and homey and totally un-Frank.

My eyes must have betrayed my surprise; before I could even open my mouth, Susan said, "Nice, eh? Bimbo Number One was an interior designer, and she did all this."

She swept her arm around the room in a gesture that signified either admiration or disgust. I think it was a combination.

"She didn't last, though. As soon as she was finished he moved on. But he did get his fifteen-percent trade discount out of her. Bimbos and Bimbettes sometimes have other talents besides being decorative and submissive."

I wondered about Bimbo Number One. She obviously had better taste in furnishings than in men.

Without another glance around, Susan headed straight for the den and started rummaging through the papers on the granite-topped desk, which had to have cost a fortune, discount or no discount.

Now that I was inside and the crime was already in progress, I had nothing left to lose, so I decided to satisfy my growing curiosity. First, of course, I inspected the master bedroom. The southwestern motif was carried through to here. A giant cactus thrived by the sun-filled window. The shadow blinds were peach, the deep carpet warm beige, and the king-size bed, topped with a fluffy patterned duvet and lots of complementary pillows, dominated the space. An intricate Indian Dreamcatcher hung in the window, its crystal center fragmenting the light into rainbows that spread across the carpet like soft terrazzo. A vase filled with wilted tulips was the only sign of disorder.

It was a restful room, designed for peaceful sleep and not the wild orgies I had conjured up for Frank.

The other bedroom was a boy's room, obviously decorated with Robert in mind. Hockey was the underlying theme, with a full set of Canadiens hockey cards, framed and mostly auto-graphed, hanging above the bed. It was visually interesting, and although the collection had probably cost a fortune in the first instance, it would surely appreciate in the future.

What engrossed me most was all the electronic gadgetry. Any eight-year-old boy would kill for a setup like this. If I were Robert I would beg to come here as often as possible and never leave this room. On the other hand, I didn't know what the atmosphere was like when the occupants were in residence. But toys like this could compensate for a lot.

For the first time I began to understand Susan's anger. If someone lived like this and made me jump through hoops just to get the meager sum promised me, I would indeed be very, very angry. And probably more than a little spiteful. Lots of big bucks had been invested in this place.

My curiosity got the best of me, and I went back to the master bedroom. Frank had surprised me so far, and I wanted to see what other facet of his personality I could uncover. So I headed straight for the closet, storage space for most of our secrets. I switched on the light and was almost blinded by the glare. Here resided the true and present Bimbo. Enough stiletto heels to satisfy Imelda, and thousands and thousands of span-gles and sequins and bugle beads. There were enough evening gowns to clothe all fifty contestants of the Miss America pageant. And clothe them well, by their standards. I was stunned. Now I'm pretty well connected, invited to probably more than my fair share of black tie galas, but not only would I never be caught dead in any of these abominations, it would take me at least three years' worth of events to run through the entire repertoire. Most of the garments still had price tags attached. Hefty price tags.

I unwillingly conjured up an image of Bimbo. A blond Mar-ilyn wannabe, standing in her closet, wistfully fingering all her wonderful new clothes. She just knew these would be her passport to a wild and exciting life. The prospect of life in the fast lane made her quiver with excitement. She felt she was very lucky.

I shuddered away the image, not wanting to feel any sympathy for Bimbo out of loyalty to Susan, and quickly snapped off the light, retreating to the bedroom. I didn't look into Frank's closet. I didn't want to learn any more secrets about him. The thought of pathetic Bimbo pinning all her hopes and aspirations on Frank made me dislike him all the more. We were getting real close to hate here.

Since my encounter with the fountain in the lobby I still had not gone to the bathroom, and it was becoming urgent. I opted for the one connected to the master bedroom, where I could continue my inspection under the guise of the call of nature. Bathrooms always fascinate me. People never expect strangers to use them, and they often reflect their owner's nature. I have rooted out other secret slobs whose bedrooms and kitchens are immaculate but whose bathrooms are to me a comfortable jumble.

This room was clearly Frank's domain. Opening all the cabinets, I counted six cans of hair spray, all loaded with fluorocarbons. Now I could add environmental pollution to the list of Frank's heinous crimes. Aside from this, there was nothing much else of interest. It was as tidy as the rest of the house, with not a single red hair to be found in any of the three styling brushes lined up with military precision beside the blow dryer on the counter. I wondered if Mme Jacqueline had a clone; I should find out who this supercleaner was and file her away as backup.

What struck me as odd was that there was absolutely no trace of Bimbo in this room. Which indicated that she was not yet secure of her tenure. True, she had commandeered the master closet, but she hadn't yet attained the master bathroom, the true symbol of incumbency.

I went back to Susan, unable to cope with Frank's life anymore. He repulsed me more and more with every passing discovery, and I just wanted to be out of there. Also, pondering Bimbo's life made me realize that Susan had said Frank was out of town but had made no reference to Bimbo. She could walk in at any moment, and that was one confrontation I didn't relish.

"Find anything?" I asked as I approached the den.

"Nothing except lots of receipts for stuff he obviously didn't buy for me. And all paid for in cash. Where is it all coming from?" she wailed plaintively. "Lots of new electronic shit since I was last here." She pointed to a large-screen TV and a tiny CD/stereo that I could guarantee delivered big sound. A camcorder sat nearby, and I flipped it open to see if there was a tape inside. Empty. It didn't even look used. Beside the state-of-the-art VCR with its handy thousand-function remote there was a collection of tapes. I thought maybe I'd find something interesting there, but on closer inspection, most of the tapes seemed to be targeted at the preteen market. The standard Saturday-morning babysitter. And I bet Robert could operate any and all of these electronic marvels like a pro.

I was a little envious.

Her brow furrowed as she looked impotently around. "I'm just so frustrated. It's so unfair." She burst into tears, sobbing quietly in the face of her husband's unfounded success.

I didn't know what she had expected to find, but clearly finding nothing incriminating was too much for her. The lack of vindication was deflating.

I tried to placate her. "Let's go. We'll figure something out between the two of us." I really wanted to get out of there. Anxiety was taking over at an alarming pace.

She gave me a baleful glare as if to say, if she couldn't figure anything out, how could I? I let the implied insult slide as she sniffled along to the bathroom to make repairs, closing the door sharply behind her. At least I was spared the agony of watching lip liner application again.

Not knowing what to do and afraid to tangle with Susan by hurrying her along, I headed instinctively for the phone. In my recent life I had spent quite a lot of time attached to it, and it was almost a reflex action. But I couldn't think of who to call. I hadn't returned any of my messages for over three weeks, and I wasn't yet prepared to make idle chitchat with anybody. This nonevent at Frank's was subtly unsettling.

So I dialed my machine, expecting nothing. I'm not one of these people who profess to hate answerers. I wholeheartedly recognize them as one of the better inventions of this electronic age. Spending so much time on the phone in my business life has left me a little shy of it on my personal time. I like to leave short succinct messages to arrange meetings with the people I want to see. Leaving a message precludes having to inquire about health and happiness until I actually see them. Since inevitably all person-to-person interchanges begin with this ritual, I'm just saving time and energy. Most of all, I like to screen my calls, picking and choosing who I'll talk to. My sense of selfimportance verged on arrogance in the latter days of my working life, but unemployment has humbled me, and perhaps returned me to a more even keel.

At the beep a disembodied voice said, "Okay, you finally went out for real. I know you're not there. I spoke to that woman in what she thinks is English. Listen, now that you're sprung, meet me at the Ritz for tea at three-thirty. I need to talk to you. It's important. Be there."

Joanne also likes succinct messages.

3

AFTER DROPPING SUSAN off at her car, neither of us any wiser about the mysterious cash, I headed off to the supermarket to replenish my barren pantry. I had lots of time before my next appointment, and I couldn't go home yet. Mme Jacqueline was surely there working her fingers to the bone, lying in wait. Too soon to face that, and too early for Joanne.

I frittered away the better part of three hours shopping for groceries, browsing through the library for new books, and reading my new treasure happily ensconced on my favorite stool at my favorite lunch counter, and I heartily enjoyed every second of it. Time was not the novelty. Space was. This outdoors was great, and I realized there were lots of other places besides my four and a half rooms. And the fresh air! And other people! And food that was appetizing!

It was heady stuff, this free time, and I felt intoxicated. I was engulfed by a positively sensual sense of freedom. Recreational drugs had nothing on this, and it didn't even cost much. It didn't earn anything either, but at the moment I chose to dismiss that fact. I was even considering myself blessed that I had chosen such a glorious day to reemerge. Nothing like a little self-denial to make you realize how great it is to be alive.

Then it was off to the Ritz. In a fit of generosity and largess I left my car with the doorman and went inside. It would probably cost me at least fifteen dollars plus tips to ransom it back, an expense I balked at even in my more affluent days, but today the sky was both blue and the limit. Besides, if I played my cards right Joanne would spring for tea, which should make it about even.

My boots clicked across the marble floors to the bar where the Ritz serves proper English afternoon tea daily in winter. In summer it's done in the garden, but since the snow was knee deep with no indication of stopping, I was relegated to the bar. Too bad, since in season the garden is a heavenly oasis in the middle of downtown, with baby ducks frolicking in the pond, surrounded by fabulous flowers and greenery, and on Saturdays it generally has a bride plunked in the middle, having her picture taken over and over as her hair progressively frizzes up. Beauty and entertainment at once.

The winter space is a lovely room with dark blue walls trimmed in cream and gold, where ladies in hats arrive daily for warm tea and polite conversation. Never have I heard voices raised there. An oval mahogany bar sits to one side servicing the small marble-topped tables that dot the blue-and-gold carpeting. At this time of day the front was reserved for drinking, but the back tables were covered in crisp white napery on which sat blue-and-gold-trimmed bone china. Silver accoutrements gleamed along with a crystal vase filled with fresh fragrant flowers, a luxury in February in Montreal.

Joanne was already installed, studiously poring over the menu, which she knows by heart. Just seeing her again made me feel good.

She has a perfectly formed head, with delicate ears usually embellished with small pearl stud earrings. High cheekbones, a good nose, and luminescent skin. She knows her strengths and dramatizes her look by wearing her honey-colored chin-length hair severely tied back off her face. On her it looks fabulous. The glasses needed to correct her severe astigmatism, which she constantly bemoans, draw attention to the deep brown eyes that peer out either sympathetically or cynically, depending on the circumstances, but always intelligently. Her body is boyish and tight, the kind that looks great in a bathing suit or pants but uncomfortable in a skirt or dress, which she consequently rarely wears.

Today the pants were brown tweed, topped with a bulky forest green sweater accenting the nubs in the tweed. I hadn't seen her in a while, and she looked great. She was glowing.

Which meant there was trouble afoot. When Joanne is annoyed or aggravated or excited she looks radiant, which lulls any opponent into a false sense of security. Equipped with a rapier wit and a level of sarcasm that surpasses even mine, she can destroy an unsuspecting vicitm easily. We've been friends since the first day of kindergarten, when, having hidden her glasses in her coat pocket after her mother had forced her to wear them to school, tantrum or no tantrum, she bumped into me and knocked me down before she even noticed me. Without those lenses she's virtually blind. Even at that tender age I recognized a kindred spirit in vanity and stubbornness. We've stuck together through school and her three marriages.

As I settled myself, she said exactly what I expected.

"I'm starved. Let's order, and then we'll talk."

Joanne is always ravenous, attacking any and all food with a gusto that suggests this is the first meal she's had in days or the last one she expects to have for the same period. Each morsel is swallowed appreciatively, accompanied by heavy chest sighs. It's very sexy. I've seen men across the room stop talking and hold their collective breath as they await the next bite. I can't figure out how she does it. I once practiced in front of the mirror but only succeeded in dribbling down the front of my silk blouse. My attempts at sexy sighs verged on the obscene, and more practice only threatened to enrich my dry cleaner dramatically. A constant admirer of this talent, I love to watch her eat.

After ordering the requisite Continental Tea with an extra pot of hot water and lots and lots of lemon, she settled back, almost ready to talk. Still, I knew I wouldn't have her full attention until the food arrived.

In her job as chief investigative reporter for the best-watched news program in the province, she carries a lot of clout. Her face is always there, at six and eleven, and she's somehow familiar to most people in the city. Out of context, off the air, people recognize her but can't exactly place her. Often I've seen someone rush familiarly over and then back away, shuffling embarrassedly. She loves these occasions, her mischievous streak inciting her to look back at them beckoningly and then go suddenly blank-faced as they approach, condescendingly tolerating their retreat. It's probably not the nicest thing to do, but it's fun to witness.

The waiter arrived, placing the three-tiered tea platter loaded with scones and sandwiches and tarts on the table between us. Joanne sighed audibly as he set down the double Devon clotted cream and assorted imported jams. The food had arrived, and now, at last, she was ready.

Spreading the napkin on her lap and buying some time to allow her to stuff her face, she said, "You first. What kind of package did you get?"

"Decent, I guess. They gave me twenty-four months."

"Get to keep your pass?" she mumbled between mouthfuls as she liberally slathered cream on a hot scone.

"Yeah. They didn't want me to, but I fought for it. Before I fell apart I negotiated like a tiger. It took two weeks to come to a final settlement. I don't think they were prepared for the opposition. They were sure I would go meekly. The pass was the one thing I had absolutely no intention of ever relinquishing. And"—I tossed my clean hair smugly—"I had it upgraded to lifetime, with first class on an available basis."

The object in question was my airline pass. Until recently my title was Vice President in Charge of Corporate and Public Relations at PanCanada Air, the premier airline in the country. As a title it was a mouthful; as a job it was stressful, exciting and fulfilling. When we were swallowed up by a huge American airline that I secretly believe will soon own all the airspace in the world, I was made redundant. That's actually the word used in my summons from the new CEO. I was called to his office on a snowy, dark Thursday afternoon to discuss my leaving and so he could express to me how sorry he was to lose me. He admired the quality of my work; but, with hands tossed to the winds, he said we couldn't support duplication in this leaner, cleaner environment. I had known what was coming, having heard the speech from some of my now equally redundant coworkers, and I had no intention of making it easy for him. If he was going to swallow us, I wasn't going to facilitate his spitting us out one at a time.

I wore my new killer Armani suit with the short, tight skirt, so impeccably tailored that it couldn't be considered anything but appropriate for business. Armani's genius is that he can make these superstraight garments become fluid entities, unexpectedly and incomprehensibly provocative and sexy.

Perched on the edge of my chair, I watched him watching my legs. They're all dirty old men at heart. I saw him assessing the possibility of keeping me on so he could "get to know me better." But he wasn't a CEO shark for nothing, and he quickly regained his composure and proceeded to do the nasty deed.

I didn't buckle easily; I left the airline with my reputation intact and my ego in tatters. But no matter—I still had my pass. And two years' severance, with all benefits. I could go anywhere they flew free, and since they flew everywhere, it could certainly be considered a genuine coup. Now that I was out of my tailspin and could look at the situation objectively, I realized I had done pretty well considering the circumstances.

It still unnerved me to talk about it, so I changed the subject. "What kind of drama are you into now?"

Joanne Cowan (née Cohen, but sanitized for professional reasons) doesn't lead a life. She directs a giant theater piece of which she is leading lady. There is always something up; nothing is ever boring around Joanne. What saves her from annoying arrogance is her sense of humor and incredible intelligence. She's the smartest person I know, and I know lots of people.

"Well, how shall I begin?" she tantalized. "The near past or the near future? Okay, the past first. I've had an affair."

Noticing the tense she used, I wasn't impressed. "So what's new about that?"

Joanne has a libido that is, to say the least, healthy. Very healthy. She's married at the moment, but that's never stopped her before. She's a sucker for tight buns, well-developed shoulders, a chiseled chin, and blond hair. She usually selects and discards her boy-toys with great rapidity. It never affects her relationship with her husband, currently a beleaguered surgeon who works as many hours as she does. To her it's just another passing adventure. I mean she doesn't talk to them, she just sleeps with them, and by telling me she absolves herself of all guilt. I am the confessional.

"What gym does he work out in?" They all work out. A lot.

"No gym. This time I've been extra naughty. I'm really stupid." I swear her eyes actually twinkled.

"So spill. I know you're dying to tell."

"Francesco Grandese!"

"What!"

Heads turned. I had raised my voice at that last "what," and the Ritz ladies with the blue hair tut-tutted in my direction, wondering who had let these young upstarts into their domain.

Usually the young-upstarts part would amuse me and gladden my aging soul, but I barely noticed. I was in absolute shock. Joanne's flair for the dramatic had paid off big this time.

"What!" I repeated like an idiot, only quieter this time.

"Close your mouth." It was the second time today someone had told me to shut my mouth. It's a good thing there are no flies around in winter.

"Do you know who he is?" I asked stupidly.

"Of course I know who he is, you moron."

Who he is, is the reputed head of organized crime for the eastern seaboard of Canada. Who he is, is a very dangerous man, although neither the police nor the RCMP have ever been able to pin anything on him. This was audacious even for Joanne.

"Isn't he married?" I seemed to be cornering the market on stupid questions and remarks. I was still reeling from this bomb-shell and couldn't think of anything remotely intelligent to say. Dozens more dumb questions flashed through my mind. I had to get a grip on myself.

"Of course he is. But then, so am I."

She actually found all this amusing. Her sense of self-pres-ervation seemed to have deserted her. Didn't she realize? I stopped myself before I said that and continued with a modicum of intelligence. "Okay. Start from the beginning. Where on earth did you meet him?"

There. At last a question worthy of a response.

"I was covering the Chamber of Commerce annual awards dinner, and he was at my table."

This was too much. "What!" I was saying that a lot. "He got the award for upstanding citizenship? He got an award for show-ing tremendous growth and profits in these recessionary times? He got an award for creative marketing?"

She giggled.

"No, dummy. He was there as a respected businessman in the community and a paid-up member of the chamber. That's funny enough in itself, but I like your take better. Anyway, he looked at me and I looked at him and it was kismet. Actually he ignored me pretty much the whole evening, but I had kismet. That isn't English, is it? Never mind. You know they say power is the greatest aphrodisiac, and I can vouch for the truth of that statement. I mean, I hardly flirted at all. I was very well behaved."

Hardly flirted for Joanne means dangerous instead of lethal.

"I was sure nothing would come of it, but the next day the floral bombardment began. Not just the regular tacky roses. One day an amaryllis, one day two dozen perfect tulips, one day a huge spray of lilacs. In January. My living room has a fortune in plants and flowers occupying every available space. I'm living on antihistamines for my allergies, but I can't bear to part with them. Let them die the natural death of neglect. If I could get my cleaning lady to ignore them, it would speed up the process and I could breathe again. I told Jacques they were from an unknown admirer, and now he's fretting about stalkers, but I can handle him.

"Each delivery came with a personalized card. I wonder if he wrote them himself or had some minion do it. *Now* I wonder. Then I was titillated. And the sexy phone calls. All innuendo. Nothing overt. He'd be interested in my health, my sorrows, my triumphs. He's really very talented at this. Probably has lots of practice."

"At least you recognize that. It's a healthy sign."

"Shut up if you want me to continue."

Everyone was bossing me around today. No use arguing; she was revving her motor and getting into gear. It was indeed shaping up to be a good story. The look on her face bespoke a punch line worth waiting for.

Nibbling at the pastries, she continued with her mouth full. "So I'll make this short and sweet and spare you all the details."

No fair. I live for her details. Joanne's stories of her sex life have been entertaining me for years. I love the graphic descriptions. She says the things other people never dare voice.

No way. "No fair," I moaned. "Come across."

"Okay, I'll spare you some of them. I'll skip the boring parts. At the end of all these flowers and conversations there came an invitation to go away with him for the weekend. All very hush-hush and discreet. Get to do the dirty out of town. More romantic that way. Or so I thought, at least. I said yes. Don't say 'What!' in that tone of voice, or I'll stop right now."

Like a good girl I held my tongue.

"We took off for Whistler."

I could only stay still for so long. "But Joanne, you don't ski."

Whistler, British Columbia, is Canada's finest ski resort. It has a world-class reputation, and lately, with the Americans on a Japan-bashing kick, lots and lots of Asians with pots and pots of money.

"Idiot. You are obtuse today. All that isolation has put your brain in slow motion. Hop to it. Who wanted to ski? I went to get laid."

"Oh." I said that quietly, afraid that if I made another faux pas she would stop telling her story, and I really wanted to hear it. At least someone had been getting some action lately.

"We arrived late Friday night. By private jet, no less. Belonging to Pacific Sugar. There's a good story in there somewhere, I'm sure, but I behaved myself and asked no questions."

I found that hard to believe but didn't dare contest.

"On the plane we talked of literature and philosophy and all that artsy-fartsy stuff. He likes Hegel and hard-boiled detective stories. What does that mean? Is it true? Well, we finally get there and are driven, by limo of course, to this huge chalet. Enormous. It could have been a hotel, but we were the only two there. Excluding the raft of servants lined up at the door to greet us. Very Victorian. Another story there, I'm sure, but again I held my tongue. You wouldn't have recognized me.

"I'm shown to my room. I figure it's for the help. Keep up appearances, you know. But no. He gives me a languid peck on the forehead, gropes my ass and sends me off to bed. Whoa, I came to get laid, and now this. What gives? Okay, it's been a long day and he's just building anticipation for tomorrow. I figure maybe I'll seduce him in the morning."

She paused and shoved a sandwich into her mouth. I said nothing, hardly breathed, afraid to break her train of thought.

Licking her fingers with very sexy audio accompaniment, she launched back into her monologue. "I wake up the next morning and wander downstairs to see if he's up yet. I decide that if he's not, I'll just go slide into bed with him. I am definitely hot to trot at this point. But guess what?"

I'm not guessing anything. I am definitely shutting up.

"He's gone. The upstairs maid tells me he had an appointment and would be back for supper. I am royally pissed. My romantic interlude is really a business excursion with a possible bit on the side. Screw him. Or not. Oh, he left me a note. There was a pile of money with it, and he said to go shopping. Don't you dare say anything."

I didn't.

"I took myself and his money to town and did some serious damage. You know I can rationalize anything for clothes."

This I understood quite well. Joanne and I share a common weakness for silk, cashmere, and designer suits—hers with pants, mine with skirts. I'm a little on the hippy side and feel comfortable in skirts. She, on the other hand, looks ill at ease in them. Stores love to see us coming, especially in tandem, since we egg each other on. The recession has somewhat curbed this for Joanne, and unemployment has halted it for me, so I can completely defend her behavior. I didn't even allow myself to disapprove, since my little B & E adventure of that morning had cautioned me not to be judgmental.

"He came in around six-thirty." Her expression was lascivious. "We had a romantic candlelight dinner, cooked by some unseen genius. We flirted. We drank. We teased. Then came the good part."

At last, details. I was getting a little impatient but was afraid to hurry her along. She was grinning from ear to ear, infuriating me.

"He leads me to the master bedroom. It's gorgeous. Huge. This house is truly amazing, but at this point who cares. He leaves me standing in the middle of the room and goes into the bathroom. Okay, I figure. The man has to pee. He sure takes his sweet time, and at last I hear him calling me, inviting me in. I enter this giant room that's the size of my bedroom, which itself ain't too shabby. It's rosy pink with divinely flattering light. Not bad. Beside the Jacuzzi is an ice bucket with a bottle of Cristal chilling. Two Baccarat champagne flutes are beside it, along with a vase with a single rose. I know. Hokey. But perfect for the occasion. Oh, did I say that he was in the Jacuzzi with lots of lovely scented bubbles? My perfume, no less. This man has done his homework. And the whole thing works. I'm really turned on.

"He beckons me."

I was sitting on the edge of my seat, holding a cream-laden scone midair and holding my breath. Now we were getting to the really good details.

"Looking him straight in the eye and never wavering in my gaze, I slowly begin to disrobe. Tantalizingly. If he can be good, so can I. We're now locked into this gaze, but he breaks first, sliding his eyes over my body appreciatively. I love this. Hell, I don't work out four times a week for nothing. These are the moments I sweat for."

She plans ahead.

"I slowly slide in beside him. The bubbles engulf me. The scent fills my nostrils. I feel gentle fingers exploring my nipples. It's great."

Now I know this is going to be good. Joanne has been known to be graphic in her descriptions, but never romantic, and the picture she was painting was unlike her. She was leading up to a big payoff for sure, and I couldn't wait. I nodded, not unlike one of those bobbing-head Kewpie dolls. She took the cue.

"He dabs a drop of champagne on each nipple and proceeds to lick it off. I finally move into action. Figure it's time for me to give something back. After all, he's worked hard setting all this up. So I sidle over to take him in my hands. And I sort of do." She hesitates, so I know I should say something.

"Sort of?" By the Cheshire-cat grin on her face I knew it was the right question. For a change.

"Well, I took hold of this little tiny thing. I mean teeny-weeny."

I couldn't contain myself. I burst out laughing. Fortunately my mouth wasn't full; I surely would have sprayed the room. More nasty looks came my way from the blue-haired brigade, but I hardly noticed.

The idea of Francesco Grandese having a teeny-weeny one was just too funny. Even his name made the idea ridiculous. But the thought of his name sobered me a little. As silly as this was, she had been in a perilous situation. A well-brought-up young lady never makes sport of a man's equipment size, much less a man as potentially dangerous as Grandese.

"What did you do?" It was a serious question, but I was still giggling. So was she, obviously enjoying the effect of her story. I'm sure it was even better in the telling than it was in the happening.

"What I did was not laugh. That was difficult enough. I mean, it was smaller than little-fella."

Joanne had once pursued and seduced a six-foot-five man with a rather big nose and extremely large feet in order to test out that old wives' tale. He affectionately called his member "little-fella," which she interpreted as poetic license. Needless to say, the experiment was unsuccessful and the nomenclature literal. Till now, he had always remained the quintessential definition of small between us. Francesco was certainly going to go down in the halls of infamy for reasons he never foresaw.

"I'm not exactly a blithering idiot yet, so I kept quiet and let the proceedings continue. I did keep my eyes closed, though. I just knew he was staring at me, waiting for a reaction. But I did understand the bubble-bath scenario a lot better. No wonder he has people killed for a living. He has plenty to be mad at.

"I earned an Oscar that night. . . .

"Next morning I wake up hoping he doesn't want a rematch, since it was such a one-sided game in the first place, and luck is with me. He has another meeting, and then we have to leave. The bad part is, he's smitten. He thinks I was wonderful. I couldn't tell. I never felt a thing. Maybe I should get the Tony award too."

"What next?"

"I don't know. I only got back Sunday. I've been avoiding his calls, but I really have to figure out how to handle this. Maybe his wife should find out. Nah, she's probably screwing around like crazy, with a husband like that, and wouldn't care. She'd probably be grateful to me for taking him off her hands, and the one thing I don't need is more flowers. Time to trot out Jacques in public again. Be a very visible couple."

Poor Jacques. Joanne's current husband spends stressful days cutting people open, and his great love is peace and quiet. After a day of being up to his elbows in internal organs, he wants nothing more than to stay home and read up on the latest computer technology. I felt sorry for him, knowing what Joanne had in store. It would be a whirlwind two or three weeks of social engagements. It would only cease when he threatened divorce.

"I hope it works." I meant that sincerely. Joanne was fun to have around.

She looked thoughtful as she attacked her food. "Yeah," she

mused, "I gotta be careful." She proceeded to eat everything remaining, including my share.

Nothing, but nothing, separates Joanne from her food. Not even possible bodily harm, it seems. Once, on television, there was live footage of a riot. The camera recorded devastation and mayhem all around and panned back to Joanne before she was cued. There she was, shoving potato chips into her mouth. I was duly impressed. Rocks were flying, cars were burning, and Joanne was stuffing her face. And the worst of it is that it never shows. She has a killer body.

"I'll deal with it." She was reassuring herself more than me. "Don't even bother to lecture me. If he had been hung like a horse I may have needed that little sanctimonious speech that's on the tip of your tongue. But he's not, and so don't."

I was a little wounded, since my lecturing her was part of our symbiotic relationship.

"In that case," I said, changing the subject before my pique could show, "go on with what you want from me. Your message said you needed to talk to me. That implies you want something, and this little story was the bait. Give."

She actually looked guilty. "You caught me. But you must admit it is a good story. Are you operating on all gears yet?"

"What do you mean?"

"Look, lady," she began. Uh-oh, I was going to get it. "You have chosen to remove yourself from the living for a selected period of time. What I wanna know is, are you back? Is that little brain working again?"

"You seem to be obsessed with little," I said huffily.

That cracked her up. "Okay, okay. I see there's nothing wrong with the cogitation procedure. Let's get more food."

She signaled the waiter for refills, and I felt the first signs of trepidation. Another full platter of food was ominous. Joanne ordered food, and Susan applied lip liner. Why didn't anyone I know do something normal like scratch or bite their nails?

The food arrived. The waiter was a little incredulous at our capacity, and I felt like pointing my finger and yelling, "It's her, she's the pig," but it *was* the Ritz. One more eruption, and the regulars might have us ejected. Sometimes I do know my place.

Swallowing an entire tart in one bite, she said, "I need you to go somewhere with me."

This was not as innocent as it sounds. Except for shopping, Joanne is a loner. She's not shy and never needs company merely for moral support. She likes to go places alone. She maintains it gives her more control of the situation. The only time she drags me along is as a beard for one of her boy-toys, and this didn't sound like that. I was sure she was going to be monogamous and faithful until she had well and truly rid herself of Grandese. She does a lot of dumb things, but she's no fool.

Very serious and all business now, she continued.

"You like adventure."

Where had I suddenly got this reputation? Susan had said virtually the same thing to me this morning. I have always pictured myself as Clark Kent, and all these people knew I was secretly Superman? How come they'd waited so long to tell me?

"Go on," I said warily. I was learning caution; after this morning I wasn't so quick to jump into things.

"It's a story I'm working on. Cigarette hijacking. Big business."

When the government imposed the goods and services tax, it pushed the price of cigarettes through the roof, a final escalation that made what was once small potatoes, big business. Trailers full of cigarettes had been hijacked regularly for the past few months. It had also gotten dangerous. On the last outing two people had been killed, one a cop, when the police infiltrated and intercepted the operation. See, I had at least watched the news and kept up to date during my hibernation.

"Yeah, go on." Definitely wary.

"There's something going down. I have a source who owes

me big and can get me in. Don't know what angle I'll eventually use, but it's interesting. It's the closest I've ever got to actual involvement without crossing the line."

"So?" Warier and warier.

"I need you to go on a run with me. To a meet."

"Me? What the hell do you mean by a run? What's a meet? I think you've been hanging around Grandese too much."

She shot me a really dirty look. "He has nothing to do with this. That's a whole other story. Drop it."

"Sure. How about the fact that it's difficult for you to go anywhere and not be recognized?"

"No sweat. Disguise. We're going undercover. Just like *Miami Vice*." Everyone was referencing canceled TV shows to me today. Do we all see our lives as an hour-long cop series? My friends seem to.

She saw the disdain on my face. "No, really, it's great. We get to dress up and everything. It's a terrific scam. It's a gay conspiracy."

This was the most ridiculous thing I'd heard in a day full of ridiculous things. I could tell she was serious, but I couldn't help but laugh. She took offense and plunged on, trying to impress me with the gravity of the situation.

"They're very organized. A smuggling ring born of the baths."

Even she couldn't resist. A smile snuck onto her lips and her mind started to wander. "I can see it all now. A bunch of guys sitting around in or out of their towels saying very seriously, 'We've got to be more careful. What with AIDS and all. We gotta find something else to do for kicks and to keep our hands off each other. I know. Let's smuggle cigarettes!' And they all let go of their towels and applaud, waggling all around."

"That's vicious." I tried to sound offended, but I was laughing too hard at the image. I do a lot of fund-raising work for AIDS and do understand it to be the scourge of the twentieth century.

Normally the stereotyping of homosexuals offends me, but I knew Joanne shared my ideas, and the concept of a gay cigarette-smuggling conspiracy was very, very ridiculous.

I came down off my high horse. "But funny," I added.

She sailed on. "It's really a great front, if you think about it. There's very little chance of being infiltrated. Especially by the police. You know what homophobes they are."

"Yeah, I can imagine the initiation procedures."

We laughed some more at this as she plowed more food into the pit that is her stomach.

"So what's our part in this?" This was a dangerous question on my part. It implied complicity.

"Look, my source can get us in. As lesbians, of course. No initiation," she said as she tried to regain her composure. "It gets a little complicated. The guy they're selling the stuff to is straight. He doesn't know they're all gay. He also fancies himself a ladies' man, and for some stupid reason they told him that the head of the whole operation was a woman. I guess they wanted to impress him, but it worked too well, and now he won't negotiate with anyone but the boss lady. Don't worry, I'll be Boss Lady and you can be butch, so I'll do all the work. You just act as my driver." A sneaky look came into her eyes. "Although . . . Never mind."

"Never mind what?" I was definitely being sucked in here.

"Well, you'd do better as the Boss Lady. Your longer hair and curves and everything."

This was dirty pool. Referring to my hips as curves was the clincher, but I didn't give in just yet. I sat there with my lips pursed. I thought it was a great poker face, but I've made that mistake before. Last time it cost me two hundred bucks and made me swear off cards, but I still fancied myself as being able to keep a straight face and give away nothing. In other words, she knew she had me.

"Tell me more."

"We're not doing anything really illegal. We're just meeting the guy and discussing price. It'll be great."

More danger. Great to Joanne implied the possible loss of life or limb. Or sex, and I couldn't figure any of that in this story.

"How'd you get involved?"

"One of my regular tipsters got me in. I told you he owes me big. I'd suggest you don't ask me why. He thought I'd like this story, so he offered me to them. Different name, of course."

"Isn't this dangerous for him once it all comes out?" I was asking too many questions for an uninvolved bystander.

"He's splitting as soon as this is over. It's his last job. His boyfriend is sick, and he's only doing this to get enough money to take him to Mexico for 'alternative' treatment. Kinda sad, but it does work to my advantage."

I had nothing much more to say.

"When?"

"Thursday or Friday. I'll call you."

Today was Tuesday.

4

MY CAR WAS duly returned to me, with lots of servile smiles and outstretched palms. Fifteen dollars, as I expected, but it did include tips. A bargain at the price, I thought, which was an indication of the great mood I was in. All these people waiting on me and hopping to at my bidding made me feel like a spoiled princess, which I liked a lot. I know they're just doing their job and everyone gets the same treatment, but they're very good at it at the Ritz. They somehow convince you it's just for you because you're so special.

I climbed in, let the doorman close the door with its attendant satisfying clunk, and headed up the hill toward home, my wheels spinning on the underlying coat of ice. I tried to digest both the tea and the unusual events of the day which had been confusing, to put it mildly. Between the hours of 10:00 A.M. and 6:00 P.M. I had been exposed to the oddest collection of facts and information. I concluded that I had lots of things I should worry about, but I felt so good I couldn't seriously fret. With great concentration I listed them in no particular order.

Was Susan going to calm down? Where was Frank's money

really coming from? Where was Frank? How could Bimbo buy such atrocious dresses? Could Joanne disentangle herself from Francesco? Why the hell did she get involved in the first place? What does one wear to a possibly criminal activity? Although I had managed that one perfectly well this morning. How small is small? How small is teeny-weeny?

That last one made me smile and realize how ridiculous the exercise was. Too much daytime TV of late. More preposterous questions flitted through my mind as I unloaded the groceries and carted them upstairs. I made a stop at the mailbox to see if any other surprises were in store for me today, but there were none. The box yielded nothing except bills as usual and a once-in-a-lifetime bargain offer for a one-hour reflexology session for the astounding price of twenty-five dollars. Too much money for someone to fondle my feet to the accompaniment of flute and crashing waves. Maybe in my next lifetime. As I opened the bills, I came to the conclusion that isolation was good for my bank account, since most of them announced zero balances. It's axiomatic: If you don't go out you can't shop. There's no Home Shopping Channel in Quebec, so I was safe on that front. The day was still looking up. I reveled in the thought of Mastercard, American Express, and Visa all being sadly disappointed this month, feverishly scanning the obits, searching for proof of my untimely demise. Pity.

And things kept getting better and better. When I opened the front door I verged on the euphoric. Inside there was pristine order. The floor was entirely visible, the furniture gleamed, there was a marked absence of litter, and the whole place smelled fresh and clean. It was almost more than I could bear. Order out of chaos makes me emotional and teary-eyed because it's completely beyond my capabilities.

In the kitchen, as I unpacked the groceries, I saw the missive Mme Jacqueline had attached to the refrigerator door. I also noticed that she had used my pig magnet for the first time. I'm sure there was a message implied, but this was the closest thing to censure that she would allow herself so I didn't take offense. It began, of course, with the eternal request for Windex, but this time I had outthought her and gloated over the two economy-size bottles in my bags. That should keep her for awhile. Not very long, but awhile. She wrote that she had done all that she could in one day, and she would be back Thursday and maybe Friday to finish. She sounded almost apologetic for not having done more, which completely baffled me. I couldn't figure out what she hadn't done. The apartment bespoke a Herculean effort on her part. It looked fine to me, but I was the one who hadn't noticed that it had degenerated into a bona fide disaster area. No, on second thought it didn't look fine, it looked fabulous.

In order not to make a mockery of her travails, I put away all the groceries, including the nonperishables, which I usually leave on the counter for her. I hoped she'd be able to find them. Very proud of what I considered my labors I headed off to the bedroom to see what miracle had been wrought there.

It was wonderful. The bed was freshly made, clothes no longer carpeted the floor and there wasn't one overflowing ashtray in sight. I shivered, noticed that she had left the window wide open, and quickly closed it. I discarded the idea of being angry with her for causing extra heating bills once I accepted the reason for it. Though I hadn't admitted to Susan that the place stank, it must have, because what I now perceived as a delicious smell was the evident lack of one.

It was so glorious that I plunked myself onto my bed with my two favorite accoutrements, a Diet Coke and a cigarette. Flipping on the television, I watched Joanne deliver a pre-recorded piece about corruption at city hall. I thought news implied something new. Obviously not. I watched without paying much attention while I silently blessed Mme Jacqueline over and over, gladdened by the knowledge that twice a week, from now until forever, my house would look and smell like this.

I wasn't very hungry after tea; even though Joanne had eaten most of my share, she'd paid the bill, and by any normal standards I'd eaten her money's worth. Yet the siren song of a clean kitchen called to me, and I couldn't resist. It stood there, all spit and polish demanding attention, so I answered by making myself a salmon sandwich with my new groceries. I sat at the kitchen table munching happily, blissed out.

I would never tire of this sight. I was so happy with my restored environment that I sort of promised myself I would make an effort to maintain it. I tried. I put the dirty dishes in the sink and wiped off the counter with a damp cloth; there were no paper towels left, since she loves those almost as much as her Windex, and I didn't feel like breaking into my new supplies. I didn't actually *do* the dishes, but I didn't leave them on the table either. She was going to be proud of me. I was. I almost believed I was turning over a new leaf.

Feeling divinely smug, I yawned and realized how tired I was. It was only seven-thirty, but it had been a very full day for a shut-in. I wiped everything from my mind and luxuriated in a long, hot bubble bath, donned a clean T-shirt, and got into a crisp, cool bed, happy to sink into lovely soft pillows. I was so mellow I automatically answered the phone when it rang.

"Hi," said this wonderful voice.

I was now absolutely satisfied. I hadn't felt this content for at least six months. A warm bath, clean sheets, and now Sam. The only improvement would be to have him here in the flesh, but since he lived in Connecticut, five hundred miles away to him and eight hundred kilometers away to me, there was little chance of that.

"Hi," I answered softly. I'm sure he could hear me smile. I tend to go all mushy at the sound of his voice, and mine definitely changes timber.

"Better?"

"Much. I went out today and everything. I'm functioning again. Thanks for your patience."

"What patience? Three weeks ago you said, very dramatically I might add, Don't call me, I'll call you."

"Well, you had the good sense not to believe me."

He'd phoned about four times—not about, four times exactly—and I hadn't picked up or called back. I felt a little guilty about that. My standard behavior patterns usually suspend themselves when it comes to Sam Levine. It had been very peculiar of me not to have wanted to speak to him. This made me realize how far off the track I had fallen and how dangerously close to the edge I had got. It was a relief to be back.

"Tonight was your last chance. If you hadn't answered—"

I interrupted, not ever wanting to know what the rest of his sentence would be. Just the thought of never seeing or speaking to him again shot a pain to what I assume is my heart. Sometimes it's hard to find.

Still mellow, I continued. "I'm exhausted. Today was very active for someone who's been a couch potato for a while. I was just drifting off to sleep. Say something nice to send me on my way."

Sam and I have a strange and difficult-to-explain relationship. We've been having an uninterrupted affair for the past twelve years. We always meet on neutral ground, never his nor my hometown, and just enjoy each other for the night or weekend. This happens about every six weeks, and it's always a delight, since it's a total suspension of reality. We laugh and joke a lot when we're together, aware that no one we know is around and we can be as silly as we please. On the phone we talk of our daily lives and how we feel about things in the world and plan our next tryst. We never talk about our personal lives.

At least *I* never do. He knows nothing about mine, and I know everything about his, even though he'd say I didn't. It's easy to get information from men. They'll tell you anything if the question is properly formed and later never realize they said it. I know he's living with someone, has been for the past fifteen years, hasn't married her, and probably never will. I don't mind this arrangement. I have no intention of ever pressing my claim and forcing a choice; we could never live together on a full-time basis. Aside from the question of relocation, we are eminently unsuited for each other. Our temperaments are opposite, and though we share the same basic values we lead completely different lives. Those things that would make him a nonstarter in my real life matter not at all when I see him for such a short period. There's no time to fight when time is at such a premium, and all those things that usually make me crazy and signal the end of a relationship don't matter. Karen doesn't pose a threat to me, nor should I to her, were she to discover the affair. Also, in this day and age I prefer knowing where it's been.

I think he's gorgeous and predictable, he thinks I'm beautiful and exciting. He's xenophobic, I'm peripatetic. A perfect match, for three days maximum. And what he does well he does very, very well. He can always make me smile all over.

"I have to be in Chicago a week tomorrow. It's such a drag. I have so much to do here."

I said he hates going places. I'm sure he had nothing out of the ordinary to do in Connecticut, but all out-of-town trips are prefaced with this speech.

"But if you can meet me, it'll be worth it. Two days."

"Of course." I'm such a sap when it comes to Sam. I'd go anywhere, anytime. That's why so few people know about him. He'd ruin my hard-boiled corporate reputation.

"I'll call you tomorrow for the details. 'Night," I said languorously.

"Dream of me."

I didn't. I didn't dream at all but fell into a deep sleep, with none of the tossing and turning I had been experiencing of late. I was healing well.

The next thing I knew, the phone was ringing, this time insistently, demanding that I wake up. I looked at the luminous dial on the clock radio and realized that it wasn't the ungodly hour I had expected. It said 10:05, not beyond the acceptable time to call someone. Feeling cheated of the opportunity to swear at my midnight caller, I answered politely.

"Hello," I murmured somewhat pleasantly, stretching in an effort to clear the cobwebs from my brain. I had been in a deep sleep, and resurfacing was presenting some difficulty. I just wanted to curl up and drift away again.

"Get over here right away. I'm at Frank's. Now!"

"What?" The cobwebs were stubborn.

"Look, just get here before I go completely to pieces. Fast!"

Susan didn't exactly slam the phone down, but she didn't replace it delicately either. Not having entirely digested the conversation but reacting to orders like a recalcitrant child, I got up slowly. I picked up speed as I replayed the conversation in my head, the underlying hysteria in her voice becoming more and more apparent.

After throwing on a pair of jeans, white T-shirt, and navy blue blazer, my standard get-dressed-quick uniform, I hastily added mascara and grabbed my purse and parka. Mascara is my minimal maintenance necessity—I can't think of any emergency that would get me out of the house without it. Descending in the elevator toward my car I remembered to brush my hair and smear on some lipstick, so I landed in the garage semi–well groomed. The stress level in Susan's voice permeated my consciousness by degrees, and by the time I wheeled out of the garage I was slightly frantic. More questions plagued me, this time none of them frivolous. Basically it boiled down to, What the hell was Susan doing at Frank's at this time of night, and what had he done to her?

It was still snowing, and as it hadn't let up all day the streets were difficult to navigate and virtually deserted. The smart people were indoors in front of their television sets or fast asleep. I didn't allow myself to consider what the really smart ones were doing. And here I was, skidding around in the middle of the night like an idiot.

I came across road crews working laboriously to clean streets that would be reburied within the hour if the snow continued unabated. The massive snowblowers prowled like hulking behemoths, puffing and huffing, ingesting white and spitting out gray. It would make a good scene in a science-fiction movie. It was icy, and the threat of plowing into a snowbank made it slow going, so it took twenty minutes to drive a distance that normally should take about ten tops.

I was cranky as hell by the time I arrived. Droplets of perspiration slid down my inner arm, and I couldn't remember if I had applied deodorant after my bath. If I hadn't, it would serve Susan right for sending me out to risk life and limb. This had better be damned good. The No Parking—Snow Removal sign was almost the last straw, and I was sorely tempted to turn around and head back home to bed. By now I was sure that only death or disfigurement could atone for dragging me out. My sense of charity had deserted me completely.

I parked anyway. The crews would alert the whole neighborhood to their presence no matter what time of day or night with their high-pitched wailing siren. I'd probably have enough time to scoot down and move my car before they had it towed. I'd better, or else disfigurement no longer counted. We wouldn't be here that long anyway. I had every intention of hustling her out of there posthaste and discussing whatever the problem was elsewhere. One visit to Frank's domicile went a long way. And what if he came home and found us there? What if he was already there? I didn't need to be added to his shit list, and I didn't put it past him to be vindictive. To date we had an equitable, polite relationship. The jerk actually thought I liked him. Joanne isn't the only good actress in this town.

I rang the buzzer marked Porter, and a little-girl voice whispered, "Who is it?"

"Me. Barbara. Let me in."

I got to the door a fraction of a second before the buzzer quit. Another elevator disgorged me onto Frank's floor, and as I stepped into the hall a now hysterical, loudly sobbing Susan fell into my arms.

"What's wrong?" I sounded worried and supportive but I did take the time to notice she wasn't disfigured, which wasn't nice of me.

"He's dead."

"Who's dead?" Today would go down in the annals of history as my all-time record day for asking dumb questions. Who else would be dead here?

"Frank's dead," she said very quietly. She was so distraught she forgot to call me stupid.

Time to spring into action and take some control. I manage things well and think of myself as reliable in a crisis. Others call me bossy, though I prefer to think of myself as professional. This was a situation that clearly called for my talents.

"Okay. Get a grip. Come. Let's go in."

At this she pulled back but then came along docilely. She had stopped sobbing and was sniffling quietly. I propped her up against the wall, since she looked like she would crumble without support, and proceeded with that great Montreal winter sport called taking off your boots and putting on your shoes. On a day of bad planning this exercise may be repeated about fifteen times. I swear, we Quebecers stay limber longer because of all that bending and stretching. In reality I was just buying time, trying to assess the situation and figure out how to proceed. Nothing clever came to mind, so I inquired, "Car crash? Heart attack?" Sensible questions.

"No. Murder."

That took me aback so far that I didn't even say "What?".

She took my hand and led me to the living room. Not letting go of me for a second, she squeezed harder and harder with a strength I never knew she possessed. She continued to look resolutely at the doorway, a refusal to confront the scene that faced me.

There was Frank on the couch, a large hole in his left shoulder.

I looked back at Susan and quickly enveloped her in my arms, thereby rescuing my almost numb hand. It was as though I could spare her the sight and thus deny the reality.

I've never seen a real live dead body. In the myriad British mysteries I've read, they tend to be neat lumps with polite wounds. Police procedurals, on the other hand, get very graphic in their descriptions of bodies, and from what I could see and mostly smell, they come closer to the truth. Judging from the large stain on the front of Frank's pants and the permeating odor, people really do evacuate at death. Television and movies never show you that. They'd lose too many viewers, and the sponsors would go nuts.

In an effort to not accept the implications of the scene before me, I concentrated on dumb details. Like, the red blood clashed with the peach sofa. Like, are blood stains removable? Like, what would Mme Jacqueline use to clean this couch? As if anyone would ever want to sit on it again.

Galvanizing myself to action, I turned to Susan to face her away from the mess on the couch, although her head was already averted. I hadn't got around to thinking of it as a body yet, much less as Frank.

"What happened?"

"I don't know," she wailed. "I was at home and got to thinking about this morning and was so frustrated and angry at him that I came back determined to find something if I had to tear the place apart."

"Looks like you did a good job," I said. I looked around the room, trying unsuccessfully not to look at what I now accepted as the body. I could see that the entire apartment was a shambles. The contents of all the drawers were strewn about, no pillow was intact, and feathers and papers littered the air and floor. Nothing was in its original place. Even the plants had been upturned, and the damp earth was ground into the pastel rugs. Someone singular but probably plural had systematically worked their way from room to room, most likely searching for something. It was a bigger mess than Frank.

"I didn't do this. I didn't do anything. It was like this when I arrived." She was dangerously close to sobbing again.

It was probably true, since we both knew the first rule of snooping is not to leave traces. Never let the snoopee be aware of your having snooped. Susan would not have made this mess. She's neat by nature and, I suspect, pathologically incapable of causing such upheaval, but mostly she's too experienced at clandestine investigating to have left such telltale traces.

"You obviously didn't kill him." I didn't add, Did you?

"Of course not, though I've thought about it often enough. But seeing him actually dead . . . He's Robert's father . . . " The tears reappeared without vocal accompaniment, which gave me a moment to think. It was more difficult than it would seem, as there was so much to take in and so many possible questions. But my first problem was Susan. Or maybe me.

"This is a giant mess. Have you called the police yet?"

"No, I just called you. And the housekeeper to make sure Robert was alright."

"You didn't say anything to her, did you?"

"I'm upset and frightened, Barbara, not stupid."

"Did you touch anything?" They ask that a lot in books.

"No. Just the phone, and after I called you I went back into the hall to wait for you. I didn't want to be alone with him. He keeps staring at me wherever I stand."

Indeed Frank's eyes were wide open and did seem to follow every movement. It was creepy.

"What will I tell Robert?" she started to wail again.

"Quiet," I ordered. "Not meaning to be callous, that's the least of our problems. We are in very deep shit here."

"Why? I didn't do anything." Aside from her annoying use of the singular, I was pleased that I wasn't the only one who said incredibly stupid things.

"Oh yeah? What are you doing here in the first place? What am I doing here? What were your intentions? Explain your placid, loving relationship with Frank. They sure as hell aren't going to buy the bereaved widow bit. We've gotta call them."

But I didn't move. I stayed rooted to the spot and continued the barrage. "Who could have done this? And why? I mean, Frank's a lowlife, but he didn't deserve this. What were they looking for? Is it a they? I don't think they found it, by the looks of things. Too messy all over. Do you think they'll come back?"

Now that last thought made me move. A twinge of fear set in, halting my motor mouth. I dropped that subject, not wanting Susan any more upset than she was, if that were possible, and trying to forestall another crying jag. I needed her in some semblance of control while I figured out our next move. I do remember thinking that if we ever got out of this I was going to kill her.

"We've got to call the police," I repeated.

"No," she said, looking scared. It was a step up from crying. "Let's just get out of here."

"No way. It's bad enough we're here now. If we leave and they find out we were here and left, we'll be in deeper trouble. I'm calling."

At that, I dug into the endless pit that is my handbag and came up with a scarf, the idea being to use it to handle the phone so as not to leave any fingerprints. I completely forgot or avoided the fact that I had used the same phone this morning, and that I had touched practically everything.

Reaching across for the phone, I accidentally brushed against Frank and he shifted, moving slightly to the left. Startled by the unexpected contact, I recoiled, banging into the end table, which in turn bumped the couch, which in turn jolted Frank, which in turn caused him to flop unceremoniously onto his side. I was horrified and for once speechless. I had been so worried about fingerprints, and now I had moved a body. Visions of prison with large, hairy women danced before my eyes. I just stood there immobile, staring at him, trying to banish those giantesses from my mind, and considered the benefits of sitting him back up. I stared without breathing for what seemed like ages before I noticed he looked strange even for a dead Frank. I couldn't figure it out.

Susan was at my side, and at the sound of the thump she looked back at Frank for an instant and as quickly looked away. She seemed to feel that if she didn't see him he wasn't there. But my eyes were riveted, and he still looked strange.

"Susan, what's wrong with Frank?" I asked, puzzled.

"What do you mean? He's dead, that's what's wrong with him. What's wrong with you?" She was certainly snippy for a person in shock.

"No, look. I know he's dead. He's funny. Look at him."

"No."

"Look at him," I ordered.

She finally looked directly at him and I could see her puzzling out the problem. "It's his hair," she said softly.

I looked again. She was right. His hair was weird. A large fluff on the side of his head almost covering his ear.

"Yeah, what's wrong with it?"

"It moved. His toupée."

"What?" came to mind, but instead I said, "I didn't know he wore a hairpiece." It fit, though. In retrospect he had too much hair for a man his age, and it never changed and never moved. I had always suspected him of being a major shareholder in a hair spray company, but this made more sense. Although I was loath to admit that I had never noticed it, I was a little pissed that she had never told me. Even in death his jerkiness was growing by leaps and bounds in my mind.

"Fix it," she demanded.

"Are you nuts? I'm not touching him."

"You already touched him. You moved him. It's your fault."

Now this was too much. She dragged me over here in the middle of a blizzard, and now she was telling me it was my fault! Shock or not, I was not shouldering the blame.

"I did not. He moved himself."

"He can't move. He's dead."

This was a totally insane conversation, and we were verging on hysteria. I know I should have just left him and called the cops, but he looked so stupid with that clump over his ear. Stupid even for Frank. Being dead and smelly, I assume he had no concern over losing dignity, yet I, who couldn't stand him, felt bad about having others, even the police, see him looking so completely foolish. I figured this last act of kindness would atone for all the hateful things I had thought of him over the years. I figured if he could see me performing this final rite of redemption he would surely be grateful, and maybe I could make some points in heaven. Although I seriously doubted that was where he was headed.

With great trepidation I approached him and tried to poke the toupée into place with one outstretched finger. But the fates were not kind to me this night. The hairpiece fell off, sliding from his head to the couch and onto the floor beside him. It lay there on the carpet, resembling a hairy rat or miniature York-shire terrier. This was worse than ever. I looked from the rat to Frank to the rat and lost control. I burst into explosive laughter. A surprisingly large bald spot had revealed itself, surrounded by puffed and fluffed sides. He was a dead ringer for Bozo the Clown.

Susan had been standing with her back to me, staring wistfully out the window, surely wishing she were elsewhere. At the sound of my outburst she wheeled around with every intention of reprimanding me for my inexcusable behavior. Before she could open her mouth, she took in the bald spot and the immobile hairy rat on the floor and couldn't resist. The two of us stood there laughing, alternately pointing to the red halo and the red Yorkie. It did dispel the fear, though, and the laughter made Frank less horrifying and gruesome. All the mystery of death deserted him. To me he now looked the fool I had always known him to be.

No longer as afraid of him, Susan picked up the hairpiece. "I'll put it back." She fluffed it in preparation for the coronation, and I was again sent into gales of laughter. Feeling and fluffing, she stopped laughing and looked quizzical. "What's this?" she asked, looking confused.

"What?" Here, it was appropriate.

"I think there's something in here." She was just touching and not inspecting, and it annoyed me.

"Let me see." I'd been successfully ordering her around so far, and it continued. She passively handed me the toupée, and I turned it over to look inside for whatever she found so interesting. The hair was hard and sticky, which supported my hairspray-stock theory. It was disgusting. But there was indeed something in there. A piece of electrical tape was stuck to the inside crown. And there was a hard object encased under it.

"Maybe this is what they were looking for," I said and proceeded to further tamper with the evidence by ripping off the tape. Never thought about fingerprints for a second.

"Look, a key." I was exultant. This surely was the key to the mystery. I prided myself on the brilliance of my deductive powers. A moron could have figured this one out, but I gloated anyway.

"Let me see that," she said and grabbed the key, leaving me

holding the loathsome hairpiece. I sensed possible mutiny as she regained her sea legs.

Not knowing what to do with the toupée and not wanting the disgusting thing in my hands a second longer, I put it back on Frank's head, adjusting it with all the care and attention of a high-priced hairdresser. I stepped back to admire my handi-work and saw that, except for that hole in his shoulder, he looked like Frank again. I could proceed with hating him all the more for getting us, and specifically me, into this.

"I think I know what this is," she said, turning the key over and over in her hand. She seemed to have forgotten about our problem lying on the couch as she inspected the key.

I didn't say anything.

"It's a key to a home safe-deposit box. My key actually. My box. See the nail polish mark," she said, indicating a red dot. "I put that on to distinguish it from the keys to the bank box. Your brother gave us this for a housewarming or wedding present when we moved into the apartment."

I knew exactly what she meant. My brother has a friend who was starting up a home-security business in that era. The com-pany supplied safe-deposit boxes destined for home use. They were touted as fireproof, theft proof, and virtually immovable if properly installed. That year, anyone who celebrated anything and knew my brother got one. Mine was bolted to the floor of my linen closet, covered with so much stuff to disguise it that I never used it anymore. It was too much trouble to unbury it.

I had to assume it had been a housewarming and not a wedding gift, since my brother wasn't invited to the wedding either.

"Aren't there two keys?" I tried to remember where mine were as I asked the question and surprised myself by knowing the exact location of both of them. I'm a slob, but I am organized.

"There *were* two keys. Frank lost his the second week he had it, but we never changed the lock, since there was no identification on it, and anyway he said he lost it in Toronto. This one should be in the vase on the shelf in my living room. I haven't used that box in ages. I piled lots of extra sheets and blankets on it to hide it, and it's too much trouble to get to."

I wasn't the only one, it seemed. I wondered if the guy who sold them was still in business and how many unused boxes covered with junk there were hanging around people's homes.

"I keep all my good jewelry at the bank. I guess in the back of my mind I never really believed Frank lost his, and I wanted my few valuables completely out of his reach." She kept turning the key over and over in her palm, staring at it. "I don't understand."

I puzzled with her for a moment, but it was too big a conundrum to work out now. We had more immediate problems.

"Look, I'm not sure we're safe here alone. If it really is the key they were after, they obviously didn't find it, and they may be back with more troops to look some more. I'm calling the police," I said as I reached for the phone, being careful of Frank but not of fingerprints. Hell, I'd already moved a dead body and seriously tampered with evidence. I couldn't get into more trouble.

But I could try.

"Put the key in your pocket and forget about it for now. Whatever you do, don't mention it to the police. We've got to check it out first. We don't know what's in there, and remember, whatever it is, it's in your house where your kid lives."

I don't know why I decided that *we* needed to know what was in the box. I was now definitely involved, both mentally and physically.

I picked up the phone, punched in 911, and politely gave the officer who answered my name and location and explained the nature of the call. He just as politely instructed me to stay there and not touch anything.

Too late.

5

I FIGURED IT might be best to pretend we were good little girls as we waited for the police, so we retreated to the front door and stood just outside the foyer. At first we waited in silence, studying the square patterns in the wallpaper, but that got boring within three minutes, and I figured now was as good a time as any to broach the subject that had been bothering me.

I looked at her accusingly and said, "I didn't know Frank wore a toupée."

"There's lots about Frank you don't know," she answered, which annoyed me further. I expect my friends to tell me everything, since I'm inordinately nosy but have the good manners not to pry overtly. That's their job in this relationship.

"You know enough about him to make me look like a fool for marrying him in the first place. How much more could I add without your writing me off as a raving lunatic and having me carted away? It's all too embarrassing and humiliating."

She had a point. "But that hair—" I sputtered and burst out laughing. "That incredibly white bald spot surrounded by that teased and sprayed halo of flaming red hair . . ."

She shot me a very dirty look but couldn't carry it through, and off we sailed into gales of giggles. The horror of what lay just inside was somewhat eased by it. We would stop, regain control, catch one another's eye, and start all over again. It was unstoppable once the cork had been pulled, and it kept bubbling over.

As we stood there giggling, the elevator door opened and four police officers emerged, guns drawn. We sobered immediately, aware that this was not the best first impression to make in a murder investigation. They seemed to agree with this assessment; the lead gun pointed her weapon directly at us and asked in colloquial French, "C'est bien vous qui avez appelé?" I noted that the only woman of the troupe took control, which pleased me. One for the sisterhood, and also it's nice to know that I'm not the only bossy one.

It didn't sit as well with Susan, though. She obviously has great disdain for women who point guns at her. Formally and haughtily, she replied, "I don't speak French. Please address me in English."

We were really making points. Susan didn't seem to realize that you don't get snooty when four people have loaded weapons aimed at you. Particularly not over language. Absolutely not in Quebec.

The lady cop behaved admirably. Ignoring Susan, she faced me and asked in heavily accented English, "Harr you de one dat call?"

I answered immediately, knowing if I left it to Susan we'd both end up behind bars forever. The policewoman was showing more grace under pressure than Susan. She was making the effort to speak English, though she didn't have to. She had the gun, which definitely gave her the upper hand.

Language is a very volatile and emotional issue in this province, and this could quickly get out of hand. The other three cops were docile enough, obviously awaiting their cue from their leader. I liked the fact that the woman was in charge and they all looked to her for instructions. I couldn't tell what language the rest of them spoke, but from the general composition of the police force I had to assume it to be French.

The language war has been in effect for many years, perhaps centuries, but the last five have signaled a dangerous flare-up. The Francophones insist that since they constitute the majority, the province belongs to them, and everyone should speak their language. Anglophones are digging in their heels and insist they are not second-class citizens. They feel that until English is completely legislated as illegal, instead of the present ban, which only includes public signage and language in the workplace, they will continue to exercise their God-given right to speak it. This point of contention has got as far as the United Nations, which recently declared Quebec an official violator of the human rights of a minority. Our own little banana republic in the middle of North America. It's a totally stupid squabble that takes up lots of time in Parliament, costs the taxpayers tons of money, and creates enormous tension between two communities who differ not at all except as to linguistic preference. At the moment the entire country is on the verge of breaking up because of this lunacy. Once again our politicians have delivered us into the fire.

Nationalism gives rise to passions that run deep, as evinced by our present situation. Susan was going to be obstinate, even though I know she speaks perfectly adequate French and mine is fluent. The upside of this language kerfuffle is that most of the English population is passably bilingual, which can only be a plus. It also didn't help our situation that the officer in charge was a woman. Susan infinitely prefers dealing with male authority figures, upon whom she can exercise her not inconsiderable charms. As I've known her for ages, I realize that this stems from a deep-rooted insecurity and probably a deep-seated jealousy of women whom she perceives to have attained position while she's been shackled to Frank.

At the moment, however, this attitude was potentially damaging. We were both on the same side, and I could murder her later.

"I called. The body is in the living room. What would you like us to do?" I answered as politely as I could without being smarmy, hoping to repair some of the damage Susan had wrought. But I *did* answer in English. I knew they were going to ask lots of questions, and it would be better for me if I answered in English and better for them if Susan did.

"Wait 'ere," she ordered, signaling Number Two to follow her and Numbers Three and Four to remain with us, although I have no idea where we might have gone.

As the four of us stood in silence, awaiting further instructions, it struck me that although there was a lot of commotion, not one other apartment door had opened to see what was happening. It was just past midnight, so although they were probably in bed they couldn't all be asleep yet. Maybe they were deaf. That could explain Frank's megawatt stereo; maybe it had rendered them deaf. Maybe they were better brought up than I and knew when to mind their own business. Or maybe lots of bad things happened on this floor and they were afraid. That was stretching it a little, but the situation seemed bizarre. I know if it had been me I would've been out there in a flash. Inquiring minds want to know. Everything.

About four minutes later the cops returned. "Entrez," said the lead lady officer. Whether she was addressing us or our two guards was unclear, but we all started to move as a body. Susan glared at her as she passed, and we all entered the foyer and abruptly halted, not knowing how far to proceed. Susan, in her new-to-me persona, huffed haughtily, her disdain implying that they were insufferably rude for detaining her without reason. Over the past five minutes she had developed quite an attitude. I worried about her acting out, causing us even greater problems, and hoped I would get a chance to speak to her alone for a second, or at least be able to signal her to firmly put a lid on it. No such luck.

"Vous," the officer in charge said, pointing to me, "Par ici."

"You," she said pointing to Susan, "dis way."

I gave this woman credit; she handled us graciously. She addressed me in French, subtly reaffirming that she was the one in control, probably figuring I was the more sensible of the two and wouldn't create a fuss. She was right.

Thus we were separated. Me with my cop, and Susan with hers, led to separate bedrooms to wait for I don't know what. Susan got the master bedroom, I assume since they thought she was the lady of the house, and I got Robert's. As we entered the room my cop looked around and his eyes became two huge orbs. Whether it was at the sight of such a mess or all the electronics scattered about I couldn't tell, but judging from the look on his face, it was the latter. He was likely trying to figure out if he could get his hands on some of the toys. Although I looked at him with disdain, I had been party to the selfsame thoughts only this morning. It seemed like a very long time ago.

I headed for the only upright chair and sat down. He ignored me and remained standing, since the only other fit place to sit was on the bed and I'm sure he considered that unseemly. His eyes flickered, undoubtedly hard at work totting up the price of all the gadgets that littered the floor and figuring how many weeks or more likely months of salary they cost. Given enough time he might have physically turned green with envy.

I would have enjoyed my feeling of superiority if I hadn't been so worried about Susan. Remembering the key in her pocket, I cursed myself for not having taken it from her. Her aggressive attitude had surprised me, and I just hoped to hell her cop spoke English, or it could get very nasty for her. Or him. There were no games in their room to distract. All she had to do was antagonize him enough and he had the power to order a search just to humiliate her and prove his domination. Even a strip search. If they did search her and found the key, they would have no way of connecting it to Frank, but it was an unusual item to be carrying around loose in your pocket. It wasn't even in her purse, which would have been more plausible.

A silent mantra of "Shut Up Susan, Behave Yourself Susan" repeated itself over and over in my head. Please, Susan.

My cop stood fidgeting, his fingers itchy. Not knowing the correct etiquette for the situation, I thought perhaps I should introduce myself and give him my card, but I no longer had a card with which to legitimize myself so I kept quiet and got depressed instead. As I sat there brooding and feeling very sorry for myself, alternately hating and worrying about Susan, my cop could no longer resist temptation. He picked up a handheld video game that had miraculously avoided destruction and busily set to playing. While he was involved with his joystick, I took the opportunity to scrutinize him.

He was very young, having not long ago graduated from toys himself. He'd grown a mustache in the vain hope of looking older than the twenty-two he probably was. His sandy brown hair showed a hat line from the cap that now sat on the bookcase beside him. The strong traces of red that streaked his moustache gave him a mismatched, unbalanced appearance. It looked pasted on. He would probably make a good cop someday, but it would take some seasoning. His uniform was well pressed and impeccable, lovingly tended to by his mother or a doting girlfriend, since he sported no wedding band, and he wore the same spit-and-polish shoes as his confreres. I wondered what brand of shoe polish the police department endorsed that was impervious to the Montreal elements.

As his game beeped away and the score mounted, his cheeks flushed, making him look about sixteen years old. He was having a grand old time while I felt sorry for myself, cursed Susan, and wondered if my deodorant was working. He hadn't said a word yet, so intrigued with his gadget I didn't think he ever would. He'd probably forgotten I was there.

So I just sat. If Susan was sitting equally unchallenged, she was probably applying lip liner.

After about twenty minutes of this noninteraction on my part and total absorption on his, the door opened and two new men entered. They caught my cop by surprise. I was feeling quite maternal by now, what with his being young enough to be my, well, let's say nephew. He jumped to, and the game fell from his hands and clattered to the floor, spewing its batteries and some wires at his feet. Abashed and red faced, he quickly retrieved the dangling parts and his hat and returned the mangled toy to the shelf, hoping impossibly that no one had noticed. He was so mortified at having been caught acting in an unprofessional manner that he looked ready to cry. I felt sorry for him, and the newcomers must have also, since they ignored the incident.

"Qu'est-ce qu'on a ici? What do we have here?" the shorter of the two asked.

In an effort to redeem himself, my babycop, at full attention, replied apologetically, "Elle est anglaise."

I had a vision of Susan's cop sounding as apologetic when he said she was English and didn't know whom to worry for, her or her cop. Who knew what kind of eruption that would trigger.

"Hokay," said the lead man, signaling to his confederate as though palming me off. He probably figured the better quarry was in the bigger room. It felt dismissive and demeaning, and I was insulted and angry. This man could learn a few lessons from the only female officer present.

Confederate turned to me, caught the fury I felt, and in an effort to be placating asked in nonaccented English, "What's your name, ma'am?"

It did nothing to placate me. Admittedly, it was the middle of the night and I had only a trace of lipstick remaining, but sufficient mascara. He could have called me "miss" if he wanted to ingratiate himself. Ma'am was for the Queen Mother, the tea ladies of the Ritz, or Jack Webb of *Dragnet*. Another canceled cop show. My brain had become a massive cliché.

I wasn't going to allow him to see how close he had come to hitting a nerve with that comment. I answered with great dignity as I took his measure. "Barbara Simons," I hissed, malevolently adding, "Sir."

Insulted as I was, I very nearly missed the fact that he was sort of cute. In another life, under other circumstances, in another universe, I may have been interested. About forty years old, wavy dark medium-length hair. Maybe a blow-dryer but definitely no mousse. Good shoulders, a narrow waist, and surprisingly long legs. He must work out a few times a week to keep that flat stomach, and I idly wondered where. He stood about six two, and since I'm five nine, height is one of the first things I notice. Well, in men. If they don't pass muster in that department I'm usually frivolous enough not to bother looking further. The clincher was his clear blue eyes, surrounded by lovely little crinkles. The suspicious bulge in his otherwise well-tailored jacket reminded me of his position, and I regained my slipping composure and continued taking inventory. His navy blue jacket with brass buttons complemented the pale blue shirt, regimental striped tie, and gray flannel pants. If I had found Gucci loafers at the bottom of all this I wouldn't have been surprised and could have nailed him as a typical yuppie. It's easier to deal with stereotypes than individuals. But he was shod in well-worn Reeboks. They even had salt stains from the snow. I did not comment on this sartorial incongruity, opting to remain silent until I could further evaluate the situation.

"Miss Simons," he continued, instantly redeeming himself. He'd probably taken a good look at me, realized the error of his ways, and decided to revise his form of address. More likely he had perceptively read my distress at being called "ma'am" in my poker face. "Tell me what happened here."

I talked, and he took notes. After the second sentence his cohort left the room without a word, presumably to visit Susan, taking babycop with him. I realized that they had come to me first and in tandem simply because this room was closer to the front door than the master bedroom. For once I'd lucked out. I'd definitely got the cuter of the two, and an Anglophone to boot.

I silently wished both Susan and her inquisitor luck. It would be a contest of wills, and only time would tell who would lose his or her temper first. I hoped her detective would exhibit the same tact as the policewoman, but I sincerely doubted it. He didn't look it, and his poker face was as bad as mine, whereas Susan's was excellent.

I couldn't dwell on this for any length, since I presently had my own problems.

I told him about Susan's call, my arrival and subsequent discovery, and pretty much everything except the toupée and key part. I omitted my morning's activities, and since he didn't ask me about the rest of my day, I felt I wasn't lying, I was simply not volunteering any information that could get me into deeper trouble than I already was. I don't just watch reruns of canceled television programs—ever the student, I learn from them. He asked me Susan's full name and relation to the deceased—his exact words—seemingly more as points of information than suspicion.

"What's your relationship to Mrs. Porter?" he asked, still very officious.

"Just friends. Good friends. Actually we're cousins. Distant cousins. Our grandmothers were sisters. That makes us either second cousins or first cousins once removed. Or something," I babbled. I was tired. Unstructured, random words poured from my mouth, and though I could hear myself, I couldn't stem the flow. I'm sure it was those blue eyes with the sexy crinkles around them. They never strayed, always looked directly at me as though I were the most interesting person in the world. It was a good technique, unnerving, and probably led people—including me—to say more than they planned.

Belatedly recognizing the tactic, I gathered myself, having remembered the ploy from my public relations press conference days. I snapped my mouth shut with a true understanding that my disconnected ramblings could potentially do me great damage if I wasn't very, very careful. I would henceforth be just as good at this as he was, and it was a toss-up as to whom had been given the better training—his at the public's expense, and mine at the hands of industry's most dastardly captains.

It took him a moment to perceive the change and accept that I would no longer ramble. He was foiled. As he took a second to reorient himself and adapt to the situation, his eyes narrowed. The intention was probably to convey menace, but it only served to make him all the more appealing. Maybe if I concentrated on his attractiveness I could deflect the peril. No, not such a good idea.

He spoke first, reassuming dominance. "Have you any idea what they were looking for?"

Dangerous ground here. No good using my poker face or I would reveal all, so I quickly went for derailment.

"Why do you think it was a them? It could just as easily have been a him." As a sometime feminist I refused to believe it could have been a her. She wouldn't have left empty-handed.

Success. He shifted tracks and considered my seemingly innocent question.

"Too many footprints for one person. They weren't careful with the flowerpots and tracked earth everywhere. We may be able to get some good prints, but I'm not sure. Stocking feet are pretty hard to match. By the looks of it there were two men, and they took off their boots when they came in."

"That means they're either neat freaks, which I doubt, judging from the way they left the apartment, or Frank knew them,"

I offered. So much for good intentions of not volunteering and only listening. Those blue eyes were putting me off my stride again and squelching my resolve. Heaven forfend, I may even have been trying to ingratiate myself.

Yet I continued. "I'd think that if you came specifically to kill someone and vandalize the place you wouldn't bother with the niceties, like removing your overshoes. Could it have been accidental? Like they broke in to rob him, and he was unexpectedly here and it went awry? Susan thought he was out of town, so others may have thought the same and figured the apartment was empty. There's lots to steal here."

I knew at my core that I was wrong, deliberately trying to mislead him, but hoped that by some miracle I was right and the key in Susan's pocket was irrelevant.

At least he took me seriously. He considered my postulation for a moment, his eyes leaving me and focusing on the over-turned plants in the corner, the earth strewn over a large radius. He returned his gaze to me and shook his head, somewhat sadly, I thought. That would have been the easy solution. Another crackhead trashing a house and killing the occupant. Big-city, modern-day crime.

"No, I don't think so. You're right about one thing. There's plenty of expensive electronic equipment that would be very easy to fence, but from the looks of it, there's still too much here for things to be missing. It looks more like they were searching for something."

And I knew exactly what that something was. Which made me very nervous, so I continued my path of diversion.

"They could have not meant to kill him. He could have surprised them, and when they realized he was there one of them got overexcited and accidentally shot him. That scared them, and they left immediately, taking nothing and leaving this mess in their wake. Junkies don't exactly think straight, but everyone instinctively protects himself, so they fled."

It sounded good even to me, but he wasn't buying any of it.

"Excuse me, Ma—Miss. I'm the detective here. I think I'm the one who's supposed to be asking the questions." He said this with a charmingly wide grin on his very good-looking face, and even though I was overtired and not computing properly, I sensed he might be flirting with me. At least I thought, or maybe hoped, he was. If they flirt with you and you don't flirt back you have the upper hand. As a feminist, in this respect, I'm pretty despicable and treacherous since I've often used this to my advantage. The present fashion for short skirts hasn't hurt my efforts either. However, in this instance I was wearing jeans, and it was entirely possible that I was flirting back, which erased the advantage.

"May I ask you one more question? Please?" God help me, I crossed my legs. He was really cute.

"Yes?"

"Who are you?"

At this he laughed. A deep hearty chuckle that revealed an excellent set of teeth that had benefited from expensive orthodontia. They were not poor teeth; the color and texture reinforced my conjecture that he didn't overindulge in doughnuts.

"Detective-Sergeant Gregory Allard at your service." He would have probably added "ma'am" if he wasn't afraid of alienating me, and if he had been wearing a hat he surely would have doffed it with a sweeping gesture.

"That's not a very English name for someone with no accent. And that's not a question, so I'm allowed."

I sounded a little like Susan, but he was still chuckling, indulging me and amusing himself. I presume I wasn't his normal kind of suspect, and he was obviously enjoying himself.

"My mother is English and my father French. I was educated in English."

The fact that he used the word "educated" indicated that he'd had a good one. Otherwise he would have "gone to school."

I was behaving incredibly. Frank was perched on the couch in the other room with a hole in him, while I was developing an interest in a man who could put me in jail. I've been known to make lousy choices in men in my time, but this was above and beyond. This man could call a halt to my physical liberty, which in one short day I had come to value highly, and I was practically batting my mascaraed eyelashes at him. There seemed to be less and less question as to who was in control.

Seeing that I was about to add something likely irrelevant, he quickly interjected, "Do you wish to add any details to your statement?"

Maybe I was in control. His renewed formality spoke volumes, and so I smiled sweetly. Maybe I was better at this than I thought.

"No, sir," I replied.

"I'll make you a deal. If you don't call me sir, I won't call you ma'am."

"Deal."

Okay. I liked this. He was starting to treat me like a person and not a suspect. Well, perhaps a suspect, but surely not a criminal. An untried, unconvicted, and potentially interesting suspect. Just like in the movies.

"Miss Simons, I'm going to have to ask you to come down to the station to sign a formal statement."

"Tonight? Can't I come tomorrow?"

"I'm sorry. It must be tonight."

As we were parrying I suddenly had a thought and spoke without reflection or concern. Incriminating someone else was infinitely preferable to incriminating myself. "What about Bimbo? Where's she?"

"Who's Bimbo?" I had his full attention again.

I explained her relationship to Frank and the reasons for Susan's nomenclature. I omitted Bimbo's taste in evening gowns.

He chuckled again. He was doing a lot of that, and I didn't

know if I was just delightfully amusing or he was mocking me. "That's a good one, I'll have to remember that. Excuse me for a moment. Wait here." Delightful was a pretty good bet.

Still smiling broadly, he left the room, presumably to confer with Susan's detective to inform him of the existence of Bimbo and the importance of finding out more about her. I doubted whether Susan would admit to any knowledge, since it might imply that Frank still meant something to her and could foster the idea she might be jealous. Mostly, I sincerely doubted that she would admit anything to a French policeman that she would never even admit to me.

And then I heard the sound that I had been half expecting and fully dreading all night. A high-pitched, intermittently screeching wail, a lot like a truck backing up amplified through a powerful microphone. Or maybe like the Gestapo. My car! They would tow my wonderful Mercedes somewhere or other unless I got outside fast.

My priorities straight, I opened the verboten door and stepped into the corridor with, I think, every intention of alerting Detective-Sergeant Allard before I bolted down the stairs to move my car. I hesitated a moment, surprised to find the apartment full of people, in and out of uniform, all looking very busy and professional. A silent alarm must have sounded, since to a person, they all stopped what they were doing and turned to look at me, Prime Suspect Number One or perhaps Number Two. It was very disconcerting, and I felt tried and convicted on the spot though I hadn't done anything that they knew about. I hoped their little detecting machines wouldn't be able to tell them I'd moved Frank. From this angle I couldn't tell if he was still there, much less if he had his hair on.

My immediate problem was the imminent removal of my car, and I had no time to get involved in a staring contest nor listen to a reprimand.

Detective-Sergeant Allard chose this moment to come out

of the master bedroom. He was surprised to find me in the hall, and his eyes narrowed once again at my betrayal of his trust. I noticed, but nothing more. He had ordered me to stay put, and from the storm clouds gathering across his brow it was obvious he was not used to being disobeyed.

My car was my uppermost concern at the moment, and I cried plaintively, "They're going to tow it. I have to move it."

He perceived the problem immediately since he was a detective, and the siren and my anxiety were a dead giveaway.

"Give me your keys."

He ordered very well. There was nothing offensive in the way he demanded. It was kind of protective and comforting. I bet no one ever thought him bossy. But then he carried a gun.

I meekly turned over the keys, and he summoned my babycop, who again reddened at the sudden attention. Detective-Sergeant Allard told the blusher to either move the car or keep the cleaning crew from towing it. Now that's real power. As far as I know, nothing stops your car from being towed if it's in the way of the snowblower. If they could figure out a way to eat it along with the snowbanks they probably wouldn't bother moving it. These guys have size and heavy machinery on their side; people fear them more than muggers. The theory is they give you ample warning and so suffer no interference. I was duly impressed at the power of the police.

"Be careful with it," I called out, and everyone looked at me like I was an idiot, except my babycop, who turned even redder and stared at the floor. I don't know why they looked at me like that; I hadn't said "what!" I guess you don't tell the police department how to drive, but I've seen them careering around corners, and this was my baby.

The master bedroom door opened, and Susan emerged with her Detective-Sergeant. From the look of things it hadn't gone very well. Susan still maintained that haughty, injured air and showed fresh evidence of lip liner application.

We all proceeded to the front door, where Susan and I went

through the boot ritual. I tried to catch her eye, but she was terribly aloof, ignoring me and treating me like she treated her cop. I wanted to throttle her; she was the one responsible for my being there, after all. That was the thanks I got. I was tempted to bare my soul and tell all just to spite her. In the elevator she took my hand, which made me realize that her attitude was a mask for worry and fear.

"Is Robert okay at home?" I asked neutrally.

"Yeah, the housekeeper is there. He let me call and say I would be very late, and I told her about Frank. Just so she'd know and wouldn't think I was out carousing," she answered in a small voice.

"No talking," said her detective.

Wrong thing to say to such a tightly wound Susan.

Her register lowered, and her voice regained strength. "Excuse me. I did not realize this was a police state where individuals have no rights. I am not as yet under arrest, so I can say what I want. Maybe if you spoke adequate English you wouldn't worry about hidden messages, which is what I presume you are implying. Typical."

Even wronger thing to say. He turned fiery red, and I was worried he would have a stroke on the spot. He looked ready to smack her good and hard, which she admittedly deserved. Greg—I now thought of him as Greg even though he'd addressed me as Miss Simons, which maybe I would point out was also incorrect—put a soothing hand on his partner's shoulder while I deliberated making points by kicking her. Just when I decided I would do both, her grip tightened and her upper lip quivered. She was about to cry again, so I ignored orders and said, "It'll be all right. We haven't done anything wrong. Stay calm. Okay?"

I actually believed it. I've always known the best way to tell a convincing lie is to yourself believe it to be the truth. Once this is accomplished you can speak with certainty. I'm not very good at trying to keep a straight face, but allow me to add words and I'm an excellent liar. Words give me strength.

Still ignoring orders, I turned to Greg and asked, "May we stay together? I think it might be best."

He was my ally, my protector. Yes, it was very late, and I wasn't thinking straight, but he was just too cute to consider an adversary. Some of my cylinders had shut down.

Greg nodded to his partner and said, "Yes, that's okay. We'll all go in my car."

My synapses now definitely misfiring, I took the time to speculate as to what kind of car he drove. This was shallow even for me, and I was duly chagrined when it turned out to be an unmarked gray police-issue vehicle with the standard dent in the front fender and rusty sides. Do they come out of the factory looking like this?

As Susan and I climbed into the backseat, I took stock of the situation and decided to convince myself Greg was ugly and not my type. Or married. Or gay. Anything to keep me focused on the issue, which was to get this ordeal over and done with as soon as possible.

I vehemently promised myself I would never again answer the phone.

THE POLICE STATION was a letdown. I had envisioned the bustle of *Hill Street Blues* or the dilapidation of *Barney Miller*. We were taken to local Station 23 rather than the ominous sounding "Headquarters." No tumult, no excitement. Just a faceless, boring modern building. Television had disappointed me again.

Westmount is an independent upscale enclave, completely surrounded by, and in the heart of, Montreal. Although it fiercely protects its independence, it shares major services such as fire, police, and garbage collection with its much larger neighbor. It is responsible for its own snow removal though, which accounts for the monster machines prowling the streets at all hours of the night. Rich people like their roads clear and their snowbanks nonexistent. So we were dealing with Montreal Urban Community policemen in a Westmount station. Unlike neighboring Station 25, which serves the downtown core and handles all the dangerous flotsam and violent jetsam therein, Westmount Station 23 is refined. They probably have their share of prostitution, but these would be high-priced call girls, protected and insulated from the police by overtipped doormen and influential clients. The pace at this station suggested a routine of burglar alarm responses, break-ins, and the occasional mugger. A genteel neighborhood that supported genteel crime.

This notion was validated when the two detectives approached the front desk and introduced themselves. The desk sergeant straightened visibly. Homicide had brought in suspects. An electric current passed through the precinct, and everyone present was curious to find out what exactly had happened and get a look at the two perps. I'm sure most of them thought we were hookers, and I idly wondered what the going rate was. It's uncomfortable to be scrutinized by so many people who think so little of you.

As word spread, I realized we were big news in Westmount and worried that when somebody figured out they could make an extra buck, they would alert the media. If it hadn't already happened. Although I was no longer gainfully employed, I still had a reputation to uphold in the business community if I had any hopes of finding another job. A bad picture of me on the front page of the local rag *Allo Police* would not enhance my résumé. I wanted out of there fast; all thought of flirting put aside, I was determined to be terse.

Once again we were separated. I was escorted to what I presume to be an interrogation room, judging by the uncomfortable hardwood chair I was given and the mirror that filled the narrow wall at the back, which would only fool a moron or a narcissistic stoned-out junkie. The knowledge that people were observing me through the one-way glass made me anxious, probably the intent.

Both detectives sat in while I gave my statement, and I presume the same routine was repeated for Susan. I was first again, this time I think not accidentally but as punishment to Susan, thus forced to sit and stew for a while. Another officer was there to take notes in shorthand.

With all these people hanging on my every word, I wasn't exactly at my most gracious as I recounted events. Detective-Sergeant Allard—I was too cranky to think of him as Greg—led me through my paces as I repeated clearly and very concisely everything I had previously recounted. It took no more than ten minutes.

They departed and left me seated on the killer chair. I was afraid to move, since I was convinced everyone was watching me through the window. My nose was suddenly excruciatingly itchy, but no way was I going to give them the satisfaction. I suffered for about twenty minutes while they were with Susan, which I took to mean she had been difficult.

Then they both reappeared, trailing a scowling Susan. Detective-Sergeant Allard, following my cue of polite terseness, thanked me for my cooperation and said I could go, he would be in touch. I went from cordial to spitting mad in a fraction of a second.

"I can go? I can go? Where? How? If I remember correctly, you have my keys. And you know where my car is. You brought me here, now drive me back. What happened to common courtesy? After cooperating with the police your 'wham bam thank you ma'am' or in your case 'miss' does not impress me."

I'd done okay up to now but I went slightly over the top when I added, sounding a lot like Susan, "I demand my rights."

Susan's detective looked like he wanted to sock me. He'd

had Susan on his hands for a while now, and I'm sure he was pretty close to the end of his tether. He opened his mouth to say something in I don't know what language when Greg burst into laughter. This distracted his confrere, who now focused his malevolence on Greg. I thought I detected steam coming out of his ears.

Greg, at his most gallant, bowed from the waist and said, "Touché. Point well taken. I'll retrieve your keys and escort you ladies back." His hand was on his heart as though it had been pierced by my épée.

He turned to his partner, who was still pinkish, and told him to lead us to the front desk, where he would meet us after he had hunted down babycop and retrieved my keys. This didn't sit too well, and the pinkish turned back to red. Greg spared him further clashes with us, announcing he would escort us and meet his partner back at headquarters, wherever that was. I must have looked at him suspiciously or strangely or some sort of "ly," since he took it upon himself to explain that they had met here at the Westmount station and proceeded in one car. His was parked in the lot. Like I cared.

I was aware that Susan's detective's ire was probably well founded and his apoplexy therefore explainable.

I took Susan's hand and followed the detective to the front desk, where we awaited Greg. Susan looked ready to open her mouth to say something that I knew would be at the least insulting, so I took the opportunity to do something I had wanted to do ever since I saw Frank dead.

I kicked her. Admittedly not very hard, but it was satisfying as hell and served to make her clamp her mouth shut and look hurt. She then fumbled in her purse, and I knew positively that if she came out with lip liner I would kick her again. Harder. Much harder.

Greg returned in the nick of time to hand me my car keys, and the three of us proceeded to leave the station. Susan, not being able to resist a final flourish, turned dramatically, focused her gaze directly on her detective, and spat out, "If you like, I'll subsidize your English lessons at Berlitz."

It was fortunate that Greg's back was to his partner when he grinned.

I feared for her next speeding ticket.

6

DETECTIVE-SERGEANT Gregory Allard drove a silver-gray BMW, which should have impressed and therefore shamed me, but I was too tired to muster up the necessary energy. We drove silently through the snow-covered streets to the accompaniment of what I think was Vivaldi. The intensity of the storm had weakened; giant flakes whirled gently around us. It was very soothing, and given another five minutes we might all have been fast asleep.

Susan and I were deposited beside my car, which was exactly where I had left it minus its adjacent snowbank. I couldn't figure out how that had happened. Allard sped away, spinning his wheels like he was in a desperate hurry to be separated from us. His perfunctory "thank you ladies" had been unsatisfying, and for some reason I felt bereft.

"Where's your car? I'll take you to it. Get in."

The possibility that Susan had walked the five short blocks never crossed my mind. There was snow.

"I left it at home. Took a taxi because of the snow. You know how I drive."

I knew, but I was astounded that she did.

"Okay. Home it is."

She got in and we left for her house, driving silently once again. Neither of us had the strength to ask the other what had transpired at the station. It could wait. I was dead tired, and thoughts of my fresh sheets filled my head. As we approached her building, I suddenly woke up.

"The key! Do you still have it? You didn't tell them about it, did you?"

Much to her credit and foresight, she didn't call me an idiot, since I would have pushed her out the door of the moving car. She looked at me haughtily—she'd had a lot of practice with that look tonight—as she slipped her hand into her pocket and retrieved a key with its telltale red nail polish mark.

"Here it is. Actually, I pretended it wasn't there and almost forgot about it throughout the whole ordeal. I was scared they'd search me, so I never even put my hand in my pocket." In one night she had learned a lesson that had taken me years to perfect. Fear is an effective teacher.

"Come. Let's see what's in there. Careful you don't wake Robert," she said, as though there were no question of my abandoning her. My complicity was tacit.

As we pulled up to her building, I was dismayed to find an abundance of newly plowed parking spaces. Trust the snow to stop falling at inconvenient times. Any idea I had entertained of postponing the next phase of our operation vanished. There were no excuses, and it was easier to face up to the inevitable than argue halfheartedly. With a sigh I maneuvered the car into the slot closest to the entrance.

Even before I switched off the ignition, Susan leaped out of the car, suddenly bounding with energy. All worries of the evening's events disappeared as she aimed for her treasure trove. I could see the dollar signs dancing above her head. I was exhausted.

It was now three-fifteen in the morning. Fortunately I'd had a nap, or I would have been nonfunctional by now. My second or third wind came when I faced up to the fact that I couldn't let Susan investigate that box alone, and I'd never get to bed until we got this over with. The situation was emotionally fraught, and the consequences of the discovery unpredictable. Or so I told myself. Basically, I was just nosy.

So we rode up another elevator, walked down another corridor, and took off our boots once again.

"Oh no! I left my shoes in his car."

"On purpose?" she asked snidely. "Don't worry, he'll bring them back. Or you can have him arrested."

This was an interesting development. Self-centered Susan, in her short interaction with Greg and me, had perceived something. I was dying to ask her if she thought he liked me, but I knew how childish it would sound. And how it was precisely the question she was waiting for, probably already thinking up a choice riposte. So once again I let something annoying she said pass without comment and silently proceeded with my boot removal. I left them on the carpet in unspoken defiance instead of putting them on the rubber mat. An unsatisfying statement.

My so-called friends who begged my attention and assistance sure were taking a lot of potshots at me today.

The housekeeper must be a light sleeper; she was already at the door when we opened it. I found it difficult to keep a straight face when I saw her waspish features, flower-flecked flannel nightgown, and frilly mob cap. She was a character straight out of Dickens.

"Mrs. Porter, I'm glad you're finally home. Robert woke up and asked for you but fell right back to sleep. I said nothing of Mr. Porter. That will be left to you in the morning. Also, Mr. King called. He insists that you call him when you arrive. I'll be going back to bed now." The frost in her voice was palpable as she turned on her incongruously bunny-slippered heel and headed back to her room, tut-tutting all the way. I translated the sounds to mean, "if these late nights continue I shall have to seek employment elsewhere. Somewhere respectable."

I heard the lock snap.

"She locks her door?" I asked, amazed.

"Only when I'm home. When she's alone with Robert she says she leaves it open. I think she's afraid Barry might wake up in a frenzy of passion and not be able to resist her. He'll crawl stealthily along the hall, enter her room, and ardently ravish her. She should only be so lucky."

Barry, the Mr. King to whom the housekeeper had referred, was Susan's current boyfriend. He'd been around for about six months, and it was still in the hot and heavy stage of romance with no sign of waning. This was a lengthy period for Susan, whose attention span generally runs to four months max. What surprised me and made me realize that Susan might be taking this one seriously was the fact that he spent nights there. Until now, Susan had always been very discreet about her boyfriends, not wanting to expose Robert to a successive string of "uncles." Susan would meet them down in the lobby or in a restaurant. The doormen in her building knew a lot more about her social life than her son did.

"That good, huh?"

"Yep," she said with a smug grin, hugging herself.

I envied her. Although I insisted I was quite satisfied with my life, I hadn't had a decent relationship for too many years, and if it weren't for my irregular doses of Sam it would have been full-blown jealousy.

We tiptoed unnecessarily through the deep carpeting to the linen closet, to the left of her bedroom, and silently set to. Her box was as buried as mine, and it took over ten minutes to unearth it. It would have only taken me two, since I would have just tossed everything over my shoulders and either left it for Mme Jacqueline or thrown it all back in a heap. However, Susan, better trained than I, carefully transferred everything to a neat pile for its eventual replacement. I strained at the bit, addicted as I am to instant gratification. My impatience must have shown, since she gave me a pitying and withering look.

"Wait for it. We can't all live like slobs, you know."

Chastened, I helped refold things.

At last the box appeared, and she inserted the key. The door swung open easily, but because of the angle we couldn't see what was inside. She knelt before it and stuck her hand in.

"There's something wedged in here. Hang on. I'll work it out."

Crouched over the box, she completely obscured my view. I wanted to shove her out of the way and do it myself, but it was her house and her box and her illicit whatever, so I tapped my foot impatiently on the ankle-deep carpeting. The thick pile forestalled more dirty looks. Both her hands were now busily at work, and she lurched backward as the recalcitrant contents finally came free.

"What's this?"

She said that; I didn't.

"Let me see," I insisted.

I could hardly keep myself from grabbing the thing out of her hands. But I was no longer dealing with the timid Susan of Frank's apartment. The experiences of the police station and her encounter with her detective-sergeant had served to restore her formidable backbone. I quickly figured out bossiness would now get me nowhere, so I didn't waste the effort.

"Move back into the hall. We'll look at this in the bedroom," she ordered, instead of me.

Just like her to procrastinate my pleasures. At this point I could hardly remember why she was my friend.

I dutifully backed out, allowing her to emerge and lead the way. I tried to sneak a peek but she wasn't having any. The whatever was kept shielded from my sight, but from her posture, my finely honed deductive skills quickly ascertained that it was reasonably heavy. Raising Robert had trained her well in dealing with overexcited children, and she was effectively applying her techniques to me, with probable just cause.

In the bedroom I closed the door a little too sharply, which earned me another scathing stare.

"Shh . . . Remember, Robert's sleeping. Here," she said, dumping a brown, well-stuffed manila envelope onto the bed. The paper had been torn in the shoving in and pulling out, yet the package had maintained its shape. A large loaf of sandwich bread. No longer Little Miss Neat, she ripped the paper off, scattering it around with no concern for tidiness. One for my team.

"Jesus!" I said looking at the plastic bag, filled with what looked like ivory face powder but surely wasn't. "What is this?"

We stood there for a moment, just staring at the package. Susan suddenly had an idea. "Taste it." She was still doing the ordering around.

Ever the foolhardy one, I carefully unstuck the sealing tape, unzipped the bag, dipped my finger, and put some onto the tip of my tongue. They always do this on television.

"Yuck. It's bitter. I don't know what this is."

"Here, let me taste it," she said as she took the bag gently from me, being careful not to spill any. Heaven forfend anything should sully her immaculate carpeting or that she should waste a gram of something potentially valuable.

In went her finger, from bag to mouth. An unattractive moue caused her lip liner to purse like a withered raisin. One taste was obviously not enough; she repeated the process. I wondered what condition her taste buds were in, since the stuff was horrible and nothing could convince me to do it again.

"I don't believe the bastard!"

"What?"

She sneered and said, "Heroin."

"What!"

"Oh, Barbara, stop being so naive. This is high-grade heroin. Two keys, by the feel of it."

Wait a minute. Since when was Jewish Princess Susan on intimate terms with heroin? Where did she learn to talk like a drug dealer? I'd better check her purse for a beeper. Against my better judgment, I was impressed.

If it had been cocaine I would have understood. It was the nineties, and cocaine had been the controlled substance of choice throughout the eighties. Susan and I were both old enough to have lived through the flower-power sixties and had survived the hallucinogenic years virtually untouched and unscathed. We had emerged as respectable, upright, responsible, and law-abiding citizens. Well, almost. I'm sure she'd flirted with drugs, as I had, and I have a distinct recollection of sharing a lineup for the bathroom at a raucous party. It used to be that lines for the bathroom meant cocaine ingestion, while in the sedate nineties lineups mean that people are reverting to their teenage behavior and sneaking off to have a cigarette. At social gatherings, bathrooms of nonsmoking households generally reek of tobacco. We've come full circle.

"How do you know that?" I may have been impressed, but I was still shocked.

"Stop gawking at me. It was a long time ago. When I was a hippie living in Mexico. Remember when I fled my upper Westmount home to find love and truth in poverty? When I found neither and I desperately craved modern plumbing, I came back and have been trying to reclimb that hill ever since."

She knew herself a lot better than I had given her credit for. I adore Susan; well, not exactly tonight, but generally. I do however recognize her for what she is: shallow, self-centered, and acquisitive. I was astonished to learn that she has a deeper, more honest side. But it was the middle of the night; I was exhausted and appalled and in no mood for enlightenment.

"You shot heroin?"

"Barbara, will you please stop sounding like my mother. No, I did not shoot heroin. It tastes awful, as you know, it snorts roughly, and the idea of sticking a needle in my arm is repellent. So I smoked it a bit. Don't desecrate the temple and all that. After all, it is a vital asset."

Aah, the Susan I knew was back.

"It was the time and place. The guys around were all snorting and shooting, and I finally got fed up with their nodding out and being sick so I split to another scene in California that was only moderately better. But I remember the taste, and this is definitely heroin. Not China White. Probably the new Downtown stuff, judging by the color."

She sounded like a drug dealer again, but I didn't pursue it. In a convoluted way I was envious of her. I thought I'd had a checkered, adventurous youth, but she'd far surpassed me. And survived it all to graduate to lip liner. No, come to think of it, I wasn't jealous at all.

There was a hint of temptation as I gazed at the bursting bag, but I quickly dismissed it. Now was not the time nor the place. I sadly doubted that it ever would be again and had a fleeting nostalgia for my misspent youth, which signaled a great trepidation for my advancing middle age. It boded boring as hell. Oh well, I was surely wiser . . .

From the way Susan stared at her finger and wiggled her tongue around in her mouth, I figured she was having much the same thoughts. She recovered first and returned to the horrible immediacy that surrounded us. She settled for donning the mantle of injured party.

"The prick. How dare he put this here. In my house. In Robert's house. I'll kill him." She was furious.

"Too late," I giggled. "Somebody beat you to it. And probably for this."

"Shit. Shit. Shit." She pounded her fists on the bed, the thick duvet absorbing all sound. Tears of anger and frustration sprang to her eyes. "He deserves worse than dead."

In an instant her visage cleared, and a look of fierce determination replaced the rage. Shoving the package at me, she said, "Here. I can't keep this in the house. You hold on to it."

"No way, Susan. Let's flush it down the toilet."

"No." I'm not sure if she was being more levelheaded or more mercenary than I, but the upshot was that she said, "Somebody wanted this badly enough to kill Frank. We can't flush it away. It's valuable, and it might come in handy."

She was cogitating extremely well for someone in her position. But what she said made sense. Someone badly wanted this heroin, which looked to weigh about two kilos. Someone had killed for it, and it must be worth a lot of money. Until we knew more about its value, we would be wise to hang onto it. Also, it might be Susan's only pawn in this game. Her interrogation had obviously not gone well, as evidenced by the redness of her detective-sergeant's face, and she could be facing serious allegations when they checked further into her relationship with Frank. The most disturbing aspect of all these conjectures was the "we" part of it. I was thinking "we" when I clearly should have been thinking "she" and getting the hell out of there as fast as possible. More cylinders were blowing.

"Hang on a sec. Let me try to reason this out. You're right. Whoever killed Frank didn't find the key or the heroin, so he's still looking for it. And obviously will go to any lengths to find it. So this stuff poses a threat to Robert just by being here. It definitely has to go," I said.

"Okay. First step. Call Barry and ask him to come over. I don't think you should be alone here tonight. Who knows what's lurking out there. Don't explain on the phone. Just tell him to get over here."

She hesitated for only a second, then headed for the phone while I tried to formulate our next move. Rational thought was difficult under the circumstances and given the hour. Barry answered on what seemed to be the first ring, and to my surprised satisfaction Susan followed my instructions. She simply said she needed to see him, and he acquiesced, asking no questions. She hung up, faced me, and calmly said, "What now?"

I shook my head, trying to ward off the idea that if I just lay down for a second I would nod off and wake up back in my own bed, recovering from a nightmare.

"I have a plan. Not a good one, but it'll do 'til tomorrow. I'll take the heroin under one condition. You have to promise—no, you have to swear on Robert's life—that you will tell no one about this. No one. Not even Barry. Sure, tell him about Frank and the police and stuff, but not one word about the key or the heroin. Or even the toupée. I mean this, Susan. Is it clear? Are we agreed?"

"Why can't I tell Barry?" she whined. I could understand her wanting a strong masculine shoulder to lean and dump on. Very nonliberated of me, but still very comforting. However, now was not the time for female fluttering, and since I was the one taking the risks we were going to do this my way or not at all.

"Because I said so," I said shortly. "That's the deal. Take it or leave it. And don't cross me, Susan. There's too much danger. The less anyone knows the safer we'll all be. Especially Robert."

That clinched it.

"Okay. I think I understand. I won't mention that stuff. It's just that I'm scared. I want Barry around for the next few days," she admitted.

"Fine. But remember, not a word."

I was belaboring the point because I was serious about the potential danger. Witness Frank's recent demise. "Get me a bag or something so I can get this shit home." This time I bossed and she obeyed.

We went to the kitchen together, peering around corners for

intruders that couldn't be there. In spite of all my assurances that no one knew the heroin was here, I was spooked. So was she. Finding a small shopping bag, we first loosely wrapped the bags in newspaper and then put them in. Perfect, nonsuspicious-size package to be carrying around at four o'clock in the morning. Sure.

We were seated at the kitchen table munching tasteless cookies when I heard the sound of a key turning in the door. Visions of masked killers danced in what remained of my brain.

I froze, but Susan rose and went to greet Barry. Once I had gotten my breath back and returned my heart from my mouth to its proper place, I considered this new aspect. Barry had a key. This relationship must be serious. His arrival signaled my departure, and I took the opportunity to grab the shopping bag and put on my coat and boots. We went through the cheek-kissing routine at the door, all of us pretending it was perfectly normal for me to be there in the dead of night. We all smiled brightly. As I left, I noticed that she was clutching his hand.

Back behind the wheel I thought about Barry to distract myself from the fact that I was now transporting two kilos of an illicit controlled substance in my beloved car. Susan's attraction to him was perfectly understandable. Susan and I were both fortyish, which meant forty-something and counting backward, while Barry was a very good-looking thirty-five. His dark hair was graying seductively at the temples, and he had the longest, thickest eyelashes I've ever seen on a man. A faint scar ran from the tip of his left eyebrow to the bottom of his ear. He was strong and slightly dangerous looking, and I sort of wished he could stay with me tonight. For protection, of course.

I made it home in one piece just as the snow finally stopped falling and the early morning city was beginning to stir.

Too exhausted to think about anything, I shoved the heroin behind some sweaters, dropped my clothes onto the floor, and fell into bed. The numerals on the clock read 5:28, and I was asleep before the digits changed.

7

THE PHONE WOKE me at nine-thirty the next morning. I reached for it, completely ignoring last night's firm resolution. The lessons of a month had been unlearned in a day, and I was back to not being able to resist a ringing telephone. It could be the call of my lifetime rather than the instrument of torture that had lately been leading me on a heart-wrenching roller coaster ride.

Joanne had seen the wires and recognized Frank's name. She called to impart the news, and I was delighted to surprise her with my inside knowledge. Surprising Joanne is quite a feat. She's plugged into every news service, under and aboveground. She can surf the Internet with ease and find all the really good stuff. If you want the real dirt, ask Joanne—or at least *I* can ask Joanne. She does have a sense of professional ethics, but we've got a lot of history and I can usually cajole information. I smugly informed her of my personal involvement, and her reaction made me glad I'd answered the phone.

"What!" she exclaimed, which I found enormously gratifying.

I reached for a cigarette to further savor my moment in the sun as I outlined the entire proceedings. She got pretty much the same version as I had given the police, but I added my morning exploratory foray to Frank's apartment. I also editorialized a lot, particularly about Bimbo's wardrobe. I did heed my own instructions to Susan, avoiding the part about the heroin and the key, but I couldn't resist describing the scene with the toupée. It was more than self-aggrandizement. She would have killed me if she found out about it elsewhere, and she surely would have.

This was a good story, and she had an in. I could envisage her grabbing pen and paper, cursing herself for not having had the foresight to tape the conversation. I leaned back into the pillows and puffed contentedly as she set to work.

"Who are the detectives assigned to the case?"

"Detective-Sergeant Gregory Allard," I answered, giving him his full title. If I had said Greg I would have never heard the end of it. It was bad enough I had Susan on my case; Joanne is more tenacious. "And you know what, the other guy never introduced himself and I never bothered to ask Susan his name."

"Detective-Sergeant Fernand Boucherville," she informed me. "He got Susan? That must have been something. I'd have paid to see that," she chuckled.

"Why would you say that?" I asked innocently, with a big grin. Since we were on the phone, she couldn't see the smirk. I was, however, surprised to note that Joanne was attuned to a facet of Susan's personality that I had previously been unaware of. They weren't close, but since they were both my friends they crossed paths often and had, over the years, established a friendly relationship. But I had never noticed that streak of Susan's, so I guess we're blind to our friends' shortcomings, the years of closeness coloring the rapport.

"Oh, come on," she answered impatiently. "I know she's your friend, but I've spent enough time with Susan to know she easily climbs onto her high horse. And he's a pip himself. Short fuse, and an outright nationalist. Did she at least speak to him in French?"

"Nope. She refused."

"Wonderful. She must have driven him up the walls. He's a strictly by-the-book guy with no sense of humor whatsoever. He usually refuses to speak any English, although it's quite good. I think he's embarrassed to admit he can. Some sort of reverse snobbery. He has a definite adversarial posture with the media, particularly the English media. The Political Policeman. His partner usually does the public speaking for the duo, but I have had the dubious pleasure from time to time. Too many times for my liking, since he brings out the worst in me. He's so easy to bait, and I have to keep reminding myself that I'm a pro. It's also not a good idea to tangle with the police."

"Oh yeah, his partner . . . What's he like?" I tried to sound casual.

"The partner, huh?" From the tone of her voice I knew I hadn't been successful. "He is one cute son of a bitch. Got to you, huh?"

Damn. I was entirely too transparent, even on the phone. It's never early enough in the morning to try to put one over successfully on Joanne, but that doesn't stop me from trying.

"Please," I said in my best imitation of Susan. "He was just my interrogating officer."

"Just?" she answered teasingly. "Come on. Admit it. You wouldn't be the first to drop."

Knowing I'd never get anywhere except in deeper if I continued on this track, I resorted to my forte, negotiation. "I wasn't aware of any danger of free fall. However, if I were to own up to some interest, what could you tell me about him?"

This was not going well.

"Admit it, and I'll spill." She was enjoying this way too much.

"There's nothing to admit," I said stubbornly.

"Okay. We'll drop it. It's obviously not important so we'll change the subject." I hate it when she's coy. This round to her. On reflection, most rounds to her.

She switched to her reporter mode. "Did you notice anything unusual last night?"

"As a matter of fact, I did. Frank lying there dead was pretty unusual." I may have lost the battle, but I wasn't giving up on our lifetime war.

"Seriously, if you can think of any details, let me know. I'd really appreciate it. Gotta go, the other line. Call you later."

It had been an unsatisfactory conversation. Not enough sleep and having come out second in a joust with Joanne contributed to my foul mood as I padded off to the bathroom for my morning ablutions. I was restored to a somewhat even keel after a shower, another cigarette, and my morning Diet Coke. Although this is the way I usually face the day, I have considered changing this regimen due to the encroaching years. It's a toss-up between my wrinkles and my disposition, and I waver daily on which ranks higher.

The discovery had come too late for the morning papers. The nice thing about Montreal, unlike New York, is that murder still rates prominent space in the papers. We have our share of violent crime, but we still have the decency to be shocked about it. After scanning the paper to make sure and checking the stock quotations to see if I was still fiscally viable, I called Susan and found her in a worse mood than I had been.

There was no grieving in her voice, only anger. She'd had a difficult conversation with Robert, explaining Frank's murder without the graphic details, and he had not taken it well. To him it was a final loss. Robert had truly loved Frank, the good-guy weekend father who indulged his only son. To her credit, Susan encouraged the relationship, and surprisingly, Frank behaved more responsibly toward his son after the separation. He even consulted Susan before broaching any major overindulgence so she would have a chance to veto it before the fact and not look the villain. I had to stop thinking like this. I might start to like him.

Barry had gone off to work, but Robert was home with Susan. Later in the day she would go to the funeral parlor to make arrangements for Frank's eventual disposal, although the date for the funeral could not be set until the police released the body. Jewish law dictates that a body be buried within twenty-four hours, but the Rabbinic Council, ever the pragmatists, long ago decreed that the law of the state supersedes the laws of the Talmud. So Frank would lie in the police morgue until someone there decided his time had come and gone. Personally, Susan wouldn't have minded if he had been buried in Montreal's equivalent of Potter's Field, but Robert deserved better, and Frank's sister would torture her forever.

"Why you? Isn't she springing for the funeral?"

"Are you kidding? Lainie spend a penny? She's good at telling me how to spend my money, but getting her to part with anything is beyond my ability. I wouldn't be surprised to discover she never went to the bathroom, the anal-retentive bitch."

Susan was venting well. Repeating my dire threats about secrecy, I hung up, telling her to call me later if she wanted me to stay with Robert while she was out. I knew she wouldn't ask, but it made me feel benevolent to offer.

My plan was to be out of the house by ten-thirty, but I took a slight detour to the wing chair by the window in the living room with every intention of finishing the newspaper to find out the other things that were happening in the world. Naturally, I didn't even get through the first page. The next thing I knew, it was eleven-fifteen and I felt great. The best thing about that chair is you can snooze comfortably and wake up without feeling stiff or sore. It has the most wonderful soporific effect. Better than Valium, and there's no chemical hangover.

Since I was awake and full of energy, I felt I should continue with my program of reinsertion into the real world. Against my will, I put on my exercise clothes and headed out to the gym, dumping my boots into the trunk of the car, as the club afforded indoor parking. I would do enough bending and stretching there. Unlike Joanne, I loathe working out. The double threat of advancing age and increasing poundage has forced me to it, so I go at least three times a week, hating every second. It makes you sweat, and your hair frizzes. Not exactly my best look.

I do not, however, go to a normal gym like a normal person. If I'm going to do this, it's going to be the least painful way possible. So I joined Le Refuge, a fully loaded health club and spa center. Large lockers, clean individual showers with opaque curtains, an overabundance of towels, hair dryers, shampoo, body lotion, and free telephones everywhere make it yuppie heaven. It does have very well-equipped workout and weight rooms, with excellent lighting and ventilation. No three-week-old air in here. All the latest torture machines and every conceivable aerobics class. Two pools, indoor and out, tennis courts, squash, and racquetball. And a luxurious spa center offering everything. The idea had been that I would pretend I was at some glorious spa in California and thus look forward to exercising. The actuality was that the high fees made me feel guilty, so I went more often than I normally would have, which is probably never. At these prices I was bound and determined to get my money's worth; knowing myself well, I paid in advance, and four more months remained in my account. This sophisticated, intricate system of personal blackmail is the means by which I do most things I have to but hate.

After parking the car, I removed my bag from the trunk and checked in. As I collected my key and headed for the locker room, my buoyant spirits began to sink at the prospect of the next hour and a half of torture.

The eleven o'clock step class had just ended, and a passel

of ladies-who-don't-work hit the locker room at the same time as I. I knew I shouldn't be so judgmental, since I had recently joined their ranks, but I preferred to consider myself as a lady-with-no-job. Nomenclature can do wonders for self-esteem.

When I saw that the locker next to mine was occupied, I fervently hoped that, whoever she was, she was busily splashing away in the pool. No such luck.

"Hi, Barbara. Haven't seen you around for a while," a cheery voice said in greeting.

Cynthia Berkowitz stood dripping beside me, having obviously taken her stepping seriously. She's a perky little bundle, standing no more than five foot three with a mop of unruly curly blond hair. Oh well, surely better her than someone with perfect nails. To her credit she's got a cheerful disposition and a job to boot.

"Not working today?" I asked, surprised to find her here at this time.

"I took two weeks off to recharge the batteries. And I figured that if I took the time now, I couldn't be persuaded to take another family vacation. David thinks they're a wonderful way to spend more time with the kids, but do you know what it's like just to pack for four boys, one husband, and myself? Ugh!" Her tiny body shuddered at the thought. "They have a great time while I cook, do laundry, and minister to cuts and bruises. Some holiday. David loves camping, whereas my idea of camping is a Holiday Inn. They all go fishing, and the boys stick hooks into themselves willy-nilly and come back covered with bloodstains. No matter what the commercials say, you can't wash out blood. My squeamish dentist husband can't stand the sight of blood anywhere except in the mouth, so he ignores them and pretends they're not bleeding all over the place. If they've done themselves serious enough damage he just hollers for me."

She drew breath. "Not this time. Two glorious weeks to myself. Look, I'm glad I ran into you. I wanted to talk to you but rumor was, you were off-limits for a while."

Gossip sure spreads in this town. "Well, I sort of lost my job and hid out for a while," I said, hesitantly.

"Glad you're back. I have to talk to you. And don't worry about work. You can get any job you want, with your talents."

I was liking her more and more every second.

"I'm sort of worried about Frank, and maybe you can set my mind at ease, even though if you're like everyone else, you probably can't stand him. I'm off to a glorious massage now. Then a pedicure. Meet me for lunch upstairs after. My treat. We should be done about the same time. Please. Ahh, life can be wonderful."

Taking my silence as acquiescence, although she hadn't given me a chance to respond, she sashayed off toward the spa, grabbing a handful of towels on the way. I wasn't quite sure I hadn't hallucinated the whole episode, it seemed to have happened so quickly. Still, I would meet her. She'd said nice things about me, and she'd said the magic word: Frank.

As I headed up to the room with the torture racks, I realized that here was another person asking for my help. I wondered what kind of trouble she could possibly get me into. Everyone else was doing an excellent job of embroiling me in chaos.

I hate aerobics classes, possibly because I smoke too much, but more likely because the classes are a bit too structured for my taste. Really because there are too many perfect bodies bouncing around near the front of the room and too much Jello wobbling in the back. My relationship with the machines is special. It's just us and no mirrors.

Since I hadn't been there for some weeks, I lowered the weights on my regular routine, but it was still hard work moving from machine to machine, completing the requisite repetitions. An hour and twenty minutes later I was back in the locker room, sopping wet, frizzy-haired, physically exhausted, and hugely satisfied. I hadn't died.

I took a long, hot shower, slathered my body with free lotion, and dried my shoulder-length auburn hair with the provided hair dryers, remarking glumly on the new strands of white appearing with alarming regularity. Once again I considered coloring it but then an anorexic bleached-blond middle-aged Nancy Reagan lookalike stepped up to the dryer next to mine, and I revised my opinion. It could wait a while. Roots would be just one more thing to fuss about, and I didn't have the patience.

Back at my locker I dressed in beige cashmere pants and a white silk shirt. A beige plaid Armani jacket that covered my butt and an hour of exercise allowed me to wear pants with equanimity. The magic of good tailoring. I know that caring about clothes is considered shallow, a reflection of one's lack of character, but I do love them. They cover my imperfect body and envelop it in a layer of sumptuousness. Good clothes are soft amour to me. I'm protected from the populace, since, contrary to what we've been taught about values, we all judge by what we see. Ask any supermarket manager; it's all in the packaging. Also, when I'm packaged in a straight and elegant manner I can get away with almost anything, since no one would believe such a person capable of anything unseemly. A wonderful masquerade, it's a helpful trick I learned long ago.

After adding a strand of pearls, I zipped up my now-smelly bag and headed for the restaurant and Cynthia. She hadn't arrived yet, so I sat down and ordered. Both Cynthia and my all-dressed cheeseburger—after all that exertion I felt I was entitled—arrived concurrently. She plunked herself down across from me and sailed into what I anticipated to be another monologue. She's suffered from motormouth ever since I've known her, but I never mind. She's usually amusing, in an Erma Bombeck sort of way, and now it would give me the opportunity to stuff my starving face. I took a big bite and settled back to listen.

"Oooh, that felt great. About time I pampered myself a little. And tonight David is taking us all out for dinner, so no dishes, and if we go for pizza there'll be no knives and forks and so no opportunities for bloodshed. Ah, the life of luxury. But you're the one I'm jealous of," she said, eyeing me critically.

My mouth was too full to say "what?" so all I could do was gulp and raise my eyebrows quizzically.

"Really. It's true. Look at you. You can eat anything. At my height I just look at a cheeseburger and gain weight. It's a losing battle. Five pounds on me is equal to fifteen on you. I used to want to be taller to go out with the football players, but now it's simply because I want to be able to eat."

I liked this woman more and more every second. Soon I'd propose if she kept it up. I took another bite with nary a thought of my thighs.

Some sort of juice magically appeared before her. I hadn't seen her order anything.

"My regular," she said, indicating an orangish concoction topped with a thick layer of foam. One sip was enough to adorn her with a mustache and send her off again.

"What's wrong with Frank?" she began, getting down to business immediately. She's always been very pragmatic. "He's acting so strange lately. Look, I know you're Susan's friend. I like her too, so I don't expect much sympathy for Frank's position, but something is seriously out of synch, and the earth-mother-nurturer in me feels duty bound to try to correct the situation. I feel I should help him. That Celine certainly doesn't seem to be the helping type. She may be the problem, but I really don't think so. I've seen Frank with lots of women since he and Susan broke up and he's never behaved so weirdly."

So Bimbo had a name. Celine.

"Last Saturday there was a bar mitzvah in the family. Of course you know that Frank is David's cousin, and it was David's brother's kid's bar mitzvah, if you can follow that. It was one of those Goodbye Columbus affairs. Well, they live in Hampstead, and you know about the peer pressure in that neighborhood.

They all pretend they've found nirvana and secretly wish they lived in Westmount. The occupation of the day is who can top who."

I didn't interrupt to remind her that her grammar could stand improvement and that she too lived in Hampstead, which, in my now relaxed and exercised and flattered state, seemed to me to be a not at all bad place to live.

"It was a huge deal, and everyone remotely related was invited. Even Susan, who is usually on the out list of that branch of the family—but Robert is in the same class as the bar mitzvah boy's brother, so I suppose they felt duty bound. David's brother did check it out with her; I mean, if she and Frank could be in the same room together without dishes flying, and I guess Susan reassured him she would behave in a decent fashion and not embarrass all their friends. But no one bothered to check with Frank."

I was surprised that Susan hadn't mentioned the event to me, until I remembered that I hadn't been very communicative of late. Which reminded me that I should call around to catch up on all the gossip I had missed.

"Anyway, Frank and Celine arrive first. He seems to be very agitated. Can't stay still. Keeps going up to people to talk to them but walks away after two seconds. And he keeps going to the bathroom, leaving Celine alone in a room full of people she doesn't know and who don't want to know her. I felt sorry for her. The nurturer again. So I took the time to talk to her. That's how I know her name—Frank sure didn't introduce us. He didn't introduce her to anyone. I don't know why he even brought her. Oh, it's Celine Plouffe. Her name, that is. She's quite beautiful and pretty okay. She's a stewardess, no, a flight attendant. She was *very* clear on that point. Frank comes back into the hall, sees us chatting, and rushes over to pull Celine away from me like I was a leper or something. I was offended. And hurt. But I felt vindicated when he suddenly had a major

sneezing fit and sprayed everyone within six feet. It was hilarious watching everyone scatter and him mumbling apologies and
muttering something about allergies. What's he allergic to? It
isn't hay fever season. Then he goes to have a conference with
the headwaiter. Maybe he's allergic to some foods and he was
checking the menu."

Nice, naive Cynthia.

"But the best weirdness was yet to come if you can believe
it. Okay"—she drew a big breath before continuing—"we all
sit down. Frank's table is next to mine. His back is to me, but
I'm facing it. I can't see his face, but he and Celine seem to be
involved in some kind of animated conversation. He's doing all
the talking and ignoring the assorted relatives seated around
him—Lainie and her husband and a bunch of others I don't
think you know.

"Then Susan arrives, late as usual. That woman has never
been on time for anything in her entire life. In tow she has this
gorgeous guy who she introduces around. Barry something or
other. How old is that guy? I'll say one thing for her; she sure
picks them good. Except for Frank, of course, but we'll blame
that on youth. On the other hand, he picks good too. Celine is a
knockout."

Before she could go on I interrupted. I couldn't resist. It just
fell out. "What was she wearing? Bim—Celine, not Susan, I
mean."

Cynthia took another gulp, this time erasing the resultant
mustache with a pert pink tongue before continuing.

"Funny you should ask. Do you know her? Who is she? It
was the most god-awful sequin-and-chiffon beaded job. Off one
shoulder, balloon beaded sleeves that sagged under the weight,
and an ankle-length chiffon skirt. Everyone else was pretty
much short, strapless, and of course black. She was flaming
fuchsia. You could see her a mile away. Everyone stared, which
naturally made me feel sorry for her. One day I'm going to sink

under the weight of everyone else's problems. Men are such bastards. Or maybe just Frank. He had to know that dress was inappropriate, yet he let her wear it."

I nodded, not particularly in agreement but to keep the story moving along.

"Well, Susan and Barry-something-or-other sit, and we all start to eat the appetizer. Some nouvelle stuff. It was gorgeous and I'm sure cost a bundle, but it was tasteless. I hate to waste the calories I ingest on tasteless food. It seems so futile. The whole affair was like that. *Très, très* when all anybody ever really wants is roast beef, potatoes, and something chocolate and fattening for dessert. We're all pretending we like the food, and Celine glances over her shoulder, notices Susan, and pokes Frank. He then wheels around and sees us all. He leaps up, knocking his chair over in the process, and makes for the door, practically dragging poor Celine in his wake. He doesn't say good-bye to anyone. Just stomps out, sneezing all the way."

Cynthia stopped talking long enough for one final swig and looked at me perplexedly. "What's wrong with him? I know he and Susan aren't usually invited to the same affairs, but I thought they had a civil relationship. I mean, he went nuts when he saw her. And why does he sneeze so much?"

I nearly burst out laughing when Cynthia said she had tried to call him the next day to recommend a good allergist, but he hadn't been home and hadn't returned her call. I wasn't going to be the one to educate her about the side effects of snorting cocaine and/or heroin. She stared at me expectantly, and I knew it was finally my turn to talk. She expected some answers or advice—but I had better.

"Cynthia, take a deep breath. The whole problem of Frank's allergies and behavior is a moot point now. Frank was murdered last night."

The effect was spectacular. Her saucer-shaped eyes opened to dinner-plate size, and her mouth formed a large *O*. Her whole face became a study in circles. She was speechless. For thirty seconds, that is.

"Omigod! I have to call David. Should I call Susan? Can I do anything?"

I calmed her, explaining that everything was under control and that she should wait a few days before calling Susan. The funeral had not as yet been scheduled and wouldn't be until the police released the body. At that the plates became serving platters. I thought the whole eyeball might drop out of the socket.

Promising to relay her condolences, I grabbed my bag and headed for the door. I left her with the bill, since she had offered in the first place and my information had surely paid for my lunch. As I was rising she put a hand on my shoulder, impeding my escape, and said exactly what I would have expected from her if I had taken the time to think about it. "What about Celine? How's she taking it?" Leave it to Cynthia Berkowitz to be concerned about Bimbo. She's much nicer than I am.

"Good question," I answered, disentangling myself from her grip. I left her sitting there looking totally bewildered. I knew it would only take a few seconds for her to collect herself and hit the phones, and I scurried out of there before she could begin a barrage of unanswerable questions.

ONCE SETTLED IN my car, I took a deep breath. The workout had left me both calm and energized. Nothing like a lot of sweat to wash away any free-floating anxiety. Before proceeding with my life, I had some phone calls of my own to make but I headed home rather than risk running into Cynthia and her concern again.

I sat down at the kitchen table with my telephone and address book. Not that I was going to call any strangers, but all the regular numbers that I called were on speed dial on my phone at the office, and the others had been handled by my secretary.

I didn't remember anyone's phone number anymore. Technology and slavery do have drawbacks.

Before I had a chance to dial out, the phone rang, startling me. I picked up, only to hear Joanne say, "Just a sec," and proceed to bark out a complicated set of orders to some lackey who was presumably standing before her. Time marched on, and I tapped the receiver impatiently, but she never noticed. I've never been able to understand why someone would call you and then ignore you completely. If they're in the middle of something, why bother to dial in the first place? The worst are the people who call and say, "Oh, you're there." Where the hell am I supposed to be, and if they think I'm not there, why bother calling? I had plenty of time to ponder telephone philosophy and etiquette before Joanne returned her attention to me.

"Hi! I've only got a sec. Two things. First, there's a preliminary meeting so my contact can introduce us to his boss before the big meet. I guess he wants to check us out and maybe brief us."

Shit. I'd temporarily and happily forgotten about Joanne's idiotic scheme. After last night's brush with the harsh reality of law enforcement, I wasn't quite as enthused as yesterday. It now sounded completely stupid, dangerous, and illegal.

Joanne is clairvoyant when it comes to my recalcitrance. "Uh-uh, you're not backing out on me now. The four of us meet, and then I'll listen to your objections. If you're not satisfied then, you can back out."

"Yeah, right."

"No, I really mean it. We're not going to do anything illegal. I promise. Nothing can go wrong."

That terrified me more than anything else. When someone reassures you about something you haven't mentioned, you know you're in deep trouble. Since Joanne had said we weren't going to do anything illegal, I was sure we were going to end up in Tanguay Prison for Women. With bad haircuts and surrounded by extremely large ladies who could hurt us. A lot.

"Isn't consorting with known criminals an offense?" I offered primly.

"Only if you're on parole. Try watching programs that haven't been canceled."

"No need for sarcasm. You're the one who wants the favor."

"And you're the one who wants information about Gregory Allard. Trade you. I'll pick you up at eight-thirty tomorrow."

"A.M.?"

"Yes, A.M., dolt. I'll be at the door on the dot. In a blue Corsica."

"When the hell did you get a Corsica?" The notion was absurd, since I was talking to Joanne of the "if it isn't a four-wheel-drive it doesn't exist unless it costs over forty-five thousand dollars" school.

"Never mind. Remember, we're undercover. I'll tell you more in the car."

"Okay," I sighed. "What was the other thing?'

"Oh yeah—they're making up the place cards and they want to know if you're coming with Stephen."

"Place cards and a date for a meeting with some gay slime-buckets?"

"Idiot," she giggled. "You're funny." She was in a much better mood than I. She saw a lark, I saw doom. "Saturday night is the Diabetes Foundation Ball. Remember? Fortunately you RSVP'd before you decided to become a vegetable. Remember? Try hard. Now, are you bringing Steve or someone else? What about your new friend Greg?"

I had completely forgotten this unwanted obligation. Diabetes runs rampant throughout Joanne's family. She's constantly having her blood sugar levels tested, having seen both her parents' gradual decline and eventual demise from the disease. It's the single greatest cause of her night terrors and may explain her promiscuity. A fervent supporter of the foundation, she does celebrity appearances, makes speeches, and generally runs herself ragged trying to raise funds in an environment where there are so many other trendier causes vying for the dollar. I'd said yes immediately, and although I now regretted it, I couldn't very well renege. I wouldn't anyway.

"We are not amused."

"Come on. Don't be mad. I promise I'll tell all tomorrow. It'll be worth the wait. You'll see. Now, you are bringing Steve, aren't you? I have to let the slaves writing the place cards know today."

"Yes, I am. Fortunately I asked him ages ago, but I'd better remind him. I haven't exactly been answering his phone calls."

"You haven't exactly been answering anyone else's either, and we're not upset, so I'm sure he'll forgive you. Oooh, did you pick up for Sam?"

"Nope. But I spoke to him last night. He's pretty pissed."

"Good. Let him sweat a little."

Joanne is one of the few people who know of Sam's existence, and although she surely isn't in a position to disapprove, she feels he's holding me back emotionally from letting myself get involved with anyone. Maybe it's true. While I was working, the last few years were so hectic, what with the buyout and contract negotiations, I don't think I had the energy necessary for a complicated relationship. And at my age they are complicated, usually involving ex-spouses and children. But I will never admit to her that she may be right. It would give her too much leverage.

"Yeah. It might be good to let him stew a little. Maybe I *have* become too accessible. I don't know."

"Excellent progress. Gotta go. Seven o'clock. Black tie. Chateau Champlain Hotel. See you."

Then I called Steve, who was fortunately not in his office, and left a message with his secretary to remind him. It served to postpone discussions about the last few weeks until Saturday.

Stephen Sonato and I have been friends forever. Ages ago we were lovers for a short time but it didn't add to the relationship. So we reverted to just being friends, although I don't regret the interlude since we're probably closer than ever. His women generally resent me, and our closeness has been known to be the cause of more than one dissolution of a budding romance, yet our friendship endures. We truly care about each other and make a hearty effort not to interfere with each other's life. Effort being the operative word, since both of us are experts at dispensing advice that we ourselves would never heed. It's not resented, since the receiver knows it comes from the heart and the advice is generally correct, but it's usually ignored. The good thing is that neither of us ever dares say "I told you so." He's quite wonderful, and no one can understand why we don't get married. Well, maybe in our dotage.

As for now, he's my professional date since he looks drop-dead gorgeous in a tuxedo. I rarely get to spend much time with him at these affairs; he loves to dance, and my friends with the reluctant husbands beset him shamelessly, whereupon he sweeps them off to Samba School and a life of hedonism in Rio. He's that good a dancer. This allows me plenty of time to catch up with people I seldom see elsewhere.

Before I could inspect my closet to snuffle out something suitable to wear, there was another call that needed to be made. Two secretaries later, I learned that Mr. Korlinski was not at his desk and was indeed not in. Would I care to leave a message? After I identified myself, the climate changed, and I easily made an appointment for eleven-thirty the next day. I could have made it anytime, and the slot would be cleared. Always make good friends with the secretaries of powerful men. They make excellent allies, and since they run their bosses' lives they can create and withdraw access at will. Again, I was glad he wasn't there. The questions I needed answered were best asked in person, even though I was loath to ever set foot in that building again. The things I do for Joanne.

After spreading an assortment of dresses on the bed and

every chair available, I decided on the short black and gold to wear to the ball. I hung it back on its hanger but neglected to do the same with the others, though I did pile them all neatly on the chair to await Mme Jacqueline.

I called Susan and got Robert at the other end. He told me she wasn't home yet and asked could I please, please come for supper. He sounded so forlorn my heart went out to him. There was no question of refusing, so I told him I'd be there at six-thirty. I also informed him that my favorite food is pizza and he should tell his mother to order some with everything on it. I was sure I could hear his face brighten. Kids have a magical relationship with pizza.

"Remember, Robert. Tell her I insist on pizza."

"Thanks, Auntie Barbara. She can't tell you no. Great. See ya later."

If only my own life could be fixed with a slice of pizza.

One more thing to do. Burrowing deeply into my linen closet, I unearthed my safe-deposit box. The lock turned easily, but it had been in disuse for so long the door creaked. As a bonus, inside I found two hundred and twenty-five American dollars that I couldn't remember ever owning. I greedily counted the cash and shoved the heroin into the box. In a reversal of form, I reburied the box with great diligence and a wide grin.

Pizza couldn't do it, but there was nothing like sex or money to make me smile.

8

AS I LATHERED up in the shower the next morning I mulled over dinner at Susan's the previous night. It effectively postponed fretting about the stupidity I was about to entertain.

When I arrived at Susan's door, I had been greeted by the lurking housekeeper. I was in the process of taking off my boots when the door popped open, and there she was. I nearly didn't recognize her in her period English drama nanny outfit. She wore a prim white blouse with just a hint of lace on the edge of the collar for that reckless froufrou look. Her dark gray serge pleated skirt was mid-calf length; unattractive even on good legs. Her piano legs were sheathed in dark tan support hose, and she wore black oxfords like the ones our mothers forced on us in grade school. All she needed was a cape to complete the ensemble. She grunted at me and disappeared down the hall, never to be seen again. I didn't know what I'd done, but she obviously didn't like me.

In the living room I found a subdued Robert. We went to his room for a private powwow and I spent some time alone with him, reinforcing the idea that neither he nor Susan had done anything wrong, stressing the fact that he was a very good boy and it was some very bad people we didn't know who killed Frank. When we found out who it was, I promised I would tell him all about it. However, I didn't promise not to edit the information. I reminded him how much Frank had loved him and how worried Susan was about him. He was all she had now, and she needed him to be brave. But it was all right to cry if he felt sad.

His eyes blinked repeatedly in an effort to hold back the tears. "Barry says I mustn't. He says I'm Mummy's little soldier, and soldiers don't cry. Ever."

I wanted to sweep this poor little boy into my arms and rock him far into the night. Instead I said, "Barry doesn't know much about boys and their fathers. His own father died when he was very young, much younger than even you, and he doesn't remember him at all. It's different for you. You're a big boy, and you loved your daddy very much, and he loved you even more. When I said you had to be brave, I meant in front of strangers. You can cry with me or your mummy if you want. I know you must be very sad."

He flung his arms around my neck and sobbed into my shoulder. I felt like crying myself, but I just blinked madly in imitation of his little soldier and held on tightly. At length, he calmed down and pulled away. Straightening himself, he looked at me with great seriousness and intoned, "Thank you, Auntie Barbara. I feel better now. I'm hungry. Let's go eat."

Taking me by the hand, he led me into the dining room and ceremoniously held my chair for me. I am constantly amazed at the resilience of children.

In an avuncular tone, Barry asked, "How's my little soldier tonight?"

Alarmed, Robert looked at me. I put my finger to my lips and smiled at him. The message was received; looking back at Barry, he answered, "Fine, Barry. Being very brave." The giggle at the end of the sentence ruined the effect slightly, but I was the only one who noticed since Susan was busily dividing up the pizza. Impressed by Robert's composure, I hoped Barry wouldn't pursue the conversation. But I needn't have worried. The discussion had moved onto the flavor of the vinegar in the salad dressing. I winked surreptitiously at Robert, and he giggled again.

He sobered and ate listlessly, paying no attention to any of the conversation. Susan let him go when he asked to be excused early with the promise that she'd come look in on him. I told her I thought he'd be fine and tried to get her not to worry. Changing subjects to get her mind off Robert, I asked what had transpired that afternoon at the funeral parlor. It was the right prompt.

"Frank's charming sister Lainie and her horrible husband, the Pestilent Phillip, were there when I arrived," she began.

"Phillip came too?" I asked in surprise.

"You know Lainie. She plays the helpless housewife role well. Helpless. Right. The woman is tough as diamonds. I'd say nails, but hers are acrylic and she likes diamonds better. She's a summa cum laude graduate of the Ivy League of JAP schools. When Phillip's around, she's a withering vine. They both took it upon themselves to grill me. She in her screechy voice tinged with sorrow, and he in a pompous 'I'm the man here' way. They were more demanding than Detective-Sergeant Boucherville. What were the perpetrators looking for? Did I think they found it? Was it valuable? And did Frank have a will? Where was it? How much money did he leave? To who? God, I wanted to sock them. They kept going on and on about what was hidden."

Panicky, I tried to signal her to shut up. I didn't like the direction this was moving in. If she mentioned the heroin, I was heading straight for the police station. We had a bargain.

Without concern, she continued. "Phil's in real estate and what with the recession he's paying a lot out on mortgages and not turning over much property. He's probably hurting for money at the moment. I hope his tenants are stiffing him on the rent," she added viciously. There was no love lost there. "They're just dying to get their hands on some money. Having Lainie as a wife is an expensive proposition."

That statement constituted the most extreme case of the pot calling the kettle black that I had ever encountered. Both their spending patterns were clichéd and legendary. But I was a brave soldier; for once I actually got away with a poker face.

"How did you answer?" asked Barry, returning to dangerous ground.

I prayed harder.

"I informed them there was more important business at hand. I implied that such questions were beneath me, but actually, I did speak to Frank's lawyer this morning."

I would have bet the bank that she'd call the lawyer within twenty-four hours, but she'd done it in less than twelve. Money is as much an obsession to Susan as to Lainie, but Susan has the good breeding to recognize it and camouflage with grace. The fact that she allowed this side of her to surface in front of Barry was another hint as to the nature of their relationship and how secure she felt with him.

"Frank does have a will. And it all goes to me and Robert. Nothing to Lainie. Or the current Bimbo. Now the only question remaining is if there is an "all." The lawyer says it's questionable even if they find some assets, there are so many liens outstanding against him it might affect the outcome. As long as his debts don't become mine, I don't give a shit. It would have been nice if there were something for Robert, but we *are* talking about Frank here, and we all know what we could expect from him. I did not, however, impart any of this information to my darling now ex-sister-in-law. Let them both stew. And hope."

We spent the rest of dinner making small talk, mostly listening to Barry describe the ultimate electronic video gizmo that he had sourced in the Orient and was bringing into Canada. I hoped he'd sell a lot of them. Susan needed the money.

As I was once again exchanging shoes for boots, my age or my recent exercise torture session betrayed me, and my bones creaked. "I can't wait for spring," I sighed. "All this bending is beginning to take its toll."

Susan laughed. "I know what you mean. Soon we'll be heading for Florida for the winter with all the other snowbirds. They claim the cold climate drives them south, but I think it's just the weight of heavy overcoats on increasingly frail bodies and the endless galoshes."

I kissed her on the cheek and whispered, "Don't forget our deal. Keep your mouth shut!"

With the disdainful look that she exhibited all too often lately, she said firmly, "Good night, Barbara," and closed the door in my face. Someday I was going to get her for all of this.

SHOVING THESE THOUGHTS aside, I got out of the shower and proceeded to dress and apply makeup in what could be deemed an alarming fashion. If I was going to do this, I would ensure my performance was memorable. Once I started to get into the whole charade it became fun. While applying the brightest, reddest, baddest lipstick I owned, I reflected on my reaction to the previous evening. I felt it had gone well, and I was almost secure that Susan wouldn't reveal our nasty little secret. She hadn't told Barry, as far as I could tell, so I decided I liked her again. Gazing at my engorged lips, I ruminated that Joanne's friendship, on the other hand, was open to question. Checking myself out, I approved of my reflection even if I did scare myself a little.

In the mirror I saw a well-dressed for day dominatrix. I had gelled and slicked my hair back into a tight chignon, which darkened it a few shades, and donned a black Claude Montana suit with exaggerated shoulders, zippers everywhere, and silver studs running down and around the sleeves. I added a black silk T-shirt to the short tight skirt, also banded with studs. Black stockings and black pumps with studded high heels completed the outfit. The ensemble screamed "Don't mess with me or I'll punch your lights out. Permanently." I bought it for a union negotiation session with a bunch of good old boys who had not to date ever taken a woman seriously. It had proven effective. Even now, whenever I run into one of those guys he looks askance and keeps his distance.

It seemed appropriate for this morning's mission. I filled a black, studded handbag with house keys, a twenty-dollar bill, and the tube of red lipstick. No identification at all. If I was found murdered, somebody would eventually figure out who I was, but as long as I was alive, anonymity seemed essential. I sported enough metal on my ensemble to send any airline scanner into paroxysms of overdrive. In the end I had to compromise, exchanging the killer spikes for some black over-the-knee patent leather boots with a platform sole, that I found in the back of my closet. Definitely a leftover from the seventies. A last glance showed that the boots enhanced the effect. The white skin I generally lament for its inability to tan looked appropriately ghoulish. Morticia and Elvira watch out.

It sure had an effect on the doorman. While I waited for Joanne he stared at me, concocting some semblance of conversation about the weather and never once blinking. I groaned inwardly. His relief would hear about this, as would the third shift. My reputation was increasing, or decreasing, by notches. I fiddled with the lipstick tube, my insecurity growing, and was at the point of beating a quick retreat when a blue car pulled up, honking. Not recognizing the driver, I continued fretting.

"I think that's for you, Ms. Simons. The driver is gesturing."

"Is that a Corsica?" I sort of knew it was, but if perchance it wasn't, I was going home, locking the door, and never ever coming out again.

"Yes, ma'am."

He's allowed to call me ma'am. He's paid to be servile.

I took a deep breath and went out the door he held for me. As befitted my attire, I strode assertively toward the car, hoping all the ice had been salted and I wouldn't ruin the effect by landing on my ass for the umpteenth time this winter.

Once belted in, I decided to get into the spirit of the adventure. I might as well make the best of it; there was no going back at this point. I extended my right hand and introduced myself. "Good morning. Justine Durrell."

Grasping my hand firmly, Joanne responded, "Pleased ta meetcha. Bobbi Berlin. Bobbi with an 'i.' "

Joanne-Bobbi was unrecognizable. Under the shearling-lined black leather bomber jacket was a faded denim work shirt open to the waist, revealing a faded black Gold's Gym T-shirt. Beat-up jeans and salt-stained work boots completed the construction worker attire. Her head was amazing. Under the backward John Deere–emblazoned baseball cap was a hennaed Buster Brown wig. Large owlish tortoiseshell glasses dominated her makeupless face. It was very simple but effective. I wouldn't know her if I ran into her on the street.

"Like it?" she asked, patting her Dynel hair.

"Like it? It's amazing! Incredible."

"Not bad yourself, Justine. Will we be joined by the rest of the quartet?" she giggled.

"Too obvious?"

"Nah. Don't worry. I somehow doubt this is a very literary group."

"Where did you get that wig? It's hideous, I love it." I was jealous. Why hadn't I thought of a wig?

"Monsieur Georges, my faithful hairdresser, lent it to me. I think he found it in the props department at the station. I also think he figures there'll be a credit for him if it gets on the air."

"Uh-uh. No way, Joanne. No cameras, hidden or otherwise.

This is just supposed to be a simple introductory meeting. I don't want my face plastered all over the six o'clock news, especially looking like Wanda the Whip. Stop the car. I'm getting out."

"Calm down. I promise, no cameras. But Monsieur Georges doesn't have to know that." She chuckled. I was terrified, and she was having fun. "I finally understand what they mean by 'Only her hairdresser knows for sure.' He's the only one who'd recognize me."

Oh great. Now we'd graduated to canceled commercials.

Driving cautiously, she began to tell me more about our adventure. It was best that I view it as such, or I'd have a panic attack. "First we're gonna pick up my source Joey. Never mind his last name. The less you know, the less you'll be tempted to tell Greg," she said with a smirk.

"Uh-huh. And what about Detective-Sergeant Allard? I thought this was supposed to be a tradeoff."

"It is. I'll tell you later. I promise. Right now I want to keep you focused."

Joanne sure made a lot of promises. "So why bring it up?"

"I don't know," she said. "This outfit makes me feel feisty."

Relaxing, I agreed. "I know what you mean. I feel I should be running the world, or at the very least a small country, in this getup. It screams domination."

We drove along Ste Catherine Street in silence, casually inspecting the shoppers scurrying in and out of the shops. Joanne was no doubt plotting her course of action, and I think she was alarmed at the implications of my garb and my attitude toward it, judging by the sidelong glances I received. The snow removal crews had done their job, and most of the roads were down to wet pavement. Constant tapping noises came from the underside of the car as it spit up salt, a sure sign that the temperature was about to drop dramatically. We passed trucks liberally sprinkling the streets, but I wasn't concerned, since it wasn't my beloved Mercedes rotting away under the onslaught, only Joanne's ugly Corsica.

Joey lived in the gentrified section of Little Burgundy, a rough neighborhood originally inhabited by factory workers who labored in the now-defunct mills and plants along the nearby Lachine Canal. Fists come readily to the inhabitants, and indeed, most of the city's prizefighters spring from this area. One particularly dilapidated section has been razed and reconstructed with medium-to-low-priced condos, leading to more altercations between newcomers seeking affordable downtown housing and the locals, who hate any change and all strangers. Families can trace their ancestors to the neighborhood for generations. Here French and English stand as one against all outsiders, and fists are the lingua franca.

Joey climbed into the backseat and introduced himself by first name only, having no doubt been coached by Joanne. He reminded me of Robert. He looked like a lost little boy bundled into an oversize coat and furry earmuffs. His frailty was not lost on me, and I speculated on how soon he would follow his friend to the inevitable. I wanted to hug him and caution him to get the hell out of there. However, given the climate, the attitude of the general public, and the paucity of support systems in the city for AIDS victims, I empathized with his desire for fast money and flight to a warmer, friendlier environment. I doubted if he could remain gainfully employed for much longer.

"My boss's name is Wayne. Jo—Bobbi said not to use last names. Sorry," he said as he patted Joanne affectionately on the shoulder. "That won't happen again. You'll see."

Joanne smiled at him. He didn't look much like a criminal. He seemed sweet and caring, but with my track record of bad taste in men I reserved judgment.

"We're going to the corner of Ste Catherine and Amherst," he instructed as Joanne pulled away. "There's a coffee shop near the corner. You can't miss it."

Oh lord. All the way out east. At least there was no chance of running into anyone I knew. My sort, spoiled Anglophones, rarely venture east of St. Lawrence Boulevard. I would, however, shine like a beacon, summoning every hooker for miles around, the neighborhood further enhancing my attire. Well, at least I'd look like an expensive one. I'm sure none of the local denizens could ever afford the ridiculous amount of money I had shelled out for this ludicrous suit.

Joanne's uncanny ability to always find parking resulted in our pulling into a spot right in front of the door, which compounded the feeling of unreality. In my experience it's only on TV and in the movies that the hero pulls up to wherever and always finds a space right up front. Never even has to parallel park, much less feed a meter. Joey dropped coins into the meter, and Joanne led our little troupe onward, Joey bringing up the rear. We marched in and froze.

My preconceptions were reasonably accurate. It was more a pool hall than a coffee shop, and at this hour of the morning it was populated mostly with working girls drinking coffee. I was staggered by what they looked like. I had imagined that such outrageous attire was relegated to the costume departments of Hollywood studios, but apparently not. They certainly advertised their wares. Skimpy was the rule of the day, even in this freezing weather. Naked midriffs jellyrolled over the tops of micro cutoff jeans, and halter tops advertised smaller breasts than I would have expected. The dominant hair color was fire engine red, which highlighted yellow complexions unfavorably in the combination morning and neon light. Not a pretty sight. I was eyed with envy and suspicion by one and all since I trumpeted "For Sale But Expensive." Montana would have been ecstatic, although I think they coveted my boots most. No one paid any attention to Joanne or Joey, which was probably better for her, but I'm not sure she was pleased to have me usurp the limelight.

We stood there for a moment until Joey took the initiative and led us to a back room, away from the scrutiny. There were three tables set up, but only one was occupied. A fey dishwater blond stood near the door, and a singularly unattractive man with acne craters sat alone, puffing on a cigar. A scruffy, graying T-shirt barely covered the beer belly that overflowed his grubby jeans. Every time he moved, his navel played peekaboo with the audience. As repulsive as the image was, it became mesmerizing. Throughout our meeting my eyes would drift to his midsection, magnetically drawn to the opportunity of viewing his innie. This was the leader of the Gay Hijacking Conspiracy? I couldn't see how anyone could find him attractive, man or woman.

I don't mind cigars. Sam smokes them incessantly, but this one was cheap and it reeked.

"Put that thing out," I ordered before we even introduced ourselves. "Or we're leaving. It stinks. Buy a better brand next time."

Joanne stared at me in horror.

Reluctantly I extended my right hand and introduced our little band. "Justine Durrell, and this is my associate Bobbi Berlin. You must be Wayne. Now what can we do for you?"

I immediately took the seat to Wayne's right as he scrambled to remove the ashtray with its offending cigar butt. Before Joanne had the opportunity to settle herself, I barked, "Bobbi, see if they have any Diet Coke. If not, some tea." I didn't offer her waitressing services to anyone else. As she had no choice but to do my bidding, she shrugged and went back into the outer room. There is the possibility that I was paying Joanne back for all the abuse recently heaped on me by Susan, but whatever the psychological implications, this was fun.

"We'll await her return. We have no secrets," I said conspiratorially. I was really getting into this.

Wayne stared at me openly. I was not quite what he expected. I was not quite what I expected either.

"How'd ya come to know Joey?" he asked suspiciously. I certainly didn't seem to be anyone Joey would ever meet.

"He's a friend of my brother." My brother would be horrified to know of this relationship, but family is there for difficult times.

Having rustled up a Diet Coke in a can and a reasonably clean glass, Joanne returned. She had got herself a cup of coffee, which Joey stared at enviously. He was too frightened of Wayne to even suggest excusing himself. She sat down, never taking her eyes off me, which further enhanced our charade. She was entirely believable in her role as doting consort; her anxiety translated into concern. Even Joey eyed me nervously. Wayne, however, seemed reasonably pleased. I had passed some unknown test, and he was fascinated.

Pushing my advantage, I opened the conversation before Joanne could jump in. "Okay, guys. Here we are. This meeting is one more than I had anticipated. Bobbi and I have now implicated ourselves in your scheme. All those people out there have seen us," I said, narrowly missing Wayne as I dramatically flung my arm toward the front room. When he flinched, power surged through me. "You know our names, they know our mien."

With both my hands palm down on the table, I stood. The boots brought my height to over six feet, and I loomed over everyone threateningly. Wayne fiddled with his dead cigar, Joey shrank, and Joanne cringed in horror.

I continued with dramatic flair. "I don't like it. Not at all. I was informed that our presence would be called for at one meeting. And here I am, dragged to this filthy hole," I said, examining my hands in disgust and displaying the multiple gold rings that now adorned my fingers. "There are now two encounters on the agenda. And who knows how often more you'll summon us."

The last implied that Wayne was actually running the show. It worked wonders. Wayne preened, so I took my cue and continued in this vein. "And you do not appear to be a person one may refuse," I said as I sat down.

Now seated, I continued in a more conciliatory tone. "We were informed that there would be a thousand-dollar honorarium for our services." I wasn't sure he understood the word, but he got the meaning.

"Yeah, that's what the rate is," Wayne said, obviously hoping it was his turn to talk.

It wasn't. I was having too much fun. I took out a cigarette and sat holding it expectantly. From the way she jerked, I know someone kicked Bobbi under the table, but it wasn't me. She fumbled in her pockets and came up with a box of wooden kitchen matches, expertly striking one on the zipper of her jeans, and leaned over to light my cigarette. I was impressed. The matches were a nice touch, and I didn't know she could do that. There must be a biker somewhere in Joanne's past.

As they sat entranced by this piece of business, I exhaled, blowing the smoke politely at the ceiling. Without acknowledging Bobbi's services, I returned my attention to Wayne.

"We want three thousand dollars. And for that I'll accord you an extra session."

Wayne blanched. "Three thousand bucks! You gals are fuckin' crazy!"

Glaring at him malevolently, I retorted. "We are not gals. We are women. I will thank you to address us as such. Your use of the vernacular is offensive. If you would prefer not to be addressed in pejorative terms I would recommend you accord us the same courtesy."

He hadn't a clue as to what I'd said, but my tone of voice spoke volumes, and once again he got the message. Joanne surely did. Ready to go for my throat at any second, she looked at me beseechingly. Power coursed.

As I looked down my nose at them I took another deep drag and continued condescendingly. "We personally have little use for men. Whether they be straight or gay. I have no sense of solidarity with the cause, so don't try to enlist our sympathies.

Fight your own battles and leave us out of it. I have a problem with the labels assigned us by men. I take great exception to nomenclature like 'gay and lesbian society.' Why are only the men gay? Are we lesbians morose? Once again sexist males, this time homosexual, are dividing our society and branding us second-class. Still not good enough to play with the boys."

I have no idea where these words came from. They tripped out of my mouth from someone else's brain. I had never, to my knowledge, given the matter any thought.

But it sure was effective. Wayne was apoplectic, Joanne terrified, and Joey looked like he wished he was dead. Clothes definitely do make the woman.

"It's three thousand dollars or nothing," I finished with a flourish.

I softened my position as I delicately stubbed out my cigarette. "Rest assured that I am proficient in the role of effective, efficient, nonthreatening, seductive businesswoman. You will not be disappointed with our performance. I can assure you that you will not be displeased."

Directing my gaze at Wayne, I smiled gently, tilted my head a fraction, and lowered my eyelashes. My whole demeanor and aspect changed instantly. As sleazy as he might be, Wayne was not dumb, and he was receptive to the transformation. Joey looked bewildered.

"Good shit," Wayne boomed, laughing. "That's great. Sold. You were right, Joey." He slapped Joey affectionately on the back, nearly knocking the frail man off his chair. The relief was visible on Joey's face. Belatedly realizing that his future had been on the line, I regretted the agony I had caused him. But I still had to finish what I had started. A few more minutes, and we would thankfully be out of here.

"As a sign of good faith I am only asking for five hundred now. I will expect the balance on termination of the next meeting. Needless to say, in cash." I intoned.

"Jeez, lady, you sure drive a hard bargain," he said grudgingly. "Here." He fished in his skintight jeans pocket and came up with a fistful of bills. I couldn't imagine how they all fit in there. He peeled off five greasy hundred-dollar bills and extended them to me. No way I was touching the stuff. Everything in the room felt infected.

"To Bobbi, please," I said with a dismissive wave of my jeweled fingers.

Joanne glared at me but took the money, stuffing it into her jacket pocket.

"The next meeting is set up for—"

I held up my hand to forestall further revelations. "Don't tell me any more. The less I know, the better. Joey can confer with Bobbi as to the arrangements. He knows where she may be reached. And sir," I said, according Wayne all respect, "there are to be no last names. I presume I may count on your presence at the next encounter?"

Where was I getting this phraseology? No one normal talks like this.

I had insulted the boss man. "Of course I'll be there. I'm in charge. I'm the fuckin' boss. Remember that." His attempt at menace was thwarted by the reemergence of his belly button. Mr. Macho struttin' his stuff. Really ugly stuff.

I rose, signaling an end to the encounter. I politely but reluctantly extended my hand to Wayne, and as he stood to shake it, said, "Thank you, gentlemen. I'm sure you will be satisfied with our services. Do not contact me directly. Interface with Bobbi."

The implication was that they knew who I was and could reach me if they wanted to. Wayne would never admit to ignorance of the fact, and Joey wouldn't be able to answer any questions, since he didn't know my real name either. But I'd cast Wayne in the role of all-knowing head honcho, a role he obviously relished, judging by his grin and the bobbing hemline of his T-shirt.

"Come, Bobbi." I snapped my fingers, no easy feat, as laden as they were with gold. I kept my eyes locked on Wayne's; we were talking boss to boss. Let the flunkies follow orders. Really it was to keep from staring at the offending navel, which had seemingly made a permanent appearance. Joanne was going to give me major shit, but Wayne was lapping up my performance. Still locked into his gaze, I delivered my parting salvo. "Don't cross me, sir." I was tempted to add "or else," but that would have been overkill.

Turning on my precarious heel, I spun around and left the room regally with Bobbi-Joanne scampering behind me. The hooker brigade in the restaurant had swelled, and all conversation stopped as we strode through the room. All I could think about was not tripping and ending up sprawled on the floor to the delight of all viewers, including Joanne. Under the onslaught of stares, I kept my back ramrod-straight and made it to the door intact, halting for maximum effect. I stood tapping my shiny, pointed toe until Joanne took her cue and rushed to hold the door for me. She must have been fuming; subservience does not come easily to her. But still, she ran ahead to the car and held the passenger door, and I settled myself in. I was secure in the knowledge she wouldn't murder me in front of so many people.

Once in the driver's seat, she gunned the motor and peeled away, spinning the wheels and burning rubber in true gangster movie style. Now that she finally had something to do, she was all action. She drove wildly as though we were bank robbers attempting our getaway. Biting her lower lip in concentration, she turned corners erratically, checking the rearview mirrors often. We caromed through streets and alleyways for about ten minutes before she relaxed, which allowed me to unclutch the dashboard and start breathing again. My concern was not only for ourselves but for the mass destruction her dangerous driving could cause on the icy streets. Also, the notion of being stopped by a traffic cop while wearing this costume did not thrill me.

"No one's following us. We got away clean," she said with all sincerity.

I burst out laughing. "Joanne, it was just a stupid meeting with a bunch of would-be criminals. Not a spy summit."

"Hmmmph. That's what you think. You realize Wayne is going to ask around about you to discover what he thinks you assume he knows."

I actually understood that.

"So what? What's he going to find out? Justine Durrell? Bobbi Berlin? A ratty Corsica, no less? Please."

"You're really seriously deranged, leaning on him like that," she said, not the least bit mollified.

Her attitude had put a crimp in my bravado. It was quite possible I had laid it on a bit too thick. Oh well, too late to do anything about that. It was her fault anyway, I told myself.

"These boots are killing me. God, I hated the seventies. The clothes were torture."

At last Joanne giggled. "What happened to you in there? Where the hell did you get 'interface'? What was all that shit about 'morose lesbians'? And when did this Barbara the Ball-buster thing first appear? Even I was intimidated, and I don't have any. Any one of those hookers would have rolled you for your clothes if they could. Did you notice they brought in the reserves to witness our departure? They were all dying for your boots. You're a walking wet dream in that getup. Try it on Greg and see how he reacts."

I moaned. I was too enervated to rise to the bait. "Get me home, please. And through the garage. If I meet any neighbors dressed like this at this hour of the day I'll have to move. The doorman is already alerted to the possibilities and wondering how to get a piece of the action for himself. Oh, following that train of thought, who gets the money?"

"You can have it. I can't take it. Professional ethics, etc. You negotiated it, you get it." She fished in her pocket and came up with the money. It looked a lot cleaner in the sunlight, so I took it. I had no ethics whatsoever when it came to this five hundred dollars. I should be paid that just for wearing these boots.

She left me off at the garage door and said she'd call me later. I let myself into the building and hobbled to the elevator. The closer I got to relief, the more my boots pinched. I made it to my apartment without meeting anyone, unlocked the door, and plunked down onto the floor to pull off the offenders. It was bliss.

Mme Jacqueline stared at me strangely as I limped to the closet, for once speechless—a bonus, since I had no time to explain. My meeting with Pietr Korlinski was next on the agenda, but first I had to get out of these clothes and clean myself up. She dutifully hung up my suit but seemed wary of the boots. They were put far, far in back.

I think she was sending me a fashion message.

AFTER SCRUBBING MY face for ten minutes, I was pleased to finally see a rosy glow replace the dead white. It made me feel healthier in all ways. The vigor I applied to the process was unwarranted, but the longer I distanced myself from the morning's charade, the creepier and more unsettling it became, which translated into my parody of Lady Macbeth. What I had taken on as a lark now assumed dark portents. The thought of bailing out became more attractive and necessary as the minutes passed. This thing was nuts!

If Joanne's plan of infiltrating and reporting didn't proceed to formula, we could be facing serious trouble on all fronts. The police wouldn't buy our innocent bystander posture if we got caught before our planned exit, and the hijackers would surely take us hostage to use as a bargaining chip, or worse, eliminate us completely should our cover be inadvertently blown. Montreal has a population of two and a half million, and the chance of being recognized is not altogether out of the question. I had more experience with infighting than overt subterfuge and therefore was probably not vigilant enough to keep proper guard against discovery. In other words, I have a big mouth and would likely say something I shouldn't to someone I really shouldn't say it to. Besides, I had a new life to lead; I couldn't hide out until this was all over.

I didn't know all the players in this scam, but I was sure they weren't the bunch of ineffectual queens I had conjured. Which upset me on another level; I've always had an image of myself as liberal and unprejudiced, and here I had fallen victim to my own clichéd preconceptions and stereotyping. All in all, I was a major idiot who should abandon this venture posthaste.

Needing to arm myself with more facts before I broached the subject of jumping ship to a potentially explosive Joanne, I prepared myself for a meeting with Pietr Korlinski.

As if in contrast to my previous attire and to counterbalance my darkening mood I selected kinder, gentler clothing. A peach wool crepe pleated skirt with matching cashmere sweater was topped with an olive-and-peach paisley jacket. With my newly washed hair softly framing my face, I looked sweet and feminine. Not generally a look I elect, but it seemed appropriate and bolstering now. Soft coral lipstick replaced the red gash.

Redressed, I couldn't find another good excuse to postpone my appointment any longer. I headed for the front door, making sure I directed a stream of mindless chatter toward Mme Jacqueline while I retrieved a coat and boots from the hall closet, in order to avoid being embroiled in another episode of the dreadful life of any one of her relatives. I only stopped talking when I heard the lock snap to behind me.

In my car, the ambivalence I had been feeling about my imminent visit resurfaced. I wanted and moreover needed to speak to Pietr Korlinski, but I dreaded setting foot in PanCanada's hallowed halls again. As I neared, bemoaning the fact that there was no major traffic tie-up, not even a minor fender bender to delay my arrival, the building loomed ominously before me. What I had always thought solid and respectable suddenly looked massive and eerie. The windows reflected the pale midday sun, making them impenetrable. Concrete and tinted glass and structural steel: badges of the seventies, and as ugly as my boots. After my musings over this morning's encounter, the building's resemblance to a jail did not escape me. Although in this mood all buildings would probably look like places of incarceration. What I really longed for were the mountains of Vermont or the beaches of Barbados, where no one knew me or wanted anything from me.

But whining never got me anywhere, and I was only toying with myself in my pretense of not wanting to go there. I could easily have met with Pietr after working hours. He would have understood how I felt and met me wherever and whenever I chose.

It was the inexorable pull of longing to be thought indispensable that drew me like an undertow. In the back of my mind and the front of my heart I had fantasies of people streaming out of their offices in great numbers, telling me what a horrible place PanCan was without me and imploring me to return. The fact that I had been fired and hadn't left voluntarily did not at all figure in my fantasy.

Wearing my best boots and dark ranch, politically incorrect mink coat to show everyone who likely cared not a whit that I was doing very well indeed, and there was life after Pancake, and a good life at that, I automatically turned in to the underground garage and pulled into my customary lane before I realized I no longer had a parking pass. Muttering profanely, I backed out, realigned the car, and drove into the visitor parking lane. My reverie already quashed, I came to the conclusion that this was not such a good idea. I was getting more upset by the second and very angry at myself for letting a simple building affect me so dramatically. As I was about to retrieve a ticket from the dispenser the gate lifted, allowing me free access. From the booth, Pierre-the-Attendant saluted and waved me in. I wasn't near enough to speak to him, so I waved back and made a mental note to tip him generously on the way out. Same bucks, but at least these would go directly into his pockets and not Waffle Iron's coffers. And no GST. I was slightly heartened to see that I hadn't already been forgotten and thankful to him for his kindness. Feeling this needy made me all the more uncomfortable.

My parking space had already been assigned to someone else. Someone from U.S. headquarters, judging by the Tennessee license plates. Malevolently, I hoped whoever it was—and I imagined a he—had a wife and family who spoke no French and would loathe living here. Mrs. Whoever would demand a divorce, take custody of their cherubic children, insist on enormous alimony, and depart, leaving him here to freeze his sundry parts off. Or she would jump feet first into the exciting Francophone culture, falling madly and passionately in love with her French tutor, who was immensely rich and just teaching to fill in the time. They would run off to his yacht in the south of France, leaving the cuckolded husband with custody of their five incipient juvenile delinquents. It made me feel much, much better.

This daydream carried me through the lobby and on up to the eighth floor. I was so involved with my fabrication that I barely noticed the indicator flash as we passed the third floor. Barely, but not quite. I had alit at three and headed for my bright corner office daily for the past twelve years, and I couldn't fight the twinges of nostalgia and longing that washed over me. One month out of work, and my life had proceeded from orderly and effective to highly disorganized and probably ridiculous. I willed these dangerous thoughts away and calmly exited at eight into an empty reception area.

This came as surprise, since the eighth floor is a bastion of security and always well guarded. The receptionist is the kind of battle-ax last seen on *Major Dad*, maintaining constant military control of what she considers her domain, dispensing passes only on receipt of some vital piece of identification.

It wasn't always like this. It used to be a relaxed, inconsequential department dedicated mostly to the inhibition of smuggling.

Everything changed in 1983, when PanCanada Air lost a plane to terrorism. Previously it had rested on the laurels of its safety record, never having had a major mishap. But after terrorists blew up a 747 midair, killing all 212 passengers and crew, a shudder ran through the organization. We had naively believed that these things only happened to American or Third World airlines and considered ourselves immune. The loss of life due to what we believed to be our negligence was traumatic. We regrouped, and the resultant changes were drastic and dramatic. In a period of less than six months, the department came to be recognized internationally as a leader in the field and premier authority, often serving as consultants to other airlines on how to improve their security systems, for which we charged astronomical rates.

This dramatic and speedy turnaround was the result of our president's prescient hiring of Pietr Korlinski as chief of security. Korlinski came to us from the Royal Canadian Mounted Police. After twenty-five years of service, retirement loomed. Although they had offered him unprecedented perks to convince him to stay, he was bored and ripe for the plucking. Pietr thrives on rising to any challenge; he loves to puzzle out and solve problems. Routine bores him, and his mind always leaps to the next contest. Our president recognized this need and offered him a most interesting proposition. He would be given the opportunity to revamp the entire operation, have an almost limitless budget, and be able to establish a department up to world-class standards. He would be given free and almost supreme rein, reporting only and directly to the president. It was too seductive an offer for a man of his personality to refuse, and he accepted with alacrity. Although the salary and benefits were generous, they were never the issue. It was the chance to create an operation to his own rigorous standards that intrigued him.

First he dipped into his pool of cronies from the Mounties. They were not standard yes men; all personally trained by Pietr, they were experts in their respective fields. Like him, they figured that what they didn't know they would learn. The RCMP would have been angrier had he not lent them his men from time to time and willingly shared information. Politically savvy, he knew enough to stay in the Mounties' good graces, realizing the equipment they possessed could be useful to him. It was a friendly arrangement that had strengthened over the years and was a contributory factor to PanCanada Air's current reputation in the security field.

All attempts to woo him away—and there had been many— were futile. He was fiercely loyal to his employer.

I hung up my coat, replaced my boots with shoes in the empty room before anyone had the opportunity to admire them, and grudgingly sat down to await the receptionist. I hate waiting for anything, and under normal circumstances I would have barged right in, but I was not stupid enough to proceed without my coded pass, ceded along with the garage card. Knowing Pietr, bells and whistles would resound deafeningly, unleashing I don't know what.

At precisely eleven-thirty a familiar face came through the forbidden door.

"Ms. Simons."

"Jennifer. How nice to see you again. How's the baby?"

"Wonderful!" she answered, beaming. "She's four months now and sleeps right through. I feel human again. And thanks so much for the gift. It was very thoughtful of you. I was really sorry I didn't have a chance to say good-bye. You were already gone when I got back from maternity leave."

Her eyes misted at the last, for which I was grateful. Again

I told myself that I had to stop feeling so needy before speaking to Pietr. Weakness was something he neither admired nor tolerated. I straightened my spine and hoped my posture would translate itself to my resolve.

"It's fine, Jennifer, and so am I. Thanks," I answered cheerfully, testing my backbone. "Where's the receptionist?"

"Where she spends most of her mornings lately. In the bathroom, puking her guts. She hasn't announced she's pregnant yet, but she can't fool me. She's got it bad," she said with a great grin. Not a lot of affection between these two.

I didn't have time to postulate about the origins of this animosity; I was stunned. I had always believed the esteemed receptionist to be postmenopausal, with her what I now understood to be prematurely gray hair, substantial girth, and matronly clothes. Mainly it was her sensible Moon shoes that put me off the scent. Nobody under the age of fifty-five wears those, or even knows what they are. I couldn't imagine her being pregnant, much less how she came to be that way.

Jennifer took the log book and handed me a special pen. Obviously some sort of newfangled device that could probably decode your life secrets from your handwriting. Pietr loved all new technology and was himself responsible for the development of a great deal of it.

"Here. Sign the book and I'll give you a badge. Never mind the vital document. Let her stew. Mr. Korlinski said to make sure you were brought straight to the office, so I can't have you sitting around while you wait for her to finish upchucking, can I? Also, he said if there's any trouble I'm to call him immediately."

"Trouble?"

"Maybe. They've denied access to anyone who was let go," she said, sneering. "They don't want them around. You didn't stop at the third?" I shook my head in answer. "Then don't. The atmosphere there is terrible. We're luckier up here. Nothing much has changed. Yet."

I felt immensely better. The place was truly going to pot, and I had a glimmer of insight that I was better off having left. If I could fan the glimmer, I could be tough as nails and ready for Pietr again.

I followed her through the swinging doors down familiar halls with no waves of regret. The glimmer exploded to flame, and I suddenly knew that I was well and truly finished with this place. My mourning had achieved completion.

In a better mood, I smiled amiably, nodding and chatting with the ex-coworkers I passed. I inquired about children, spouses, and significant others. It took about ten minutes to reach the end of the corridor, since Jennifer presented me to all and sundry as though I were a trophy. I guess it was her way of reassuring everyone that it was possible to successfully survive Pancake.

Pietr leaped to his feet the moment I entered his cavernous office, which resembled a war room, with charts and maps pinned to the walls and spread neatly over every available surface. He grabbed me in a big bear hug, squishing all the air out of me.

"Babs, you look great!" he thundered. "Here, sit!" he said, directing me to a big leather visitors' chair that has been the terror of many during his tenure. Pietr does not suffer inefficiency or stupidity with equanimity. The thought of the many who had sat quivering in this seat made me smile as I arranged myself comfortably.

"Babs," he repeated, totally unaware of how I felt about this. Pietr's the only person on the face of this earth whom I allow to call me Babs, a name I have detested since it was bestowed upon me by my second-grade teacher, whom I loathed with a seven-year-old passion that I can still summon every time I see an age-appropriate little girl. Joanne and I were the smartest kids in the class, but we were girls and she favored boys. It was my first taste of sexism, and the Babs nomenclature was rightly perceived as demeaning to my small self. But I knew Pietr didn't mean it in the same way, and aside from having a very real and deep affection for him, I'd be afraid to correct him.

He's a six-foot-three bear of a man with huge mitts for hands. Advancing age has beefed up his already hefty frame, but none of it is flab. Any football team would still sign him on the spot. His posture is always ramrod, and on seeing him you can't help but wonder why he's not wearing a uniform. Depending on his mode of dress, he's more often taken for a mob enforcer or armed forces general than the sophisticated technocrat that I know him to be. Acknowledged worldwide as a leader in his field, he's constantly on loan to other airlines or out inspecting his troops, and so I considered myself fortunate to find him in town.

Since his old RCMP connections have been rigorously maintained, he's a font of information about most illegal activity and therefore was in a position to help me. If he chose to. If I played my cards right. He's very protective of me, so if he sensed any doubt or if I evinced any hint of possible self-destruction he would clam up, denying me all information that could, in his view, harm me. Fortunately, the warm greetings in the corridor had bolstered my previously drooping ego, and I felt strong and capable of choosing my words carefully.

He flapped his bushy eyebrows and ran his huge hand through the Marine flattop as he held the chair for me. There was nothing sexist in this action. He's astute enough to never underestimate the intelligence of women; to him it's an act of common courtesy. A gentleman always treats a woman as a lady until she proves otherwise. And then the trouble would begin.

"You're lookin' great, Hon," he roared. "Gettin' away from this zoo seems to agree with you. Good for you."

I was thankful that his enormous desk was between us, or I would have had to suffer one of his famous pats on the back. If you weren't well rooted you could be sent sprawling.

"May I smoke?" I asked innocently. I love lighting up in this building. It makes me feel naughty since Waffle Iron is a well-enforced nonsmoking environment, which means that everyone has to head outdoors to feed their habit, no matter what the weather. In winter, clusters of people hang around the front door shivering and puffing, promising themselves daily that they'll quit rather than continue to suffer this freezing indignity. In the spring, as the snow melts, layer upon layer of soggy cigarette butts is revealed. It's odoriferous and disgusting, a particular embarrassment for visiting dignitaries, but we smokers have always taken perverse pleasure in the eyesore.

Pietr had heeded the advice of his doctor, who must be a twelve-foot-tall Sumo wrestler, and cut back to six carefully meted out cigarettes a day. Best of all, no one has the nerve to order him not to smoke in the building. In the dead of winter, when it was too cold to go outside, I'd come up here for a conspiratorial fix and chat, from which we'd developed a warm friendship.

"Of course, Hon. Here," he said passing me the oversize ashtray. "Aim the smoke toward the vents, please. Give 'em a hint of what's goin' on here."

Subversive talk from one so loyal.

I lit up and asked after his family. A widower who had lost his wife to breast cancer many years ago, he never remarried and had raised his children singlehanded. I'd often speculated about his sex life, but I sure didn't dare ask, and there was never a whisper of scandal or even gossip. His parenting skills were obviously exceptional, since all his children were now married, upstanding citizens with well-behaved children of their own. Moreover, his extended clan had a deep, abiding affection for him and insisted on including him in everything. A *Bachelor Father* success story if I ever saw one.

"Okay. Small talk over. What can I do you for?"

I hate that phrase, but there was no way I was going to tell him that. Size brings entitlement.

"Well, it may be out of your field of expertise, but I may have gotten information about something dumb and dangerous."

"Information my foot, Missy. If you're here, you're involved, and it's serious. Do you need protection? Boyfriend harassin' you?"

I put up my hand to stop him. I hadn't chosen my words as carefully as I had planned. Time to regroup.

"No. Nothing like that." I had forgotten just how protective of me he was. He'd always maintained I was too pretty for such a tough job and it was one that only necessitated the use of my brain. Wait until he found out about this.

It is, however, interesting that I have never taken offense at his assessment of me. I've seen pictures of his late wife and consider him a connoisseur of pulchritude. I like that he thinks I'm pretty. I guess vanity sometimes supersedes my sense of sisterhood.

"I'll get right to the point. You won't let me hide anything anyway. Do you know anything about cigarette hijacking?"

I lit another cigarette to avoid looking at him, trying to avoid a lecture about keeping my nose out of things that don't concern me. But the ruse didn't work. He was much better at this than I.

He waited patiently while I finished fiddling with the match and when I could stall no longer I looked up to find him sitting straight up with his index sausages steepled under his chin.

"Yes, yes, I do. Aside from all that has been in the papers recently, I went to an RCMP seminar about it just last week. Keeps my hand in. And I go to them when I'm feeling depressed."

"You depressed?" Even though I was shocked, one small part of my brain had registered the fact that I hadn't said "What?" I was making progress. But returning to the matter at hand, I was surprised to hear that Pietr even knew the meaning of the word *depression*.

"All the crap, excuse me, the garbage that's been goin' on around here's got me down. But it doesn't concern you anymore. I'm really pleased for you," he said sincerely.

I was again surprised. The morale at Pancake must be pretty low for it to have reached Pietr; he tends to be oblivious to office politics. I was about to pursue the subject, but I noticed his embarrassment at having revealed this much, so, with a sensitivity I don't often evince, I changed the subject.

"Well, I'm happy, I think. It took a while but I finally accepted it, and I guess it's for the best. It's time to move on."

"Sounds like you're tryin' to talk yourself into that, Babs. But you're right. Although I'm not sure how I'm goin' to handle it when my time comes," he said, eyebrows lowered.

"Your job is endangered?" I was floored. Pietr Korlinski is one of PanCanada Airlines' chief assets and likely a bargaining chip in the negotiations that preceded the takeover. Any airline in the world would happily hire him away, letting him write his own ticket. I know. It's been tried. The idea that he could be fired was inconceivable.

"They brought up my opposite number from Memphis to 'share information.' Bull rot! They really want me to teach him everythin' I know and introduce him to my contacts on the outside. They want all my secrets. Then they'll dump me. I'm no fool. I can see the writin' in their agenda. The good thing is that this guy's a horse's patoot and couldn't understand anythin' technical if I explained it to him ten times. Which I won't even once. I don't know who's runnin' their security department from behind the scenes, but it sure as hell ain't this turkey. If I saw a future for myself here I'd get me on a plane to Memphis, make some discreet inquiries, and pirate the mastermind guy away. Their department is good, and this guy sure ain't it."

"You can't be right. They couldn't get rid of you. You're the best in the world."

A large smile creased his face, immediately relaxing it and

sending his eyebrows skyward. It's a wonderful smile, generally reserved for his children and theirs.

"They want me to move to Memphis. I won't. Plain and clear. So anyway, I got depressed, what with all this political garbage and the idiot bureaucrats involved, when my buddy invited me to an info session on cigarette hijackin' and I went. It's the hottest thing these days. You goin' into a new line of work? Don't."

The eyebrows came back down menacingly.

"No. Nothing like that. It's just research," I said as innocently as possible with my best poker face. It had the usual effect.

"Which means you won't tell me," he answered, moving his eyebrows to midlevel. His serious look. "Just remember, I'm here if you need me. Anytime. I'm serious, Babs. You can count on me."

"I know. And I'm truly grateful." I was beginning to mist up. I tossed my hair to clear my head and returned to the subject at hand.

"Well then, tell me what you can." Pietr understood my phraseology, since he never told everything. He plays his cards close to the chest and only reveals enough to satisfy his questioner that he's been fully briefed. Generally some vital detail is omitted. Pietr maintains a firm upper hand in all his dealings, and I knew his tactics well enough not to push for more. An adversarial relationship is not recommended when dealing with Pietr. The man from Memphis was in for a difficult time.

"It's a dangerous business, Babs. Growin' at top speed. The final straw was the goods and services tax, which raised prices to the breakin' point."

He then proceeded to regale me with enough facts and figures to send an actuary into orgasmic paroxysms. I listened carefully, understanding most of it but not particularly interested. Finances are only fascinating when they're mine.

"People are just fed up," he continued, "and in a way it's a form of individual tax revolt that the players are taking advantage of. But the public's still smokin', so they're buyin' their butts illegally. The most honest and well-placed citizens have their sources and buy contraband regularly.

"If you asked these citizens if they were breakin' the law, they'd laugh and deny it. They'd probably sail through a lie detector test, so sure are they that they did nothin' wrong. Cheatin' the government is always considered fair game, and nobody realizes how many people get hurt in the deal."

He was right. The newspapers said that one in three packages of cigarettes was bought illegally, and if the government released that figure it was probably a lot higher. I myself often bought a carton of cigarettes from Pierre-the-Attendant at a very good price and without qualms. No wonder he'd waved me in so generously. Probably thought I was coming back for more. And now that I thought about it, maybe I was.

Pietr was all business now, expecting and receiving my rapt attention.

"There's lotsa money to be made at not too great risk, so everyone's gettin' involved. There are too many housewives goin' over the border, buyin' cigarettes, and resellin' them to their friends at a profit to bust 'em all. They're a small cog in the general problem of cross-border shoppin'. Anyway, they're penny ante as individuals but even they add up to big bucks, and they're the smallest players in a huge system. They're simply indicative of the general dissatisfaction with the hierarchy. And as we all know, when there's a buck to be made the big guys move in."

"Organized crime is involved in cigarettes?" I was surprised. The motley crew I had met with this morning certainly hadn't seemed connected. To anything.

"Sure, Babs. The same guys who run the drugs run the contraband. At first it was in the hands of independents, but it's just too lucrative and they got hustled out. The distribution network from top to bottom is similar in drugs and cigarettes. And the end pusher is less likely to get arrested, and if he should, at most it'll be a slap on the wrist and a fine. So it's easy to recruit people. Everyone wants to make some money these days, and most people have no compunction about what they perceive as cheatin' the government that they feel is responsible for the recession and their predicaments. The justification is that they're just hurtin' the system that hurt them in the first place. Naive thinkin', but perfect targets for the guys at the top, the big guys who're rakin' it in. And very tight with their control throughout the distribution system."

I sat there filling the air with blue smoke as my anxiety grew. Pietr was now pacing, choosing his words, carefully deciding what he should allow himself to tell me. The care he took with his words inspired more fear in me than the actual things he said. The omissions were ominous.

"I don't like that you're askin' me about this." He frowned and peered directly at me, having surely used some invention of his to read my mind. More likely it was my poker face at work again.

"Hell, the way it's set up it's easy. Forget stealin' the stuff. Just buy the merchandise bulk in the States, where it's legally sold by the manufacturer to a distributor without any taxes since it's exported, and then smuggle it back into Canada. Remember, 'Five thousand miles of undefended border' is one of our mottoes. Who can patrol all that? And the Indian reservations are used a lot. They fall under separate jurisdiction and often straddle the border. In in the United States, and out in Canada, with no real border crossin' between. The Indians, or Native People as they're called today, take such pleasure in screwin' the government, which they consider the oppressor, they don't ask too many questions. Basically the dons use 'em as disposable pawns. The Indians feel they're needed and in control, but once again they're manipulated and badly exploited.

"Or it's even more brazen, and they bring it up across the border in flatbed trucks, usually loaded with logs or lumber. The crossings are busy, and what with all the cutbacks, understaffed. So no one checks too carefully. Load's visible. Nothin' to hide. Except the inside is hollowed out and stuffed with cigarettes returnin' home."

The pacing continued as he warmed to his topic, eyebrows frantically flapping.

"It works pretty much like this: One receiver buys the whole load, breaks it up to distributors who deal it out everywhere. Vending machines, convenience stores sufferin' the effects of the recession, gas stations, factory workers who're tryin' to put somethin' away in case they get laid off, housewives whose husbands are already laid off. Dealers aren't too hard to find. It's perceived to be a victimless crime, but in truth it's vicious and often bloody. Like the drug trade, once in it's hard to get out and stay healthy."

Now he planted himself in front of me, his large shadow blocking out the sunlight that filtered through the tinted windows. I didn't know whether the drop in temperature came from the sudden shade or the menace emanating from him.

"Which leads me back to my primary concern. Why the hell do you want to know this, Babs? What kind of idiotic adventure are you contemplatin'? If you're short, I can lend you a few bucks to tide you over. Don't get involved. It's not worth it," he said, his voice stern.

My future health depended on my response.

"No, no, Pietr," I reassured him. "I promise not to go into it." And I meant it. I was going to bail out of this whole charade as fast as I possibly could. The first call I was going to make when I got out of here was to Joanne. If she wasn't there, I was going to defect to whoever answered the phone. Her whole plan was nuts. I didn't even want to hear any more.

So I don't know why I asked, "But what about the stuff that

doesn't come back over the border? The trucks that get hijacked directly from the factory?"

"Look, missy," he glowered, his eyebrows lowering ominously. "I don't like this line of questionin'. Where exactly are you leadin'?"

"Nowhere. Like I said, it's research. I just want to know. I won't do anything dumb, and I don't need the money. Waffle Iron was very generous in its dumping."

"Really?" With his interest piqued, his eyebrows returned safely to midlevel. "Maybe you can give me a few tips on that subject. Might come in useful."

"Come on, Pietr. You're a fixture around here. They're certainly not going to do anything to you."

"You never know, you never know," he mused as he sat back down behind his desk, and I breathed easier. His looming presence had been intimidating. He surely never had to worry about being thought bossy. One look at him in his threatening mode would make anyone jump to without asking questions. One's sense of self-preservation was always very much to the fore when dealing with Pietr Korlinski. I almost felt sorry for the man from Memphis. Almost.

His fingers steepled as he considered his alternatives. I took his concern seriously.

"Look, you can get a job anywhere if worse comes to worst. You're internationally respected. Anyone would hire you. You're famous," I blustered. I hated to see this confident man so suddenly insecure.

And to my great surprise, this time my tactic of deflection worked. He was no longer lecturing me about my safety. My stature restored, he considered my bargaining capabilities. My forte was negotiation, and if he moved his cards a little bit farther from his chest I might be able to help him should he eventually leave PanCanada Air. To each his own expertise, or blackmail.

"Okay," he said resolutely, as though we had struck a deal.

"I'll tell you about the independents. I won't harp on the subject, but believe me, Babs, you should be careful. These wiseguys are the most dangerous, the most unhinged."

That opinion I could second, if Wayne was exemplary.

"They're hot-rodders," he continued, his great sausages flexing up and down, his eyebrows immobile. "They're in it for a quick buck with no concept of the consequences. They antagonize the police, but mostly, the Organization doesn't like people who invade their territory, and in an unprofessional fashion to boot. And when these gentlemen frown, someone gets hurt. You're too pretty to tangle with them. I presume you'd like to stay pretty?"

I nodded assent, realizing that further protestations were useless. In a way it was touching that he was so concerned for my welfare, and the decision to furnish information was all his. I couldn't push him.

He decided to tell.

"The independents are usually loosely organized. Or disorganized, I should say. More often than not, a gang set up for a one-shot deal. All they see is big bucks and a quick hit. There are different ways, but generally they'll bribe a dispatcher and/or a driver to let them know when the load is leaving. About ten minutes after departure they'll hijack the truck and knock out or drug the driver. If he's implicated, they'll do it anyway to allay suspicion. They then have two hours to unload the cargo. Any more than that, and the truck will be reported missin'. The best way to do this is drive it straight into a warehouse and unload quickly. Then drive the truck back out and abandon it anywhere, leavin' the driver bound and drugged inside. It'll be found fast enough.

"Next comes the part these jerks often don't know. They're excited about their success, and the first part is usually easily completed, so they dig right into their booty. What they should do is get out of there and watch the buildin' for a couple of days to see who's nosin' around. The driver or dispatcher may have gone over and cut a deal, and the police could be waitin' for 'em to come claim their goods. About a week will generally do.

"Then comes the part that takes even more patience, which goofballs rarely have. Every single case has to be carefully gone over with a detection probe. The equipment isn't hard to get. Those mail-order houses for would-be spies sell it. All those macho magazines have plenty of ads for these companies. It has to be done slowly and carefully and can take up to two weeks to clear a load."

I must have looked perplexed, because he slowed down and smiled at me expansively. He was now the teacher explaining things to a not-too-bright student. I didn't care. This was fascinating. If he left Waffle Iron, maybe we could team up, like in *Scarecrow and Mrs. King.*

"At least two of those cases are bugged," he said as he stared significantly at me, revealing his trump card. "As soon as the seal is broken, a locater signal is sent back to the factory, and by now the police. It's inserted randomly at the time of packin', and from the outside it's invisible. The hot-rodders aren't usually well enough plugged into the operations system to even know these bugs exist, and this is the point where they most often screw up. You hear of the police making arrests, but what you don't hear is that the tobacco companies have very tight security and sophisticated toys to protect their merchandise.

"Another effect is that independent hijackers royally piss off the organized boys. They feel that these upstarts give their business a bad name, if you can believe it, and they don't like anyone movin' into their sphere. They protect territory zealously, and if the police don't make an arrest you've got to be nervously lookin' over your shoulder for the mob. They don't concern themselves with civil rights."

Storm clouds reemerged across his brow. I thought it would be prudent to say what he wanted to hear.

"Sounds much too dangerous for me. I promise to use this information judiciously. I won't compromise you, don't worry," I said, though he never even considered that I would or, for that matter, could.

But this man was not from Memphis. "Babs. One more time. Stay away from this. Even information casually dropped can be dangerous. I don't want anythin' happenin' to you. You're one of the good people. Just remember one thing; if you need me I'll be there. Anytime."

And the eyebrows rested.

"Thanks, Pietr, I really appreciate this. And I'll be careful. I still have some good years left, and I have no intention of jeopardizing them." I'm not sure whom I was trying to convince.

"Can't interest you in lunch in the executive dinin' room, can I? It's just after one, all the big shots will be there, and they'll choke on their food when they see you. Might be fun."

"No, thanks. I can live without the indigestion. And, as I remember, the food ain't great. Free, but not great. I'll pass. But can we have dinner next week? My treat."

"Sure, missy. But it'll be on me. I still have my expense account. Let Pancake give us a final blowout."

Pietr seemed to be resigned to his fate; I was less sure. It would damage the airline's credibility to fire him. I couldn't see them justifying it to the press. It would have been my job if I were still there, and I couldn't have done it. Some new American with no favors to call in would get eaten alive. If Pietr weren't the potential sacrifice, I would relish the confrontation. I had to work on this spiteful trait that had recently emerged.

"You're on. I'll call you, and we'll set it up. My love to all the kids."

He pushed a button somewhere, and Jennifer arrived to escort me out. I hugged Pietr with sincere affection and, after regaining my breath, allowed Jennifer to lead me docilely down the corridor back to the reception area.

"Ms. Simons, how did you find him? I'm worried about him. He's so depressed."

"He'll be okay," I tried to reassure her. "I think the changes around here have affected everyone. When the dust settles, he'll be his old gruff self. Remember, he's a star. He'll come shining through."

I didn't believe a word of it, but it seemed to make her happier.

10

ON FRIDAY MORNING I was snugly ensconced in the wing chair by the window, relishing the silence and basking in the warming sunlight that streamed in through the tinted, UV-treated windows. My condo fees paid for some luxuries that I used. I looked out at the crisp whiteness that was everywhere, happy to be indoors, since the temperature had dropped dramatically as predicted. The radio announced a high of minus twenty-two, eight below zero in the olden days before we went metric and could no longer figure out if we were supposed to be hot or cold nor how fast we were really going. Many an argument with a citation-wielding traffic cop has been lost over this. Sue Grafton's new book lay in my lap, to be cracked open as soon as I solved the vagaries of the metric system and decided if I was pro or con. In my blissful state of lethargy it was a weighty problem.

My whole house gleamed. Even the silver had been polished and sparkled in the sunlight. As a result of Mme Jacqueline's quick and diligent work, I now had a morning's peace, blessed quiet, and pristine order to revel in.

And then someone knocked at my door. I should have known that I had not been a good enough little girl to have earned a brief oasis of calm.

AFTER LEAVING PIETR'S office the day before, I had descended to the garage and stopped at Pierre-the-Attendant's booth to thank him for his consideration and with the idea of tipping him for having given me the Dutch courage to proceed into the building. Before I could say anything he welcomed me back and asked if I needed any cigarettes. The notion that he too was feeling the recession flitted through my mind. The layoffs at PanCanada must have seriously affected his sideline; the shrinking personnel resulting in diminished sales. The influence of non-nationals probably put a further crimp in his income. White-collar Americans smoke a great deal less than French-Canadians, who treasure their Gallic sense of adventure and doom. I dismissed the idea that he had only been nice to me because he smelled a potential sale. Garage marketing.

The discussion in Pietr's office should have dissuaded me, but avarice is a very strong emotion. I told myself I would consider the transaction as a psychological exercise. And Pietr was right. I felt absolutely no qualms about cheating the government. Moreover, it was my civic duty, and thus I felt only very slightly guilty as I forked over twenty-three dollars each for two cartons of king-size Matinee instead of the forty-six and something each that they cost at the local discount store. And not a blessed cent went to the government. Well, I hadn't voted for them anyway. I actually hadn't voted at all, but if I had it would have been for the other team. Who probably lost because too many people behaved in a similar fashion, and so I deserved the government I got, but I still hated giving them money I righteously felt they didn't deserve. This convoluted reasoning process helps me rationalize behavior I know to be unacceptable. And it saves money.

Plus, I was so caught up in conflicting reasoning that I neglected to tip him, saving me another three bucks. I love a good bargain.

Buoyed, I didn't feel like going home. Who knew what awaited on the answering machine? And Mme Jacqueline was likely still there. Mostly I was hungry. It had been an eventful morning with no sustenance and lots of costume changes.

Lunch alone in a restaurant seemed too risky, since it would only lead to serious reflection. I didn't want to think of the ramifications of Pietr's information nor about Wayne's bobbling belly button nor about dear departed Frank and absolutely not about the booty stashed in my house. I decided to deliver myself over to mindless drivel.

Since I've steadfastedly refused to get a phone in my car I stopped at a corner pay phone to call the beauty salon. After ascertaining that Jean-Jacques could take me immediately, I ordered a sandwich from the lady who runs the costly concession and headed to another parking lot, where this time I would have to pay. I did balk and refuse the suggested manicure that, on examining my fingertips, I realized I badly needed. Well, we all have to make adjustments and economies in these recessional times, and doing my own nails seemed an appropriate penance. I hoped I would get around to it before the ball on Saturday.

I feel it important to emphasize that I am not a slave to my hairdresser. I only go when I need a haircut, which is about every three or four months, so I don't consider it an indulgence. Although I must, since I always seem to be justifying my visits to myself.

A good haircut really is one of life's necessities. It is even encouraged in executive circles and can be the clincher in job interviews and political campaigns. John Kennedy had a great one. Richard Nixon didn't. I've yet to figure out when women's hairdressers came to be considered such a symbol of feminine overspending. Probably when they changed their nomenclature to coiffeurs or stylists and started charging astronomical prices, which we continue to fork over without complaint in sheeplike fashion and great fear.

Jean-Jacques has been my hairdresser forever, since I'm too terrified to go to someone else. I've always considered that having your hair cut by a new hairdresser is a lot like having sex with a new partner. You know exactly what you want, but for fear of offending the so-called expert you're afraid to spell it out. So you drop hints. First gentle hints. Then broader hints. After that you close your eyes and pray for results. A good hairdresser is like a good lover; responsive to subtle clues.

Jean-Jacques is the best. I trust him implicitly, which is more than I can say for most of the lovers I've had, and although I'm not a frequent customer I'm a loyal one, so he likes me.

The next two hours flew by in a flurry of eating, having my hair washed and conditioned and trimmed, and gossiping with Jean-Jacques. Susan is one of his more frequent customers, since her expertly done natural-looking streaks need constant attention. So he had lots of questions, which I answered judiciously. The grapevine sure works fast when it comes to murder. I guess infidelity and disease are old hat. Nothing like a good murder to quicken the pulse of gossip.

His turquoise contact lenses nearly popped out when I told him Susan and I had discovered the body together. It was too complicated to tell the story in proper sequence, and I was targeting effect, not accuracy. Every time I see him he has a new eye color. He is to contact lenses what Elton John is to glasses. Personally I think it's some sort of competition with his assistant, whose hair color changes apace. He'll lose in the end, since she can have her color redone as often as she likes for no charge—one of the perks of the otherwise slavelike job— whereas he has to fork over big bucks for all those lenses. I never have the temerity to discuss the economics of this relationship with him. It's more fun to gossip.

When I finally got home, feeling wickedly pampered, the message button was flashing. It was someone called Celine saying she'd like to meet with me. The accent and sentence structure bespoke a Francophone who spoke English rather well. In Quebec, sizing up people along linguistic lines and fluency is vital in deciding how to approach and deal with them. In my corporate life it had been an absolute necessity, and I still did it out of habit. It took two beats to realize that Celine was indeed Bimbo, so well had Susan trained me. She didn't leave a number, just said she'd call back later. First I wondered what she wanted, and then I worried about how she knew who I was and where she had got my phone number. It made me uneasy.

A long, hot bubble bath restored my calm. I was careful to keep my hair dry, as I'd just spent all that money and it would be truly wasteful to undo Jean-Jacques' labors so soon. My mother hadn't raised a spendthrift.

Safely in bed, I had decided it was time to think about the direction my life was taking when I remembered it was time for *Law and Order* on television. It seemed an apt choice. Then I fell asleep, once again forgetting to call Sam.

I WOKE UP full of energy, and in an unusual fit of domesticity I diligently chopped vegetables and seared ground meat—a combination of lean and medium beef and veal, although I would lie to the person I served it to and promise it was all lean—in preparation for a giant pot of chili. I make enough for about twenty people and then freeze it in single and double portions. It keeps me fed for a few months and helps when unexpected people drop in at mealtimes. It's my version of the nesting syndrome, and I felt like Donna Reed as I puttered about the kitchen, except I was wearing sneakers instead of heels. I even sort of cleaned up, putting everything in the dishwasher and wiping off the counter. The spots on the floor, I chose to ignore.

As the chili burbled on the stove I retired to the wing chair to read and contemplate the metric system. It had thus far been a wonderful day. I should have known it was too good to last.

At the sound of knocking I stared malevolently at the door resolving positively to move and leave no forwarding address. No one in this building was getting tipped next Christmas, that was for sure. All and sundry seemed to have liberal access to my front door.

Yesterday's dress-up charade probably abetted the situation, since maybe the doorman perceived my uninvited guest as a john and thought it tactful not to ask his name nor announce his presence. He probably figured he was being discreet and would pocket something from me in return. Well, I'm on the condo board, and the security in this building would be at the top of the agenda at the next meeting. Unless of course there was a petition demanding my expulsion before the meeting.

With a sigh of resignation and frustration I went to the door and looked through the peephole. Not a john. A Greg. Detective-Sergeant Gregory Allard. So much had happened since our last encounter that I had almost forgotten about him as a person. He'd floated back into the vague pool I labeled as Police. I instantly flashed on the fact that Joanne hadn't furnished her promised information. Nor was she returning my phone calls.

My mood deteriorated rapidly as I continued to peer through the peephole. Better to take inventory before opening the door. Even through the distortion I could tell he was attractive. I wasn't. I was wearing a duster that would have done my mother proud, and I had no makeup on, not even mascara. I'd definitely have to change my solitary habits now that I no longer had the insulation of doormen. At least my hair looked good, the offending ragged edges expertly scissored away. If I hadn't espied my sunglasses carelessly left on the entry table, I might not have answered. One of the advantages of untidiness is that, although things are rarely in their proper places, they're usually in convenient ones.

After quickly donning them, I opened the door and said, "How did you get in?"

"Good afternoon, Miss Simons. I've come to return your shoes," he said politely, ignoring my rudeness.

Chastened, I invited him in, took his coat, which I actually hung up, and politely led him to the living room. I then excused myself and made a dash for my bedroom to apply some badly needed mascara and exchange my pathetic duster for jeans and a T-shirt. Not the most glamorous of looks, but nineties instead of fifties. The aim was to shed June Cleaver and reach for Cindy Crawford.

It also gave him the opportunity to do what I think is instinctual to cops: inspect the premises. I'm sure he'd taken complete inventory of my living room when I emerged, scarcely five minutes later. I'm a fast dresser.

"Smells good," he said, sniffing the air.

"Chili. Lots of it," I replied with no further explanation. Let him think I was having tons of people over to partake. He didn't have to know I was planning to eat it all by myself over the next three months. It would sound too pathetic.

I offered him the drink I knew he would refuse, reminding myself that I should stock up on mixers for my phantom or real guests in case someone should ever take me up on my offer. I rarely drink, hence I have a fully stocked bar, culled from various duty free shops over the years. The only things that seem to move are the scotch and the cognac, and those slowly.

After seating himself on the couch he tried to figure out what to do about the throw pillow he had neglected to move, which was mashed uncomfortably beneath him. While enjoying his discomfort, I noticed he was still cute. I again vowed that as long as I lived here I would never face the day without at least mascara.

Annoyed at being caught off guard, I took the offensive and demanded, "How did you get in?"

"Just flash a badge and you can go almost anywhere," he said with a lazy smile. In a spate of tit for tat he was enjoying my obvious discomfiture.

Great. I mentally calculated personnel and their shifts, and reluctantly came to the conclusion that he'd shown his badge to the very same doorman who had salaciously savored my Wanda the Whip attire. The whole building was probably on red alert, glued to their windows in the expectation of my being led off in handcuffs and disgrace for nefarious activities. If I didn't move of my own volition, the condo association would now surely petition for my departure. I tried to remember if there was a morals clause in our agreement.

"I thought I'd surprise you," he crinkled.

"Well, you did." I didn't twinkle back. "I'd have appreciated a subtler approach. The doorman network in this building is better than Ma Bell's. The whole street knows you're here by now," I grumbled.

Since he had no inkling of Wanda's existence, he must have thought that I was overreacting, and I had no intention of elucidating. It was my house and my life he was screwing up, and I was pissed off.

Uncomfortable, he decorously held up a brocade shoe bag and said, "Here are your shoes."

He looked so silly brandishing royal-blue velvet that I started to laugh, and we both relaxed as I took it from him and tossed it carelessly onto the loveseat. He probably figured I would put the shoes away later.

"Where's your sidekick?" I asked, now all smiles and pleasantries. After all, a good-looking man in your living room is worth being pleasant to for at least a little while.

"I'm not on duty yet. Dropped over on my way in to the station. I'll hook up with him there in about an hour. I didn't mention that I was planning to visit, since I didn't tell him you'd left your shoes. He doesn't have many kind words for you or your friend. I think he'd like to make a case against Mrs. Porter. She sure gave him a hard time, and he's not used to that. I'll say one thing for her, she doesn't bully easy. He hasn't come up against too many like her."

"There aren't too many. Susan is special."

I intoned those last words with great seriousness as I looked him directly in the eyes, and we both burst into laughter, completely at ease in each other's presence. This was not normal behavior for me. I'm unused to having good-looking men in my apartment in the middle of the day and should be suspicious of any who appeared.

"He probably deserved it, the sanctimonious prick."

A look of true horror crossed his face as soon as the words had slipped out and he realized what he'd said. I doubt he'd ever admitted that thought in public or said it aloud before, and I was intrigued that he'd let his defenses down. It made me feel powerful and attractive. I smiled comfortingly.

"Don't worry. I won't tell him you said that. I have no particular desire to even see him again. But isn't that out of character? Aren't partners supposed to be willing to go to the wall for each other, to die for each other? Don't they place their lives in each others' hands daily? Don't they love each other more than their wives? In a masculine, nonsexual way, of course. Isn't there never-ending loyalty? I watch a lot of television," I prattled. Maybe I wasn't as much at ease as I'd imagined.

Still smiling and showing lots of excellent teeth, he answered seriously. "I do trust him to protect me and cover me in all instances. As I would him. We've been partnered for three years now, and I know his every move. I have no wife, he's divorced for the third time, so there's no competition. I am loyal to what he stands for. Law and order. But on a personal level, I can't stand the bastard. He can't even begin to relate to me in any way except professionally. Can't decide if I'm the enemy or not. A very political policeman."

"Those are the very words my friend Joanne used. Joanne Cowan."

"You know Joanne Cowan?" he exclaimed, reddening.

Aha! No wonder she was holding back. Guilty knowledge. There was definitely a good story there, and as soon as he left I was going to drag it out of her. I almost felt like throwing him out to rush to the phone, but the knowledge of what was hidden on my very premises persuaded me to act like an adult. I was in a precarious situation, and I had better behave. And put the heroin out of my mind lest my poker face somehow reveal its existence.

"We've been friends forever. Even longer than Susan," I said. "And she has nothing nice to say about Detective-Sergeant Boucherville either."

"Most people don't," he sighed, looking weary. And cuddly. "I'm getting tired of defending him. It gets harder and harder."

He looked defeated, and I felt it my womanly duty to cheer him up. I still remember some of the things my mother tried to teach me. Or was it *Father Knows Best*?

So I stupidly offered, "Celine called me. She left a message saying she'd call back."

"Celine?"

I preened. I knew something he didn't. I could now be said to have been helping the police with their enquiries. If I lived in England. In Canada it could be said that I was just showing off and trying to ingratiate myself.

"Celine. Bimbo. Celine Plouffe."

I saw the lightbulb click on above his head as his body tensed. We became all business. A ferocious intensity overtook him as he discussed his case, giving him a scary, dark edge that made him cross the line from cute to very attractive. That, coupled with the information that he had no wife, should have set alarm bells ringing. Instead, I blathered on.

"She's Frank's current girlfriend. Ex-girlfriend now, I guess. You know, Bimbo." I shouldn't have added the giggle, since it earned me a sharp, scornful look. I must remember to have more respect for the dead. Even the obnoxious dead.

"How do you know who she is? Mrs. Porter denied knowing anything about her. And there was nothing in the apartment to indicate who she was."

Not having learned my lesson, I teased, "No secret drawer filled with dirty Polaroids? No happy snaps or love letters tied in red ribbon? No mechanical aids?"

That sharp, rebuking look again. If I thought this was flirting, I needed a refresher course; I was losing him quickly. Time to be serious.

"Susan told me she knew nothing about Bimbo." Truth on my part. Lies on hers. I'm sure she knew everything about Bimbo. "Someone else told me. Someone inconsequential." I don't know how Cynthia Berkowitz would feel about that appellation, but I do know she would want to be left out of this. She'd want to know all the gory details, of course, but I don't think she'd take kindly to being questioned by the police. I'm certain her kids would, though.

"It was part of a story and came up only as a sidebar. I also know she's a flight attendant. I don't know which airline, but it's not PanCanada."

I had checked her out on the computer during my visit there and could find no trace of her.

"And how do you know this?" I think he was fishing for Cynthia, but I elected to misinterpret.

"I still have some friends there. Until recently I was VP of public relations and corporate affairs. So I had someone check." During my previous interrogation I had only offered that I was currently unemployed, not from where.

"You're *that* Barbara Simons!" Now he blushed. A pretty, light shade of pink.

"What does *that* mean?" I demanded. He squirmed.

"Oh, nothing . . . I guess I've seen you on the news or something."

Bad save. But the last remark brought Joanne back to mind. Somehow she was the cause of his discomfiture. Again I felt like bundling him out the door and heading for the telephone.

We both behaved like adults and reverted to business, letting the embarrassment slide.

"Look," I started. "I gave you some information, and now I'll offer some speculation. Then I want something back. Celine obviously has another residence. No woman lives somewhere without leaving more traces of herself than that apartment had. Her clothes were there, but she wasn't. And they were mostly fancy clothes. Where were all the jeans and T-shirts? The ratty sweatshirts that everyone has? And the makeup?"

"I see you looked around before we arrived."

Oops!

"Well, yes. I was checking to see if anything was obviously missing. Or if anyone was still there."

Medium good save.

"We had the same impression. When Mlle Plouffe calls back, please encourage her to contact me. Or at least report to me what she says. She's probably scared and likely knows more about this than anyone. Please do not meet her anywhere alone. It could be dangerous. Call me."

So Celine is Mlle Plouffe, Susan is Mrs. Porter, and I'm Miss Simons. Formal bastard, wasn't he? However, Joanne was just Joanne.

"You really think she might have done it? Killed Frank, I mean?" Perhaps I should have said "Mr. Porter."

He looked deeply into my widened eyes and virtually drawled his response. Now he was flirting, and loath as I was to admit it, he was much better at it than I.

"No. I don't think so. We assume there were two people

present besides Porter. Two men, judging by the size of the footprints. And I don't think they meant to kill him."

"What!"

"Mrs. Porter will be informed as soon as the report is concluded, but preliminary results indicate he didn't die of a bullet wound. He died of a heart attack."

"What!"

Stop saying that, I screamed silently to myself. Just as I was digesting this information and preparing to ask something intelligent to counteract my "What"s a pinging sounded. It was either my smoke detector, the microwave oven, or a beeper. And since the chili was on the stove tightly covered and I wasn't even smoking, it had to be a beeper.

"May I use the phone?" he asked, fumbling to turn it off.

"May I" instead of "Can I." What school *did* he go to?

"Certainly. You can use the one in the kitchen if you want some privacy." Or at least a semblance of it. I was glad there was no music playing and I could probably hear everything perfectly without even moving, should he choose to close the doors behind him. Which he did. Louver doors leak noise brilliantly.

As I watched him fumble with his beeper I thought of how ridiculous I've always found them. I once dated a hospital administrator who secretly envisioned himself a trauma surgeon and never went anywhere without his beeper lest his services be needed on a moment's notice. He always put it in a prominent place, announcing to anyone who would listen that he was "on call" and might be summoned momentarily. We never went anywhere where this wasn't his opening gambit. In the three months we dated—my usual limit—the stupid thing went off four times. Much to his deserved chagrin, each and every time it turned out to be his mother. I wondered if Gregory Allard's mother ever beeped him.

Smiling, I strained to listen. The conversation was pretty

much one-sided and not my side. He could have used the phone in the living room for all the top-secret information I was gleaning. The call was short; upon reopening the kitchen doors he returned to the living room to find me innocently lighting a cigarette.

"Those things'll kill you," he said as he regained his seat.

"Oh no! Not another holier-than-thou reformed smoker. Who has the nerve to tell me not to smoke in my own house," I exclaimed in mock horror.

"Sorry. How did you know? The reformed part, I mean."

"I'm usually pretty good at rooting them out," I said cheerfully. "A certain jealous-vigilante gleam appears in the eyes. They always sound like they're trying to convince themselves instead of me. How long?"

"Three months and two days and I don't know how much longer."

"Well, that's honest at least. Keep it up. It really is a disgusting habit. And expensive." But not if you buy them on the black market, I didn't add.

"Now tell me about Frank's so-called heart attack."

"Not so-called. Very real. That was the lab on the phone with the first of the toxicology reports. The initial suspicion was that he died of his wound. He was shot with a Glock-17."

"Never heard of it. They don't have them on television."

He laughed. "It's a nine-millimeter weapon that takes standard ammunition. It's a fashionable weapon with the gangbangers these days. Since it's made of polymer, which is a kind of plastic, it's lightweight and flashy looking."

"Oh, I do know about those," I interrupted. "They're a joke at the airlines. We catch lots of drug dealers because of them. The schmucks think that because the gun is plastic it won't appear on security scanners, but they're wrong. They show up in all their glory, just waiting for their owners to be arrested. You know, it's amazing how many people pack guns in other people's luggage. Or so they maintain as they're hauled away."

"Right," he said, rubbing his chin. "You're that Barbara Simons. I keep forgetting what you do for a living."

"Did. And that's the second time you've said that. What does it mean?"

"Nothing. Never mind." He shrugged his square shoulders and smiled ingratiatingly to distract me. It worked.

"The Glock was fitted with a silencer, which accounted for why none of the neighbors heard anything."

"Yeah," I interrupted again. "What about the neighbors? How come none of them showed up in the hallway, with all that action going on? No one is that uncurious."

"There are only six apartments per floor. The inhabitants of three of them are in Florida for the winter. Another couple was away skiing, and the last tenant swears he heard nothing and slept through it all."

"I don't believe that," I said.

"Neither do I, and we'll continue checking," he added.

It didn't make sense. There had been elevators full of people coming and going all night long. And from my firsthand observation, the cops weren't too considerate about not disturbing the residents. Also, they must have done a door-to-door canvass at the time. They always do on *NYPD Blue*.

"When did he tell you this? Didn't you canvass the neighbors at the time?"

"You *do* watch a lot of television, don't you?"

Damn. Caught again, and a double problem. Now he would think that I spent all my time at home glued to the tube rather than out gallivanting with the beautiful people. It made me appear lonely and miserable, with nothing except the excitement and romance of cop shows and sitcoms to entertain me. Also, it's fine for me to say it in a flippant manner, but I hate having it coming back. It was *my* living room, and he should know to play by my rules. Only I had forgotten to post them at the door.

I ignored the comment and repeated the question.

"There was no answer at his door at the time, so we went back the next morning and spoke to him. He said he'd taken a sleeping pill and had slept through the whole affair. He was asleep from nine o'clock on and didn't hear a thing."

"Hmmph," I snorted.

"That's what he maintains."

"Hmmph," I repeated, which made him smile again. At least it was an improvement on "What?" "Who is this man? What's his name?"

Now he laughed openly.

"I'm afraid that's really none of your concern. This is an official police investigation, you know. I really shouldn't be discussing any of this with a civilian."

The phraseology fascinated me. They really use words like civilian. Although I would have normally belabored the point, I wanted more information, and since he was being nice and open I saw no sense in closing him down, the inevitable result.

"Then tell me about this heart attack stuff," I said pleasantly as I stood to go into the kitchen to fetch a Diet Coke for me and some bubbly water for him. I used the best crystal glasses.

He took his gratefully. "Thanks. How did you know?" he asked, no doubt impressed by my psychic powers.

"Just a guess," I demurred. Ex-smokers are always thirsty at first. I know. I've been one on numerous occasions. And doesn't everyone who is anyone drink bubbly water these days? Except me, of course, as I'm faithful to my Diet Coke. Actually, I'm probably addicted to it, a fact I rigorously deny to all interlocutors. I seem to spend a lot of my life in denial.

He sipped gratefully and continued.

"As I said, we initially presumed the bullet killed him, but on further investigation it seemed unlikely. He was shot in the shoulder, and that's not generally fatal. It can tear the hell out of bone and muscle, but it shouldn't kill you. The preliminary X rays gave us our first clue."

"X rays?" I interjected. "I didn't know that bodies are X-rayed. I can't remember Quincy ever doing that."

Drat! That TV stuff again. This man was going to think I was really pathetic. But he didn't seem to have noticed the slip.

"No. It's not general procedure. At the moment there's some sort of experiment going on in conjunction with the medical schools and teaching hospitals in town, and so for the past two months all bodies have been X-rayed on arrival at the morgue. In this case the technician actually looked at the film before sending it off and brought it to the attention of the pathologist."

I sipped politely and did not light a cigarette so as not to distract him.

"He found evidence of talc granulomatosis, which led to further investigation."

"Evidence of what?" I asked. An actual proper usage of the word *what*.

"Talc granulomatosis is a favorite of the medical profession, although it's reasonably rare in these sophisticated days. Interns especially like it because it's simple to detect, flashy, and makes them self-righteously feel the unlucky stiff deserved his end, or the living patient can be pompously lectured to. Makes them feel omnipotent."

He certainly had no great respect for doctors. I wondered why.

"What is it?" I asked impatiently.

"Cocaine is generally cut with another substance to increase volume and profits. Rarely does it hit the streets pure. In fact, never. It's cut with lactose, Novocaine, baby laxative, and many other fine white powders. This is called being stepped on, and before it hits the streets it's stepped on many times."

I didn't bother to tell him I already knew this. Some information is best kept to oneself. Certainly when talking to the police.

"Sometimes, especially in the early eighties, it's cut with

talcum powder. It's a cheap filler and readily available. The substance is inert and shows up on X rays as tiny calcitic densities scattered diffusely throughout the lungs. It glows. Impossible to miss."

"And Frank had this?" I asked, giving him the opportunity to drink some water. I wondered why he was telling me all this but had no inclination to ask. That gift horse thing. Or maybe it was "Beware the Greeks . . ." I hoped the former.

"Mr. Porter showed smatterings of talc throughout his lungs."

I knew it. Mr. Porter.

"Yeah," I offered. "I can believe Frank was into coke."

I sure could. I had two kilos of heroin in the other room to support the fact that Frank was conversant with controlled substances, but it was unwise to dwell on the thought at the moment.

"He always wanted to be trendy," I said with sympathy that surprised me. "He thought of himself as being on the cutting edge, whereas he was always outdated. Cocaine was the drug of choice of the so-called fast crowd in the eighties, and I know it's now the nineties, but as I always said, Frank was a slow learner. But what does this have to do with a heart attack? How did that happen? I didn't know he had a weak heart. I don't think Susan knows either."

"No, it's unlikely she would know. There was no indication of any preexisting condition. In short, he simply overloaded. Blew his fuses. The toxicology screens show that he had recently ingested some very high-grade cocaine. Close to pure, judging by the traces left on the table. It was virtually uncut and surely more potent than anything he would have been used to. That, coupled with the trauma of being shot, sent his heart into overdrive, and there weren't enough cylinders functioning to keep him pumping. So he expired."

His choice of words likened the process to a car breaking down rather than a person meeting his eternal end, but I was in no position to get involved in a discussion of semantics. The information began to sink in. "That would mean they didn't expect to kill him. They just meant to scare him into telling something," I mused.

"Correct," he beamed. His student was apt.

"So, do you think they found what they were looking for?" I asked innocently.

"No. We think he died before he could tell them. That's why the search was so thorough."

I longed to ask him about the toupée. Traces of tape must have been discovered on the inside. How did they explain that? Still, Greg had said the police thought nothing had been found, and surely the tape would indicate something had once been hidden there. It was too great and dangerous a conundrum to ponder at the time, so I simply sat there, hoping I looked suitably puzzled.

At which point he rose.

"I must go now," he said formally. "Thanks for the drink."

I jumped to my feet and made small talk about the cold as I escorted him to the door and delivered his coat.

"Thanks for the shoes," I said shyly. As reluctant as I had been to let him in, I now didn't want him to leave. The pit of my stomach was behaving oddly.

"It was nothing. It's been a pleasant interlude."

Now what did that mean?

"Remember, don't meet Mlle Plouffe without first checking with me. Well, I'm on my way to meet my partner, and then we'll go talk to Mrs. Porter again."

"Good luck," I said with heartfelt meaning. "A hint. You do all the talking. I get the feeling that just walking into Westmount Square will set your partner on edge. Oh, whatever you do, don't let him get embroiled with the housekeeper. She's ten times worse than Susan. She may just be lethal to Detective-Sergeant Boucherville. Might cause his arteries to burst."

"Thanks for the tip," he said, grinning.

I loved that smile, and my stomach was weird again.

There was an awkward moment at the door, where we both fidgeted like teenagers. It didn't seem right to just say good-bye and never see each other again.

I could tell by his shuffling that he was about to say something that I likely wanted to hear when the door across the hall opened and my nosy neighbor appeared with the smallest bag of trash on earth.

"Garbage room," she said brightly as she brandished the bag and pottered down the hall. The building tom-toms were rumbling.

Greg said thanks again, although for what I didn't know. I doubt he did either. He headed briskly toward the elevator under the steady scrutiny of my neighbor.

I closed the door quickly and paced for a while. There was a lot of information to assimilate and try to sort out.

Since the previsit languor had dissipated and I was now sexually energized without any hope of relief, I changed my clothes and headed for the club, having remembered to turn off the burner under the chili. It smelled delicious and only needed cooling before being put into containers and shoved into the freezer. It could wait.

Mercifully, I encountered no one I knew as I worked out all my aggression on the machines. There was a close call in the locker room, but I hid out in the shower until the offender left. I was quite prunelike, and my hair was completely destroyed, but I felt calm and relaxed as I drove back home.

The first thing I did was call Joanne, who wasn't home. I didn't have the heart to browbeat her husband. Him I liked. Her, I wasn't so sure. I also called Susan to find out how the encounter with the police had gone, but she wasn't home either. Barry answered, which shouldn't have surprised me by now but did. He told me Susan had gone to the funeral home to make the final arrangements. The police would release the body today, and services would be held Sunday morning. He added that he was looking forward to seeing me at the Diabetes Foundation Ball. I thought to myself that Susan's decision to go to the ball wasn't all that strange. She wasn't exactly in mourning, and she would be the center of attention. Susan doesn't mind doing a star turn every now and then.

I ate some chili, put away the rest, did not wash the pot, and got into bed to watch TV. Very soon I fell asleep.

I forgot to call Sam.

11

SATURDAY MORNING, AFTER awakening refreshed
and at peace, I found myself back in my wing chair, surrounded
by the detritus of the newspaper, musing that despite my problems with the building, I could never move. I'd probably be able
to find a great apartment somewhere; due to the government and
the economy, the city was loaded with them at relatively cheap
prices. But I'd never find a particular spot as comfortable as this
one. It was warm and cozy sitting in the yellow ribbons of sun
that belied the subzero temperature and snowpacked streets
outside. At that particular moment, this was simply the best
place on earth to be.

So far this morning I had accomplished nothing and was
quite content with that. So much interaction lately had left me
exhausted, as habituated as I was to solitary confinement and
inertia. I puttered around the apartment for a while doing not
much and spent an inordinate amount of time safely ensconced
in my trusty chair by the window reading the deliciously fat
newspaper.

I was working on the crossword puzzle and it was proceeding

easily, which lulled me into a sense of intelligence and competence. I could handle anything. Weeks of lethargy had dulled my instincts, and I felt well and very laid-back. It was even possible that I might consider looking into that crystals stuff if this cloud of well-being continued to envelop me. Or maybe buy a New Age tape to tinkle dissonantly in the background.

I should have been warier.

The first thing that happened was that the phone rang. Well, actually it sort of bleeped or blurped. My living-room appliance for interactive communication is improbably shaped like a Mercedes 560SL and emits an unnatural sound. My brother, the purveyor of unusual gifts, decided that while some people have phones in their cars, I definitely needed a car in my phone. I love it. It's stupid and makes a ridiculous sound that is a reminder to take nothing mechanical or electronic too seriously. A utensil of the absurd.

I lifted the hardtop that serves as the handpiece, fully expecting to find Joanne at the other end. I could now get to the bottom of this Gregory Allard thing. If it was a thing. I was still undecided.

It was the elusive Celine Plouffe, which was even better than Joanne, even if she is famous. She introduced herself politely in a firm, clear voice and asked if she could meet with me. Intrigued and at the same time eyeing the elements outside, I suggested lunch at my house. I had no inclination to venture out into the freezing cold unless my destination offered indoor parking, and none of the current trendy lunch places did. She seemed surprised by my hospitality but accepted. We set the time for noon, and she rang off.

It was only after hanging up that I reflected on the intelligence of asking her to my house. She was an unknown factor, and laziness had once again predicated my response. But I decided it was all right. What could happen to me in my own apartment? Never mind what had happened to Frank.

However, I *was* wary and responsible enough to alert Greg. I shifted my bones and went to fish his card out of my purse. It was very official looking and impressive, and only slightly mangled. It took about an hour to ferret out the phone number, cleverly hidden in a corner. I think the dual-language, information-packed card was meant to intimidate its recipients, not to actually invite them to call. Of course I was put on hold and forced to listen to abysmal, static-filled music followed by a commercial in French for a hemorrhoid preparation. I was familiar with it in English, and translation hadn't improved its disgusting message.

I fingered the card with all its official-looking insignias and reflected that, unlike most people, detectives probably use up all their business cards. I personally don't know anyone else who does. People order cards in the hundreds and thousands because of the significant price break for quantity, but generally, before they have time to distribute them all, they move or change jobs. This should have attuned me to the conspiratorial forces that surround us, but I just thought it was a great scam and a business opportunity that warranted further contemplation.

I was about to launch into further exploration of the topic and its endless possibilities when an actual live person came on the line and babbled something totally incomprehensible.

"Pardon me? What?"

" 'Omocide. Sergeant Larivée 'ere," the voice slowly and politely translated, having pegged me as a unilingual Anglophone.

I went with the assumption and proceeded in English. "Detective-Sergeant Gregory Allard, please."

" 'E's not 'ere. Massage?"

Her voice cooled perceptibly at the mention of Greg's name. Did lots of women call him? Or was she jealous of any female who asked for him, having secretly lusted after him for years? It was something to ask him about. I understood "massage" to mean "message" and not that he was out getting himself shiatsued and anointed with fragrant oils. He wouldn't have told her if he was.

"Please tell him Barbara Simons called. It's not urgent."

"Dat's a new one," she mumbled as she rang off. The police department must give lessons in speaking in riddles; her answer was totally incomprehensible to me. Something was definitely out of synch with those two, but it was not my problem, and I had discharged my civic duty.

I prepared a salad, heated some of the chili, and wept as I chopped raw onions for the condiments. Although my waterproof mascara lived up to its advertised promise, I'd need lots of toothpaste to rehabilitate my breath before I faced the public— but it was well worth it. Chili loaded with raw onions and freshly grated cheddar cheese is so very comforting on a day when the temperature has dropped below zero. Celsius and/or Fahrenheit.

To my great surprise and satisfaction, the doorman announced Celine's arrival. I might decide it wasn't necessary to move after all.

Celine arrived at my front door looking like a frozen Michelin man. Her puffy red down coat matched her red hat and bright red cheeks. She was rosy all over. She had evidently walked some distance, judging by her ruddy color.

She took off her red, shearling-lined mitts and extended her hand in a stiff manner, not really appropriate to the informality of the occasion. Her handshake was firm, her fingertips cold in spite of the warm mittens. After removing the red boots, exposing natty red-and-white-striped socks, she came in and began to disrobe. First came the hat, from under which tumbled masses of shiny blond hair. It looked real and Miss America–like. Definitely an expensive haircut. From the bulk of her coat emerged a lithe body clad in jeans and black turtleneck. Cotton. But not a blend. She was about five foot six, which gave me some inches on her, which for some reason pleased me. Her eyes were deep blue, and she had high cheekbones and a rosebud mouth. She looked like she came off a Victorian chocolate box.

The most distressing thing was her legs. In her tight jeans they seemed to go on forever, ending in taut, shapely buttocks. A definite head turner, this girl could cause car pileups. If I hadn't been curious as to what she wanted I might have slammed the door in her face. I really don't like perfect women. Particularly perfect women who have fifteen years on me. They're just *too* depressing and always succeed in making me feel inadequate. No litany of accomplishments nor enumeration of strong suits can ever compensate for the freshness of youth.

One trap I've never fallen into is the one that assumes that all blond beauties are dumb. Anyone born looking like that has to have some modicum of brains, if only to deal with all the attention focused on her throughout her life. I've discovered that blonds tend to be smarter than they look or let on. The really smart ones, like Jennifer Marlow on *WKRP in Cincinnati*, work the system for all it's worth. On the whole, they make me very, very wary.

"Would you care for something to drink?" I offered. No reason not to be polite just because she was gorgeous. I'm above all that.

"A beer, please. Lite if you have it," she answered, sizing me up as she spoke. Her eyes took in everything, likely comparing the way we filled out our respective jeans. Well, at least my black turtleneck was cashmere, not cotton.

I looked in the fridge and said, "Sorry, I forgot to restock." There was never any in stock in the first place, never mind restocked. I must remember that not everyone has my peculiar drinking habits and start to shop accordingly. But I wasn't letting her know that. Let her imagine that I'd had a houseful of fabulous people last night who'd depleted my supply.

In my daydreams I imagine my apartment overflowing with glamorous guests, whereas in reality, the thought of all those people invading my space horrifies me. Ten people for dinner max. And once every ten months seems a good idea too.

"Anything else?"

"Okay. A martini, then."

A martini? Who the hell drinks martinis at home, much less knows how to make them? I knew it was either vodka or gin with vermouth, but how much of each? So far, every word she'd said—and there hadn't been many—had unsettled me. Not only was she breathtaking, she was bringing to light great gaps in my education.

"Vodka or gin?" I ventured.

"Vodka, please."

Good answer. I went to the freezer and extricated a bottle of excellent Russian vodka. I knew it was excellent because the man who had given it to me had not only told me so, he'd left the price tag stuck to the bottle to reinforce the information and to make sure I appreciated his largesse. I hadn't been quite as appreciative as he would have liked. I did know enough to keep it in the freezer, though. How very sophisticated of me.

After retrieving a bottle of vermouth from the well-stocked, seldom-used bar in the den, I returned to the kitchen with both the bottle and a beautiful crystal martini pitcher with matching crystal stirring rod.

On reflection, a martini was a great choice. I'd finally get to use this silly set. It had been a gift from the union members two years back, which was unusual in itself, since it's not often that labor buys management a gift. The employees had felt that during the difficult contract negotiation I had dealt fairly and honestly with all factions, including the insidious press. When all was finally settled to their satisfaction for the next three years, they'd chipped in and bought me a thank-you gift. Since the windup coincided with Christmas, and the company was equally satisfied with the outcome, I was allowed to accept, as management decided it couldn't be construed as a bribe, and should the media decree otherwise, the company could counter with how wonderful and unusual labor relations were within their organization. I made sure the press never found out. I do not like being used, even for a healthy paycheck.

Anyway, if I were going to sell out, it wouldn't be for an expensive but ridiculous martini set. Who uses these things? The store had surely seen the purchasing committee—everything in a union is always done by committee—coming.

It sure impressed Celine. She eyed it with envy. Maybe this was a new status symbol that I hadn't hooked onto yet. I'd have to get out more.

"Here," I said, shoving the bottles and pitcher toward her. "You mix it. You know the proportions you prefer." Thus I was perceived as hospitable rather than ignorant.

She mixed an entire pitcherful, which staggered me. Could this skinny little thing possibly drink all that and remain standing? At lunchtime? Now it was my turn to be impressed.

She poured some into the glass I provided. It wasn't a regulation triangular martini glass, but it was Baccarat crystal. For some reason I was pulling out all my good stuff for her. I'm not so acquisitive as to have run out and bought an entire set of proper martini glasses when I received the gift, although I did consider it for a not-too-brief moment.

I realized how nervous she was when her hands trembled as she lifted the glass and took her first deep gulp. And I discovered something not perfect about her; her nails were unpolished and bitten to the quick. This surprised me and gave a hint that she wasn't ever all that calm. I never consider that women who look like her could be nervous. It's the others around them who are.

We sat at the kitchen table and proceeded to eat and chat. Well, it started as chat. We talked about the chili (she liked it and heaped it with onion, so now we would both reek) and the cold (she didn't like it). She spoke well, her English grammatical and polished, which indicated extensive lessons. After a short while of meaningless musings the tone of the conversation changed as I tried to turn it into something more like an inquisition, with me firing the questions.

Throughout the small talk my confusion had grown. Even from her frivolous conversation I could tell she wasn't an idiot. I just couldn't figure out what a beauty like this would want with Frank. Properly packaged, she could have anyone, and Frank was not at the top of anyone's list of great catches. The only conclusion that made any sense was that she was dumber than she seemed, or up to something nefarious. Her ongoing nervousness ignited my suspicion as to her role in the whole affair, as aside from her atrocious taste in evening wear, she did not seem a credible victim.

"Why me?" I started, sensing the time was right to get down to issues. "Why do you want to talk to me? And how do you know who I am?" I was about to continue and ask her directly what it was she wanted to tell me when she interrupted. Although she wasn't in Cynthia Berkowitz's league, silence didn't seem to be her long suit, and she filled the air with words at every pause. If I was going to get all my questions in, I'd have to talk a lot faster.

"I know you and Mrs. Porter are good friends. Frank says you're Robert's godmother and that Robert loves you." She said this openly and with seeming honesty. Not a flinch or a flicker.

I didn't have her equanimity. I'm sure my eyes registered the shock I felt. I was nonplussed. Her opening statement was short but spoke volumes. Mrs. Porter? Celine referred to Susan, Frank's wife, as Mrs. Porter? I would have expected and preferred "that bitch" or something of that ilk. Mrs. Porter illustrated dramatically her subservient role in the relationship with that bastard Frank. How dare she look like that and allow herself to be so submissive? I wanted to shake some sense into her, but I was afraid her brains would rattle. It was time to revise my position on the dumb-blond stereotype.

And Robert spoke of me? What instigated that conversation? I was so off balance that my mental list of questions eluded me. Consequently, I neglected to ask her how she knew my phone number and address, since I'm not in the book and I have no recollection of Frank ever calling or visiting me.

All I could muster was, "How long have you known Frank?"

I shouldn't have asked. The answer was so pathetic I wanted to cry. The instincts I had about her as I fingered her evening clothes at Frank's had been accurate.

They'd been together for six months. She'd been living with him for three. She loved him very much, and they had been planning to get married as soon as Mrs. Porter would grant him a divorce. He'd recently taken her to a family function so she could meet his family, which she took as proof positive of his noble intentions. They hadn't stayed for the whole evening though, since Mrs. Porter showed up and Frank said he didn't want to be subjected to her begging again, so they left soon after Susan and Barry arrived. She called them Mrs. Porter and Escort. Mrs. Porter had been very difficult about her relationship with Frank, and could I please tell Susan that Frank loved her, Celine, very much and would never, ever have taken Susan back, no matter how much she pleaded.

Now I was the one who needed a martini to help digest that, but I settled for a Diet Coke. I thoroughly and absolutely detested Frank; he was lucky he was already dead, because if he wasn't I would have run out and killed him. Susan would never have taken Frank back under any conditions, not even the promise of stacks of money, which in itself indicates how much she loathed him. The idea of living with him would make her gag, if not actually retch.

Frank had filled this pathetic child with such a load it was tragic, although it graphically illustrated his talents as consummate salesman and disgusting person.

I had to change the subject fast. No contradictory words were appropriate. Let her keep her illusions, since she no longer had Frank.

"You know the police are looking for you," I said.

"*Oui*. I figured. I know I should go see dem but I'm ascared. I'll lose my job if I get hinvolved wit dem."

As she presented her case and drank more of her martini, the last vestiges of control deserted her. The more nervous she became, the more accented her English became. On arrival it had been a trace, but with the mounting tension it was thickening. The martinis must have worked on me too by virtue of proximity, because I felt sorry for her. I was well aware that airlines are not sympathetic to flight attendants who get in trouble with the law.

"Who do you fly for?" I figured that was a good, nonthreatening question.

"Hair Quebec. I don't know why de police want to see me. I don't know nothing. I weren't even here. I was up to Tuktoyaktuk on Monday. I come back Tuesday."

Under different circumstances the disintegration of her speech would have been hilarious. Now it was unsettling, since it made me worry that she was going to fall apart at any second and I'd be charged with putting her back together or having her carted off, to the extreme delight of all my neighbors.

I know Air Quebec. It's a well-run regional airline that specializes in northern Quebec and the hinterlands of the Arctic. It has always amazed me that enough people travel these routes to make it a lucrative proposition, but, unlike most airlines today, Air Quebec is operating healthily in the black. The routes are not exactly glamorous, and any suspicion that I harbored that Celine was involved in smuggling drugs for Frank evaporated. The frozen tundra is not exactly the port of entry of choice.

"I can't get hinvolved wit de cops. I need my job now. I need de money. Frank's gone." And predictably, she burst into tears.

I couldn't figure out what to do. She sobbed daintily, using her napkin to blot her eyes. I hoped her mascara was waterproof, as the napkins were linen. I didn't know if she was crying for Frank or for her job. And I didn't want to know. If it was for that creep Frank, I'd have jostled her small brains out of her.

The only thing I could think of was to refill her glass, which took the remains of the pitcher. She'd polished off the whole thing. How come she wasn't drunk? I'd have been comatose on half the amount.

As the sobbing abated, I noticed that she cried more gracefully than Susan; her eyes didn't turn rabbit-red like Susan's had. I wondered what brand of mascara she wore; it remained intact, and there were no traces on the napery.

She told me she'd arrived late Tuesday afternoon and had proceeded home as usual. There was a tape across the door, but she'd assumed it had been the exterminators announcing their presence. How dumb *was* this girl? She assumed that an orange police cordon was like a Sani-Seal in a cheap motel? Couldn't she read? And I further doubt that there was a roach alive in Frank's neighborhood. Maybe I was wrong, though. Maybe Frank's mere presence attracted them. It wouldn't surprise me.

She insisted, a little too vehemently for my taste, that when she saw the mess in the apartment she'd left immediately. I was still mulling over the police Sani-Seal, and I neglected to ask more salient questions. Like, where was her other home? How did she know that Frank was dead? I guess I just assumed that one of her friends had told her, since she'd surely called around after fleeing the premises. And by now everyone knew. Also, where had she gone?

I was about to ask the last one when she plowed on, and I didn't want to interrupt, since I think we had finally reached the main point of her visit. The biggest hint that the climax was nigh was that the accent disappeared as she proceeded. Her brows knit in concentration, and she even relinquished the grasp on her glass for the first time.

Her clear navy blue eyes looked directly at me without wavering as she said, "It looked like someone was looking for something. Did they find the money? Is that why he was killed? Because he wouldn't give it to them?"

Had there been some hesitation before the word "money" or was I grasping?

"Money? Frank had money in the apartment?"

No "What" for me this time. This was my interview.

"Yeah, sure," she answered matter-of-factly. "There was usually about five to six thousand dollars in cash hidden in the bottom of the dirty clothes hamper. I saw right away that it was overturned. Do you think that's why they killed Frank?" she repeated. "Because he wouldn't tell them where the money was hidden? Maybe the cops have it. Do you know if they do? Do you think they would give it to me, or will it all go to Mrs. Porter? I sure could use it," she ended wistfully.

When she'd finished her questions, she took a last long gulp, which effectively drained the entire contents of the martini pitcher. Then she sat back, folded her hands daintily in her lap, and waited for answers.

I tried to sort out this information quickly so that I could form a response. She sat there patiently, her pretty face open and without guile. I had not known about the money, and likely it had been claimed by the killers. An occupational bonus. But I knew that it wasn't the intent of their search. I kept my eyes focused on her, although they longed to stray to the linen closet with its cache of heroin worth a fortune on the street.

"I don't know anything about any money," I said truthfully. "I guess you should ask the police about that. And you're right; it might explain everything. It might have been some burglars who were cranked and killed him when he wouldn't cough up the cash," I lied. Although I didn't think I sounded at all convincing—more like a bad version of *Barretta*—she seemed to accept it. Or maybe she hoped that was it.

"Celine, you really should go to the police and tell them your story. As it stands, you're a suspect now, but if you just explain your absence I'm sure you'll be in the clear, and Air Quebec need never find out." I wasn't sure of any such thing but it seemed like the appropriate thing to say.

Anyway, she appeared to be convinced. "You're right. I'll go see them later. It would be better than hiding."

I didn't ask where or why, which should strike me off the cast of *Police Woman*.

Now that the food was consumed, the martinis drunk, and she saw that I had no idea where the money or anything else had gone, she got up and began redressing for the elements. Slowly and surely her taut body metamorphosed into a puffy red cocoon. I marveled again at her capacity for alcohol; she didn't even wobble as she stepped gracefully into her red, salt-stained boots.

At the door I posed a last question. "Do you know any of the neighbors on your floor? The single guy down the hall? Do you know who he is or anything about him?"

Her face shut down. I'd finally said something threatening. This *Columbo* stuff worked.

"No," she said carefully. "I don't know hany of de neighbor. We didn't socialite much." She turned and proceeded down the hall, studiously trying to look nonchalant. I expected her to whistle, but I guess her mouth was too dry.

I'd hit a nerve, and this girl had the worst poker face in the history of the world. Much, much worse than mine.

This mystery neighbor seemed to be key; he would bear further investigation. First step was finding out his name. That seemed simple enough, so it went to the top of tomorrow's agenda. Actually, second on the list. Frank's funeral was scheduled for ten o'clock in the morning. He *would* be inconvenient, even in death.

But if I went back to Lainie's house with the mourners after the service, I might be able to look over the list of attendees as people signed in at the door to attest to their devotion by their presence. I was positive I would be welcome at the close gathering, at least by Susan, who would appreciate my presence in a hostile environment, and I was sure Robert would be happy to see me. At last, a concrete plan.

After I had tidied up the kitchen and loaded the dishwasher, it now time to do the same to myself. First I decided that I was in this thing too deep to rely on Greg—who hadn't called me back as yet—to get me out. When I realized that I had neglected to ask Celine so many important questions it became clear that it was time to get organized and make a list of the things I needed to do and needed to know. I was not going to be caught unprepared again. I was miffed that Greg hadn't called, even though my message had said that it wasn't urgent. He had seemed so concerned about my meeting Celine, but maybe I misinterpreted his warnings.

Anyway, for some screwy reason, I felt I had to get to the bottom of this whole thing. And for some totally unfathomable reason, I was sure I was the only one capable of it. I was watching way too much television and had definitely read too many mysteries.

I tucked the list into my purse, feeling that now things were under control. Lists are very comforting to me, although I seldom consult them except to check the items off with great pride once the task has been completed.

There was too much time left before I had to get ready for the ball, so I decided to be a healthy person and go exercise. I could work out some of the frustration I felt about overlooked questions to Celine and the inexplicable sadness I felt at Greg's neglect. I would punish myself and my body in the name of physical fitness. I changed into a tacky exercise outfit, grabbed my gear, and headed for the garage.

My snoopy neighbor across the hall opened her door at the same time. I swear she lies in wait.

"Nice to see you, Barbara. You're looking better. And receiving lots of visitors, I see. How lovely to be so popular."

"Thank you, Mrs. Brooks. You're looking well as usual."

"How nice of you to say that. My arthritis has been acting up, but we mustn't give in, must we. We must keep up appearances."

I hate her. She's one of those iron-willed little old blue-haired ladies who simper. Passive-aggressive to the max. And she was the keeper of the tom-toms in my building. The way she stared at me, I knew she was keeping an eye on all my activities. Once again, I'd have to consider moving.

In my car, instead of going to the club I found myself heading toward Frank's building. The unknown cipher of the neighbor intrigued me, and it was just possible that I might find the keeper of the tom-toms in his building and learn something of his and Frank's affairs. Since I wasn't dressed for the freezing cold, as I had expected to drive directly into another underground garage, I took it as a good omen and felt munificently blessed when I found a parking spot right in front of the door. For a second I felt like Joanne.

My inordinately expensive sneakers afforded no purchase on the ice as I slithered my way in an ungainly fashion toward the door, only to be confronted by a burly doorman. The building had obviously beefed up security since Frank's demise. I pretended I belonged and knew where I was going as I tried to sail by him. No go. He stopped me and asked who I was calling for, and since I didn't know my quarry's name I used the only one I could think of.

"Frank Porter," I announced as I continued toward the elevator.

A beefy arm stopped me.

"Mr. Porter is out. Leave a message."

Since when were doormen secretaries? I very well knew Frank was out—permanently. And the doorman didn't fit the profile. His uniform pulled across his barrel chest and looked like it came from a costumers, with too much gold braid to be credible in this neighborhood. His accent was Brooklyn. Something was definitely wrong here, and I thought it best to make the fastest nonsuspicious exit possible.

"Well," I began hesitantly, gathering speed with every word. "Tell him his cousin Carol dropped by. Carol E, not Carol A." I thought this piece of business might be sufficiently confusing. His thuglike appearance led me to the probable conclusion that his brain was pea-sized. I hoped I was right, since if I was truly Frank's cousin I would surely know that Frank was dead by now, as I'm sure the pseudo-doorman was well aware. The Carol E and Carol A stuff I thought a clever touch. Too clever for this idiot. I was hoping he might think it was some kind of code and grant me access.

Well, I was a novice at this.

All this brilliance was ruined by my unceremonious plop as I veered round, strode purposefully out the door, and splatted down on a patch of snow-covered ice. I'll give him this; he didn't smirk as he rushed out the door to help me to my feet and watched me thread my way carefully back to my car, all the while trying not to cry. But I'm sure I saw evidence of a spreading smirk as I drove off.

In my car I was furious. I'd ruined my tights, and my knee was bleeding. The cute gold-and-black strapless number I had designated for tonight was now unwearable. Scabby knees have not been a major fashion statement in my circles since I was four.

Having abandoned all thought of exercise, I went home to tend to my wounds. Then I hunted through my closet for something appropriate to wear and came up with a long slinky black velvet number with a dangerous slit up the front just to the left of center, which would do since my right knee sported the bandage. It was form-fitting, to say the least, and I was glad of my aberrant eating habits during my period of excommunication, which had caused me to lose some weight. Every extra ounce showed in this dress.

Having checked for droopy hems and finding none, I went

to the kitchen for a Diet Coke before indulging in my toilette.

More news. The message button on my answering machine blinked, and I was sorely, literally and figuratively, tempted to ignore it. It was probably Greg, and I wasn't up to repeating the story of Celine. I certainly didn't want to rehash my ungainly exit from Frank's building. I didn't need him chastising me about my stupid nonplan and how it hadn't worked. I could do that very well myself.

Nevertheless, there was no point in postponing the inevitable, and with a huge sigh I pushed play.

"Where are you? You were supposed to call me back. Chicago is off. I settled the thing by fax. Technology beats the Midwest. Which gives me two scheduled days off, and now I'll take you up on your standing offer. I'm coming up to see you Thursday. I'm leaving now, so call me tomorrow after five. And organize lots of free time from whatever it is you seem so busy with. I'm planning to wear you out. Bye."

Sam. He'd slipped my mind completely, and I hadn't called him back. And now he was coming to Montreal. I knew I should be ecstatic that he was making the trip just for me, but I was filled with trepidation. I was not sure that Sam on my turf was a good idea. Out of town we managed to create a never-never land atmosphere to our trysts. Now I was going to be presented with reality, and I was apprehensive.

Whatever possessed him to suddenly come here? And why now, when I was surrounded by all kinds of lunacy? This man never went anywhere he didn't have to, so what the hell did he want? He surely wanted something.

I retired to a bubble bath to soak away the encroaching stiffness in my limbs and to dispel the cloud that hung over me. Celine had left me with more questions than answers, and the ersatz doorman had seen my car. Sam was on his way, likely to tell me it was all over. Things were not going well.

I was a dismal failure in the role of Jessica Fletcher.

12

STEPHEN ARRIVED PROMPTLY at the stroke of seven in an excellent impersonation of Prince Charming. Instead of a chariot led by six white steeds, he whisked me, Cinderella, off in a billion-horsepower, charcoal-gray Rolls-Royce.

For a change, the doorman was impressed. Although he wasn't the man who'd witnessed my recent characterization, I was sure he'd heard all about it. If he thought I'd been bought and paid for this evening, he must have been speculating on the price with wonder. Cinderella should make more money than Wanda the Whip. Or maybe not.

As I looked at Stephen, devastatingly handsome tonight, I reflected that he was the only person I knew who had a car this luxurious. And it was wholly owned, not leased nor written off to some business. I could tell by the license plates. In my new potentially reduced circumstances I began to evaluate the possibility of reinstating our romantic relationship. It's nice to feel like a fairy princess once in a while. However, that would only validate the opinions of my doormen, a satisfaction I couldn't see myself granting. Anyway, I could always borrow some money or his car from him. I think.

"How's the latest?" I asked, sinking comfortably into the butter-soft, pearl gray leather as he pulled away into the freezing, star-filled night. The snow crunched beneath as we glided through the crystalline-clear air that accompanies subzero temperatures. The luminous sky and moonlit shadows added to the magic of the evening.

"Her name is Ellen, as you well know, and she's fine," he answered not very amiably, eyes riveted to the road.

"Ooohoo! I sense some hostility here. Perchance a lady on the precipice of making an exit? Come on, what's up?"

"Nothing's up. Look, I have to concentrate on the road. There're patches of black ice everywhere."

"Sure." I sneered and remained silent, trying to seem acquiescent. There was no black ice. I'd found the only piece this afternoon. There was only lots of salt-and-gravel-strewn pavement dusted with snow, but I thought it gauche of me to point that out. Anyway, the traction on his car is excellent; he has ABS brakes, multiple airbags. and mega-dollar snow tires. I wasn't the least bit frightened of skidding into anything dangerous. Neither was he.

After forty-five seconds, which I deemed the proper length of time for him to regain his fragile concentration, I plunged ahead.

"Which, I take it, means she's putting pressure on you and you're not quite sure how to react," I said, exercising the premise that we were engaged in a two-way conversation. He had only two options at this point. Either to answer me or tell me to shut up, both of which I could handle. When he surprised me and showed no sign of saying anything, I blustered on. "Okay. Cut to the chase. How serious is it? I mean how serious is she, and how serious are you? Two distinct questions."

"I thought I made it clear that I didn't want to discuss this," he snarled, giving me the evil eye. My determination must have been evident; he gave up. "You're not going to let me off the hook, are you?" he sighed, downshifting into a steep decline.

"Nope." I kept my eyes glued to the road so as not to let him see my victory grin. He's always been so easy.

"Could you please get a life of your own, so you can stay out of mine?"

"Nope again. Yours is more fun. Give."

"May as well, if I expect any peace tonight," he said with a body-heaving sigh. If these were the sighs of small annoyances, I'd hate to be there when there was a real tragedy. "Let's just say that she's more serious than I."

"So what's new? They're always more serious than you are."

This wasn't a reflection on his inability to commit to or maintain a relationship, it's just that he has a sign saying Patsy of the First Order pinned to his sleeve, immediately visible to every single woman and divorcee he meets. And married women, on occasion. He's nationally classified as a major catch, with his combination of good looks, personality, and pots of money. Women always fall head over heels for him and land panting at his feet. When the usual ruses don't work, they have been known to resort to all kinds of outrageous behavior in the hope of ensnaring him. His life is infinitely more interesting than mine, and I have no qualms about grilling him over it. Being the object of desire of so many has never been one of my major preoccupations. Too bad. Therefore I feel that those who have must learn to share.

As part of this ongoing saga of Steve's Seductions, there was my all-time favorite gambit, which I dubbed the Camille Caper. The appropriately named fragile beauty, who I'm sure watched the movie endlessly and never read the book, managed to sink her delicate pearl pink claws fairly deep into Stephen. The withering vine approach was effective, arousing all his protective instincts. This damsel-in-distress routine is not one I can abide, and it took all my willpower to keep my nose out of it. Since he seemed content in his adoration, I mostly did, making fewer snide remarks than normal. However, it all came to a head when she arrived at his house one day to announce she'd just been to the doctor, and he had given her the test results. She was devastated. She had only a few months to live. Dabbing her eyes gently with an Irish lace hankie, she informed him of the tragic news and told him she had only one dream left in life. She'd never had a wedding, and she wanted to die a wife. Stephen ached and agonized over her fate, and the good-natured schmuck acceded to her wishes. Wedding preparations were begun.

But Stephen has a vast fortune, and he felt that with better medical attention perhaps her life could be extended, or she might even be cured. I never did find out what the mysterious disease was. He got in touch with the Mayo Clinic to make arrangements and asked that they jointly consult with her local physician to discuss the evaluation and ask him to transfer her files. Surprise. Somehow the doctor was endlessly unavailable or out of town, and it only took Stephen twelve beats longer than a normal person to figure out something was fishy. Sometimes he's such a naïf.

I swear I never said anything. I would have gone over the edge and damaged our relationship forever if I dared open my mouth at all about this one.

I guess you don't make all that money by being an idiot, and he finally smartened up and recognized the ploy for the farce it was, and with lots of hearts and flowers and expensive jewelry he severed the relationship. He even dumps them nicely. Maybe that was just what she needed, because Camille miraculously recovered and quickly took up with an eighty-three-year-old trillionaire who was besotted with her and, best of all, had no children.

I'm totally awed by some of the ruses that women can concoct, and if I hang around Stephen long enough I'll have enough material for a book, and then I'll get to be a guest on a talk show; the first one with good hair. I marvel at the creativity and energy these women devote to their endeavors, and I can't bring myself to denigrate them. It's a full-time occupation and should be respected as such. Some of them are really good at their jobs.

And I guess Stephen's worth the effort, I thought as I again noted how handsome he was and thought of what a good friend he'd always been to me. But it didn't stop me from prying.

"How badly have you been leading her on?" I asked.

Stephen loves to shower women with flowers and trinkets. He says it makes him feel good, and he loves the look of wonderment when they receive the gifts. Except the word trinket has different connotations to different people. I buy trinkets in Woolworth. He prefers Cartier. No wonder these women are so easily besotted. What I can't drive through his impenetrable skull is that most women are not used to this sort of behavior and they're understandably overwhelmed and enthralled. They tend to feel they've hit the motherlode. What's really pathetic is that perfectly intelligent women go to pieces when an attractive man pays them court. It's so unlike what they've been trained to accept as normal that they latch on, gasping. Stephen and I have had this discussion often, and I've tried to illustrate how unfair he's being and urge him to tone down the indulgences. He always says he'll try, but I've yet to see proof of it.

He resents my incursions into his spending patterns, so he answered abruptly. "No I haven't, Miss Cheapness. Only flowers, no jewelry. Well, maybe a little something."

I thought about this for three beats.

"Now I understand all," I said, my head bobbing like a rear-window toy dog, pushing the envelope. Since both his hands were on the steering wheel and he greatly values his extravagant machine, he couldn't sock me. "My superb deductive reasoning has led me to comprehend your ill humor and its root cause. No need to consult with my man Watson. I've solved the conundrum singlehandedly. Not only do I now know that you've had your first big fight, I know exactly what it was about. Me!" I trumpeted triumphantly.

He stared at me like I was either psychic or completely loony. But his hands stayed firmly on the wheel, so I was safe from the swat I deserved.

"Eyes back on the road, please. Remember, black ice lurketh." I edged toward the door in case he forgot his good breeding or vehicular investment and decided to mete out deserved punishment.

"Look, it's simple. It's Saturday night, and you're out with me. Me, I reiterate, not her. Off to a glamorous event, and we'll no doubt be mentioned in Monday morning's social columns, which I'm sure she reads avidly. Fool, you're at the point in your relationship where Saturday night is considered a given. You, typical insensitive male that you are, have not picked up on the signals and nuances. You've neglected to heed the telltale clues. And when you innocently mentioned that you were busy tonight, you were unprepared for the major explosion. Were the tickets on your dresser for the past month? In open view? To have her assume that she would accompany you and you just forgot to mention it? And when it turned out that you were going with me to this event on a Saturday night, she exploded. And I bet you just stomped out, figuring a raft of flowers would fix everything. You stupid ninny." I shook my head as a sign of disappointment.

"I really didn't foresee this kind of complication when I asked you to escort me. Uh-huh, I think this calls for a bauble."

I gave him a moment to digest all this, then gleefully poked him in the ribs, with nary a thought to black ice.

"Huh? Huh? I'm right, aren't I?" It was unfair of me to take such pleasure in his discomfiture. I was probably retaliating inappropriately for the humiliation of my afternoon splat. Anyway, I didn't like Ellen. She had been barely civil to me on the two occasions we had met. Although Stephen has never mentioned it, I gather that she was doing her not-so-subtle best to sever our relationship. Which is very stupid. We've been friends for too long to drop one another because of third-party demands. She should have known better. She wasn't a dewy-eyed ingenue but in her mid-thirties, the survivor of two failed marriages.

She should have realized that she was on dangerous ground if she was going to tangle with me. Empirical evidence would suggest that I have more staying power.

So I was not altogether upset at this turn of events.

"Shut up," he muttered. "It is unbecoming for a lady to gloat. And by the way, you look very becoming tonight. Great dress. Great body."

"Dirty pool. How can I keep sticking it to you if you're gonna be nice? However, as a parting thought, be aware that the departure of Ellen is nigh. No great loss."

We had just pulled up to the front of the hotel with the great fortune of not having encountered a single patch of the dreaded black ice. The quick work of a car jockey who attended to my door precluded a riposte from Stephen, so I had the last word.

I waited under the heated canopy as Stephen and the jockey, who had stars in his eyes at the prospect of piloting such a machine, engaged in a serious discussion. Most probably a warning. Beautifully cloaked people glided through the doors in total denial of the antifur lobbies. Practical people. It's easy to be antifur in California. I'm sure all their militancy would wane drastically after spending a winter in Montreal. And visiting the dying trapping settlements in the north to see the animals starving to death from overpopulation. It's not a politically correct position, but it's a pragmatic one.

One of the features of the Chateau Champlain is its sweeping staircase which allows people to make grand entrances. It's probably its only good feature. The hotel was built in the sixties and still stands out in the Montreal skyline. Local pundits have likened it to a giant cheese grater, though I consider it to be a grumpy monolith, reaching through the clouds with hundreds of frowning windows evoking displeasure at their surroundings. The sullen panes trumpet that nothing wonderful or magical could ever occur inside, announcing their displeasure to the world. The hotel mainly services business travelers whom I always imagine to be frantically engaged in lackluster, sullen trysts, trying desperately to compensate for the enervating windows that frame their every vista.

I banged my knee as we went through the revolving doors that grace so many of our public buildings in response to the elements, cracking the scab on my knee, and winced. I had had the foresight though not the deftness to envelop it in a thick bandage, which was clumsy though I hoped absorbent enough. Stephen caught my grimace and raised his eyebrows quizzically.

"I slipped on the ice. Tore up my knee."

"Surprised you landed on your knee and not your most padded part. The one with the lowest center of gravity," he said in retaliation for my having had the last word in the car. I should have known better than to believe he'd let me get away with anything. We're well-matched and well-practiced affectionate sparring mates.

We joined the queue to relinquish our coats and perform the regulation boot-shoe dance in which the most elegant and graceful of ladies is reduced to pantomime. Disencumbered, we took our place in the swift-moving reception line, smiling brightly at no one in particular. To the right of the esteemed governor-general stood Joanne, gracious and relaxed. Tonight she was the personification of the society lady who sits on endless committees and has regular manicures. Not a trace of Bobbi Berlin. The pressures of her daily routine showed not a whit as she greeted each of the five hundred guests with a personable word. The queen herself could take lessons, and I noticed that Her Majesty's representative was as impressed as I.

We proceeded to cocktails, where Stephen and I mingled, banalities tripping easily off our tongues. We work well as a team, having honed the skill at all the functions I had been compelled to attend in my past life. We could do it without ever being accused of being vapid, which is more than I can say about the myriad I prattled to. The best thing is, I forget everything anyone says as soon as I move on. It's a negligible social skill, but we're so practiced we pride ourselves in our perfection.

Sometimes Stephen and I can be insufferable.

When the lights flickered in signal, we entered the main hall and searched out our table. The normally glitzy ballroom with its hideous chandeliers and heinous carpeting had been transformed into an eighteenth-century chateau grand hall. Joanne's committee must have worked like demons. The lighting was now subdued, emanating mostly from the thousands of candles scattered about. The flower arrangements were simple and low and the tapers high and thin, flattering everyone. Somebody must have paid the fire inspector big bucks to allow this dreamy scene, and for a brief moment I feared the triggering of the sprinkler system. Actually, it could be rather fun to watch the society belles scampering frantically, trying to save their expensive dresses and coiffures. It could degenerate into the winning entry on *America's Funniest Videos*. I have to get a life and sell my television set.

To my surprise, I was having a great time. I couldn't dance much because of my knee, but I slipped in a few and indeed felt like Cinderella. Our table was pleasant, and the music was kept at a level that enabled easy conversation.

Of course, Susan and Barry arrived late, causing a slight sensation. I'm sure she stage-managed the process, knowing the value of a good entrance. On the other hand, I'll admit it enabled them to go directly to the table and thus avoid the cocktail-hour chatter, which could have been painful. The gossip network works quickly, and I'm positive that within five minutes of their arrival the twelve people in the room who didn't already know what happened had been informed.

She looked beautiful if a little frantic, having uncharacteristically selected a sapphire blue satin slip dress that fell straight to her knees, giving her a fragile, gamine look. Susan is always in black, possessing the largest collection of black garments I've ever encountered. Her nod to color comes from her accessories, and she can be easily identified by her startlingly colored shoes, purse, or belt. The effect has become her signature, so I can only assume tonight's departure was premeditated. An "I'm not mourning, so don't offer me sappy condolences" statement.

I'd never seen Barry formally dressed before. He's generally a jeans and sweater guy with a sometimes nod to a sports jacket, if necessary. He really should do this more often, because he was devastating. The formality of the tuxedo was offset by the reckless scar, which gave him the look of a romantic swashbuckler. A soap opera talent scout would salivate, and Brad Pitt had better watch out. He politely held Susan's chair for her and then took his. As he sat, he shot his cuffs like a self-conscious child who has just learned his first grown-up maneuver and, knowing that the crowd is watching, can't wait to show it off. All with a serious face and laughing eyes. Familiar gold and lapis cuff links appeared. Susan's late father's. This was the final stroke, and I now knew for sure she was a goner. Head over heels. Hopelessly devoted. Likely irretrievable. But I had no time to ponder the implications of this latest discovery, since Jacques, Joanne's husband, asked me to dance.

In spite of my aching knee we essayed a few twirls. I could see Stephen, his head nobbing in assent as he cha-cha'd Cynthia Berkowitz into intricate patterns. He wasn't saying much, but she was, as usual. He didn't look bored, his smile not at all forced. She was a cute little bobbing sausage stuffed cheerfully into a red dress that should have been too young for her but wasn't. The conversation looked like fun, and I'd have to ask him what juicy tidbits she'd imparted. When Jacques saw me wince for the third time and knew for sure that he hadn't stepped on my foot, he suggested we sit down. Not in a hurry to return to the head table loaded with formal bigwigs, he steered me to a big soft leather couch near the bar. It was deep and comfy and once installed I didn't know if I'd be able to escape.

He got straight to the point. He earnestly begged me to get Joanne to slow down; his life was being upended. This ball seemed to have injected her with social energy, and she'd taken up the whirl in a major way. She'd booked them solid for the next month and had even bought him two new tuxedo shirts, saying the old ones would begin to look frayed due to the incipient repeated washings. She was overdoing it.

I reminded him that he'd been through this before; the behavior was spasmodic and would surely soon subside. I didn't mention that the last occurrence was the result of a short affair with her personal trainer. With a wry look he said, "Barbara, just tell her it isn't necessary. It's all right."

It was a comment made casually, but it made me uncomfortable and led me to suspect that he was aware of Joanne's philandering and resigned to it. I didn't want to think about the dynamics of the whole thing. I assured him that I would talk to her if I could ever get hold of her and, with great effort and some pain, pried myself out of the sofa and headed back on the petal-strewn carpet, which was beginning to mulch. I could see they were starting to serve dessert, and since I had paid a fortune for the tickets, I was determined to get my money's worth.

As I hobbled my way back to the table, squishing my way through the petals, I saw Joanne sequestered in a niche, not exactly hidden but not quite public, talking to an attractive man. The candlepower enhanced her features, and the fortuitous choice of floaty cream chiffon softened her generally tougher mien. She said some sharp words I didn't catch, spun on her dyed-to-match high heel and tottered unsteadily toward her husband. The man with the thick white head of hair and too-wide-lapeled tuxedo sighed and watched her departure wistfully. Another dream squelched.

Age hasn't altered Joanne's appeal; men still proposition her regularly. She's not overtly sexy, dressing as she does in trousers and loose sweaters, yet she seems to have a devastating effect on men. She hadn't exactly left a trail of broken hearts, but rather a vatful of crushed libidos. She finds it annoying, resents the presumption, and considers it an insult to her professionalism. Or at least that's what she says.

Maybe that was what Jacques had been alluding to. I certainly hoped so.

The rest of the evening was more of the same. A little dancing, lots of talking, good wine, and delicious food. I had the good fortune to encounter Cynthia Berkowitz in the ladies' room as I inspected my deteriorating bandage. She looked at the clumsy mess I had wrought and immediately took charge, commandeering the attendant's first aid kit, shoving me into a chair, and proceeding to redo me, unbidden. Her experience with fish hooks had paid off. She worked deftly, and when she was done I had a neat bandage, thinner and less bulky than my previous effort. Somehow she'd managed to make it less visible, more flexible, and sturdier. I'm always impressed with talent.

Of course all this was accompanied by a constant stream of chatter about who would and would not likely come to Frank's funeral the next day. I hadn't known that a large portion of Frank's family disliked him as much as I. They must have loaned him money.

She also told me about the latest skirmish in the escalating war between Susan and Lainie. Now that Frank was dead, I was sure that all gloves were off and the proceedings would provide us all with a great deal of entertainment for the next few months. Lainie had launched the first sally. It seems that there had been some discussion about where the mourners would adjourn after the funeral for the traditional repast. The logical place was Lainie's. She had a sizable house and could quite easily accommodate the twenty or so people who felt close enough to actually come back to the house.

Lainie went ballistic. She screeched that she would not stand for all those people tramping through her house and manhandling her precious antiques—her words exactly, according to Cynthia. "Antiques" was questionable; to me they looked more like an eclectic collection of garage sale offerings, but then I'm no expert. Whatever they are, they're ugly now and were probably just as ugly a hundred years ago.

Cynthia said Lainie remained adamant, and the poor man from the funeral home who had innocently asked the question was mortified. She insisted her threadbare rugs (not her words) wouldn't bear the trampling and her chipped dinner service (again not her words) was not intended for such casual use. She refers to her odd assortment of dishes as her "Rosenthal," thereby elevating it from the standard bric-a-brac of others.

So Susan, the future-ex-wife-widow, had offered her apartment, if only to quell that distressing voice. She couldn't have cared less if there had been no funeral at all and Frank had simply been buried quietly, but she felt Robert was entitled to the civility of a proper bereavement and also she could better control any histrionics he might be exposed to if the reception were held in his own house.

"That's probably why they got here late. She was making the arrangements for tomorrow and fighting with Lainie," Cynthia said. Then she giggled. "I'm a real star tonight. Everyone wants to ask me questions. I feel like Cinderella at the Ball."

I wonder if all little girls grow up to be women who still yearn for the magic of fairy tales and dream of being fairy princesses. I'd had the selfsame hankering just a few hours before.

"People have been pumping me to find out everything I know about Frank's being snuffed. It's been more fun putting on a grave face and saying mournfully 'I can't discuss that at this time' than it would have been blabbing. If I knew anything. And if it were any of their business. I decided on that phrase before I came and practiced in front of the mirror. Smart, eh? It's been such a giggle."

I really like Cynthia. I like her whole attitude toward life. It's all a large entertainment, and there's humor and fun to be found in everything. You just have to be able to see it.

I collected Stephen from the dance floor where he was now samba'ing with a large, tiara-topped woman I had never seen before. He introduced her as the Duchess of Somewhere, which I sincerely doubt, and I'm sure he was enormously grateful that I had arrived to rescue him from her size-eleven feet. But I didn't think grateful enough to earn me a trinket.

It was a successful evening, my first large social foray since I had rejoined the world, and as we waited for the car to be brought round—hopefully for the car jockey without nicks—I leaned into Stephen and sighed contentedly.

"You're more fun than Ellen. You're even better in bed. Or were. I had a good time, considering the foul temper I was in at the outset. Thanks," he said as he patted my ass affectionately. I was so mellow I actually liked it. Maybe I could angle for a bauble.

As we got into the unscathed car I spotted Mr. Leonine Whitehead watching us, or at least the car, enviously. Poor man. He'd had a difficult, lustful night. First Joanne, now the Rolls.

Stephen saw me to the door, kissed me pristinely, and patted my ass again. I had thought about his bed comment on the way home and once again considered reigniting the fires, but I was too exhausted tonight. It had been fabulous. We'd dazzled, we'd chatted, we'd danced, we'd eaten well, we'd drunk moderately, and I'd had my knee bandaged by an expert.

My dress fell to the floor in a puddle, and I flopped into bed with a contented sigh.

13

AFTER MUCH WAFFLING I finally decided I wasn't in mourning nor had I any great respect for Frank, so I dressed in a navy blue suit with an ankle-length skirt that covered my knee bandage. It was very dernier cri, my last major purchase before I got the sack, and so I felt it was appropriate to wear to a funeral.

I figured a nine-forty-five arrival for a ten o'clock funeral would be just about right. Since it was Sunday morning and the stores were closed, there should be no difficulty parking. I was mostly right, having neglected to factor in the imposing Catholic church that faces Paperman's funeral home, but after only one circle of the block I spotted a slot and made a beeline for it, nosing out a very irate churchgoer who had thought God had led him to this very parking space. Those who visit the dead are obviously more driven than holy rollers. I sincerely hoped he'd confess the inflammatory and downright obscene names he called me, having lowered his window in the freezing cold to make his point audible. His wife reinforced his sentiments, flipping me the bird as they drove off to seek a spot elsewhere. I chuckled at the departing digit. The whole episode cheered me enormously.

The best thing about Jewish funerals in Montreal is that they're prompt and quick. Twenty minutes to a half-hour tops before they clear the room to make space for the next influx. There aren't many Jewish funeral homes in this city, and Paperman's efficiently handles the great majority of burials from their Cote-des-Neiges Street location, famous for its dearth of parking. The whole deal is sign in, take your seat, sniffle a little at the appropriate words, and leave.

It must have been the first service of the day, as there were no leftovers littering the lobby or front stairs. While fulfilling my first and most important obligation by signing the visitor sheet, I remembered my mission. As I entered the chapel I was surprised to see that it was already almost full and people continued to pour in. I looked around for a place to cram myself, blocking traffic as I surveyed the territory. An officious but not unctuous attendant pointed me toward the front and gave me a gentle shove to get me moving. Maybe it was my funereal fashion garb that earned me the honor of being directed to the second of the two rows in the front marked "Reserved." It was a good seat, as the crowd was now mostly behind me, thereby eliminating the need for social chatter with the many familiar faces I recognized on my solitary journey down the aisle. All I had to do was hunch my shoulders in mock bereavement, and I would be left alone.

But I couldn't even fake it. Before me lay Frank in his closed, polished mahogany coffin, which must have set Susan back a tidy sum. Lainie sure wouldn't have sprung for such a nice piece of wood. Since the coffin was closed, I couldn't check to see if he was wearing his hair. I had no feeling of loss. I disliked Frank too much at this point to even pretend sorrow, and I was still pissed off that he'd dragged me into his tawdry departure. His legacy of two kilos of heroin secreted in my apartment didn't help either. In life I usually managed to avoid him, but in death he'd landed the final "gotcha."

I was surprised by the large turnout. The folding side doors had been peeled back to accommodate the overflow, and by five minutes to ten every seat in the house was taken and the side aisles were filled with somber standers. The only available seats were in the two "Reserved" rows, where few dared venture, and I sat virtually alone. I don't think the lack of people up front signified any great love or respect for Frank, the dearly departed, it's just that nobody would own up to being close enough to him to merit a favored place.

Yet they all wanted to be present. A relatively young man of their acquaintance had met with a violent death, and curiosity abounded. The hordes massed as though their very presence might illuminate the mystery. This wasn't a furtive AIDS burial, it was a splashy murder with untold elements of violence and excitement. This was a white-collar crime crowd, leaning more to insider trading and income tax evasion. Frank's funeral was the closest that most of these people would come to living a television experience. However remote, there existed the possibility of rubbing shoulders with a murderer, and the atmosphere was more electric than somber.

I spotted many revelers from the previous night who had traded their finery for sober black but were still dressed to the nines. There was even a scattering of hats with delicate black veils, to theatrical effect. Considering my own attire I wasn't one to point fingers, but as I waited for the procedure to get started so we could get it over and get the hell out of there, it did cross my mind to augment my depleted income by writing a piece about the correct attire for a funeral of the larcenous dead, using this crowd for visuals. There was an absolute fortune on these backs. Perhaps if we were to knock off a few more marginal people, we could turn the economy around and finally put a halt to the recession. I don't think it's proper to wear the same thing to consecutive funerals.

Joanne insinuated herself into the pew beside me. Dressed

in charcoal pants, brightly printed silk shirt, and slate blue blazer she called to mind neither last night's froth nor today's requisite dignity. She looked cheerful and very much alive, having topped her outfit off with electric-blue-framed glasses, and I heartily approved. Joanne was being Joanne.

"Great seat. Thanks for saving me one."

"Hi," I said surprised. "I didn't expect to see you here. Especially after last night. By the way, it was fabulous, and it seemed like everyone was having a great time."

"Well, it was a great financial success. We raised more money this year than last—the year, you will note, that I wasn't in charge. Problem is, I'll probably be sucked into it again next year, and it's a lot of work. Thanks for saying it was fun, although I have doubts about your ability to rate things social, since your most recent interactive experiences have involved the dead, the police, and navels named Wayne."

"Thanks for reminding me. That isn't an episode I like to dwell on. What's happening there, anyway? Are you sure you want to go through with this? Do you realize the possible consequences?" I became more and more agitated as I remembered that other involvement. Pietr's warnings loomed large in my head; my life was complicated enough with Susan and her woes and illegal substances in my possession. The whole thing made me dizzy.

"No way you're backing out on me," she answered as she grabbed my arm and squeezed. Hard. "You must see this through to the end. The big meeting with the big boss is set for Thursday night. Look, we'll discuss this later. It's not exactly the right time," she said, loosening the grip. I would have black-and-blue fingerprints on me.

"Big turnout, eh?" she continued breezily. "I had no idea Frank knew so many people. They certainly can't all be his friends."

I gracefully allowed Joanne to change the subject, since winning an argument with her is not easy in the best of conditions and the second row of a funeral was not the optimal situation. I'm well aware that Joanne will never back away from a public scene. One of us had to be the adult.

"Maybe he's screwed them all," I said, warming to the topic.

"Judging from the number of women here, I'd say literally and figuratively."

"Ugh! Can you imagine actually screwing Frank?" My whole body puckered at the thought. "Those liver lips slobbering all over you?"

"Good point. Ask Susan if he knew how to use those lips. Did they work like some large suction cup? And was his tongue just as big?"

"Joanne! We're in the second row!"

"Oooh," she said, shuddering. "I can't decide if the image is a turn-on or disgusting."

"But it's a huge turnout. And if it's not for sex, it's likely for money. You're the brain, and you're good at math. Let's try to estimate how much he's taken from all these people. Maybe they all came to see him actually planted so they can finally write off the debt, moral or physical."

"What's most amazing is that these schmucks kept financing him. I can't imagine so many people being so stupid. Well, well, well," she said incredulously. "Look who's coming. And heading straight for you. A gentleman caller."

I whipped my head around to see Detective-Sergeant Gregory Allard standing stiffly at the end of the row.

"Good morning, Miss Simons, Miss Cowan. May I sit with you? There doesn't seem to be any room left."

"Sure. Scoot over, Barbara," Joanne said, giving me a shove with her hip. At least she'd laid off my still-tender arm. She orchestrated the seating arrangements so that when we were all settled, Greg was somewhat uncomfortably wedged between me and Joanne. Now there was no possibility of returning to the subject of Wayne, and I'm sure she was delighted.

Someday I'm going to have the occasion to get her, and I'll make it good.

"Wouldn't you be more effective at the back, scanning the room? And what the hell are you doing here anyway? Is there something I should know?" Joanne peppered, donning her reporter's cap.

"No, Ms. Cowan." Either his tendency toward formality or her intimidation finally evinced the proper form of address. "There is nothing you should know, as there is nothing I know."

Joanne rolled her eyes at that one.

"I came to catch a glimpse of the family, and when I spotted you I hoped you could place them for me," he smiled at me. A big crinkly smile; just for me.

"They should be filing in any second now. They're all in a room off to the side waiting for the proceedings to begin. Here they come. I'll fill you in," I said obligingly.

Well, he looked good this morning. The banker at leisure. Gray flannel pants, charcoal blazer, white shirt, and colorful silk tie for that debonair touch. I assumed he wasn't wearing sneakers today, since he had on overshoes and I don't think they make them big enough to cover Reeboks. And he had smiled at me.

"First in, of course, is Lainie Herman, Frank's sister, followed by Phillip, her husband. He's in real estate. Then Robert, Susan's son, and of course you remember Susan. The second row has some aunts and uncles I've never met. They're from Ottawa, where Frank is from originally. His parents passed away within six months of each other a few years ago. It's not much of a family. Never was," I explained with sadness, which surprised me. Maybe if he had come from a less dysfunctional family Frank might have been a fully functional, live person.

The aunts and uncles looked like they were present under duress, exhibiting no great sadness. They were probably annoyed that they'd had to drive two and a half hours to Montreal for this funeral of a nephew for whom they had little regard. Frank had likely hit them up for money too.

The officiating rabbi made the requisite noises about Frank. He didn't have much material to work with but managed to acquit himself adequately. As a rule, he was known to be pompous with his congregation, but on this occasion he was gentle and sympathetic. I commended him for his unexpected sensitivity. Robert sat stoic, periodically glancing at Barry, who sat not with the official mourners but in the row in front of us, dressed formally in a black suit, looking dark and brooding and surely fueling the speculative gossip that would emerge from this event. Not fully understanding the import of what was happening, Robert was doing his very best to be a good little soldier, having recognized the solemnity of the service; the rabbi directed a great portion of his remarks in his direction. Susan held Robert around the shoulders reassuringly, and her gaze rarely wandered from him.

"Is he the boyfriend?" Greg whispered, indicating Barry with a tilt of his head.

"Uh-huh. Not bad, eh?" Joanne whispered back. "Hey, which one is Bimbo? Point her out to me," she ordered as she reached across to poke me.

"Yes, is Celine here?"

"Shh!" came a chorus from behind us. They were right. This was neither the time nor the place for conversation, but talking to each other was infinitely preferable to listening to someone extol Frank's nonexistent virtues.

If it was a trap, I didn't fall into it. I didn't dare scan the gathering in search of her since I supposedly wouldn't recognize her. Likely she was hiding at the back, the only genuine mourner in the bunch.

"How should I know? I've never seen her," I answered, annoyance flooding me. I turned to my supposed protector and whispered, "You didn't call me back."

"Sorry. I was out on a case."

"Shh!" came the chorus again, drowning out my protestation that I thought *I* was his case. It's a good thing the chorus was voluble; it was a stupid thing to say. Greg surely had more than one case, and it would only have fueled Joanne. However, this time we attracted the attention of the rabbi, who shot us a decidedly unholy look. We shut up. The rabbi wrapped it up eloquently, the cantor sang the blessings melodically, and mercifully it was over.

The casket led the procession down the center aisle, attended by Phillip-the-brother-in-law, two uncles, and three pallbearers I'd never seen before. Must be cousins.

"I promised Susan I'd go to the cemetery. Come with me?" I asked Joanne. Or rather begged. A dreary, freezing graveside ritual was not something I relished.

"Nah. It's too cold. It's below zero out there, and I have to get my battery jumped, since my car was dead this morning and I had to shell out money on a taxi to come to this event. I phoned but you'd already left. I feel I've already gone beyond the call of duty, so I'll just take a cab back home and get Jacques to give me a boost."

"Please," I whined. "I'll drive you home after, and I even have jumper cables in the trunk."

"Big deal. So do most people who live in this city, although I am a little surprised you do, knowing your garage-to-garage winter experience. But okay, I guess I'll go. It's the only way I can ensure that Frank is put away permanently and can no longer annoy me."

"I didn't know you hated him too."

"Well, he once came after me for a celebrity endorsement poster. It was when he was into swimwear, and he wanted a picture of me in a bikini. Yeah, right. Excellent for my image as a serious journalist. When I refused, he tried to go over my head to the station manager, promising big advertising bucks. The slime."

She'd never mentioned this before, and just the thought of Joanne in skimpy attire plastered on an auto shop wall made me giggle, earning me another poke in the ribs.

"Decorum," she hissed as she turned to Greg and asked, "Will you be joining us? I could use the time to interrogate you."

And Detective-Sergeant Allard actually blushed.

There was history here that I would drag out of Joanne if it meant smashing her glasses, or better, shoving her into Frank's grave so they could spend all eternity together.

Regaining his composure, he said, "Sorry I won't be able to make it. I have to get back to the station." He turned his full attention to me, which made me only slightly weak in the knees, and said, "I'm very sorry I didn't return your call, but I will speak to you later." He removed the skullcap that he had acquired at the door and inspected it, debating whether to just leave it on the pew or appropriate it. In the end he stuffed it into his pocket, looking furtively around for possible witnesses to this heist. The rosiness returned to his cheeks, making his eyes all the bluer.

As we'd been near the front, we were among the last to reach the door, so we had to hurry to the car. We made it in time to join the funeral cortege just as it pulled out. It was short. We passed the so-called mourners who dotted the front steps awaiting the departure of the hearse with mock reverence. The frozen condensation of their collective breath gave the scene an eerie look befitting the occasion. A few early arrivals for the ten-forty-five threaded their way through the crowd toward the double doors, heads bowed. Business was good at Paperman's today. Slowly the procession crawled through the frigid streets to the cemetery nestled into the side of the hill that we Montrealers refer to as a mountain.

It was painful going, crunching over the frozen packed snow in my too-thin-soled boots. I hadn't taken into account that the subzero temperature would be accompanied by a crisp northerly wind, which made the whole thing unbearable. I stood there shivering, stamping my feet in an effort to retain some feeling. Most of the others present were likewise engaged, and we looked like Indians doing a little burial dance.

"The windchill factor must make this forty below, and you're gonna pay for making me come here," the ex-weathergirl bitched.

The elements contributed to the speed with which the interment was processed. Frank was mechanically lowered, and Robert threw in the first handful of frozen earth, which made a decided clunk as it hit the coffin. Robert recoiled at the sound, and Susan wrapped her arms tightly around him, trying to envelop him in warmth. Barry stood faithfully at Susan's side, looking as though he should be elsewhere and trying not to shiver. He wasn't suitably dressed for the climate, and I think cemetery detail was something he mistakenly thought he could avoid. His sneeze punctuated the end of the service.

As soon as the proceedings were deemed concluded, Robert squirmed out of Susan's grasp and ran to me.

"Auntie Barbara, Mummy says Daddy's at peace, which means he's resting until we get to see him again in heaven."

If Frank was in heaven—which I sincerely doubted, since I do believe in a just God—I didn't want to go there, but I didn't tell Robert this. Joanne snorted and looked away as I avoided the topic by taking his hand and heading back toward the cars.

"Can I go with you? You have a neat car, and I hate Uncle Joe. He keeps punching me in the arm and telling me what a lucky boy I am that Daddy was my daddy. How can I be lucky if my daddy is dead? I don't understand what that means, and I don't like it when he makes me sit on his lap. Please?" He wasn't whining, but his apprehension was obvious as he faced me with his hands on his nonexistent snowsuited hips.

Memories of Oprah and her bad-hair guests recounting childhood abuse at the hands of family members flooded my mind. Robert was likely overreacting but who knew for sure, and now was not the time to probe further.

"Susan," I called over. "Robert's coming with me. Is that okay?"

She nodded her assent, and I turned back to find Robert and Joanne pitching snowballs at the tombstones. One small child and a rather overgrown one.

"You're both babies," I said, exasperated. I could see Lainie glaring at me from her post beside Phillip. She never lets go of him for a second. I guess if you look and sound like Lainie, the fear that your husband will vanish with a more palatable woman is understandable. It's a real and definite possibility.

"Come on, you guys. It's freezing out here, and anyway, I think if you knock over a headstone the ghost of the person inside comes out to haunt you."

Robert stopped cold, looking from me to Joanne, who shook her head in rebuttal and signaled with her foot. Not the fool his father was, he received the message loud and clear on his juvenile antennae, and they both rounded on me and lobbed their balls. Figuring that there was now no way to make a dignified exit, I yelled, "Last one to the car sits in the back!"—in my two-seater, no small feat. We all tore off apace, and I nearly had to cede the driver's seat to Joanne until she slipped and fell into a convenient snowbank. Robert and I found this hilarious and proceeded to attempt to give her a snowbath. We'd completely forgotten where we were, and appropriate behavior eluded us. It was nice to hear Robert laugh.

The tsk-tsking of the passing rabbi brought us back to the present. He had resumed his officious stance and saw three individuals being disrespectful, not a child trying to maintain his delight in life. We did however heed his signal, and Robert and I helped brush Joanne off, then filed off to the car, suppressing giggles the whole time.

Joanne was shivering so much from the melted snow Robert

had forced down her neck that he felt guilty and generously offered her his rightly won front seat. He crawled gracelessly onto the back ledge, which was more suited to a body his size anyway.

"So you'll drop him at Lainie's and then help me jump my car?" Joanne inquired, unbuttoning her coat to allow the warmth from the heater to penetrate the chill.

"Not Lainie's. We're going to Susan's."

"Susan's! What's wrong with Lainie's? She's his sister," she said with great indignation.

"Nothing. Not now," I said to ward off further discussion, indicating Robert with my head. He was happily rubbing his face in Joanne's fur collar.

"Okay. Message received. Drop him off at home."

"No!" came a muffled cry from the back. "You have to stay with me, Auntie Barbara. You're supposed to be taking care of me!"

Children are adept at pushing the guilt button. Joanne's dead battery was the perfect excuse for not spending more time with Frank's family, especially my particular least favorite, Lainie. But there was dear Robert, nuzzling mink and insisting I be his protector.

"Joanne—"

"Never mind. He got to me too." She turned to face him. "You do pathetic very well." To me she said, "Drop me at home and get on with it."

At last I had the advantage. An eight-year-old kid had furnished me the opportunity to thwart Joanne. For once I would not be at her bidding. But I still didn't get the last word in. As we pulled up to her door, she got out and delivered her sally.

"Thanks for the lift. I'll see you soon. I know Wayne's looking forward to it. And do send Greg my regards when you speak to him later. You whisper too loud," she said as she slammed the door.

I winced at the thunk and drove on to Susan's slowly, ruminating on my obligations and the messes I was into on two fronts. Robert hummed.

The visitor parking spaces in front of Robert's building were all full. For an instant I thought this would be my perfect out and I could just drop Robert off and split, but it wasn't to be. He directed me into the indoor garage and began major negotiations with the teenage attendant. This involved a lot of hero worship on Robert's part and a lot of preening on the other kid's. He treated Robert as a nuisance, but clearly enjoyed every second of the adulation. I was personally escorted to a choice space, the owner being in Florida with the rest of the intelligent population, and we got out and made our way to the bank of elevators, waving to our abettor all the way.

Upstairs we took off our boots and added them to the jumble that littered the hallway. The coats were dumped on Robert's bed, which was already buried.

"Hey, if Uncle Joe wants a hug you can hide under this pile. He'll never find you."

It was the wrong thing to say. I'd meant to be light and breezy, but a look of genuine apprehension crossed his face, and he reached for my hand.

"I'm sorry. That was a stupid thing to say. If Uncle Joe comes anywhere near you, come find me. I'll take care of it. I promise. And I'll keep my eye on him. Don't worry," I said, ruffling his caramel hair.

Children are so easily assuaged. He let go of my hand and bounced out of the room, having entrusted his safety to me.

The tour-de-ville involved in dropping Joanne off had caused us to be latecomers, and I headed into a living room full of people bearing overladen plates. An enormous buffet had been set up on the dining room table, and liberties were being taken. The cold had piqued appetites, although I did notice some faces that had not been visible at the cemetery. The gathering consisted of a collection of aunts and uncles, including some of Susan's family and Lainie's friends. I was the only one of Susan's friends present, but then I also qualify as family.

Bad luck. The first person I encountered without a full mouth was Lainie, who blocked my way, all narrow and pinched. Her pointed elbows projected through her black sweater, and her bony knees protruded below her black, slack skirt. Black was clearly not her color, accentuating the sallowness of her skin. Standing appointments at the hairdresser, manicurist, and electrolysis helped a little, but there was always the drift of incipient fuzz spreading across her chin, now accentuated by the black garb. Her face was the antithesis of her brother's. Tight and puckered as opposed to open and fleshy. Frank, in all his clownishness, was the better looking of the two.

I'd never actively disliked Lainie until recently, when she'd tried to aggrandize herself at my expense at a mutual friend's third wedding. It's a long, boring, stupid story, but the upshot was that she'd disgraced herself and had made enemies. My friends are loyal.

I opted for polite but wary. It was, after all, her brother's funeral, and I do have respect for ritual. I couldn't very well snub her or be seen to avoid confrontation or back away. I can be as childish as the next ten-year-old, and the bitch wasn't going to get the better of me.

Lainie is ten times the control freak I am, but she hasn't learned the social grace of camouflage. It would be difficult for her anyway, since her dissonant, grating voice raises hackles. Poor girl was pathetic in her incarnation as the Wicked Bitch of the West. She hadn't been that bad before I'd decided to hate her; then she'd merely been a dismissible annoyance. I'd gone from passive to active.

"Barbara," she squawked, "I must speak with you. Come into the kitchen."

Without waiting for a reply, she grabbed my arm and propelled me through the swinging door to our destination. Her grip was surprisingly strong for such scrawny fingers, and it was in the exact place where Joanne had landed her strongest pokes. We exploded into the small space, to the surprise of the three maids who were laboring to keep up with the flow of food and dirty dishes.

"Attention, attention!" She clapped her hands in accompaniment. "You ladies will now excuse us for a few moments. Go empty ashtrays or serve food or something. Now!" And she clapped her hands once more to punctuate her order. In the small space it made a loud and fearsome crack.

Either they were afraid that the next clap would be about their bodies, or they were being well enough paid to suffer this indignity. In any case, they dropped everything and filed silently out of the room, eyes downcast. Well aware that every circle has its gossip network, I savored the thought of Lainie trying to get help for her next party. But then I remembered her precious antiques and realized with sad disappointment that the occasion would never present itself. It was an amazing performance: it wasn't even her house, and she had assumed command. I decided I'd waited too long to start hating her. All those years wasted in indifference.

She backed me against the refrigerator and came directly to the point. "What did Susan take from Frank's apartment that night? Where did the money go?"

I was appalled and frightened. Was she aware of the heroin? Were they—whoever they were—in it together? I could envision her manipulating her brother into a treacherous situation, but I couldn't visualize her actually pulling the trigger. Or maybe if I rethought the situation I could. After all, Frank hadn't been expected to die, and she does have huge feet. Of the two siblings she was the smarter, if not the more likable. And since Frank was detestable, that's saying a lot.

"Susan didn't take anything," I said in technical truth. I had taken the something. My brain was trying to work, but black fog had taken over. Celine had also mentioned money. Maybe money was a euphemism. If it was, I was in big trouble.

"Frank always had piles of cash on him, and he must have kept it somewhere. I want it. I consider it mine since he owes me a bundle."

"You and the rest of the assembled crowd," I answered with no great grace. "Get in line. I don't know nothing about no money," I said in a bad imitation of Butterfly McQueen and an attempt at levity.

She's always been short on humor.

"Susan," she snorted. "She'd never give me a penny." And rightly so, I thought, neither would I. "All she's good for is spending Frank's money. Grieving widow, hah!" She snorted again. An underfed, ugly horse. "What about the will? What's in it? She won't tell me anything, and even Phillip couldn't get it out of her." She must be more self-aware than I've given her credit for; realizing her own artlessness, she had sent in the troops in the form of Phillip, affable enough but too much of a Milquetoast to carry any weight.

"Lainie, what the hell do you want from me? If you have any problems, speak to Susan or Frank's lawyer. I know nothing, and I wouldn't tell you if I did."

She didn't hear a word I said.

"I know there's money. I just know it. Susan's going to steal it all. That Barry's advising her, and by the look of him I can tell he's trying to get his hands on it too. He had the nerve to ask me which bank Frank kept his safe-deposit box in. Susan never loved Frank. She just wanted to take him for all he was worth." Her voice rose by the octave throughout the tirade. Another sentence, and only the dogs would hear her.

"Get away from me," I said, pushing her bony shoulder to clear a path. "You should try harder to hide your true nature. It's as ugly as you are," I said in what I hoped was a disgusted tone. I hadn't had a good catfight since high school, and I was beginning to warm to the idea. "Your brother Frank never made an honest dollar in his short life. He never spent money that wasn't someone else's. He was just better at getting it than you are. He at least had some charm, you only have venom." At this, I shoved her hard into the stove and glided triumphantly through the swinging doors. Right into Phillip.

"Your wife is in there," I said, motioning behind me.

He impeded my progress and took me semi-gently by the arm. The whole family must practice block and tackle on weekends. They also have a propensity for arm grabbing.

"Don't be too hard on her, Barbara. She's under a lot of stress. I told her not to approach you, but she's convinced that Susan and you took something from that apartment. She says that Susan intimated as much, and she feels that it's hers since she's been so supportive of Frank in his difficult time lately."

A loaded monologue. I doubt Susan hinted anything after my dire warnings. She swore she hadn't told Barry, and she'd surely confide in him before Lainie. What was it that Lainie knew or suspected? Or did Susan decide to exacerbate their tenuous relationship by dropping broad hints, therefore sending Lainie into her shrew act? And what kind of support had she been giving Frank? If he was flush enough to buy a Rolex, why did he need money?

Once again I'd acted before I thought. Lainie could have furnished some information on Frank's recent activities, but I'd slammed that door shut. If I was ever going to find anything out, I'd have to tone down the physical aggression and not lead with my mouth. This job was harder than I had anticipated, and the circle of suspects kept widening. It was all very confusing.

Phillip's arm was still resting on my shoulder when Lainie opened the door into my back as she exited the kitchen. One look at us in that intimate position was enough to launch her again, so heeding my own advice about antagonistic behavior, I slipped away without responding and left him to appease her.

It would be a very long time before she would think of me with any grace, much less affection. I tried to assess if she could do me any real harm, but since I was already unemployed she couldn't threaten my livelihood, and her friends are marginal in my life. Which was too bad, since I might have been able to pump them for information if I'd handled myself better.

I decided I'd had enough of this unfortunate day and headed back to Robert's room to retrieve my coat and get the hell out of there. Only to be waylaid by Susan's mother.

She was a perfect over-the-hill china doll. Two splotched circles of rouge adorned her cheeks, metallic blue eye shadow embellished her eyes, spidery black false eyelashes crawled across her hooded lids, and carmine red enlivened her lips. Once known for her beauty, she was making a desperate effort to extend her halcyon days. Coquettishness is not attractive in a seventy-something squishy woman. Relations between her and her daughter have always been strained and fraught with emotion. I suspect a great deal of competition for Susan's father's attention years earlier, but I've given up trying to delve into my friends' and particularly their parents' psyches. Formative years are long gone, and the personalities are now gelled into adulthood, so it's better to accept them for what they are now. Or not.

After effusive greetings accompanied by a well-padded hug, she asked after my parents. She and my mother call each other daily in the summer, but since it was the dead of winter and my parents had absconded to Florida for the duration, she hadn't heard from her. Nor had she called. In the battle of the penurious it is a toss-up as to who is the tighter. Susan and I have spent many a hilarious afternoon relating Bitty and Sally stories. Yes, she's called Bitty, although lately she's begun requesting to be called by her given name. When she reached seventy-five she realized she was a tad too mature for Bitty and elected for more dignity. Maybe at eighty she'd twig to the makeup overload.

Throughout the exchange of pleasantries and chitchat about my parents, she seemed to be looking past me. Either there was something compelling happening behind me, or she was smashed. Finally I turned to see what captured her attention and followed her gaze to Barry, leaning against the wall, drink in hand, taking in the whole scene. His expression was one of benign amusement and his dark eyes were in constant motion, sweeping the room. He looked gorgeous.

No longer feigning politesse, Bitty now stared at him openly. She sighed like a deflating inner tube.

"Isn't he marvelous. Such a dashing young man, and so good to Susan. I understand he has a successful business."

Which I translated to mean: He's good-looking, he's Susan's junior, he's rich, and if Susan plays her cards right all that can be ours. She really thought "mine," but she's an old lady, so I try to be generous.

I'd have deemed it impossible, but the morning was becoming *more* distasteful. Whatever happened to dignity? Only Susan was handling herself well, circulating among the assembled, making polite and caring noises, with Robert glued to her side doing his good little soldier routine adorably. Well, at least Bitty's daughter and grandson had manners.

I excused myself and made it to the coat room without being further accosted. Cynthia Berkowitz stood at the foot of the bed, staring at the tangled pile. When she saw me she broke into a sunny smile.

"Awful, isn't it. No one in there gives a shit about Frank. They all just want to know who gets his money and how much of it there is. Schmucks. If he had any money, Frank wouldn't owe them all, would he? How's the knee?"

Leave it to Cynthia, the supposed bubblehead, to cut to the heart of the matter and astutely sum everything up.

"Much better, thanks. Root out my coat and let me out of here."

"I'm coming with you. Could you try to sorta hide me or something so I can avoid Bitty? She grilled me about the will. Like I'd know anything. Everyone seems to think I know something because I was the only person in this room who was nice to Frank. I know he was an idiot, but he could be charming and fun and my kids loved him."

It was the nicest eulogy of the day, and certainly the most sincere.

We unearthed our coats, dropping a bunch onto the floor in the process. When I saw that Lainie's was one of the crumpled coats on the ground, I refused to let Cynthia pick it up. It seemed inadequate revenge for a morning of torture, but it would have to suffice.

Shielding Cynthia as best I could, we made it to the front door.

When I finally got home after giving Cynthia a lift, I was astonished to find it was only one-fifteen. It felt lifetimes later. Happy to be back in my safe haven, I needed to indulge in something mindless to restore equanimity and give me the opportunity to sort out the information I'd absorbed recently. I settled on washing and ironing the silk shirts I didn't dare entrust to Mme Jacqueline.

As I sprayed and pressed, I came to the logical conclusion that there were too many interested parties, and a closet full of heroin would do nothing to enhance my continued safety. Never mind what Joanne was dragging me into. I wondered when I had last updated my will. And if I got knocked off, what would people think when they discovered two kilos of smack in my apartment? The same thing I thought when I found it. For the first time, I had the sense to be afraid.

Maybe confession would alleviate the terrors. I picked up the phone to call Greg and recount the episode of Celine. But that's as far as I intended to go. The heroin would remain Susan's and my little secret for a while longer, and I prayed fervently that Susan was behaving accordingly. I'd call her later to give her a pep talk and remind her whose life she could be endangering. I know I hadn't done much with it lately, but I did have hopes for the future.

Once again he was out. I left my name and number, wondering if he would ever call back.

I went to dinner with Stephen, where we dished about last night and I regaled him with an embellished version of my conversation with Lainie. I had lots of fun and lots of wine and went home and fell into bed alone but no longer frightened. Just a little horny.

14

THE RADIO JOLTED me from a pleasant dream that evaporated the moment it clicked on, announcing another freezing day before I had a chance to reach over and snap it off. This time my thoughts of moving ran to the island of Mustique, where I knew no one and could cavort with princes. I stretched languidly, trying to recapture the lazy mood that had preceded the unwanted intrusion, but to no avail. Free-floating anxiety filled all the space around me, and before I surrendered to complete panic I got up and headed for the shower, where I sometimes do my most creative thinking. As the warm water pelted me, I tried to formulate a specific game plan for the day. Yesterday I had lost too many opportunities because my mouth engaged before my brain; I couldn't afford a repeat performance. My month of solitary confinement had slowed down my thought processes, and now I was suddenly embroiled in a bunch of mayhem and needed to think clearly.

The water washed away the apprehension and soothed me. I stood there until I felt the onset of prune skin and then reluctantly turned it off. It felt so safe and mindless in there.

Dressed in my jeans uniform, having exchanged the regulation T-shirt for a wool turtleneck sweater in deference to the February cold, I began my day's adventures by calling Susan to arrange to drop by. In the kitchen I made toast with the bread I had bought on my first foray, which was now stale. I refused to dwell on the metaphor.

For my amusement and pleasure I decided against the newspaper and opted for the news on television. So much more concise; today just felt like a concise day. I wanted facts, not editorials.

Gregory Allard surfaced in the corners of my mind as I listened to the litany of overnight murders. Two women and one man had perished. One bullet, one knife, and a bathtub. Normally, most of this would have only caught my peripheral attention, but my recent close association with murder had made me more attuned to my brutal surroundings. I wondered if Gregory had caught any of these cases, which would mean he'd have even less time for mine—I considered Frank's death my case. I decided I didn't care. Thinking about him would only impede the day's schedule, and I was determined to stick to the agenda.

I used to think I lived in a safe city. After lecturing myself, I decided I still did. Compared to Detroit and even Toronto the Good, Montreal is pretty tame. Most of the major violence is labeled as a "settling of accounts," although lately the scorekeeper seemed busier than usual. On my night of infamy, only Frank had bought it. Perhaps his murder would set off an explosion in the crime rate, although I hadn't as yet met anyone who was truly sorry he was dead, except perhaps Robert and maybe Cynthia, so I couldn't really believe anyone would hasten to even his score. Even Celine and Lainie seemed more interested in the financial implications of his death.

Maybe it was just open season on fools, as supported by the case of death by bathtub.

I'd spent so much time at Susan's lately that the doorman

and I were on friendly terms. Ever since I'd been kind enough to ask him how he was doing in school, we were best buddies. He seemed to think I was clairvoyant, but it was just my detecting skills honed to a fine edge and the large pile of textbooks that surrounded him at his station. If he could miss the obvious that easily, I feared for his success in the career of his choice. When he told me he was in law school, I quaked for his clients.

Sucking up to doormen has its rewards, and he motioned for me to leave the car in the clearly marked No Parking space right by the door.

I did the elevator trip and performed the boot dance perfunctorily. It's a rite so often repeated it becomes part of you, an automatic repetitive ritual from the middle of November to the middle of March. We must be cretins to live here.

Susan had warned me she wouldn't be in, so the housekeeper answered the door as expected and grudgingly allowed me access. She didn't say a word, just opened the door, nodded to no one in particular, and turned around and walked away. Going under the assumption that she meant for me to enter, I headed for the living room.

There was no evidence of yesterday's gourmand repast in sight. Not a dirty ashtray, no crumbs on the carpet. I can never figure out how people manage to maintain such immaculate surroundings. I would pursue the quest for this knowledge with diligence now that I had more time to wreak havoc on my home.

The housekeeper silently reappeared, brandishing an envelope. Another brown manila envelope, but this one benign. She did a quick surveillance of the room to see if anything had been disturbed or pilfered and seemed disappointed to find everything untouched. If we'd been standing in the dining room, I wouldn't have been surprised to find her counting the silver spoons before she allowed me to leave.

"Mrs. Porter is not at home."

Yes, she is, I thought. You've tied her up and are holding

her hostage. You're performing evil and cruel experiments on her. I didn't say that. I didn't say anything, not trusting my mouth. She really was obnoxious, and she obviously hated me. Although I hate to admit it, she scared me.

She handed me the envelope and admonished, "I'll expect this back in one hour. No later."

I took it meekly, and before I even had time to stuff it into my bag she put one hand on my shoulder and propelled me back to the front door and escorted me to what she considered the right side of the sill. I turned to say something polite and untruthful and was greeted by the door slamming in my face. It happens often on television, but I was totally unprepared for the shock of the insult.

I stood frozen, perplexed. I'd never offended this harpie in any way except perhaps to poke fun at her nocturnal garb, and I doubt Susan had repeated that to her. I think she somehow felt I was responsible for the mess she'd had to clean up last night. She should have seen the mess at Frank's. It was beyond my fathoming, and since I had only an hour with my manila envelope, it was time to hop to. I sighed under the weight of the acrimony and put my boots back on.

She'd effectively terrorized me with her dire warnings, and the sixty-minute limit resounded in my head. Although I knew there was nothing mysterious or deadly in there, I handled the envelope gingerly, grasping it by the edges so as to avoid touching and possibly detonating it in the enclosed space. The elevator got smaller and smaller as it headed down to the shopping concourse. Three more floors and I might have been blown to smithereens. She'd really spooked me. When I got to the bottom unscathed, I put my imagination in check so I could get on with it.

I headed straight for the drugstore, which has a photocopier available for public use at a dime a pop. Now that I no longer had an office, such locations of previously taken for granted pilfered services are valuable information.

On checking the contents of the envelope I discovered there were sixteen pages to copy, and the machine took exact change only. Two choices. Return the lists later than the prescribed hour so I could run home and raid my cache of loose change, or try to cajole dimes from the crater-faced teenager behind the counter.

It took two candy bars that I didn't need but would eat anyway to get the requisite number of dimes, and time was marching on. Pizza Face had an attitude, and it was only because of my ineffable charm and the threat of the imminent arrival of Immigration that he conceded to give me my change in dimes. He sullenly checked the register and was thrilled to find there were only two dimes in it, so he figured he'd won and couldn't help me after all. But I'm tough when I'm single-minded. My threats escalated to those of major violence. In the back of my head I wondered if I could get Wayne's boys to pay this guy a visit. Now that I personally knew some bona fide heavies I pressed my claim with vigour. It was great; completely cowed, he scuttled off to the back to return with the needed change. He couldn't look me straight in the face as he handed the dimes over, and I loved it.

If that old bat upstairs could terrorize me, the least I could do was pass it on. I had never realized I was such a bully. And I resented to the ends of the earth laying out my hard-earned money for Frank. Even if it was only a buck sixty and two thousand calories, it rankled. I considered keeping a ledger, and when this was over I could take it out in heroin, but then I'd never know how to convert it to cash. Maybe Wayne. He seemed to be cropping up in my thoughts a lot. Scary.

Twenty-five minutes later I was back pounding on Susan's door. The machine had eaten three extra dimes that it refused to release even after a series of well-placed kicks. My toe hurt like hell, and someone was going to pay. Zitface had grinned through the whole charade, which hurt even more. After I calmed down, I realized that it was Frank I was angry with, and since he was dead there wasn't much I could do about it. No more expending useless energy and doing myself bodily injury. He wasn't worth it.

This time there was to be no advance announcement by the doorman. If Susan could sneak into my building, I could repay the effort in kind. I reentered at the concourse level on the heels of a grocery-bag-laden matron. It was probably the maid's day off and she was unused to all this toting, because she was not balanced and foodstuffs were threatening to spill at any moment. I gallantly came to her rescue as she fished in her purse for the keys. This, coupled with my most ingratiating smile, gained me easy access. She studied me as we ascended in silence, memorizing everything about me to report to the police if she should hear of a burglary in the building. I dazzled my teeth at her as the elevator reached Susan's floor, and she breathed a sigh of relief as I got off. I was not stalking her.

The tiny glass peephole was dark for a very long time as the housekeeper surveilled me. The very audacity of my having bypassed security was a personal affront to her, and she jerked the door open to confront me. She wasn't happy to see me, even though I had made it with eleven minutes to spare.

"Hi there. Made it in less than an hour." I showed so many teeth my cheeks hurt.

"Hmmph," was the only reply as her hand snaked out from behind and snatched the envelope. Within two seconds of this scintillating exchange the door was once again slammed in my smiling face, which turned bright red at the repeated insult. Fortunately there was no one around to witness my humiliation. As I waited for the elevator I plotted intricate scenarios, all of which climaxed in the ignominious death of the housekeeper, mob cap perched on her head for all to scorn. The most attractive plan was the fantasy wherein I fed her to the snowblower.

Next stop was food, so I headed up the street to Nick's. It's only around the corner and half a block up from Susan's, but an intricate pattern through a series of one-way streets ups the ante to about a kilometer. The city planners are obviously in cahoots with the petrol purveyors. Of course, I should have left the car where it was and walked, but it was cold and I'm lazy and didn't think it out. This brilliant flash of hindsight became obvious only when I was stuffing the meter with quarters. On the bright side, this was Westmount, where a quarter bought you thirty minutes, unlike Montreal, where the going rate can be as high as twenty-five cents for ten, which enrages a lot of people, who then mangle the meters, which leads to more price hikes and more bad temper, leading to domestic violence and severe tranquilizer addiction. One of my many unsolicited solutions to the problem of urban violence and crime is to do away with parking meters and hang all the meter maids by their pantyhose. I get a lot of parking tickets.

Inside Nick's I was confronted with a major decision. The counter or a table? Serious consideration. When alone I usually opt for the counter. Depending on the time of day, it's either Schwab's counter of opportunity or Edward Hopper's counter of despair. In any event, always a romantic notion. But today was too cold for romance; every time anyone walked in, a cold draft blasted the counter sitters. I could tell by the intermittent involuntary hunch of shoulders, so I took a booth, which would give me plenty of room for the sixteen pages I had to peruse.

The ponytailed, hennaed waitress saw to me immediately. She was just a little too old for that hairdo but clung desperately to the ingenue look of her high school days. Today she sported a bubblegum-pink bow, which clashed dramatically with her hair but did make a statement and perfectly matched her pink lipstick. It was tacky as hell, but remarkably cheerful. It would be easy to spot her in the crowded restaurant.

"The regular?" That meant a vegetarian sandwich and a Diet

Coke with no ice. I love having a regular. It makes me feel so plugged in and connected.

"No, not today. I'll just have plain dry toast and the Diet Coke."

"Too bad," she said saucily, turning her perfect bottom to me as she sashayed into the kitchen. Wait until she turns forty and starts to thicken. Twenty's voluptuousness is forty's liposuction. And her face was too old for the rest of her anyway.

I went through the lists carefully, again surprised at how many of the community's upstanding aging Boomers had dressed up on a freezing Sunday morning to attend. As testament to their presence, most of the assembled had completed the column for addresses, which was loaded with Westmounts, Hampsteads, Outremonts, and downtown condominiums. Their need for a written thank-you made my job a lot easier. A good question was, who would write the politely worded notes? Susan or Lainie? Who would look up all the missing postal codes? Who would spring for the stamps? As long as it wasn't me I didn't much care, but I could see a huge fight brewing. Maybe Barry could be persuaded to tell all.

I crunched my sawdust, scattering crumbs everywhere. Anything that has no fat and few calories is guaranteed to be tasteless and should be banished from the face of the earth, but it was food and I like food even in its worst form. Except for beets.

Bingo! On the eleventh sheet, three quarters of the way down, with no toast left, I found it. Or sort of found it. The address was the same as Frank's, and the signer had conveniently appended his apartment number, which placed it on Frank's floor. Only the signature was virtually illegible. The closest I could come up with was Lawsomething McSomething. Maybe Lawrence, maybe Mc . . . The guy must be a doctor. Impossible. I'd better stick to first names only.

I paid the meager bill, smiling at my frugality and detecting skills. Another career opportunity opening up. I left a big tip, bundled up and headed out into the sunshine. I even smiled at the stranger getting into the car parked in front of mine. Smug isn't an attractive word, but it was an apt description. I tossed the lists into the trunk again, congratulating myself for the good sense of not just dumping them onto the passenger seat to be stolen by any passerby. I didn't bother to ask myself why anyone but me would want them, but never mind. I was a borderline genius with a real flair for this kind of stuff.

Now to confront the target.

As I drove to Frank's, it dawned on me that I hadn't seen Celine's name on the lists. When I first learned of her via her garish wardrobe, I would have bet that she would have been present front and center. I pictured a vision in black bugle beads gliding silently to the front, dabbing a delicate tear with the tip of her white-gloved finger, bordered of course with black sequins. But that was the Bimbo of my fantasy. The one who had visited me I would expect to try to melt into the shadows. She seemed so timid. Or maybe frightened.

I had conveniently forgotten the new bruiser doorman, since my knee seemed to be healing. I hadn't inspected it since Cynthia had bandaged it Saturday night. It was too difficult to repeat her ministerings, and I had left it exposed to the elements, air drying; well, it was exposed to the inside of my jeans.

There he was, dressed in his stupid uniform looking stupid, positioned front and center and glaring at all passersby. This was obviously not his idea of a great job, and he made sure you knew it. I don't know who was paying him, but I'm sure he was making way more than minimum wage. The tenants must be really delighted with this attractive new addition.

Since he'd already seen me once before and I have great fearful respect for people whose heads grow directly out of their shoulders, I kept on driving. Even though I doubted his pea brain could retain most information for any length of time, I had created enough of a scene with my splat on the ice that even he might remember me. Which was a pain in the ass, since Susan had enclosed a key to the lobby door in the envelope.

I decided to try her trick. It had worked in my high-security building, so it should work here. I ditched my car around the corner out of sight of Neckless and walked around the block to see if I could approach the building from the back. I discovered that by climbing over a mountain of snow, I could get to the garage door without having to present myself from the front. There was likely a fence under that pile, but the plows had shoveled everything against and onto it in an effort to maintain access through the lane.

It was great fun. I had the right boots on and fell into the King of the Mountain game I hadn't played since I was ten. In the olden days, before they carted all the snow away in huge trucks in the name of progress, they used to blow the filthy muck onto people's lawns, to the dismay of the homeowners who had to contend with the sludge and debris when the pile finally melted sometime in May. But for the kids it was fantastic. We were all Sir Edmund Hillary in the making, scaling precipitous heights on our way home from school, which often turned out to be a two-hour trek after a fresh blow.

I wanted to stake my claim of the mountain in the name of all fired people in the land, and probably would have had I not spotted some children eyeing me nervously. Grown-ups do not climb snow banks, and I was likely deranged, so any second they would run home to tell their mothers about the crazy lady on the snowpile and the police would be called and I'd had enough of jails for a while, so I silently scooted down the other side and found myself at the garage door with no place to hide.

Frank's building was meticulous when it came to snow removal. Not a snowbank in sight to crawl behind. Any car coming down the lane would see me lurking, and the driver would challenge my access. At least I would if it were my building, and this was Westmount, where the citizens were for the most part upstanding and perspicacious. I wandered up the lane, searching for a good hiding spot, and finding none, I decided I'd better come back later when I could dress even more warmly if that were possible. The cold was eating into me. Another option was coming back on garbage day, wrapped in a green bag. Neither alternative pleased me. Night was scary, and that particular shade of garbage-green did nothing for my complexion.

As I moped back down toward my snowbank and inquisitive children I noticed a side door. In my building there is only one key for all doors leading to the common areas, and maybe it was the same here. It worked. I couldn't believe my luck. Even better, it led to a service elevator, so there was little likelihood of having to stop at the lobby level and chance an encounter with No Neck. I exited the elevator on Frank's floor and started down the hall, which looked dingier than ever. Someone had replaced the orange Sani-Seal of Celine's fancy. How had she gotten by the bruiser in the lobby? Maybe he hadn't arrived on the scene yet when she'd come. And surely she knew the side-door trick. No point pondering.

I got to the door I wanted and banged on it. Not tapped, not knocked, but banged hard and loud. The idea was to unnerve the guy and try to bully him. No answer. Bang, bang, bang, and in my best *Miami Vice* voice I yelled, "Open up. I know you're in there."

Not very original, but to my complete astonishment it worked. The door opened halfway, and an emaciated string bean said, "Look, officer, I told the other cops all I know. I was asleep the whole time. I didn't see anything."

He didn't say he hadn't heard anything, and he thought I was a cop, which could work to my advantage if I didn't blow it. My immediate concern was that someone would call Neckless to complain about the noise. Since the murder the tenants might be a little nervous and more vigilant.

"Look, we can talk in the doorway and have everyone listen, or you can let me in and we'll do it quietly. I have the kind of voice that gets louder in the gloom."

The only answer was "Huh?" but the door opened and I entered a bright, overheated apartment.

"See, sunshine and modulation," I almost whispered.

"Huh?"

Either he was a moron or he was stoned. Likely the latter.

"Officer, I don't know anything."

"Not Officer. Lieutenant. Lieutenant Tulipe LaFramboise." Not fancying myself a detective-sergeant, who usually comes with a partner, I gave myself a promotion. Now I was Greg's boss, and I liked that. The silly surname ensured that if the guy complained about me to the real police, the officer who took his statement would write him off as a nut. Also, as far as I knew there were no women lieutenants in the entire Montreal Police Department.

This guy bought it.

I took out the pad I keep in my purse to make my lists on and flipped it open to a page of expense account items that I no longer needed. I studied it.

"Your name is Lawrence MacIlveny," I said more as a statement than a question, although I was guessing.

"MacInery, ma'am, uh, lieutenant, ma'am."

I couldn't tell you who had previously questioned him, but I would bet on Fernand Boucherville. The guy was scared shitless.

Power coursed. This being a cop was a real trip, and this time I had no objection at all to the "ma'am" nomenclature. Authority to the max. "Let me take you back a little. Have you noticed any unusual activity in the direct vicinity of Mr. Porter's apartment recently?" Cop talk. Extraneous words.

"Huh? Uh, no." He was the worst liar in the entire universe.

"Look, Larry, I'll level with you. I don't care crap all about you and your tawdry little life. I mean you no harm, and I'd like to keep your name out of the press. And I can. I have connections."

I was good cop/bad cop all rolled into one.

"You can?" He was incredulous. His thin body was clad in a pair of torn jeans, which maybe were cool but more likely shabby, and a yellow hooded sweatshirt, even though the apartment was heated to a thousand degrees. He looked defeated and cornered, as though he were used to being browbeaten. I put his age at around thirty, although his downtrodden mien made him look older.

"You don't work?" It seemed a good bet, since he was home on a Monday morning. Yet he lived in an expensive building, and unemployment insurance does not afford a continued Westmount residence, even lower Westmount.

"Getting disability. I had a breakdown a few months ago. And my parents help me out."

"What was your occupation?"

"Futures trader."

The breakdown must have been massive; I couldn't imagine anyone in his right mind giving this scrawny excuse any money. I'd heard the burnout rate was high in the field, but I'd always envisioned a trader as looking more like Michael Douglas than Barney Fife.

"So you're at home a lot. You must have been aware of the activities in the Porter residence." I had to remember to keep up the cop talk.

"Can you really keep my name out of this? No newspapers? My parents will cut me off if I do one more thing."

More to this breakdown than revealed.

"You have my total assurance. I'll discuss this with no one, not even my superior. He's a pig, and so I'd like to crack this one myself and get that promotion I've been wanting."

I had no idea what I was talking about. I had no superior, since I was as unemployed as this poor jerk. But I could make good on not reporting him to the press or involving him. What the real police would do was another story.

Tulipe LaFramboise was a great liar with a fabulous poker face.

"Tell me what you saw Tuesday night."

"Nothin'. I told you."

"Okay, we'll do it another way. We'll get technical. Tell me what you heard. Everything. Or I'll ask for someone else to interrogate you."

Just anticipating another visit from Boucherville was enough to make him shiver in the heat. This guy was so easy.

"Well—"

"Yes?"

"Well, there was a knock on Frank's door."

So he knew Frank on a first-name basis. "And you were out in the hall at the time?"

"Uh-uh, no way. I was here in the kitchen, which is beside the front door. The carpets in the hallways are thin, and the doors are hollow. Noise leaks like crazy. People are always banging on the walls to tell their neighbors to turn down the television. Frank's stereo system is the worst. Great sound but really loud."

"So how did you hear the knock if his stereo was blasting?"

"I never said it was, I just said it could," he said, beaming that he had confused me.

He was regaining confidence, and I didn't like that. I sighed audibly, and made the motions of tapping my nonexistent truncheon in my hand impatiently.

"I'm getting a lot of words here and little information. Stick to the point and I'll be out of here. At this rate we'll have time to send out for pizza."

"Okay, okay. I heard the knock and was surprised Frank was there. He'd told me he'd be out of town for a few days. I'm supposed to watch the place for him when he's away, so I opened my door a crack and peeked down the hall."

"And?" He seemed to have run out of steam or else decided he'd imparted all the information I needed and it was all over. I was tiring of this space cadet fast.

"If you'd like I can search the place. See what kind of controlled substances I find. Then see what your parents have to say."

Panic stricken, his eyes darted to the wooden inlaid box perched in full sight on the coffee table in the living room. His stash. Downers, from what I could surmise from this specimen. Heroin?

"I'm trying. Really. I don't know what you want to know."

"Everything."

"Okay, okay. I went to the door and cracked it open a bit to see what was going on. Like I said, Frank was supposed to be away, so when I heard the knock I wanted to see if he was home."

"Why?"

"I wanted to talk to him."

I'd pursue that later. He was speaking in almost complete sentences, and I didn't want him to lose his fragile train of thought.

"Go on." I'd need a cattle prod soon.

"I didn't see Frank, but I heard them talking and I was glad he was home. There were two men, but they were already inside by the time I got to the door."

"If you didn't see them, how did you know there were two of them and that they were men?"

"By the boots. Two pairs of men's boots. Frank doesn't keep his outside. Doesn't wear them much anyway."

No, of course not. Too cool.

"What time was this?"

"I dunno. After nine, I guess."

So Susan had just missed them. I shuddered.

"That's really all. I was going to listen for them to leave so I could go see Frank, but I got tired of standing by the door and went inside and fell asleep."

An attention span to rival mine.

I hitched my purse higher on my shoulder and made leaving motions. "Thanks. You've been cooperative, so I don't think it will be necessary for you to make the journey downtown." I started for the door, and at the last moment, in the best *Columbo* fashion, I pivoted and added, "So what exactly did you need to speak to the deceased about?"

Sheer panic.

"Umm, umm, I wanted to remind him to water his plants. It's very dry here."

That was the most pathetic excuse I'd ever heard, and having dealt with management and labor for many years I'd heard a ton of them. It was right up there with "the dog ate my homework."

I tapped my foot on the thin carpet. He was right about that; the resultant sound was sharp instead of squishy.

"All right, changed my mind. Get your coat. Downtown."

What I would have done if he'd actually gotten his coat is beyond me, since I had nowhere to take him, and a Mercedes isn't your standard issue police vehicle. It never was a question, because this time he escalated from panic to absolute terror.

"No, wait a minute. My folks'll kill me. You promised you'd leave me out of it."

"I warned you to cooperate."

"Okay, okay. I used to do a little weed and sometimes some coke—"

"And?"

"Well, I've been sort of depressed and thought maybe I'd start again."

Yeah, sure. "And you wanted to speak to Frank as part of your Twelve-Step program?"

"Huh? Uh, no. Umm, Frank used to get it for me."

Annoying, disgusting Frank was now drug-dealing, revolting Frank.

"Look, kid," I said although he was close to my age, "get yourself into a rehab program. Speak to your parents. Tell them you want to try. Otherwise you could end up like Mr. Porter, who no longer resides down the hall."

This time I left. I descended in the elevator, alit back at the service level. When I got outside I relaxed. I hadn't realized how tense I had been through the whole charade. This detecting stuff was nerve-wracking. I took a look at the snowbank and realized I'd have to rescale it from the wrong side. The incline facing me, while not 90 degrees, was a damn sight close to it, and I no longer had any adrenalin to spur me on.

Lawrence MacInery had enervated me in more ways than one. First, he was a pathetic druggie who'd thrown away his whole career and future. Second, he'd confirmed that Frank was dealing, which made me furious and murderous. Third, because of Frank I was embroiled in an unholy mess. And fourth, if I had thought that two keys of heroin stashed away in my closet was somehow romantic and exciting, it now dawned on my middle-aged mind that it was neither. It was simply foolhardy and dangerous and would have to be addressed soon. Larry had wasted his life on drugs, and I wasn't going to perpetuate the legacy if I could help it.

To hell with the snowbank. Fed up with the whole distasteful affair, I walked up the lane to the front of the building. If the doorman recognized me, let him. He'd never have an inkling I'd come through the side door, since that took reasoning skills and I suspected his abilities in that area. And if he did figure it out, so what? I didn't care anymore. I just wanted to be as far from this place as possible.

I regained my car, feeling eyes following me. There was a man in a car parked three behind mine, and I was sure he looked familiar, although I couldn't have placed him on a bet. The escapade had me spooked, and the whole world seemed suspicious.

As I drove to the safety of my apartment a huge depression settled on me. This whole affair had sunk to depths of depravity that I couldn't abide. I went upstairs and plotted how I could restore my life to an even keel. In a week I had complicated it enormously in a tawdry and disgusting fashion. I wouldn't let this continue, and there was one aspect over which I had some control.

I called Pietr and squealed on Joanne. She'd kill me if she found out, but I knew Pietr would be discreet and resolve the whole thing with his buddies at the RCMP. No way I was letting Joanne go further with this. The world is an inherently dangerous place, and I wasn't taking chances with her life. Or mine either.

Pietr, of course, lectured me no end, and I apathetically sat through it. When he realized that there was no fight in me, he eased up and thanked me, promising to attend to it and vowing to keep my and Joanne's names out of it. If she didn't know I was the one who snitched, she wouldn't be ticked off at me. I hoped.

We made a date for lunch, which I accepted on the grounds that he no longer browbeat me. I baited him with the Wanda the Whip adventure, and I guess a good story is irresistible, since he swore that was the last I'd hear of it. Except for its resolution, of course. As I hung up I realized that I still had some of my bargaining skills left, which made me feel a little better.

I spent the evening taking a long bath and watching lots of mindless television. On *ER* there are plenty of gunshot wounds but only medical mysteries and no macho cops or P.I.s.

15

WHEN I WOKE up, I realized I hadn't called Sam back yet. He was expected on Thursday; just two days away to the end of my life as I knew it. It couldn't be good news. He would never come all the way to Montreal to tell me something wonderful. He'd sweep me away to a fabulous destination to impart the news on a beach at sunset. Why I absolutely knew this to be an irrevocable truth is beyond me, since he'd never swept me anywhere—Stephen was the sweeper—and I couldn't imagine any good news that I'd want to hear. Only bad.

I was depressed. I listened to the news on the radio, but there was nothing about the arrest of a hijacking ring and the morning paper was no help either. I wanted it to be public so I could speak to Joanne again. While all was still in limbo I didn't dare face her; Joanne's wrath is not a pretty sight. I've seen her turn grown men to quivering jelly with words. She wasn't the smartest kid in school for nothing.

My heightening depression threatened a throwback to my month of seclusion, so I decided that as appropriate penance, I would do the thing I hated most. Well, the second most hated thing. The first obviously is cleaning up, which reminded me Mme Jacqueline was due any minute, so I'd better brace myself for a diatribe or get the hell out of there. I opted for the gym and exercising. As I loathe both the place and the activity, it seemed fit punishment for all my transgressions.

A lot of other people must have felt guilty that morning; the parking garage was packed. Of course, the only space I could find was about five dreary miles away. By the time I got to the entrance I was ready to pack it in and turn around, feeling I'd already paid my karmic dues.

For the next hour and a bit I sweated and slaved. By the time I hit the showers I felt much better, but I would have never admitted it. I like to carp that I hate working out, which I do, and I'm loath to admit that it never fails to energize me and lift my spirits. We've been told that fit is in, and we've come to accept that the only method that gets us there involves a lot of perspiration and money.

Although I wasn't depressed any more, I was obviously still cranky. Nothing that a nice cold Diet Coke wouldn't cure.

First surprise of the day was seeing Susan perched at the bar, drinking coffee. It wasn't even ten o'clock yet, and here she sat sipping cappuccino, looking refreshed.

"What are you doing here? In the morning? I thought you only came in the afternoon."

"Yeah, usually, but I woke up early and didn't know what to do with myself. With all the stress of the last few days, I'm back to not sleeping very well. And rather than take it out on Barry I thought I'd take the morning stretch class to try to calm down. I'm a wreck."

Susan has suffered from occurrences of sleep disorder for a few years now. It seemed to me it was always coincidental with Frank's most outrageous transgressions. She once went into an experimental insomnia program at McGill University, but when she discovered it entailed seeing a psychiatrist on a regular basis she quit. Susan guards her secrets dearly, and to have to admit to anyone that Frank had the capacity to upset her to this degree was unthinkable. I'm not sure she herself realizes the dire effect Frank has on her. Also, she'd have to tell a stranger what a jerk he was, which would lead to the question of why she'd married him in the first place, which would force her to voice the fact that she'd had visions of mink-clad, dollar-dripping sugarplum fairies.

It was perfectly in character for Susan to have chosen stretching, of all the classes and disciplines offered. It's the least strenuous, you never break a vulgar sweat, and it's populated with golden-agers whom it benefits enormously. And princesses with long nails and hairdos that would be imperiled in other classes.

"You look relaxed enough," I said. It was true. Her skin was clear, her dark eyes shone; she looked suspiciously satisfied.

"I feel better. It's been a difficult weekend as you can imagine, and I'm concerned about Robert. He seems to be handling the whole thing okay, but I'm worried about long-term effects. He's withdrawn from everyone. Barry's tried to talk to him, but I think Robert's resentful. I don't want him to feel that Barry is trying to take Frank's place as his father, but I don't want him to hate him either."

"This Barry thing is starting to sound serious, Susan," I said with a small twinge of envy.

"Maybe. We'll see," she said noncommittally in a quiet voice. Then she lifted her head, and her eyes flashed. "Hey, did I tell you what happened with Bitch Lainie? No, I haven't had a chance to talk to you. What did you *do* to her? She's really furious. Told me you'd never, ever set foot in her house. Notice the word again wasn't in that sentence, since I don't think you've ever been there yet. But you really and truly pissed her off, for which you have my eternal gratitude."

With an arched, French-manicured pinkie she lifted her

cup for another sip, leaving no hint of a milk-froth mustache on her lined upper lip. She had accomplished her mission. Susan's agenda means that she'll tell you what she wants you to know when she wants to. Otherwise she'll casually change the subject with the drop of a tidbit that you absolutely have to follow up on. The present state of her love life was not up for discussion at the moment, and the deflection was successful.

"So she hates me that much, eh? Let's go right over there. She'd really dislike that. And we could accidentally smash some of her bric-a-brac. She'd have a coronary, and we could forget to call the paramedics."

Not up to my usual standards but ultimately satisfying. I launched into the tale of my encounter with Lainie in the kitchen, with the emphasis on her interaction with the waitresses. I turned it into a funny story and was rewarded with a big smile and hearty laugh. One of my jobs as a friend is to lighten things, and Susan had been weighted down the last while. No matter that she'd dragged me along with her, she was still the primary victim. Excluding Frank, of course.

I took another satisfying sip. The wonders of chemical substances.

"What else did she say? There has to be more to this story," I said. What she'd told me didn't qualify as good stuff, so there had to be more.

"She screeched at me about a safe-deposit box!"

"What!" I did it again.

"Relax. She doesn't know anything. Her brother Frank would certainly never tell her anything. She was always after him to tell her what his financial situation was. As if he had one."

"So why did she ask?" I was still suspicious.

"When we were all at my house, either just before or after your little encounter, she got Barry into the kitchen, her base of operations it seems. I just bet there's a horde of waitresses out there right now plotting revenge. Maybe they'll poison her soup at the next dinner party. We know it won't be hosted by Lainie, but these women work the circuit and they'll find her soon enough. Maybe they'll just salt it, which would be good enough, or better yet spit in it. Yes, poor Lainie's going to have a difficult time with her next free meals."

Susan verily twinkled when she said that. I wouldn't put it past her to call one of the hapless waitresses and suggest just that.

This time I wasn't distracted.

"What did she do to Barry?" I asked, not sure the danger had passed.

"She cornered him. Literally. She had him wedged between the fridge and counter. She ordered him to find out if there had been any money or anything found in the apartment and where it had gone. Even if he did know something I can't imagine why she would think he'd tell her anything; she assumes everyone will do her bidding. She certainly has no problems with self-esteem."

The elusive money again. Lainie and Celine were convinced it existed, and that it was the cause of Frank's demise. I knew for a fact that it wasn't the reason that Frank had bought it. I even knew he hadn't even been supposed to be shopping. In the technical sense, I guess his death could be classified as an accident. As to the money, either his killers had taken it, or some cop now had a new big-screen TV and fully loaded VCR. This avocation had turned me into a bigger cynic than ever.

"Barry insisted there was no money, that I hadn't taken anything. He stuck up for me. I like that."

"Then why the safe-deposit box question? Where did that come from?" The leeriness was still there.

"Barry told her the money, if there was any, was probably stashed away in a box somewhere that I didn't know about and asked her if *she* knew where it was. Turned the whole thing right around on her to get her off my back and out hunting banks. So she took it on herself to confront me, quizzing me about a box. I guess she figured I might keep some secrets from Barry."

When it comes to money Susan keeps secrets from everyone, so it was a good guess on Lainie's part.

I took another long swig before saying anything. This talk of boxes kept reminding me of the heroin in my house. A sense of dread spread through me again. If only I could figure out what to do with the damned stuff.

"Uh-uh." Susan cautioned, looking me straight in the eye, her back rigid. "You're not flushing it."

"How—?"

"The furtive look in your eye. And the fact that you just downed three quarters of your Coke in one swallow."

"Diet Coke. Not that you'd understand the nuance."

Have I mentioned that Susan still weighs the same one hundred eight pounds that she did twenty-something years ago?

"How did you answer Lainie?" I pressed.

"It was terrific. I acted horrified. Did Frank have a secret box hidden somewhere? Who could I get to tell me where it was? Who could he have confided in? Then I clammed up; went stony silent. She interpreted that to mean I suddenly remembered something, which of course I hadn't. I really got to her when I said 'Gotta go. Speak to you soon' and slammed the phone down. She's probably still sitting with the receiver in her hand trying to puzzle out what it is I know and how she can get her hands on it. Most fun I've had in weeks," she finished, a giant grin illuminating her face.

"Good job. Here," I said as I took the check, an equally wide grin on my face, not as vivid as hers since I had no lip liner on. "I'll buy."

"Big deal. A whole cappuccino. I at least deserve lunch."

"Don't push it. Remember whom you dragged into this saga."

We chatted for a while, discussing who wore what to the funeral and speculating on each one's motives for being there. It was mindless and served to entertain and to avoid the larger issues. As we finished up I spotted something out of the corner of my eye.

"Quick. Let's get out of here. I think I just saw Cynthia Berkowitz, and although I love her dearly I'm not up to a monologue or inquisition at the moment. The sight of the two of us together will send her into spasms of ecstasy. We won't get out of here until dinnertime. I think it was her. I'm not sure."

Susan grabbed her bag and made a dash for the side door. "We're not taking any chances. Let's get out of here." As she got to the door I saw she'd held me to my word and left me the check. I threw too much money on the table, unwilling to take the time to wait for change. The tab on this escapade was increasing daily.

We penetrated the garage, deeply engrossed in frivolous conversation, mostly her pumping me about Stephen's latest. Too bad Stephen and Susan never got along all that well. They seem to sniff at each other like suspicious dogs, circling. He's certainly got enough money for her.

In an instant we were at her car. Front row, right near the door of course, since Susan never walks any distance.

"How'd you do that?"

"What?" Her, not me.

"Get a place so close to the entrance."

"I don't know," she said, not really understanding the question. She just assumes a great parking spot is her due and somehow always gets one. She must share some genes with Joanne. "Some executive was just leaving as I pulled in. I could tell he was an executive because he was driving a Volvo and wearing Johnston & Murphy shoes."

I knew my friends were car snobs, but shoes?

"Mid-level executive. If he wants to go higher, he'd better get a pair of Guccis."

"Enough," I interjected. "You'll disillusion me."

"Can I ask you a favor?" she said, changing the tone. "Can you come for dinner tonight? Maybe Robert will open up to you."

"Sure. I'd like that. What time?"

"Seven-thirtyish. Barry doesn't get home 'til seven or so."

Time to have a discussion with Barry. I liked him well enough so far but would have to sound him out further. Susan made light of the relationship, but her refusal to discuss it on any other plane led me to believe it was quite serious, and I wasn't letting her make another mistake like Frank. Why this was my responsibility or business I don't know, but it was.

"Need a lift to your car?" she asked facetiously, reverting to our previous lightheartedness.

I really could have used one since I was way the hell at the other end, but I knew what it would have entailed and declined. I hesitated while she got in, and sure enough the inevitable ensued. As she adjusted the rearview mirror and uncapped the lip liner, I made my escape. So far the day hadn't been bad, and I wasn't going to hang around and ruin it by witnessing the primp and preen routine.

The hike was longer than necessary, since I took a wrong turn, lost in my thoughts. They weren't very deep, but they were worrisome. Whenever I had some time alone they seemed to return to the same theme. I hadn't called Sam back, and Thursday was only two days away. What could the man possibly want, and were all those comfortable and happy assignations about to come to an end?

I never saw them coming. That's a line you hear a lot, and one I'm always skeptical of. More likely a clever plot device, accompanied by appropriate dramatic music. But I swear, I never saw them. Suddenly there was a car beside me, boxing me between two cars. The doors popped open, and out jumped two men.

I looked around; I was the only person in sight, so they had to be there for me. I had no idea what to do, so I stood there, hoping it wasn't happening.

"Get in," one ordered.

"Why?" I asked, honestly perplexed. In retrospect, I guess asking questions was not appropriate behavior, but I'd had no schooling in the etiquette of being kidnapped.

"I said get in," he repeated, this time grabbing my arm and starting to drag me. His cohort had by now come around the car and was beside me, reaching for my other arm.

Something snapped. The innocent passivity I had displayed dissipated; I was truly angry. How dare they accost me in broad daylight—well, broad neon light—and try to shove me around? Enough was enough. How many more indignities was I going to have to endure? In the past few days I'd gotten a scabby knee, sold out my best friend Joanne, harbored drugs, tampered with evidence, convinced my neighbors I was a hooker, and possibly lost what I on the spot decided was the love of my life. I'd had it.

I can't remember exactly what I did, but the next thing I knew the second guy was doubled over, wailing. Damned if I hadn't kicked him smack in the balls. Lucky shot, fortuitous footwear. I was delighted I'd taken the time to change into street clothes before leaving and had selected a sturdy pair of brown Italian oxfords to complement my ensemble. But there was no time to dwell on my sartorial cleverness. Number Two was recovering and mad as hell. Number One had me firmly by both arms, and I was sure Two was getting ready to sock me.

One evidently was of the same opinion, since he said, in a deep enough bass to resound through my tense body, "Cool it." For a second I thought I was in the arms of a white Barry White.

"The bitch kicked me," whined Number Two, adjusting his private parts gingerly.

"Help me get her in the car before somebody comes," the mellifluous voice intoned.

I couldn't see what the guy who had me pinned looked like. It had all happened so quickly, and he had me positioned with my back to him. Number Two had a ruddy complexion that I was sure would even out as the pain in his lower parts diminished. I'd landed a good one, and the topper was that he now had a very visible treaded footprint adorning the front of his tan pants. He would have done better to have selected a long overcoat this morning instead of a brown shearling leather jacket. Until he had the time to go home and change, he'd brandish my badge of honor. Even in my precarious situation I took time out to be proud.

They shoved me into the backseat of the idling car. I rued the fact that I was as big a car snob as my friends and had no idea of the make of the vehicle. It was beige and boxy like every other car on the road. What happened to very identifiable fins and lights? Have we all learned to aspire to mediocrity and only want ordinary, boring possessions? My brain was not in top form. This was not the appropriate time to ponder the decline of the mores of modern civilization.

Fortunately, Two was the driver and so was in the front seat where he couldn't bop me one. There was a final fleetingly satisfying moment when he tried to brush himself off and winced at the touch. I'd landed a really good one.

"Who are you, and what do you want?" I asked as the door locks clicked around me.

"Just behave, Miss, and you'll come to no harm."

I just knew Number One was a good guy. He'd called me miss.

"Where are we going?"

"Someone wants to speak to you," he said in accentless English. Another stereotype blown to smithereens. Obviously thugs were not all semiliterate French-Canadian or Italian ape men. The French-Canadian assumption had been there because a) they're the majority and b) I've previously speculated on the government's plot to turn us all into closet racists. The Italian angle comes from television. At least I didn't include blacks in my narrow vision, so maybe I'm not such a racist after all.

Beside me sat an Anglophone, smartly dressed in a navy topcoat, pearl gray leather gloves, white silk scarf, and a voice to die for. I bet his friend up front would later try to cajole him into swapping outerwear.

We sped out of the garage into blinding light. The reflection of the sun off the snow was so bright that both One and I shielded our eyes. In the front seat, Two was not similarly afflicted, as he had donned sunglasses. Big, black, menacing shades. If he'd have worn them when he came at me, he might have spared his jewels.

We drove west along Van Horne, passing strollers and shoppers. People didn't seem to be in a hurry, although it was very cold. The sun was deceptive, making everything seem warm and friendly, so no one showed any interest in the car that passed, traveling within the speed limit. How could I expect them to take notice when even I didn't know the make and model of the car I was being abducted in? This would be very embarrassing to explain to the police, okay, to Greg, if I ever got out of this alive. For a very split second death seemed preferable to abject humiliation. Something was definitely askew with my values.

I peered over the seat, searching for any identifying marks, but could find none. Some detective.

We pulled up beside a white limo parked on a residential cul-de-sac. I noted the license plate number—JRW 638—with some satisfaction. If I lived through this at least I'd done one thing right. If I didn't forget it in all the conflicting thoughts flying around in my head, bumping up against each other like pool balls in a break.

My abductors must have practiced the next maneuver a million times, judging from the precision with which the move was executed. The rear doors of both cars opened simultaneously, coming within millimeters of each other. I was roughly shoved from my seat onto the floor of the other car, landing on my knees and elbows. Now my knees would be a matching pair, as I could feel the scab rip off the healing one and sure scraping of the other. People were taking great liberties with my legs, and I was once again angry enough not to be afraid.

As I lay sprawled on the roughly carpeted floor of the limo, sputtering profanities, a well-manicured hand reached for mine. Soft fingers, buffed nails, and the most god-awful huge diamond ring I'd ever seen. If that rock was real it was worth a king's ransom. The pope's ring is more subtle.

I looked up to find myself peering into the concerned face of Mr. Leonine Whitehead, the man who had cornered Joanne at the ball. Who was he, and what did he want?

"Who the fuck are you, and what the hell do you want?" The sputtering had turned to phrases, albeit still profane.

"I do apologize to you, Ms. Simons, for your discomfort. This was the only way I could arrange to speak to you. Let me help you up."

The silky hand reached out again, and this time I grabbed it and hoisted myself up onto the soft glove leather seat, executing a cursory inspection of my knee area. Shit, the expensive, fully lined, 100 percent virgin wool, made in Italy, navy blue trousers were ripped. They cost a lot, and I no longer had a lot; my knees would heal, but my pants wouldn't. I was fuming.

"You owe me money for these trousers," I announced. "Big money, mister."

That outburst elicited an amused guffaw. His bejeweled hand snaked into his pocket and came up with a hundred dollar bill. Just like that. Loose in his pocket. No wallet. No money clip.

"More," I demanded.

Another quick motion and another hundred dollar bill.

"Another one." I pushed my luck.

He sighed and came up with one last bill. Okay, I'd only paid a hundred and fifty, but they'd been on sale and marked down from three hundred, so I felt entitled. Also, my indignity had to be worth something.

"Thanks. Now I'll reiterate. Who the fuck are you, and what the hell do you want?"

"No need for foul language, Ms. Simons. I will explain all in due time."

Civilized clichés from a cultured voice, actually a seductive cultured voice, accompanied by the proper form of address. On inspection he was quite attractive, with a full head of white hair, piercing, widely set black eyes, bushy white eyebrows tamed into arched submission, sharp aquiline nose, and full rosy lips. Not bad at all for a man his age, which I assessed to be early sixties.

"Allow me to introduce myself. We have been in each other's presence but have not been formally introduced. My name is Francesco Grandese."

He punctuated this speech by grasping my hand and kissing it. Really. I was momentarily ashamed that my fingers weren't festooned with any impressive rocks. All I had to flaunt was one measly ring on my pinkie. But it *was* a Cartier three-gold-roller ring, so I hoped he'd at least recognize quality. Sam had given it to me on our fifth anniversary, and I rarely took it off. In my day-to-day existence I never gave a thought to its provenance; it had become a part of me.

So this was Francesco Grandese, Mafia kingpin. He of the small organ. I had to banish that thought quickly lest I smirk. Irking the person who's kidnapped you is not the wisest course of action.

"That doesn't explain what you want," I said, still pugnacious.

"Ah, Ms. Simons, now that you have cleaned up your language we may converse. Vulgarity does not suit a woman so beautiful as you."

Joanne was right. This guy was trite but good.

"I'm sorry if I have offended you. It's just that I'm not used to meeting people under such stressful circumstances. An encounter preceded by a proper introduction would have been preferable."

My speech pattern mimicked his. If he could be formal, so could I. It was ridiculous. His two goons had hijacked me, shoved me around, and likely eliminated countless people for this man, and he recoiled at a measly little "fuck." They say our values are out of kilter, and for once I had to agree.

"I have come to plead my case," he said, lowering his eyes in a gesture of submission.

"What case?" I asked, not falling for this routine one little bit. I was still mad about my pants, even though they'd netted me a tidy little profit.

"Let me rephrase," he said, taking a whiter-than-white, what looked to me to be Egyptian cotton handkerchief from the breast pocket of his English-tailored charcoal gray pinstripe suit. He had the equivalent of three months' average person's earnings on his back. I couldn't see his shoes from my vantage point, but I'd bet money they were handmade. The wages of sin sure do enable you to dress well.

"You are a good friend of Joanne Cowan."

"How do you know that?"

"I know much about Ms. Cowan. She is the most exciting woman I have ever met. She is a vision who floated across my path, but, like the elusive butterfly, I cannot contain her."

Shit. This mobster was bonkers over Joanne, who was going to be one dead person as soon as I could get my hands on her. Hadn't she gotten me into enough trouble for one week? Now I had to deal with a lovesick capo. If I played my cards right I could negotiate with Mr. One and/or Mr. Two to do the hit. Just being in the presence of this gangster made me think like one. However, Joanne did deserve everything I could mete out for this one.

"What do you want from me?" I asked warily. I had been led to understand that these type of people were not easily refused, so I feared his request.

"I have come to beseech you to press my suit."

My first thought was, *ironing*? Me, the disciple of Mme Jacqueline? At a million bucks a pop for a suit he wants me to press it? I think not. Still and all, I had no idea what he was talking about.

"What? I don't understand." I blustered. "What do you mean?" It isn't wise to feign ignorance with a man like Grandese, but I wasn't playing stupid.

"It is the beautiful Joanne. She has beguiled me. I cannot think of anything except her. My business is suffering."

My life had reached a new apex of absurdity. Francesco Grandese, Mafia chief, was madly in lust with Joanne Cowan, my near-blind childhood friend. I had new respect for her acting abilities. She must have been very, very good, and damned if I wasn't going to pump the breath out of her to get her to tell me exactly what it was she did. I mean, how many variations on a basic theme can there be? Along with the Oscar and the Obie and the Tony, she'd earned the Dumbest Move of the Century award that night. And how small was it?

It took every ounce of my willpower to keep my eyes on his face.

"I'm sorry. I really can't help you. You see, Joanne's husband is a very dear friend of mine, and I couldn't possibly place myself in the position of separating them. He loves her very much and needs her. She is the reason for his very being as I'm sure you can understand. I would be endangering the lives of his patients if I tried to fracture the relationship, and that's a responsibility I couldn't bear."

What the hell was I talking about? The words spilled out of me, formal and earnest. They had no validity, or maybe they did, I didn't know. I just knew this whole thing was fraught with danger and I only had my mouth to get me out of it. I've used it successfully before, and now I needed all my skills. My brain was working overtime for a change.

"I understand your attraction to Joanne, but I pray you forgive her lapse. The interlude with you was a slip, an error in judgment. No doubt she was swayed by your charismatic personality; I know she was impressed by your intelligence. When she confessed the affair she was shamed by her transgression yet still intrigued and tempted. However, she loves Jacques, and after much soul searching we decided she must never have anything to do with you again for the sake of her marriage and all the people Jacques might still save."

I've seen too many reruns of *Casablanca* on the Late Show.

"Ah, Ms. Simons, I am wounded," he said with his hand over his heart. This melodrama was taking on serious overtones of farce. I only hoped he wouldn't wound *me* and that he hadn't been to any film society showings lately and went to bed early.

"Please sir, this is all said with the greatest respect for all concerned. I understand what you are asking me to do, but you must see the greater picture, accede to the greater good," I said in finale, hoping I hadn't taken it over the top. That was it. I'd shot my entire bolt, and now I could only hope he wouldn't terminate me. I knew I was going to kill Joanne, and I wanted to live to see the moment.

He looked pensive for a moment, sad for another, and finally a big smile spread across his face, showing teeth as white as his hair and handkerchief.

"You present your argument well, young lady." I might be able to learn to like this man. Ms., young lady—we were off to a good start if you could ignore the kidnapping part. There was also the distinct possibility that in his continued company, one might not last long enough to earn the appellation "old lady."

"Ms. Cowan has meant much to me, as I see she means much

to mankind. I must release her." He really looked sad when he said that.

Joanne the Slut had been elevated to the ranks of Joanne the Saint. And all my doing. Dead was way too good for her. At least now if she ever found out about my snitching to Pietr about Wayne, I'd have a bargaining chip. She owed me big.

"I will be sorrowful for a while, but I will recover and keep my distance. Perhaps you will relay the message? I would not like to be an intrusion in her life."

Yeah, just in her body—if you could, I thought without the hint of a smirk. It's amazing what a life-threatening situation can do for a poker face.

"Mr. Grandese, sir? I have a request of my own," I dared.

"Yes?" he answered, making it sound like a question and looking down his aquiline nose at me in suspicion.

"Please take me back to my car in the limo. I don't wanna go with those two guys. Please," I whined. I realized that I was scared of Two, who had by now inspected his genitals and plotted revenge. The idea of being isolated in a car with him—even with One present—was frightening. I was terrified for the first time. I seem to have panic attacks after the fact rather than when they could save me from doing something stupid. I'll have to work on my timing.

I think he took my request as a personal compliment. He preened and said, "Certainly, Ms. Simons. And let me say you are as beautiful as your dear friend. You must look wonderful together."

Oh shit. Either he was transferring his affections from Joanne to me or he was fantasizing some kinky sex scene involving me, Joanne, and maybe him. Any one of the above combinations was distasteful. How had I talked myself into this? I mentally examined my statements and could find nothing suggestive. This wasn't my fault, and Joanne was in danger of having every last pair of her glasses pulverized to tiny little bits that

I was going to force down her insatiable gullet. Now I had piqued Francesco Grandese's interest. And I had worried about Wayne!

I don't know what button he pushed, but the divider came down, revealing a gorgeous driver of the Bimbo ilk. If those were real I'd give her my car. And if those were his, what did he want with Joanne, who barely had any and relied on the miracle of the Wonderbra?

"Giselle, please take the young lady to her vehicle. Then we will have lunch."

The divider rose and we drove silently back, he no doubt thinking about dessert. The car carrying One and Two preceded us, while another followed closely. We were our own mini-cavalcade, gliding through the streets of Outremont. We all drove into the underground garage en suite, the last car stopping in the entryway blocking access to anyone wanting to enter or leave. Those noon Level IV Aerobics students were going to be incensed.

I arrived at my destination. Grandese kissed my hand, said nothing at all, and was driven away. I hoped I'd never hear from him ever, ever again. The last car followed, with Number Two taking the time to give me the finger. I stood there watching the procession depart. After they were gone, six cars peeled into the garage and shoved themselves haphazardly into the first slots available. I ducked instinctively, thinking they might intuit that I was responsible for the detainment.

Eight ladies raced for the entrance, practically elbowing each other through the door as they sped to the locker room. They had probably expended more calories in stewing over the delay than they would in class. I wondered if Two had shown them his digit on the way out.

I headed home, only to find Mme Jacqueline getting ready to leave. Bad timing. She took in my disheveled attire without comment, no doubt inured by the Wanda charade. I listened to a story about her third daughter being thrown out of the nunnery for a bad attitude and a biker boyfriend. They must be really hard up for novitiates these days if she'd lasted so long. I muttered banalities in French, listened to platitudes, and bade her farewell, assuring her that all would be right in the world again. For her, maybe. I still had two keys of heroin to dispose of.

As soon as she was out the door, I headed for the phone. All my rage returned as I punched in the numbers, only to be rewarded with Joanne's voice mail message. She was out, leave my name and number. Not even a please.

"It's Barbara. If you don't call me the second you get in, I will tell everyone about your trip to Bermuda last year. I mean it. This is no idle threat."

Joanne's trip to Bermuda was really a trip to Los Angeles and an ultra-chic plastic surgery clinic to have her eyelids done. The on-camera news business is brutal, and Joanne was concerned about a cute, perky newcomer to the station. She came back looking the same but better. It appeared that the vacation had left her rested and energized. This was a deep, dark secret that she had shared only because if anything went wrong either here or there during her absence, someone needed to know where she was. Even Jacques, her husband, thought she was in Bermuda. Or at least he said he did. It was such a serious secret that I'd never mentioned it again, much less threatened her with disclosure, so she had to know I wasn't kidding.

After slamming the phone down I went into my bedroom to change. It was nice and orderly and fresh smelling, unlike my life.

I retrieved the three hundred dollars from the pocket before I threw the pants in the trash. It was a sad farewell; I hate parting with clothes I still like. I inspected my knees and saw they were now both encrusted, and green stuff was oozing out of the first wound. Infection—the perfect metaphor. I rinsed and soaked both in salty water for half an hour, applied a liberal slathering of antibiotic cream, and bandaged myself up following Cynthia

Berkowitz's teachings. Kind of dumb looking but I was proud of my nursing abilities.

Then I noticed my elbow was also damaged. Worse, my shirt had blood on it. In a fit of materialism I was glad I'd opted for cotton instead of silk or cashmere. I repeated the medication routine on my elbow in an abbreviated fashion, since this was getting very boring. Then I discovered another truth; Cynthia Berkowitz was right. It is impossible to remove blood stains, and there was no infomercial on the air at the moment to sell me something that someone devoutly swore would. The shirt was hung up to dry and would go to Mme Jacqueline instead of the trash. The biker nun might be in need of clothing and was probably no stranger to blood. After some quick calculations I figured I was still a few bucks ahead, so it wasn't a complete loss.

Lunch consisted of Lean Cuisine that I found in the freezer and Diet Coke. I was famished, but of course there wasn't anything appetizing in the refrigerator section. It was already after two, closer to three, the kitchen was getting messy, and the bathroom was a shambles. And Mme Jacqueline hadn't even been gone two hours. I didn't know if I should be angry or depressed.

16

I SPENT THE next while in my wing chair with Sue Grafton and her alphabet, absorbed in someone else's conundrum. It was a happy time.

When the phone rang I jumped for it, a rush of adrenaline pumping me up to let Joanne have it.

"Miss Simons?"

Greg. And I didn't care. It seemed like lifetimes ago that I had even considered him. The police and the bad guys had all become rolled into a ball labeled "them"; they were indistinguishable.

"Oh hello, Detective-Sergeant Allard." I wished for the millionth time there was a male equivalent for Miss. "What can I do for you?" Formal, polite, disinterested.

"Have you heard from Mlle Celine Plouffe?"

"Well," I equivocated. What to do? Another lie would only compound the task of keeping things straight. I had learned from telling my tale to Pietr that unburdening helped me sleep. From now on I was going to come clean.

"Yes, actually. She came to visit me Saturday."

"Saturday?"

"Yes, Saturday afternoon. She was here for about an hour."

"You didn't tell me about this. I asked you to keep me informed."

"Well, excuse me, Your Policeness. I *did* call you. I left a message, and you never called me back. Check your facts, buster."

I'm not sure where all the aggression came from. I think I was just tired of being pushed around, mentally and physically.

I could hear the rustle of pink slips while he hunted for proof of my words.

"Did you find it yet? I'm waiting." I tapped the phone with my Cartier ring to signal impatience. Now that I was in the right and he was in the position of having to apologize, I could enjoy the conversation. And lighten up.

"You're right. Here it is. Two of them. However, you didn't say anything about this when I saw you on Sunday."

"It was a funeral, for chrissakes. And you were busy making eye contact with Joanne." He hadn't been, but it never hurts to discomfit them some. I still hadn't got to the bottom of that story. It was something else to add to the Blast Joanne List, which was growing proportionally with the length of time she was taking to call me back.

"I'm waiting," I said, resuming the tapping. It might not be as large as Grandese's ring, but it still had its uses.

"For what?" he asked, puzzled.

"An apology, Detective-Sergeant Gregory Allard. I'm waiting for you to drop to your knees and beg forgiveness. Also, either call me Ms. Simons or Barbara."

My tirade elicited a hearty chuckle. I was happy I'd made him smile, since he *was* kind of cute. And single. And I was insane.

"I offer you my sincerest apologies, Ms. Barbara Simons. If you were here I would proffer a rose."

"What color?" I was getting close to flirting again.

"White?"

My favorite color of my second-least-favorite flower. If he'd said carnation the conversation would have been terminated. At least the color was right. Red would have been too pedestrian and personal.

"Perhaps an iris would be more appropriate. A more delicate bloom," he added, getting into the mood.

The man was a clairvoyant detective. I love irises.

"Apology accepted. Why do you suddenly want to know if I spoke to Celine?"

"May I remind you that I am the detective here, and I think it's my job to conduct this investigation?" he said with a twinkle in his voice to indicate that this wasn't an official reprimand.

"So conduct."

"What did Mlle Plouffe say? What was it she wanted from you? And why did you do something so stupid as to ask her to your house?" I could hear the anger in the last line.

Three good questions. The nuance of the last one piqued my interest. Not that he was mad at me, but that he had called my apartment my house, not my home. This raised him another notch through the class system. Middle-middle or up, and what was I doing thinking these things?

I told him all about Celine's visit, about her inquiry and concern about missing money. I admitted I had been too dumb to ask her where she lived when she wasn't with Frank. I had just been nonplussed by her seeming fragility, so unlike the Bimbo of my imagination. I also mentioned that Lainie was obsessed with anything, particularly money, that might have been found at Frank's and told him about the scene in the kitchen, this time omitting the details about the waitresses. Let the police, hopefully Detective-Sergeant Fernand Boucherville, give her a hard time for a while. In recounting my tale I realized that Celine had revealed nothing, nor had she accomplished much from her visit, since I had nothing to offer. I topped it off with the anecdotal information that she had put away a pitcherful of martinis and still remained standing. I didn't mention that she was gorgeous. No sense diverting him from me.

"So that explains it," he said cryptically.

"Explains what?" Hard as I tried, I couldn't figure out what I had imparted that was elucidating.

"Her stratospheric blood-alcohol levels."

Ominous words. There was only one way he could know about her alcohol level.

"What happened to her?" I asked, alarmed.

"What makes you think anything happened?" he asked with suspicion.

"Stop treating me like an idiot. You said blood-alcohol levels. How could you know anything about that if she was still missing?"

"You're right. That just slipped out."

"Look, tell me what's going on. The time frame puts whatever happened to her soon after she left here, about three-thirty Saturday afternoon. Someone may have followed her from here, and that makes me very uncomfortable. I want to know what happened to her. And why."

All this getting shoved around lately was making me reassert myself. The mushy mind of my withdrawal from the world was banished.

"We've just identified her. She came in as a Jane Doe. She was found by a drunk in an alley behind Laval Street in the Plateau late Saturday night with no identification. It took a while to get a match on her prints."

"She has a record?"

"No. Air Quebec fingerprints all its employees as a matter of course and sends them in to the national register. It isn't my case, but I was having coffee with the detective whose it is when the identification came through. I got worried about you."

That was nice, but now was not the time.

"How did she die?" I asked. It seemed a callous question even to me.

"Shot through the heart. It would have been instantaneous."

Thank God for that.

"Greg, was it the same gun that killed Frank?"

"No. Wrong caliber. However, I haven't eliminated a connection, since I'm not a great believer in coincidences."

"What was she doing on Laval? Or at least, behind Laval?"

"You were right in your original speculation. It was her other apartment. The airline confirmed a address on Laval and I'm on my way over there now."

"Can I come?" Like a ten-year-old asking her older sibling to tag along to the movies. With the expected response. "Of course not. This is official police business, Barbara."

"Will you let me know what you find? Will you describe it in detail for me? Please?"

"Why?" The leery voice.

"I just can't seem to get a handle on her. She came here the innocent postulant, full of grief and concern for her future. It just doesn't jive with a blond beauty who has two addresses and a closetful of sequins. Something is screwy with the whole picture. And she sure can drink; she learned that somewhere. I'd like to know how her other persona lived."

"Sure. I'll call you later. In the meantime, be careful. I don't know if and how you fit into the picture, but I'd like you to stay alert."

"Right. I'm going to Susan's for dinner, so either call me there, call me later, or leave a message where you can be reached. And thanks for telling me."

"Just don't inform my partner. He doesn't like me telling civilians anything. Especially Anglo civilians," he said in an effort to keep things light. "I'll speak to you later."

I replaced the receiver and sat down to think about what I'd just heard. Even though the conversation had been short, I'd learned a lot. First and foremost, Celine was dead, probably killed right after she'd left me. Maybe if I hadn't plied her with alcohol her reflexes would have been better and she could have defended herself. No. Beating myself up was wasted energy. I had to think forward.

So she lived in the Plateau. That fit. It's a neighborhood in the city core that has been a stepping stone for countless generations of immigrants. In the eighties the cold-water flats and industrial lofts began to be attractive to young artists looking for cheap digs. The inevitable followed, and gentrification set in with a vengeance. It's still cheap and uncomfortable, albeit loaded with modern appliances, and the young trendies are the major tenants. I could picture Celine there, in a corner coffee bar drinking a latte. I altered the image to a proper bar and a martini and bade her a silent farewell. No matter what she had been involved with, she was too young and beautiful to die.

Why did she have two apartments? Was it her safety net in case it didn't work out with Frank? Did he know about it? Questions that would probably never be answered.

Greg had called me Barbara at last and said he was worried about me. That was sweet. *Was* there anything to be worried about? I know I had something to fret over. Two kilos of it. My nerves got the best of me, and I got up to check that the front door was locked. On reflection, I had had the feeling of being followed the last two days. I dismissed it as paranoia; if I had been shadowed it would have been Grandese's boys working out their kidnap plan. Now that I had explained it to myself I felt better.

The conversation had infused me with fear, but damned if I was going to let Frank spook me. I changed my clothes in an effort to discard the fear with the frocks. If I didn't get a grip soon, I'd need Mme Jacqueline four times a week, and I couldn't afford it.

The phone rang, and again I jumped for it. Time to deal with Joanne, and it was preferable to vent anger than live fear. At last I'd get my licks in.

No such luck.

"Hello, Ms. Simons, it's Jennifer, Mr. Korlinski's secretary."

"Hi, Jennifer. What's up?"

"Mr. Korlinski asked me to tell you to watch the six o'clock news."

"Okay, I'll bite. What's this about?"

"I really don't know. He's been out of the office all day, so I didn't speak to him. Look, it's going to be on in a second, and I want to watch it too, so I'm gonna go. Okay?"

"Are you still at the office at this time?"

"Nah. He left the message on my machine, and I found it when I got home."

So Pietr didn't trust the phones at Pancake and left a message on Jennifer's machine. That meant he'd been out doing something extracurricular. But why not my machine, or even me in person? Was there something wrong with my line? Until I spoke to him from a call box in the morning I was going to be wary of what I said over the lines. Paranoia was winning.

I went into the bedroom and flicked on the TV. There sat Joanne, calm and cool with her hair slicked back, making stupid opening small talk with her male coanchor. Then he looked into the camera and said, "Today the RCMP broke up an interprovincial cigarette smuggling operation. As a result of a tip to the Mounties, six men have been arrested in a most unusual raid."

The screen flashed to the inside of a warehouse somewhere, with Joanne standing in the middle, microphone in hand. She'd been called out at the last minute, because she was wearing the same thing as she was in her anchor position. She never does that. Every segment that she's in shows her sporting a different outfit. Some nights it's a veritable fashion orgy.

Joanne proceeded to tell us that on a tip from an unidentified informant, an organized cigarette-smuggling ring had been broken up. Hints of organized crime connections. There followed a list of numbers and calculations about the cache. While she was talking I saw that in the background, not six feet away from her, Wayne was being led off in handcuffs. He wore a different T-shirt, but his belly button still made random appearances. Joanne looked unfazed as she continued her report, confident in the assumption that he would not connect her to the Bobbi Berlin of Amherst Street. She really is fearless.

Well, she got her story. Maybe it wasn't as exciting as the one she had planned on, but it was the lead story and good enough to alleviate some of the guilt I harbored. I hoped that was the end of it. Wayne would certainly tell the police about Wanda and Bobbi in an effort to spread the blame, but I think we'd covered our tracks well enough on that front. Anyway, it was such an absurd tale that no one would believe him. They'd check it out though, and it remained a question of just how observant the hookers in the bar had been. Hopefully, my boots had distracted them from my face. I hoped poor Joey hadn't been caught in the dragnet.

Joanne finished her report with the usual comment about the police looking for further suspects, and the screen came back to her at the anchor desk. Her opposite asked, "Do the police know who provided the information, Joanne?"

Stupid question. Even if they did, Joanne would never disclose the name to a million or so viewers. If the anchor didn't smarten up he'd be looking for another job soon. A pretty face will only take you so far.

"No, John. They've ascribed it to an anonymous informant. I'm sure they wouldn't reveal a name, in any case." She didn't add "you fool" but her tone of voice intimated it.

Good for you, Joanne, I rooted. Score one for the intelligent guys.

The newscast continued with the rest of the events beclouding our city and world. I wasn't interested in anything except the weather, and I should have skipped that as well, since the pretty weathergirl, who had to be a thorn in Joanne's side, informed me that on the upside it was going to warm up a little but on the downside another dump was headed our way. She used those exact words, so I figured Joanne didn't have much to worry about.

My snow tires were earning their keep this winter.

Two seconds after sign-off the phone rang, and this time it was Joanne at last.

"Hi. Did you see it? I don't know why, but everything went down today. I'm on a lucky streak because at three o'clock I got a call from the RCMP telling me to haul ass over to Fullum Street with a crew immediately. I was the only one there when it all happened and the first one on the air with it. It was a close call whether I would get back here in time, but I did it. They edited like mad, and we made it with only seconds to spare. The other stations had to settle for interviews with the Mounties after the fact. A scoop!"

She was ecstatic and flying in the stratosphere. I could detect no hint at disappointment at not being able to complete her original plan, whatever that may have been. I was so glad the episode was closed that I wasn't even interested in what it had been. Maybe when we were old and sitting in our rockers I'd ask her about it, and if she could still remember anything we'd have a good laugh.

Pietr had evidently listened to my confession with both ears, and had saved my butt by throwing the exclusive Joanne's way. I could also deduce the provenance of the call that directed her to the site. It would have felt good to deflate her bubble and admit my part in the story, but that would have meant admitting my deception. Although I knew I was in the right and she was reveling in her story, she'd lecture me, and I wasn't up for that. I could do that very well myself.

"What was that message all about? So I haven't called you for a bit. Big deal. No need to get nasty."

"Joanne, we have to talk." That's a line one spouse usually says to the other before she or he walks out.

"My, aren't we dramatic. Look, I'll tell you all about Greg tomorrow. This time I swear. I'll meet you at the Pizza Hut on Decarie at noon. Gotta go. I've got some spots to do to promote the late newscast. My story's gonna be picked up by the national feed. Bye."

She hung up. Oh well, let her have her moment of glory before I laced into her. It was insufferable how self-righteous I was becoming over the whole Grandese interlude, and I would find it more satisfying to have her present in living flesh to bear the brunt of my planned tirade. I was sort of glad I hadn't been able to get a word in edgewise. She thought I was pissed about Greg, and I couldn't wait to lambaste her about Grandese. I needed to see her face. Also, in the back of my mind there was still the suspicion that my phone might be tapped. Greg and Pietr were turning me into a raging paranoiac.

The choice of Pizza Hut is not so unusual if you know Joanne. There's an all-you-can-eat buffet at lunch, and Joanne sure does like to eat. They see this thin thing coming and think they've nabbed a good one; she'll just have a nibble and they'll make a pile of money on her. Wrong. She packs away enough for two truck drivers but does have the decency to leave a generous tip. Large enough to assure her seating as soon as she arrives, to the annoyance of the assembled queue, who cry Foul! or Celebrity Preference! when they recognize her. It isn't her renown that gets her a seat, it's her money.

On a certain level I was disappointed that I had to postpone my gratification until tomorrow; I'd been anticipating the pleasure of being one up on Joanne. I put on my coat and boots and headed out the door to the inevitable elevator. Wouldn't you know it, Mrs. Brooks opened her door the instant she heard the snap of my lock.

"Barbara dear, I just saw your friend on TV. Very pretty she looks. Do you think you could ask her to bring me an autographed picture next time she comes by? Have her sign it to Agatha. Thank you."

I had no time to say anything before the door closed. She hadn't said one snippy thing for a change, although to my surprise, I preferred the haughtiness to the treacly syrup she dispensed today. Joanne was going to pay for this too. The tab was mounting.

It really wasn't worth thinking about for more than half a second, and a good dinner beckoned. I immediately forgot the whole interchange.

An unfamiliar doorman guarded Susan's building so I was forced to park indoors and pay for the pleasure. For some reason I don't mind extravagantly tipping for a free service, but I hate being made to pay. Same money, different privileges. Since I had joined the ranks of the unemployed, I had gained a new perspective on the employed classes. They pay for fewer things and have more money. At this pace of dissatisfied cogitation, if I didn't find a job soon I'd turn into a Marxist, albeit a well-dressed one.

You can't visit a resident and park underground in Westmount Square without venturing outdoors. You can only get as far as the shopping level from the garage, and then you have to exit and walk around the building. In the evening there are few residents on the concourse behind whom you can sneak into the residential areas. During the few minutes it had taken me to drive in, find a spot, take the escalator to the shopping level, and pause to select the door that would get me closest to the entrance of Susan's building, it had begun to snow. Hard. While I was driving over in my car I hadn't been aware of the wind, but as I crossed the open plaza that Mies van der Rohe had obviously designed for warmer climes, it blew at me with gale force. The little bits of snow felt like BBs as they pelted my face.

When I finally reached the lobby I could feel a healthy glow on my face.

The doorman took my name and announced me before he let me get into the elevator. Another building with the semblance of tight security. Over the past few days I had learned the ease with which it could all be bypassed. In a building like Westmount Square, false security, probably costs a lot, I thought.

Susan was waiting at her door, looking wonderful in a pair of khaki pants with matching silk camp shirt. Casual chic that cost as much as the building security and equally meaningless. I shook my head to clear the cynical thoughts. The little person inside me is nicer than that, and it was time to look for her. I would not allow Wayne and Grandese to shape my soul.

"Hi, you look great," she said.

"Thanks, so do you."

At least we didn't air kiss three times in the Montreal fashion.

"Here, let me take your coat while you take off your boots."

"Where's the witch?" I asked in a voice I realized was too loud the second I heard it. I heard snickering in the distance and for a moment panicked, having every intention of bolting for the elevator if I saw her. However, it was only Barry, who obviously shares my affection for her.

"Come on, she's not that bad. Robert likes her." Maybe she was a split personality, and I got the evil twin. "Anyhow, she's off tonight, so it's just us."

"Good," I said as I handed her my coat and took off my boots for the twelve-millionth time this winter.

Robert came bounding in and flew at me. I caught him mid-leap and whirled him around, ending in a mutual bear hug.

"Hi there, kiddo. How'ya doin'?"

"Fine, Auntie Barbara. Put me down and come with me."

As Susan and Barry watched, he solemnly took me by the hand and led me into the bedroom, taking pains to ensure the door was tightly shut. His bedroom here wasn't as heavily loaded as the one at Frank's, but I noticed that he did have more than his fair share of toys. Susan may claim not to have any money, but she sure has the right address and all the accoutrements.

"Okay, what's up? What's the problem?"

"Well, it's not really a problem," he said, considering carefully.

"It seems to be. You've got everybody worried."

"I do not. I've been good."

"You certainly have, and that's the worry. You're very serious these days. What's on your mind?"

I get along well with Robert because I treat him as a quasi-adult. I try not to talk down to him and never tell him how adorable he is. I just tell everyone else, since I'm madly and passionately in love with him. He's just the most precious thing in the whole wide world, and I adore him to death.

"It's the kids in school, Auntie Barbara."

"What?" Not an astonished interjection. A simple request for more information. Perfectly acceptable for once.

"They're saying things about Daddy."

"What things?"

"That he was a bad man and he got punished. They say I must be bad too." No wonder he'd been behaving so well.

"My best friend Joshua says his mother won't let him play with me until they get the guy who killed Daddy. She says it's too dangerous. Is it, Auntie Barbara?"

Poor thing. Such a big burden for such a little child. First the loss of his father, and then the loss of his best friend. If I ever got my hands on Joshua's mother she'd hear it from me. Didn't she see the cruelty of her words and actions? Probably not. She was concerned with the safety and well-being of her own precious package and wasn't taking any risks. I could see both points of view, and both were right in their own way, but Robert was mine and Joshua wasn't.

"Sweetie, you're not in any danger. Nobody is going to hurt you. You know how careful your mother is."

"But what if someone hurts her? I'll be all alone," he said, his little body shaking and tears brimming.

The crux of the matter.

"No one is going to hurt Susan," I said, possibly lying. "Frank's death had nothing to do with you or her. She won't leave you, Robert. She'll be with you until you're very old."

The talk show psychiatrists say you're supposed to level with children; be brutally honest to prepare them for the hazards of life. However, this wasn't the occasion for that. For all I knew, a bus could flatten Susan the very next day, but that wasn't likely, since she wasn't one to walk the streets in winter. Robert was immersed in loss, and I wasn't going to aggravate the situation.

"And Barry's here to protect the both of you."

"Yeah." A discordant note in that word.

"What's the matter? Don't you like Barry?"

"He's all right, I guess. He's not very good with kids, but I can see he tries. And he likes my mother a lot. Most of my friends' parents are divorced, so I know a lot about this and Barry isn't bad. He just tries too hard."

Robert was indeed a sagacious eight-year-old. It is a reflection of our times that he could handle the situation with such sophistication and aplomb. I was very proud and impressed.

"You're right. Your mother likes him a lot too, and you're very smart to recognize that he's trying with you. Give him some more time. Maybe he'll learn how to do it better."

"Okay," he said, mollified. He's so adorable.

"Most important of all, you'll always have me. I'd kick butt for you."

That earned me a huge smile.

"Yeah, you'd be good at that. You're tough."

I chose to accept that as a compliment.

"And I love you a whole bunch, Robert."

"Me too, Auntie Barbara. A whole lotta bunch."

"One last thing before we go in for dinner. I'll make it quick because I'm famished. Don't worry about what Joshua and the other kids say. I know it's difficult to hear, but it too will pass. Everyone's just a little nervous these days so the mothers are being extra-careful. Wait it out, and when they find the bad guys it'll all be over."

"Are they gonna find them soon?"

"I hope so. Now let's eat."

He opened the door and tore off to the dining area, leaving me miles behind.

"Let's eat," he trumpeted. "Auntie Barbara is hungry."

By the time I reached the table, Susan and Barry were already seated, big grins on their faces as they looked affectionately at Robert, who stood behind my chair, holding it for me. This kid had manners.

Dinner consisted of a huge salad, rosy leg of lamb with a choice of mint sauce or jelly, and plenty of side dishes. I love eating in houses where there are men and children present. Lots of red meat and good stuff.

In deference to Robert, we kept the tone light. We learned a lot about astronomy that I didn't know but was colloquial to Robert, who was disgusted with our ignorance. Barry regaled us with a reading of the operating instructions for a hair dryer that he was importing by the crateload from China. Those people sure are creative with the English language. I offered to translate it to English and then retranslate it to French for him. He accepted, sweetening the deal by offering me two hundred and fifty dollars for my work if I could deliver in a week. And there would be more to come if I did a good job. This was great news. At last a source of cash besides my bank account. I was in such a good mood that, with nary a thought to my spreading hips, I tucked into a large piece of blueberry pie. On the side of caution I eschewed the ice cream.

Robert left us as Susan brought out coffee, which I don't drink but everyone else does, so I pretend. He declared that for my information, now that he was eight and a half he was old enough to take a bath all by himself, which he was planning to do right now.

"Alone? What, no ducky?" I asked.

"Auntie Barbara, I'm too old for duckies," he said, the exasperation visible all over his cute little face. "But I do have water guns," he added with a sly laugh.

Susan shrugged her shoulders and called to his departing form, " If you get water all over the bathroom floor you're in big trouble, monster." To us she said, "Now that he's allowed to bathe unsupervised it's a lot more work for me. I think more water goes on the floor than down the drain.

"How did you find him?" she asked, concern evident.

"He'll be fine. He's just had a lot on his plate lately. The kids in school are giving him a hard time, and he's concerned something will happen to you. But don't be too worried. He's well grounded, and he'll be okay. And by the way," I said, facing Barry, "he likes you, so that's not one of his problems."

Barry preened. This relationship was serious indeed if he cared so much about what Robert thought. I'd better be invited to this wedding.

"Listen up. I've got some serious scoop . . . "

I told them about most of my conversation with Greg. They were both alarmed and appalled at the news of Celine's death. Susan was so shocked that she forgot to ask who Celine was, inadvertently revealing at last the fact that she knew she was Bimbo. Somewhere there's a list of names hidden—a list with the name, current phone number, and birth date of every single Bimbo and Bimbette that has crossed her path over the years.

As I told them the gruesome details, maybe embellishing them a little for effect, Susan rose and went to stand behind Barry with her hands on his shoulders. Envy coursed through me. They asked hundreds of questions to which I had few answers, but I got an appreciative laugh when I told them how I'd sicced the police on Lainie.

Susan and I cleared the table and left Barry in his place, poring over his Sino-English manual perplexedly. I wasn't as confounded. I mean how hard can it be to outline the use of a hair dryer to someone who won't read it anyway? All anybody remembers is the dire warning not to use it in the bathtub.

As soon as the door swung shut behind us, I whispered, none too softly, "Susan, I have to get rid of that shit in my house. It's scaring the hell out of me. Celine's dead, Frank's dead, and I've got what they were probably killed for. I'm really scared. It's one thing for me to tell Robert everything's going to be fine, but I'm terrified."

"Calm down. You're right. We'll think of something."

"Not good enough. If we don't think of *something* by tomorrow night, I'm going to flush it."

In the back of my mind there was the niggling knowledge that the heroin had to be out of my house by Thursday. It took a few seconds but I thought of why: Sam. No way was I going to cope with him and heroin. One problem in my house at a time.

"All right. Tomorrow night we'll do something. I don't know what yet, but something. I promise we'll get it out of there."

"Okay," I acceded, somewhat placated.

I helped her load the dishwasher and we went back out only to find Barry still seated, still puzzled.

"Who writes these things? How do they expect to compete in a world market with this crap?"

"Barry, they know people like you will hire people like me to fix it. Besides, it's good for the economy; I need the money. May they continue forever," I said, giving the Chinese translators my blessing.

I wondered if he had overheard any of the conversation in the kitchen, but he didn't seem to have, so I tried to dismiss the thought. My paranoia was running amok.

I bade them good night, got splashed by a giggling Robert as I bent to kiss him good-bye, put on my boots, and began the trek to my car, looking over my shoulder every step of the way. If someone was following me, he was doing a good job.

At home, safely in bed behind locked doors, I fretted about Sam. I was too chicken to pick up the phone and face the music over the wires. As I wavered about calling, I remembered the possibility that my phone was tapped, and that clinched it. I nearly believed me.

17

BY NINE O'CLOCK I had read the paper, done the two crossword puzzles in the *Gazette* after reading all about yesterday's raid on the warehouse and learning nothing new, showered, dressed, and had two cigarettes and one Diet Coke. I thought about making my bed, but it seemed too great an effort so I just threw up the covers, leaving all the decorative pillows piled on the floor. Mme Jacqueline could sort out their correct placement on Thursday. It's my house and my bed, but she manages to make it look better than I can. I guess that's why she's the professional.

Following the application of mascara, I went downstairs to the doorman's desk and asked to use his phone. I pulled it as far away as its long wire allowed, to get some privacy. His distrusting eyes never left me, though I couldn't walk off with it as it was firmly attached to the wall behind him. It's boxy, black, and ugly, so I wouldn't have any use for it in any event. However, if he kept up his staring I'd sneak down one night while he was off peeing, cut the wire, and abscond with it. He must pee sometime; it just seems he's always at his post. I decided I hated him.

Since my Wanda episode, all the doormen had been observing me with suspicion. If I kept my nose clean for a while, maybe I could convince them that I was still my old boring, conventional self. From the way this one followed me with narrowed eyes, I could tell it was going to take a long time.

I got Jennifer on the line directly; I guessed the receptionist was at her post over the toilet bowl.

"Hi, Ms. Simons. I watched the news last night and didn't see Mr. Korlinski. Couldn't figure out why he wanted you to watch. What was it?"

"I don't know either," I lied. "That's why I'm calling. Is he in?"

"He's on another line, but he shouldn't be long. Do you want to hold?"

"Sure."

I was forced to wait to the accompaniment of a commercial about the wonderful destinations that I could fly to at unbelievable discounts. I wasn't interested. The one perk I had left was that I could fly anywhere I wanted for nothing, and the idea of a vacation sounded mighty attractive, but until I got rid of the two kilos of heroin stashed in my house the probability of leaving town was slim. As I half heard the virtues of warm beaches and sunny skies, I became more bound and determined to get that stuff out of there today. Susan had promised to come up with something, but that wasn't good enough. If she didn't take it somewhere by tonight, it was going to join the receptionist's last night's dinner while I danced a jig of joy as I watched it swirl away. If it's true what they say about the sewers, there were going to be some very stoned alligators and rats prowling tonight.

"Hey, Babs, didya see it?" a voice boomed into my ear. I snapped to attention. Even on the phone Pietr has that effect on me. "Got the Cowan woman an exclusive in the bargain, so that should square things for you."

"Thanks," I started saying. It was no use. He barreled along, obviously in a great mood. I was happy I'd been able to lift him from his depression, if only for a little while.

"Also got to make points with the Mounties. They were in shock about the whole thing; had no idea what was about to go down. This was big, Babs. Much more organized than I'd ever expected from your information. We found their warehouse still loaded from the last run, and a big one was planned for next week. The narcs didn't initially believe me when I came to them, but I've got what they call credibility."

"How'd you find them so fast? I gave you nearly nothing."

"That was the easy part. We picked up your pal Wayne Grandese at the coffee shop you mentioned, put a tail on him, and he led us right in. For being so well organized he was pretty stupid."

"Wayne Grandese! That's his last name?" I said that a little too loud and saw by the size of his eyes that the doorman had heard me. Grandese is a famous name in this town. Rehabilitation was going to take longer than I had envisaged.

"Is he related?" I asked, still shocked but with lowered volume.

"Yup. The prodigal son. We always knew Francesco had another kid and he was gay. Old Frankie chucked him out of the house a few years ago in disgrace. That kind of lifestyle don't sit too well with a fine old Italian family like his. Murder and mayhem are fine, but a gay son, no way. Little Waynie had lived in that house a long time and learned a lot. Decided to freelance and go into competition. Show Poppa up. The names'll be on the air today as we didn't release them until this mornin', so it's gonna fly in the Grandese household tonight."

He was having a merry old time telling me this. He sounded more relaxed and happy than I'd heard him in ages.

"Gotta thank you for this one, Babs. The most expensive dinner in town. You pick the place and name the time, and I'll clear the decks. I'll be there, and I'll even bring flowers. Irises, if I remember right."

"That's great, Pietr. You sound terrific."

"I am, Babs. That was fun, and there hasn't been much of that around here lately."

"In that vein, is there something wrong with my phone? Why did you call Jennifer instead of me?"

A raucous laugh came down the lines. "You're gettin' paranoid, little lady." I knew that. "I didn't have your number on me, and Jennifer had stepped out of the office when I called there. Didn't wanna leave the message with the battle-ax in the front. Don't trust her much. I knew Jennifer would follow through.

"Nah, you can say anythin' you want on your phone. If you'd like, I can have it swept for you, though I don't think that's necessary. You can have your conversations with that long-distance boyfriend of yours."

Shit. He knew about Sam. How? I'd never know. I have to remember that Pietr usually knows everything. He didn't know about the heroin though and I was still suspicious about my line, but I couldn't ask him to check it for me because that would signal I was up to something, and he'd dig and dig until he found out.

Poker faces can't give you away on low-tech phones. "Thanks for the offer, but I don't think it will be necessary. And never mind about my so-called boyfriend. It's none of your business."

"Haven't minded 'til now, Missy," he said, still gregarious. "Have to go back to work. See you next week. Thanks again for the adventure. Made me feel like a young buck again."

He rang off and left me with a smile of wonderment on my face. Wayne Grandese. I wondered if Joanne knew that before she got into the sting. I doubted it. She's stupid sometimes, but not dumb. And she likes being alive a whole lot.

Well, at least Francesco Grandese now had more on his mind than Joanne.

I went back to my apartment whistling dissonantly. I'm not

very good at it but that's never stopped me. I did some paperwork for a while, balancing my checkbook and checking on my investments. I have discovered that it takes a lot of work not to work, because if you don't manage what you've got carefully, you won't have it for long. As a bonus, I also had eight hundred Grandese *père et fils* dollars to deposit. Not shabby for a few hours' inconvenience.

Pietr's good mood was infectious, and I was in fine spirits when I drove out of the garage to meet Joanne at Pizza Hut. It was a minor inconvenience when I realized the weathergirl had been right; *dump* was the appropriate word. It was coming down in blinding waves, but being the Montreal driver that I am, it didn't faze me much, nor the other drivers, who were skidding and sliding about, pretending nothing was wrong. It was slow going, and when I finally arrived I found Joanne already seated with her first platter of food in front of her, nibbling delicately, having had the good manners to await my appearance before she tucked in with a vengeance.

I shook the melting snow from my coat and hung it on the hook attached to the booth to let it dry out. The place was steamy from all the drying outerwear, and the aroma of pizza was counterbalanced by the odor of wet dog. We're so used to it we hardly notice anymore.

As I slid into the booth and prepared to pull out a cigarette to heighten my pleasure at the anticipated interchange, I saw that we were in a non-smoking section. I should have known better than to let Joanne arrive first. If I'd been the one, I could have jumped the queue at the drop of her name and chosen a table more suited to my vices. She hates when I smoke but has given up the battle of reprimanding me. It doesn't work, and she isn't enough of a paragon of virtue to be in a position to lecture me. But first come, first served was the order of the day in our never-ending subtle competition for one-upmanship. She stared into the distance as I replaced the pack in my purse, the hint of a smug smile gracing the face that I felt like bashing.

"You got here early," I said.

"Yup. I'm famished." Tell me something new, I thought. "I was the star of the newsroom this morning and felt entitled to the time off. Did you see the *National News* last night? My story was the lead. I'm eternally grateful that no country chose yesterday to invade another, nothing flooded, and nothing major burned down. Mine was the biggest story of the day. Do you want to hear the most amazing part? Do you know what Wayne's last name is?"

I did, but I wasn't admitting it, or I would have had to explain how I knew. I had no intention of involving Pietr or mentioning my part in the proceedings. She was satisfied with her scoop. After all, I had my health and body parts to consider.

"Grandese!" she exploded. "He's Francesco's son! Can you believe it!"

I must have looked suitably shocked, because she prattled on.

"Did you hear what that idiot John asked me on air last night? About the anonymous caller? He sure got a lecture about that bit of idiocy. I swear, the guy looks great, has a fabulous voice, and can read the teleprompter without glasses, but he has the IQ of a squirrel. I think his time is up. Have you noticed the cute guy who does the sports? I think he's about to be promoted. His credentials are too good to stay in sports, and word is they've been trying him out there to gauge the public's reaction. Pretty soon he's going to replace John-Boy at the anchor desk. And isn't it great that Beth is on holiday and I got to sit in for her last night? Anchor and lead story. Doesn't get much better.

"But back to matters at hand. They think the tip was from Grandese. Not Francesco himself but one of his guys. It seems Wayne doesn't get along too well with his father and was planning a little freelance. Daddy got wind of it and pulled the plug.

I'm not convinced about that, though. I don't think he'd turn in his own son, no matter how much he disapproved of him and his lifestyle. I would think he'd handle the matter himself.

"Whoever it was, God bless him."

I was a "her," and I'd accept all the blessing I could get.

I sat through her monologue patiently, knowing I would get to top her, since her story was already public knowledge. She needed to crow, but it was okay, she deserves a few accolades every now and then as she's good at her job. Some of the facts I already knew, but I was treated to a different take on things. I had the real one, I thought. For a fleeting nanosecond I even felt sorry for Francesco Grandese. First his son was far out of the closet and into a cell, and second, the speculation was that he'd turned Wayne in. There would be much soul-searching in the hierarchy today. The nanosecond expired quickly. A mobster is a mobster, and how he got his comeuppance was no concern of mine.

As she wound up, I said demurely, "Joanne, I think you'd better eat something before I tell you a story that's going to make you choke."

"Like you could," she said, still flying. Her need to fill her stomach got the best of her, and we both went to load our plates. We split up to forage separately, and the next time I saw her she had three different slices of pizza, a huge portion of lasagna, a bowl of spaghetti, and a starstruck busboy in tow to transport it all for her. I had settled for a self-service single slice of pizza with a small side salad. Not quite diet food, but a zillion calories less than Joanne's feast.

She piled right in, gracefully shoveling the food into her mouth. It all looked so polite and mannerly, yet she was consuming the food at an alarming rate. I didn't say anything because I was sure she'd choke for real. All of it, every last morsel, disappeared down her gullet, not a drop landing on her cream silk shirt (white is too bright on air). I kept hoping for a tomato sauce disaster, but none was forthcoming. When we finished at the same time, she smiled in the direction of the busboy, who was at our table in seconds, clearing the empty platters.

"Jeff," she said, having taken note of his name tag with her reporter's eagle eye and thick lenses, "would you be a dear and bring me some coffee and a dessert? The buffet table's so crowded. You select something delicious for me. Please."

The boy was apoplectic. He belatedly realized that he hadn't drawn breath since he'd arrived at the table and took a huge gulp of air, which he promptly swallowed in embarrassment and joy. To his further chagrin, this resulted in a bout of hiccups.

"Yessir, I mean yes Joanne, I mean Mrs. Cowan, I mean Ms. Cowan (hic)." If he got any redder he'd pop a major artery.

"And Jeff, hon, bring my friend some tea. No dessert," she said to his departing, ticcing form.

The bitch. Dessert for her, none for me because I was in danger of getting too fat. Which made me angry and in the perfect mood to lambaste her.

I had to postpone my tirade and calm down a little, as Jeff was back in twenty-two seconds with tea for me and coffee and a very large piece of something smothered in whipped cream for Joanne. He'd made it a point to bring only one fork.

"I was kidnapped yesterday," I said nonchalantly. We were going to do this at my pace.

"What? Somebody stole you and returned you when they realized you'd lost your job and weren't ransomable?"

The bitch wasn't taking this seriously.

"No Joanne, I was cornered in the garage at the club and forced at gunpoint into a car." I'd added the gun part for effect. They could have had guns; I just didn't see any.

"What!" Now I felt a lot better.

"It's true. Two thugs pushed me into a car and drove me off. Although I got one smack in the balls with my heavy brown oxfords "

"Ouch!" she winced.

"That's not what he said. Much more colorful vocabulary. They drove me off and transferred me to another car. In the middle of Outremont. In broad daylight. You know, more goes on in this town than you'd imagine. Hasidim were strolling by, kids were playing, and I was being victimized. Some community watch. There was a sign posted right in the window of the house we were in front of, for all the good it did."

I was making up a lot of this to further embellish my story for dramatic effect. I'd been too terrified to take notice of the name of the street I was on, much less the buildings and houses. The Hasidic touch was good, I thought. Never hurts to inject a little religion into the proceedings.

"Quit editorializing and tell me what happened," she ordered in true reporter style, without the manners she generally displays toward the victims she interviews. I was Barbara, and she was used to pushing me around.

However, this time it was my story, and we were going to do it the way *I* wanted.

"Inside the other car someone was waiting for me. A man. A well-dressed man with white hair and very black eyes." I paused, waiting for a suitable reaction.

"Who?" she asked, picking up the cue.

"Think about it. Who do you know who rides around in a white stretch Pimpmobile and fits the description?"

I mentally kicked myself. It was too good a clue, and I had planned to draw this out more; make her beg.

"No!" Still and all, a good reaction.

"Yes." Calmly.

"No!" Even more incredulous.

"You're repeating yourself. Yes, none other than your ever-loving minimal-membered boyfriend, Francesco Grandese." Not a bad turn of phrase, if I do say so myself.

"What!"

Perfection achieved.

I got down to basics, telling her about him pressing his plea on me. I even told her how I'd extorted three hundred dollars from him to pay for my navy pants. The best part was when I recounted how I'd implored him to give her up for the sake of mankind, how I'd appealed to his nobler side by intoning that countless lives were at stake, that Jacques would crumble and innocents would die. It was so dramatically well told that she didn't even notice the whipped cream that dribbled off her suspended fork and landed with a silent splat on her shirt, front and center. I rejoiced and ignored it, leaving her to survey the damage later, and finished with my knockout blow, telling her that Grandese fancied me too and would consider a threesome if we would only make it so.

"He barely has enough for one, what would he do with the two of us? Expect us to entertain each other, I guess," she said, smiling dolefully.

We stared at each other warily for an instant, but the moment passed and she polished off the rest of the something on her plate, lost in thought.

"I owe you for that," she said grudgingly. "Although you managed to turn a tidy profit from the adventure. I was with you when you bought those navy pants.

"Thanks," she said softly, taking my hand. "I really mean it. He could have made big trouble for me, so I appreciate your getting me off the hook. You're a true friend."

Having dispensed with the humiliating realization that she was now in my debt, she made motions to leave, gathering her purse and briefcase.

"Just a damned minute, sister. We're not through here."

"You mean there's more?" she asked innocently, prepared to listen. She relaxed the grip on her belongings and turned her attention back to me.

"There sure as hell is more. More for me. Now tell me what

you know about Gregory Allard. All of it. Now. Or I'll do something drastic. You've been tap dancing around the issue for days, and I want to know immediately. Or else!"

There were a lot of "or elses" I could think of off the top of my head, and so could she.

Jeff reappeared to clear the table, a major hiccup escaping as he reached us. Joanne dismissed him with a waggle of her fingertips, then called him back and ordered another cup of coffee. She called him "sweet'ums" which sounded to me like an insult, but he departed in raptures. I was sure he'd never miss one of her newscasts ever again and would take the same liberties in recounting the story to his friends as I had taken with mine. She forgot to order me another cup of tea, but he brought one anyway. Anything for the queen's lady-in-waiting.

"It's nothing, really," she began in a dismissive tone.

"Spill," I ordered. It was nice being in charge for a change.

"Right," she said, organizing her thoughts. I was going to hear this at last; I could tell by the set of her chin.

"It was just before Jacques and I got married. We'd just moved in together, and I was passionate about him. And faithful. I still love him to death, by the way. Anyway, infidelity was the furthest thing from my mind when Greg crossed my path. It was at a particularly gruesome murder that had gone unnoticed for a few days so the air was ripe, to say the least."

The slut. She wasn't even married yet, and she was off boffing Greg. I know all about life-affirming sex after horrible deaths. I'd seen it just the other night on TV. I didn't say anything, deciding to allow her more rope before I strangled her.

It seemed all my fantasies had been violent this last while. I returned my full attention to her. I wasn't going to miss a word.

"I thought I was going to lose my lunch and thus embarrass

myself, when this cute guy offers me a V Versace-scented hand-kerchief. When I realized what I was smelling I took a closer look at him. Isn't that what you wear?"

"Yeah," I said. Me and some other girlfriend of his. It isn't your run-of-the-mill perfume; hard to find just anywhere. Time to change.

"What I saw I liked. He's good looking and well turned out. English, too. We flirted a little. Even though I was in a monoga-mous phase, I never gave up flirting. I wouldn't know how. After I recovered and my bile returned to its proper place, we went out for coffee and talked and flirted. Of course he asked me out, and I daresay I was tempted, but I ruefully admitted I was getting married in two weeks and told him to wait a couple of years."

Double slut. She knew she couldn't last.

"The scent of the handkerchief put me in mind of you, and I thought I'd offer you to him. It was time you hooked up with someone else besides Sam. You could use getting laid more often. It's good for the complexion."

"What's wrong with my complexion?" I demanded. I know I'm not gorgeous, but I haven't had a zit in years. As a matter of fact, I'd always considered my skin as one of my better features.

"Nothing's wrong with it. Sometimes you do get a little pasty looking. Nothing like a little hanky-panky to start your blood rushing and give you a little color. You have heard of afterglow, haven't you?" she asked, teasingly.

"Shut up and continue." Oxymoronic but appropriate.

"He was a little leery. After all, remember all our horrific blind dates in high school."

Mine, not hers. She never needed to be fixed up, thick glasses notwithstanding.

"I had just covered one of your press conferences and knew it would be on air that night, so I told him to watch and call me at the station the next day. We parted, and I fully expected never to hear from him again."

"And?"

"And the next afternoon he called. It was a long time ago, over four years, so don't get upset."

"I'm not upset. Go on."

I was, though. What was coming was not going to be pleasant, and I'm really bad at rejection, which might help explain why I don't date locally more often. If they reject you out of town you can slink back home and pretend nothing happened.

"Grow up. Stop looking so glum. It isn't that bad."

"So quit stalling and spit it out."

"He'd watched you carefully during the segment. Even taped it and reran it to get a better feel."

"And?" I repeated, bracing myself.

"He found you too tough. He was afraid of you."

"Me?" I was shocked.

"Yes, you."

I thought about it for a moment and decided he was probably right. It had been a press conference, and when it came to work I *was* tough, never giving an inch when I knew I was right. I was earning big bucks and worth every penny of it. I casually wondered what I had been wearing to enhance the image. Often I'm so shallow; it's just so much easier to attack the visuals.

Joanne was right. It hadn't been that bad. I wasn't even upset; I thought it was funny.

"The wuss," I said, sputtering with laughter.

"My sentiments exactly. Just think how embarrassed he was to be finally confronted with you. The two of us together must have sent him reeling. Good thing for him it was a funeral and we were in front. He can't know what I've told you, and he must be humiliated at the prospect of discovery, since my reporter's eye tells me his interest in you is more than casual."

"It isn't." I waved the enticing idea away.

"Is too."

"Is not."

"Is too. You seem to not dislike the notion. What about Sam? Spoken to him?"

Panic set in. "Shit. Joanne, he's arriving tomorrow."

"Here?" she asked, genuinely shocked.

"He left a message that he was coming. Said he wanted to tell me something. I haven't had the nerve to call him back to ask him when he's arriving so I can pick him up at the airport."

"Let him take a cab."

"He'll have to. I'm scared. What could he want? This can't be good."

"I don't know what good is when it comes to Sam. You know how I feel about him. I just don't want you to get hurt. Look, it can't be horrible. Men can never face you when they say something devastating, much less travel hundreds of miles to do it. They phone or fax. So don't worry; you'll know soon enough. Call me the second he's gone. Or before, if you need me."

With that we got up to leave, Joanne once again picking up the tab.

"Business expense. We did talk about Wayne and his connection to Grandese, didn't we? I can swear to that in front of the grand jury when they indict me for income tax fraud."

"Joanne, this is Canada. We don't have a grand jury."

"Whatever—"

She flashed Jeff a warm smile and left him a copious tip. My dried-off coat was instantly covered with snow the second I hit the outdoors. Joanne declined my offer of a lift and hailed a cab that magically appeared. I, on the other hand, spent the next ten minutes sweeping snow off the hood and roof and scraping the windows before I could get my car to a drivable state, getting soaked and sweaty in the process.

She was probably warmly ensconced in her office, hard at work jabbering on the phone, with an open bag of licorice bits at her elbow, by the time I drove away.

I'd forgotten to ask her what had happened to Joey, but it could wait. That chapter of my life was behind me, and it was going to stay there. Driving conditions were too dangerous for me to even have time to consider the possibility that someone was following me, so I went home free of paranoia for the first time in five days.

18

BY THE TIME I got home I was sopping wet. The weather-girl had underestimated her dump, and I found myself navigating through a blizzard, sweating as much as in an hour at the gym. My hair was plastered to my skull from the snow I had collected while cleaning off the car. I was badly in need of a shower and the opportunity to start my toilette all over before I saw anyone else or they saw me. I wanted to be ready for Susan, who was definitely on the agenda. She'd promised, and I was going to hold her to it no matter the elements.

The garage was full, which led me to believe that we were in for worse weather. Cars that should have been at the office were parked in their home spaces, dripping dry. My deductive reasoning led me to believe that offices had closed early, a rare occurrence in a city this well prepared for the hazards of winter. It was going to be a bad one. Still, no way Susan was begging off. Tonight the heroin was leaving my house, one way or another.

I squished myself out of the car and started toward the interior entry to the building and elevators, fumbling through my pit of a purse for a house key.

Surprised to hear my name being called, I looked up to find Barry hailing me. Changing direction, I went to meet him halfway.

"What are you doing here?" I asked, sidestepping a puddle that had formed from the melting car snow.

"I came to talk to you about Susan. I need your advice," he said pleasantly.

Good answer. I love giving advice.

"How did you get in?" I'd asked that a lot lately, and it always elicited a disturbing response. It was no different this time.

"I used Susan's method. She told me how she did it when you wouldn't let her in last week."

Big mouth. Did she tell him everything? Again I reverted to the mood that seemed to be the flavor of the month. I was pissed. I decided, rehabilitation or not, I was going to have to move. Security in this building was a farce. Everyone appeared willy-nilly, disturbing me. Still subject to the aftereffects of telling my tale to Joanne, I was prone to exaggeration.

"Why didn't you just call?"

"I did, and the machine picked up, so I didn't know if you weren't home or screening your calls and decided to come over."

"In this blizzard?"

"It wasn't snowing so hard when I came, though I'm sure my car's buried by now."

Which meant he'd been here for some time.

"I don't understand. Why wait for me in the garage when you could have sat in the expensive, newly decorated lobby? We spent a lot of money to make it attractive for just that purpose. Why bother to sneak in?"

"This is why."

He pulled a gun and pointed it at my heart region, or at least where it could cause great damage if it was indeed real and were to go off. The gun was big and menacing and looked suspiciously like one of Robert's water guns. My mind couldn't accept the reality, and I sloughed it off as a lousy practical joke.

"That's not funny. Put it away and go home. I don't feel like talking to you now. I'm wet and cranky and want to take a shower. Next time try a more civilized approach, and I'm sure you'll find me more receptive."

As I turned to walk away, giving him the cold shoulder he deserved, he grabbed my arm, forcing me to face him head on.

"This is serious, Barbara. It's not a toy," he said, brandishing his weapon, waving it around to punctuate his sentences. "Just do as I say, and you won't get hurt."

Famous last words. For once television viewing came to my aid and made me realize what a perilous position I found myself in. Barry had a real gun and intended to use it. On me. I'd be dead in the garage. I had to buy some time.

"What do you want?" The last time I had posed that question it had been of Grandese and the answer had been semireasonable if somewhat farcical. I didn't think I would be as lucky this time.

"Let's go upstairs and discuss it. Behave."

He spun me around, and I now found myself directly in front of him, a cold gun pressed into my back. Through my coat and my blazer and my T-shirt, it felt cold. Icy. The mind truly is a wondrous thing.

"March."

My brain disappeared to a netherworld. All the books I had read, all the cop shows I had watched, all the movies I had seen, replayed themselves in lickety-split motion at the same time, resulting in a series of jumbled images of surreality. This couldn't be happening to me. It just was not possible.

I marched. We proceeded single file, with me praying the garage door would open and somebody would drive in and save me. No such luck, of course. Everybody seemed to already be in or waiting it out somewhere, probably in a warm cozy bar surrounded by convivial people.

Next I prayed the elevator would stop at the ground floor to let someone in. God was busy elsewhere.

The only thing I could think of was to buy some time. At my doorstep I wouldn't let Barry in with his boots on, and he was so ingrained with the habit he didn't balk. The ritual took forever, with me going first, my shaky fingers fumbling with the laces, then him, trying to kick his off without taking his eyes from me. We left the boots in a puddle by the door, a definite no-no in this building. I could only hope Mrs. Brooks across the hall would complain to the doorman and he would in turn come complain, albeit diplomatically, to me. Or she would pound on my door herself to demand their removal and at the same time snoop to see who was with me. Which meant Barry would take her hostage too and kill us both. The idea of taking her with me was the only bright light in the whole escapade.

Once in, I didn't know what was expected of me. Barry kept the gun trained on me and led me to the living room, where he ordered me to sit on the couch. Seated, I had the sensation of deja vu. This was exactly the same position on the sofa Frank was in when Susan and I found him, only I didn't have a bullet hole in me. Yet. I popped right back up.

"Did you kill Frank?" I blurted out as I shrugged off my coat and tossed it on the sofa. Not the brightest question in my position.

"No, I didn't. I wouldn't have been that stupid. The two gentlemen who were responsible for that error have been dealt with. People who work for me don't make mistakes."

"You killed them?" I was incredulous. People I know don't kill people. They just think about it a lot. "Never mind. Don't tell me," I said. I didn't want to know. My brain cells were in overdrive trying to assess the situation, and the intelligence portion seemed to have shut down, leaving my mouth in control. That's the only excuse I have for the dumb thing I said next.

"Omigod! You killed Celine." Valley-girl words uttered with

an ominous inflection. "You killed her after she left here. With that gun! You followed her from my house, then shot her. Why?"

"I didn't follow her. I sent her here in the first place. How do you think she knew where to go? And what makes you think I killed her then? I saw you Saturday night, didn't I? Did I look like a murderer?"

So that's how she knew where I lived and got my number, and no, he hadn't looked like a killer. And he didn't look like one now, which threw another stereotype out the window.

I didn't say anything about the autopsy report, which had closely pinpointed the time of death. I focused on a remembered anomaly.

"You and Susan arrived late. I thought she was making an entrance, but it was your fault, wasn't it? You were pressed for time and got dressed quickly. That's why you were wearing her father's cuff links. You'd forgotten yours at home or lost them on the way or something and had to borrow some. I should have known. Susan doesn't give jewelry; she takes it."

"Very clever, Barbara. It's too bad you didn't think of that earlier. You mighta saved your bacon."

This clichéd conversation convinced me we shared the same shortcoming. We both watched too much television.

"What about Susan? How can you do this to her?" If I were going to die I'd at least get all the facts first. It would kill me to die full of questions.

"She need never know, will she?" Syntactically wrong, but I wasn't going to correct him.

"I don't get it." Keep him talking. My brain was getting into gear again.

"The one misstep in the whole affair is that I genuinely care for Susan. And Robert. He's such a good little kid, and I'm sure he'll make a very good son. Susan was supposed to be disposable along with Frank. I'd use them for the duration and then move on. But's she's something special, and I fell for her big." Even

Mike Hammer never used so many clichés in sequence. I'd never noticed that Barry spoke like that. Maybe holding a gun has that effect.

"I still don't get it. Why kill me?"

"I'm not going to kill you. I just want you to give me that package you're holding. Then you'll disappear suddenly. You can manage that, can't you? Use your pass and go somewhere warm and start all over again. If you come back and say something, I'll kill Robert."

I bet. How stupid did he think I was? He knew how much I loved Robert, and I guess he figured it was a good enough threat to satisfy me temporarily and get me to accede to his request. However, if he thought I'd ever let Susan marry him, he was crazy. I'd kept my mouth shut, and she'd married Frank. I would never let that happen again, and he knew it. Barry might very well be crazy but he wasn't an imbecile. I knew I was going to die.

"I remember now. You didn't ask who Celine was at dinner last night when I said she'd been killed. I never once called her Bimbo, yet you knew who I was talking about. I'm so dumb. I should have realized it at the time." I wanted to pound the side of my head in disgust, but I didn't think any sudden moves were wise. "And you were probably listening while we were in the kitchen. You heard us, didn't you?"

"Yes. Do you think I'd sit there for ten minutes for some Chinese hair dryer? You should have known better. I've had a tail on you since Susan called you in the middle of the night. She shouldn't have gone to Frank's."

So someone besides Grandese *was* following me. I wasn't paranoid. There must be some way out of this, I thought furiously. Keep talking. My interior conversations were overlapping the exterior ones.

"How did you know she went there?"

"My guys came to report their tragic error to me, and after

I dealt with them I hightailed it over to Frank's to resume their inept search. Frank wasn't too bright, so I was sure I could find the stuff. I arrived just as you did. Figured out you wouldn't be there without Susan having summoned you, so I phoned her house, and the housekeeper told me she wasn't in. Stayed around until the police came and then went home to wait for Susan's call. Figured I could get the info from her. I didn't think she'd hold out on me, but when she didn't say anything about the police finding anything, I knew she'd taken it. And probably given it to you. I didn't toss your place because it was easier to just wait for you to lead me to it. This building's got better security than Frank's. So here I am. Now go get it."

"Go get what?"

"Don't be coy, it doesn't suit you. I want the heroin."

"Since you're going to kill me, no matter what you say, will you answer some questions first?"

"You've sure got spunk. Shoot."

It was an unpleasant choice of words. I couldn't believe the situation. He looked so normal standing opposite me, chatting. We could have been at a cocktail party discussing the political situation. Except for the gun.

"Why Celine? What was her part in this?"

He chortled. I was going to die, and he chortled. If he wasn't brandishing that thing I would have smacked him.

"Ah, the beautiful Celine. She was stunning. Celine and I have known each other for years. I met her when she was at flight attendant school, still so young and alive but with her eye on the prize."

"And you were the prize?" Shut up, I screamed silently. Don't antagonize the man.

He chuckled rather than chortled this time. He was having a grand old time.

"In a manner of speaking. Curvaceous Celine had a taste for the finer things in life, things she could never afford."

I hadn't noticed any curves on her, but then Susan doesn't have any either. Barry liked them model-thin.

"We went together while I began my 'other' import business. So much more lucrative, you know. I'm not greedy. I don't do it on a big enough scale to upset anyone. Enough for some extra spending money and ready cash. At first it was just cocaine, but Celine persuaded me heroin was the wave of the future. At about the same time I was considering the product switch, I met Frank in a bar and we got to talking. He was in need of money for a new venture, as usual. Sure it would be a loser, but I saw a conduit and an opportunity. I invested heavily, and after a few months I called in my marker. Of course Frank couldn't come up with the money, so I persuaded him to do some importing for me."

"But how?"

"That cheap fabric he uses has to come from somewhere. I have it layered in the bolts. Bring it in a little at a time. Then I set Celine loose on him to monitor the operation."

"So she was after the heroin, and all that stuff about cash in the hamper was a bluff," I mused.

"I sent her over here to find out what you knew. It was a silly waste of time, since you're smarter than her."

I was so scared and confused I barely heard the compliment.

"Celine watched his every move and reported back to me. As an extra perk she got him to buy her things."

"You and Susan. How did that happen?"

"That was another of Celine's ideas. Frank whined to her about Susan and her clinging ways, and she was curious. Asked me to investigate, which I did, and I liked what I saw. The perfect setup."

"What went wrong?" I was going to feed off his gregarious mood for as long as I could.

"A couple of things. Frank, being Frank, had to come up with his own angle. An endless supply of free drugs wasn't enough for him. I even let him deal a little to his friends on the side, but he got greedy. Started skimming quantity. The night he died he was supposed to deliver up the two keys of H he'd taken, and break a leg in the process. My last shipment had come up short, and it didn't take a genius to figure out where it had gone. It was to be the final chapter of our arrangement. I wanted Susan, so it was time to get rid of Frank. The plan had been to get him to return the product and leave town permanently."

"I get it," I said, flashing on another remembered item. "Frank left the bar mitzvah in a panic because he saw you there, not Susan. He was scared because he knew you knew about the skimming."

"Righto."

He didn't ask how I knew about that event, which was good, since this time I was positive Cynthia Berkowitz would want to be left out of it.

"You said a couple of things went wrong. What else?"

"You're a nosy one, aren't you?" He waved the gun under my chin, tapping it lightly on the underside. When I came to the conclusion he was just playing with me, enjoying the recitation and the sound of his own voice, I started breathing again.

"Celine had been with Frank for too long. She'd learned from him, emulated his avarice, and gotten even dumber. Frank seems to have that effect on people. They sink to his level.

"She met me at a bar in the Plateau to report on her visit with you and how she'd come up empty. She liked you, by the way. Wanted to be like you. Now that Frank was gone, she figured we'd get back together, but by now I was in love with Susan. She was furious and threatened to expose me. I'm sure it was all a put-on, but it got me to thinking there were too many loose ends out there. I want Susan, and I want out, since I have enough money, even for Susan. My regular business is doing well, and I've got some stashed abroad. Celine was not going to mess it all up. Better to eliminate her. So I drove her home and let her off at her back door and shot her."

He finished with a shrug of the shoulders, as though it were the only logical conclusion to the chain of events. Lately I had fantasized about killing a lot of different people, but to actually do it was something else. He made killing Celine seem a minor inconvenience, a pesky cyst to be excised. Frank's two killers were dead, and I was the next to go.

I worried about what was coming. It irked me that I always skip over the action parts in books, having trouble deciphering who does what to whom. I should have realized they were educational manuals, and the time would come when I would need the information.

Barry decided he'd done enough talking, and I sat there, looking cowed. He flicked the gun in signal and motioned for me to get up. Where were we going?

"Enough jabbering. Where's the heroin?"

So concerned was I that he was going to shoot me on the spot that I had completely forgotten the reason for this intrusion.

"Where was it?" he asked, curious. His guys hadn't found it, and Susan and I had, which no doubt peeved him.

If I spoke I didn't have to move. I stood rooted and said, "Right under your nose. In a safe-deposit box in Susan's apartment."

"What!"

First Joanne, now Barry. I could die a happy woman.

"Yep. All tucked in neatly under a bunch of blankets."

"Susan knew all along?"

"Of course not. We found out when we were at Frank's, and then we went back to her house later, and I took it and brought it home. Remember the small shopping bag I had with me when I left? Right in front of you."

That's me, cow or crow.

"I thought it held your shoes. You women always carry bags

with shoes in the winter." He returned to the business at hand. "How did you know where to look?"

"Susan recognized the key."

"What key?"

"The one stuck to Frank's toupée."

"I didn't know Frank wore a piece."

"Couldn't you tell? It was so obvious."

Even in a life-threatening situation I lied, not wanting to admit that I hadn't known either. Susan kept secrets from him, and he didn't know her well enough yet to know that she always would.

He was aggravated. I had known something he didn't. I guess it's not a good idea to annoy your potential killer, because this time he whipped me around and shoved the gun in my back. Hard.

"Ouch. I know it's there, you don't have to hurt me."

"Where's the heroin?"

"In my box. I have the same one as Susan. My brother gave them to us. You didn't know?"

I was a dimwit, toying with him.

"Shut up and show me."

"It's in the linen closet."

"Where's the key?"

"In my bathroom."

"Let's go."

Off we went down the hall. There was a minor snag when he tried to shove me into the guest bathroom, but he accepted my explanation that the key was in the other one without shooting me, and we proceeded.

The room is large, so there was ample space for the both of us.

"You're a slob," he said, taking in the between-Mme-Jacqueline's-visits surroundings. A shower or bath means a fresh towel every time, and I keep my person clean, so there were quite a few plopped all over the floor.

"And you're a murderer," I retorted.

"The key," he said menacingly. I have to learn to be more careful in my choice of words.

"Okay, okay. It's in the medicine cabinet. In the box of Band-Aids."

He found it first shot, as would any burglar, but until lately there hadn't been much in it worth stealing so I hadn't bothered to be clever about hiding the key. It seemed more important to put it somewhere where I could find it.

"Now the box."

We went to the linen closet, where I pointed out the pile on the floor.

"Move back a little," I said. "I have to crouch to reach it."

"All right, but don't make any sudden moves. I'm right behind you, and I'll shoot if I have to."

More TV banalities. It *must* have something to do with guns. Macho crap. Middle-class men don't learn that language in school. At least not when we went.

I got the package out of the box and stuck my nail through the plastic, creating a small hole. Barry had me straighten up, and we backed out, as there was no room to turn around. He pointed me in the direction of the adjacent den and shoved me along while I worked the hole larger and larger. When we entered the den I stopped short, forcing him to come around to face me. I quickly removed my finger and hoped I'd made a big enough puncture.

"Hand it over," he ordered, anxious to inspect his merchandise.

I did exactly what he told me, but, with the same technique I use in storytelling, I embellished the action. I swung the package in an arc at him. He flinched, although my intention had been not to hit him but to strew the contents. If the hole was large enough.

It was. Ivory powder flew out onto the floor. Barry reached

out to snatch the bag from me just as I dropped it. The tape must have loosened with all the manipulation because it landed with a whoosh, spewing heroin. Barry bent to inspect the situation, and this time I was ready. I took off like a rocket and managed to make it out the front door. As I hit the hall, with Barry at my heels trying to draw a bead on me, I started to yell, hoping someone would come to my rescue. I aimed for the fire exit, praying all those hours spent at the gym would give me the necessary wind and speed.

As I barreled around the corner I came to a crashing halt. Literally. The next thing I knew I was on the floor on top of Gregory Allard. Not a bad position to be in, but this was not the time. I could hear people around me, and when the stars cleared from my head I rolled off and sat up to see Barry being handcuffed by Fernand Boucherville as three very large men in flak jackets pointed offensive weapons at him. I decided I loved Boucherville a whole lot and would give him my firstborn.

Greg had by this time recovered his stance, and he gallantly helped me to my feet.

Around me, doors opened and people stared.

"We'll step into your apartment, Ms. Simons," Greg said, steering me down the corridor.

"There's nothing to see here. It's all over. Everyone back inside," trumpeted Detective-Sergeant Boucherville at high volume in French, and all the doors snicked shut at the same time. I would have a lot of explaining to do.

To Greg he said, "I'll take him in. You get her statement, and I'll meet you back here."

The last I saw of Barry, he was being escorted into a waiting elevator.

Greg followed me back to my apartment and into the living room.

"How did you know?" I asked, puzzled. In real life the cavalry doesn't ride in at the last minute to save you. See, I was learning.

"You have very good security in this building, Barbara."

Hah! But he called me Barbara.

"So?"

"The doorman saw you being led away at gunpoint on the monitors and called it in. We considered it a hostage situation, alerted the SWAT team, and took all the necessary precautions. If you hadn't come out of there like that we were about to begin contact by phone."

The cameras. Last year we had installed hidden cameras all over the garage, to be monitored by the doorman. I had maintained that an obviously positioned visible camera would act as a deterrent, but I was the only one. I had been outvoted, and a concealed system had been adopted. Thank God.

"Why didn't he call you when he saw Barry sneak in? Why wait for a gun?"

"He didn't see him. It must have happened when he was at what he euphemistically called a 'comfort break.' He admits to taking one an hour before the excitement."

So the doorman does pee. And Barry had waited a long time, probably hunkered down between cars to avoid being seen by the legitimate residents as they arrived home from work early to avoid the storm.

"Now tell me what happened." He took out his book to take notes.

"Can I tell you first without your writing anything down? I'll repeat it all a second time for you, if you want. Just listen. Don't write anything and don't interrupt. This is difficult enough."

I was still shaky so I sat down. When I realized it was the same position Barry had forced me into, I moved to the wing chair, where I felt safer. Greg played along with the musical chair routine and sat on the accompanying hassock.

This time I told the truth. In a dirgelike monologue I recounted all the relevant events from beginning to end, without embellishment or omissions. When I finished he just stared at me.

"Are you nuts?!" he exploded.

"Yes," I answered meekly.

"Why didn't you tell me all of this before?"

Why hadn't I? I didn't know. I'd just got caught up in the whole thing.

"I dunno. I'm stupid, and I'm sorry." I was as contrite as I sounded. Every bone in my body was regretful. Sorry wasn't enough.

He sat pensively for a bit and then faced me, looking deadly serious, and said, "This is not about to happen. Remember that."

He stood and went to survey the heroin mess.

"Where's your vacuum cleaner?"

"In there," I said as I pointed to the linen closet, shivering. I didn't want to go in there again.

He got it out and assembled it as I watched. It's a good thing he didn't ask me to do it; I wouldn't have known how. He plugged it in, and it came to life with a roar that startled him. Mme Jacqueline doesn't seem to understand on/off switches. He vacuumed up every ounce or gram of heroin and did the hall and foyer to boot. Then he changed the bag, vacuumed the living room to get some stuff in the new one so it wouldn't look so fresh, unplugged the machine, and replaced it. I took the old bag and threw it down the garbage chute.

The rest of the heroin, one intact bag and a half full one, we solemnly flushed down the guest bathroom toilet—something I had been wanting to do ever since I had been stupid enough to bring it home.

When all this was accomplished, he led me back to the wing chair and pulled out his notepad.

"You say he admitted killing Celine Plouffe?"

I took the hint and recounted an edited version of events.

I couldn't believe it. In order to keep me out of trouble he'd compromised himself. This was a man who thought I was too tough?

I spoke and he wrote, and by the time we were finished Fernand Boucherville reappeared. He said nothing about any heroin, so I assumed Barry had kept his mouth shut about that, hoping to incriminate me. At some point he would say something to someone, and I would be questioned. But he couldn't have known Greg would save me. I hadn't known that.

Boucherville asked a few more questions in an unpleasant manner, and I answered politely, not wanting to irritate him. I even spoke in French. By the time they left together it was close to dinnertime, and I was starved. All that adrenaline played havoc with my blood-sugar levels, and I craved food.

As they departed, Greg turned back, flashed a warm smile, and said, "I'll call you." It didn't sound very official to me.

After stuffing my face with anything I could lay my hands on, I knew I had some phone calls to make.

The first was to Susan; it wasn't easy. I told her pretty much in detail what happened; she'd find out sooner or later. Even though Barry had been going to kill me, I stressed how he felt about her, that he hadn't been leading her on or using her. He was a murderer, and here I was, extolling his virtues.

Susan listened silently, and when I was finished all she said, in a soft voice, was, "The prick. They're all pricks."

"Susan, do you want me to come over?"

"No. Thanks, Barbara. It's better if I stay home with Robert alone. I have to figure out how to tell him. I'm so sorry I got you into this. I'm just glad you're safe and still alive. Robert and I need you. I'll speak to you in the morning. Thanks for calling."

I felt like a heel. I felt like I had personally disappointed someone I loved. It was irrational, but there it was.

I decided to call Joanne to cheer myself up. Bombshell number two for the day.

It was as much fun as I had hoped. I gave her the bare-bones story, the same one Greg had written down, and it was good enough for her. She made me repeat it into a tape recorder, and then hustled me off the phone.

"I'm going down to the police station right away. It isn't often that someone I know gets carted away. Gotta get a crew. Thanks, Barbara."

Everyone was thanking me for nearly getting killed. Some friends.

I took a very long shower, breathing in the steam in an effort to clean my insides. After drying myself off and anointing my body with expensive creams I felt I deserved, I put on a clean T-shirt and crawled into bed. It was early, but I was exhausted, and tomorrow would be another trying day.

Tomorrow was Sam.